# THE SWIM

## JANET HOGGARTH

Boldwood

First published in Great Britain in 2025 by Boldwood Books Ltd.

Copyright © Janet Hoggarth, 2025

Cover Design by JD Design Ltd.

Cover Images: Shutterstock

A CIP catalogue record for this book is available from the British Library.

Paperback ISBN 978-1-83678-455-5

Large Print ISBN 978-1-83678-454-8

Hardback ISBN 978-1-83678-453-1

Ebook ISBN 978-1-83678-456-2

Kindle ISBN 978-1-83678-457-9

Audio CD ISBN 978-1-83678-448-7

MP3 CD ISBN 978-1-83678-449-4

Digital audio download ISBN 978-1-83678-450-0

This book is printed on certified sustainable paper. Boldwood Books is dedicated to putting sustainability at the heart of our business. For more information please visit https://www.boldwoodbooks.com/about-us/sustainability/

Boldwood Books Ltd, 23 Bowerdean Street, London, SW6 3TN

www.boldwoodbooks.com

*To my brother, Peter, and my sister-in-law, Sarah.*
*Thanks for all the cold-water therapy!*

If you don't become the ocean, you'll be seasick every day.

— LEONARD COHEN

# 1

## SHAKESPEARE BEACH, 6 JULY 2023

I had essentially been dared into swimming the English Channel. That was the official story if anyone was curious enough to ask, though in reality it was only partly true. No one had actually forced me, either. It wasn't like when Mum had suggested the Duke of Edinburgh bronze award as an after-school activity so she could have the run of the house, allowing her shabby affair with school head-master, greasy Mr Kilburn, to continue under the radar. Known as Mr Klingon behind his back – an overbearing forehead cross hatched with an unfortunate combination of pockmarks and wrinkles did him no favours. Children could be cruel.

'All that fresh air will do you good. You could do

with the exercise, Cordelia,' Mum had said at the time, scanning a critical eye over me, having previously set the tone for the rest of my teenage years. The affair's emetic disclosure (and many other truths) was something I was only introduced to post watershed teenage years when Mum decided we were now officially friends, dissolving our tenuous mother-daughter contract (signed with invisible ink in the first place).

I pondered my mottled feet, water pooling on the concrete, imagining how Stephen, my brother, felt, unable to recall life unencumbered with kids trampling through his carefully curated life straddling bulging nappies, projectile vomiting, bringing home every bloody virus from the nursery petri dish. Rose-tinted pre-swim life had been laden with gloriously lazy Saturdays with the *Guardian* and a creamy oat latte from Ruby's; tramping along the rolling downs or across the iconic Seven Sisters with excitable Kevin; the Tiger Inn on a crisp autumnal afternoon anticipating the sun's dive below the partly dressed trees; the occasional dinner out... Wine! Instead, life had taken on a distinctively regimented mantel. Laps in the pool at the Sovereign three times a week, bi-weekly weight training, and swimming in the biting sea come rain, shine or indifferent cloud. I'd reluctantly taken up running under Desi's instruction, my hefty boobs pinned down like a couple of Just Stop Oil protestors inside a brutalist sports bra. The problem with running was it churned up my already delicate tummy. Only last week I'd been pounding country lanes around Jevington when a number two threatened the status quo. Christ! Taking my chances inside a thick hedge just at the crucial moment, head hovering at an ungainly angle avoiding losing an eye to vicious hawthorn branches, I crouched and let go...

'Morning!' an elderly gentleman called out, dog on a lead, giving me a nod. *Where the Jeff had he sprung from?*

'Morning,' I'd blustered, praying he was half blind. We could easily have been exchanging pleasantries outside the Post Office. But then I unintentionally started peeing and watched in horror as it trickled out from under the hedge where the dog began lapping it up before wildly barking, clearly disgusted I'd marked my territory right under its very nose.

I shivered. Why hadn't Cathy sounded the horn yet? The short swim to the shore from *Boudica* (a handsome thirty-six-foot navy and white Dutch steel flybridge motor cruiser) had anesthetised my skin,

the shock robbing my breath when I hit the devil-
ishly cold water. Being a lugubrious landlubber, it
was a relief to leave the queasiness behind.

Standing on the steps awaiting the signal, icy fingers jammed their way into my muscles like jack
hammers. With no sun to toast the chilly sea breeze,
my only protection on top of sun block was the unc-
tuous layer of Vaseline spread liberally over my entire body by Desi – *'You could have waxed, babe! It's like
spreading butter on a gorilla.'* He'd paid particular attention to the chief chafe points of groin, armpits
and underneath my swimming-costume straps
where a tiny green swim light was attached. A corresponding light was clipped to my goggles strap like a
docked dog's tail.

Just like the gentle waves I was about to hurl myself into, the actual swim signalled the culmination
of the journey, not the dawn. Like migrating birds,
waves travel impressive distances, disturbing all
manner of mariners while innocently stirring up
schools of plastic jetsam and docile sea creatures in
equal measure. Wisps of foam snapped through the
damp air, waves breaking on the curved steel
handrails, reminding me of the ones at the lido.
Cathy, the pilot, had suggested swimming to the
steps as they were more agreeable than picking my

way over the vestigial sliver of shingle like a crab walking on a Lego carpet.

Historically, most swimmers began their Channel attempts from either Shakespeare's shore or Samphire Hoe further along the coast. But an hour before high tide, all that remained was a landscape of jagged rock armour protecting the adjacent railway line from rapidly encroaching coastal erosion. Its eerie resemblance to the ramparts of an offshore prison brought to mind *Escape from Alcatraz* with Clint Eastwood on his make-shift raft – the sharks though, urgh! *Do not think of sharks, Cordelia. They don't exist.* Well, of course they existed, just hopefully not in the English Channel. But what if a *Carcharodon carcharias* mistakenly turned right at the Cape of Good Hope, aimlessly swimming north up the African west coast until it hit Europe, confused by the rapidly warming oceans, venturing into the narrow mouth of this very Channel? Delirious with starvation, it would be primed to chomp down on any moving target it could lock its jaws onto.

The Hollywood actor, Richard Dreyfuss (shark expert, Hooper, in the film, *Jaws*) burst into a rabid monologue inside my head listing every shark's Latin name and their bite radius after examining a potential shark-attack victim in the morgue.

The predawn blush bled into the clouds clotted above the terminal wall, *Boudica* bobbed fifty metres ahead, her lights throwing down a jittering glitter path. The translucent half-moon hung heavily in the sky, ready to slide off stage. Someone, maybe Desi, began jumping up and down on the stern waving their arms. I scraped out an earplug.

'You need to go!' The horn had been sounding the entire time in fierce competition with my clamouring heart. Ramming the plug back in, I picked my costume out of my bum, straightened my goggles, checked the lights and crouched down, pressing my fingers against the rough concrete – a silent goodbye. I followed the steps into the water, jettisoning off once in waist high. One stroke at a time, my mantra (actually Desi's mantra). He had stolen it from a re-tired Channel swimming coach he'd discovered in his collection of books and open-water podcasts. Accompanied by the smacking of hands slicing the surface and the faint gush of bubbles rushing past my ears after each exhale, I ploughed through the water like I had on countless occasions, my smooth red swimming-capped head trained like an Exocet missile in *Boudica*'s direction. *It's just another swim...*

When I reached the boat's port side, muted cheering broke out on deck, so I raised my head, catching Desi twirling and clapping enthusiastically while Alan punched the air. Having successfully swum the Channel to mark his sixty-fifth spin around the sun, Alan genuinely understood the untold trials lying in wait. It was rather optimistic cheering before I'd even sprung out of the gate. *Woeful wabbit never won the race*, not that this was one.

*Boudica* pursued me until we inched past the terminal wall in unison, a hulking ferry crowding the skyline ready to shuttle passengers choosing a more congenial passage to France.

'The cliffs take an age to disappear so you can feel like you're going nowhere,' Alan warned last week after the usual Sunday swim. 'I wouldn't look back... It's also best not to keep asking where you are or how long you've been going. Just keep your head down and swim. Hours have ways of wrapping themselves in knots in the Channel. Proof we live in a matrix! Time is definitely in the eye of the beholder.'

Clearing the towering terminal wall, the sun finally breached the horizon on the left, casting an orange slick over the water's surface in a *Game of Thrones* cinematic panorama. I could just about determine the sandy sea floor while powering towards the Dover Straits and the Inshore Traffic Zone while below, shoals of needle-like silvery fish darted between tendrils of light. Once the seabed disappeared, I knew I'd have to overthrow all nightmarish thoughts of sea monsters.

Without warning, Mum's voice rang between my ears: 'You never finish anything, Cordy. I'm not being mean; I'm just stating a fact. I hope you do it, I really do.'

Earlier, I'd woken to a cluster of well-wishing texts, one of them from Stephen, sent at five past midnight.

Good luck today. Hope it goes well and you prove the crone wrong. That would make me so proud! Though I am proud already. I can't believe you're going to swim the Channel! See you in Dover. Kallie and the kids send their love. Go Aunty Go! Xx

'Aren't you scared of drowning?' Stephen had asked a few weeks ago.

'I wasn't, but now I am!'

A family of waves caught me off guard, repeatedly slapping my cheeks, mouthfuls of seawater unavoidable. Glancing up, the sun pierced my goggles;

a small white vessel cut ahead, generating enough swell to sway the little yellow rib roped to *Boudica*'s stern.

On one of the more extensive sea swims (nine hours, NINE HOURS!) thrashed out in a continuous loop from the Langham Hotel to the pier on Eastbourne seafront, I'd been struck down by the monotonous chorus of 'Baby One More Time'. By hour six, Britney had all but moved in, suitcases in the hall, when the plangent opening bars of *The Godfather*'s back room piano and tremulous mandolin finally outplayed her. That was how memorising film plots to block torch songs from circling like buzzards was born. Hasten to say recounting *Jaws* was *not* on this tedium-bashing roll call.

Alan had concurred: 'I replayed episodes from *Frasier* once I'd been going a couple of hours. I think I managed to stretch the one where Diane returns between two feeds trying to piece together everything in the right order. It was the only thing that worked to beat boredom and obsessing about the cold. That and treating the swim like a giant therapy session. You're trapped with yourself for thirteen plus hours. That's a lot of shit to face.'

After shoving my head in the sand for decades, perhaps this was an opportunity to pull on the tiger's whiskers. At the very least, I could lay some ghosts to rest...

'Practise makes patterns, not perfect,' was another of Desi's borrowed swimming mantras. I was due my first feed two hours in today but was arbitrarily forbidden from touching either boat or human, such miscreant behaviour invalidating the swim. We had worked out a system of plastic bottles tied to sturdy string filled with various sugary liquids, Desi or Alan hurling the line like fishermen hooking catch of the day. Memories surfaced of the one and only enforced morning service with Mum in the Tin Pot Cathedral (St Saviours Baptist church), a Bible story of the apostles facing another unsuccessful fishing expedition in the Sea of Galilee until good old Jesus (multi-tasking as fisherman and King of Expletives respectively) suggests digging deep and throwing the net one last time. Would you believe it – they were rewarded with a mighty haul; it was as if he knew.

This swim had more in common with religious zealotry than I cared to think about. Just the act alone of voluntarily plunging into freezing-cold water in the deepest corner of winter reflected shades of John the Baptist.

*Head down, four strokes, breathe out. Bubbles.*

## 2

SINGIN' IN THE RAIN

A strict vetting system had been mandatory for this timetable of films I had to re-watch. For a start, I needed to be able to confidently recall their plots so that I wasn't just left staring hopelessly into the abyss. Being a woman of a 'certain age' (forty-nine – why weren't men ever described as a 'certain age?'), my short-term memory was shot. This meant I'd have to plunder the archives from an era when stories sank into the subliminal mind and settled there until called. The eighties and nineties were perfect then.

I soon realised fictional tales alone weren't going to be enough to sate the gnawing boredom of the Channel. Luckily, pertinent memories had attached themselves to these films like limpets, subplots if you please, and that forced my hand to choose a chronological running order for the swim, allowing the past equal leverage.

Most films throughout the 1980s had been discovered courtesy of BBC Sunday afternoon programme planners, occasionally Channel Four; ITV was frowned upon.

'Children, ITV is for the uneducated. If you'd ever seen *Tizwas,* you'd understand.' Stephen and I knew better than to ask how Mum had arrived at that conclusion if she'd never watched it. Button three on the television remained untuned so when pressed ('*Don't use the remote – it's lazy!*'), the screen filled with snowy interference and a tantalising ghost ship of voices. Mum had refused to rent a VHS player in an endless battle to stave off what she called the 'dumbification of the masses'.

'Society's sliding into the mire; everyone's so idle, sitting around watching TV, piling on the pounds. Next there'll be machines that suck fat out of your body instead of walking to the shops or doing Jane Fonda!'

Dad had bought the TV outright, an act of insurrection, its permanency hard to rail against. ITV needed to be pinned down in real time when Mum was at the afternoon service or on a Wednesday evening when she taught Slimnastics (a boisterous aerobics/gymnastics hybrid) at the Tin Pot Cathedral. She had been hiring the Tin Pot Cathedral's hall for her Slimnastics class for three years and had managed to resist the calling of Jesus so far. Yet once Pastor Michael (outrageously suave for a churchy person) took stewardship of the place, not only did she find herself attending church but offered a new job that fitted round us. Pastor Michael (who preached in jeans!) also happened to moonlight as Mr French, manager of the local Spar and conceived the job title, Checkout Executive, just for her. Mum cajoled us only once into joining her at a service, but the smell of stale feet, eggy bleach and burning dust from the pre-war electric heaters made Stephen projectile all over Pastor Michael's lectern halfway through a sermon. Halleluiah!

The day we watched *Singin' in the Rain* was memorable, least of all because of the film itself, though it remains a firm favourite nearly forty years later. June 1986, I was eleven, nearly twelve, Stephen almost ten. Mum had just left for her second bout of worship; Stephen was retuning channel three when the doorbell rang. Mum had cautioned against answering the door whenever she was out.

No. Matter. What.

I ignored the bell, watching the TV screen flicker onto a Persil advert; Stephen stopped turning the tiny dial. The doorbell rang again. Then again.

Burdened with being in charge, I crept into the hallway, feet squeaking along the dimpled clear plastic protector shielding the swirly beige and mud brown carpet. A man pressed his glasses against the rough rolled glass panel at the top of the door.

'Cordelia, is that you?'

I shrank back against the bannisters, a balustrade digging into my spine.

'Cordy, it's me, Dad.'

Stephen joined me.

'Let me in. I want to speak to you.'

'Dad?' Stephen hissed. 'Isn't he in Austria?'

'No, Australia.'

'I said that!' Stephen eagerly made a move towards the door.

'Mum didn't mention he was coming home,' I whispered restraining him like a boxing referee. 'I don't think it's him; it just sounds like him.'

'I want to see,' Stephen said in his outside voice.

'Stephen, it's Dad. Let me in, will you?'

I tightened my grip but couldn't gag him.

'Cordelia won't let me.'

'Cordy, it's me! I have a key here somewhere.'

At the sound of shuffling, I sprung towards the door, pulling the chain across.

'How do we *know* it's you?' I asked in my best grown-up voice.

'Who else would it be?' the voice said, straining to contain impatience.

'I dunno. A robber? Strange Colin from Donnington Crescent?'

'Strange Colin can't talk!' The voice pledged allegiance: 'I know your mother has said not to open the door, but I'm here to say you can. It's OK.'

*What would Jesus do?* Not that Jesus was a particular role model; it was just something Mum said. Over the last few months, since Dad had left for work in Australia, life had changed so subtly, like looking beyond my reflection in a mirror. Because of the opposing time zones, Dad was apparently asleep when we were awake and vice versa; only Mum was allowed to talk to him. He'd not even said goodbye, just left a letter. On a more thorough inspection, the 'a's all sprouted a funny little squiggle as if trying to hook onto the line above, just like Mum's did. Stephen had been properly upset, having been reduced to a minority in one fell swoop. *Stephen's now the man of the house*, 'Dad' had written in the letter. It wasn't like Dad influenced the intricate fabric of our lives so that in his absence the whole place fell down like a badly hung curtain pole. It was more what he represented. A solid presence in the house, a backbone. After the trillionth time of asking Mum if we could talk to him, we gave up. Considerable clumps of hair started falling out on Stephen's pillow and in the bath and the GP said it was stress-related alopecia.

'Look, I'm sorry I just disappeared,' Dad pleaded through the front door. 'I didn't really have a choice. I promise it's me. I'll prove it: Cordelia's favourite chocolate is Cadbury's Buttons and Stephen has a birth mark on his tummy shaped like the Isle of Wight.'

'It's him!' Stephen sang. 'Let go!'

He ran to the door and scrabbled with the chain, flinging the door wide. Dad wasn't an emotional man, his cards practically stapled to his chest, but he rewarded Stephen by scooping him up in his arms, holding on just that little bit too long; in the end, Stephen wriggled free.

'*Singin' in the Rain* starts in ten minutes,' Stephen said, looking between Dad and me. 'Do you want to watch?'

I'd wanted to see *Singin' in the Rain* since catching

the eponymous dance scene on a 'best of' compilation programme on BBC Two. Films acted as cinematic escapism; visceral emotions typically squashed down flowed freely when watching a film. I was permitted to get upset at films, but not if I fell over in the playground or if Mum scolded because I'd asked why her top was on back to front on returning from afternoon service. 'It's rude to ask questions, Cordelia!'

Sitting on the sofa in the front room fifteen minutes later, the TV blaring, a sashaying Lina (grating Jean Hagen) and a penguin-suited Don (slick Gene Kelly) arrive at the premier of their latest film, *The Royal Rascal*. A glacial two months had passed since Dad had left.

'When did you get back from Austria?' Stephen asked as Lina broke her compulsory vow of silence, her fish-wife voice setting everyone's teeth on edge.

'I never went to Austria,' Dad answered.

'Australia, silly,' I corrected.

'I never went there either.' Dad paused, his coffee cup suspended in front of his face. 'Did your mother tell you that's where I was?'

'No, you told us in a letter,' Stephen explained. 'You went there for work.'

'I didn't. Let me see this letter.' He set his mug

down on the wonky coffee table without a coaster, liquid slopping over the rim.

Stephen jumped up, eyes still on the screen, briefly watching the pandemonium play out as Don left his premier alone, before running upstairs to his bedroom.

'Where were you then?' I asked. Kathy (vivacious Debbie Reynolds), a new character, had inadvertently rescued Don in her car and was mercilessly teasing him about his commercial film career when serious actors like herself were solemnly treading the boards.

Stephen reappeared brandishing the letter, thrusting it at Dad, who scanned it, his features creasing in concentration.

'You know this is your mother's writing?'

Dur yes! Stephen vehemently shook his head. Dad carefully placed the letter on the sofa next to me while Stephen sat on the floor in front as if awaiting a story. 'Mum doesn't know I'm here. I promised her I'd give her three months to decide, but I can't wait any longer.'

'Decide what?' I asked, Kathy's pink-frilled can-can dancing filling the rapidly appearing cracks in our conversation.

Dad opened his mouth, then closed it with a sigh

before speaking. 'I've been living elsewhere for a while. Your mum wasn't happy...'

No way! As a rule, this type of coveted information only traded between grown-ups. I flicked my eyes towards their black and white framed wedding picture on the sideboard. Both posing for the camera on the steps of Brighton registry office, Dad's chunky glasses hogging the limelight, his young bride nervously glancing at the camera from underneath her perky veil, not quite smiling in her white, three-quarter length ballerina dress with capped sleeves and a demure high neck. All the rage for 1970. Mum looked exactly like Elizabeth Taylor in *National Velvet*, if you covered up her more robust jaw with your finger and only considered her from the top lip and above.

'I rang twice a week but she said you didn't want to speak to me. Anyway, none of it matters now. Your mother wanted it done this way. I was hoping...' He shrugged, the realisation slamming into me that he was disappointingly weak. It didn't matter that he resembled a mildly handsome professor and sold medical textbooks to shops and universities all over the south of England, once winning 1982 Salesman of the Year and a gold Parker pen with his name engraved on it. So what if he had met George Michael at a publishing party, or that he could play 'The Saints Come Marching In' with his armpit.

'But she's not unhappy,' Stephen whispered, a single tear sliding down his reddening cheek. 'Pastor Michael made her laugh.'

Dad slowly brought his hand up to his mouth while Kathy hurled a cream pie, smacking Lina in the face, missing supercilious Don. I poked Stephen before he let anything else slip, prompting more tears.

'Pastor Michael...' Dad said and slowly shook his head, patting Stephen like he was a dog.

Later on, a key turned in the front door just as a bejewelled Lina was asked to sing 'live' at *The Dancing Cavalier* premier in front of a packed auditorium.

'I'm back!' Mum was early.

Stephen jumped up to meet her in the hallway. 'Dad's here!'

Meanwhile Don, Cosmo and RF gleefully hauled up the stage backdrop curtain, revealing a miked-up Kathy providing the mellifluous singing voice of lip-synching Lina in a *Cyrano de Bergerac* deception.

'What do you mean your father's here?' Mum's pinched voice bounced down the hallway. I leapt off the sofa, fumbling with the dial, hastily tuning out

Don and Kathy's triumphant final duet, flipping to BBC Two and a black and white film I couldn't immediately place.

'Dad said you're lying,' I announced, standing the same time as him.

Mum's eyebrows flinched. 'Good to see you're back from Australia,' she responded. 'When did you arrive?'

'Lois, they know.'

'Children, he was in Australia, weren't you?' Mum pursed her lips and raised her eyebrows, trying to prompt an agreement.

'No. I've been in Eltham with Tony from marketing. He let me stay in his spare room but he needs it back for his brother's visit.'

Within the silence, a jaunty yet soulless zither escorted a woman on the TV as she wandered from an impersonal burial and into the final scenes of what I now recognised as *The Third Man*.

'We need to talk on our own. Kids, do you want to go out and play?' Mum clenched her hands, her eyes flicking towards the TV screen.

'No thanks,' I said. 'I'd rather stay in.'

'I'd rather you went out. Your dad and I need to chat.' Mum stormed over to the TV and switched it off at the wall.

'You said we can't go out on a Sunday unless it's to go to church. You said so, remember?'

'Cordelia, don't disobey me. Out now.'

Stephen edged towards the door.

'But it's against—'

'Kids, outside.' Dad eyed Mum warily, digging into his trouser pocket and pulling out his battered wallet. 'Here's a fiver. Don't spend it all at once. You've got half an hour. Stephen, you got your watch on?'

Stephen proudly waved his steel Casio on his wrist.

'I'll still be here when you get back.'

My stomach whirled like a fairground waltzer. What on earth was going on?

# 3

## THE CHANNEL

Alan's whistle tore through my childhood. *Had two hours passed already?* Film therapy definitely worked! I dropped my legs, treading water, sparkles dancing like birthday candles, the sea a smoothly iced cake. Wispy clouds scooted across the sun. I swam closer to the port side where Desi stood gripping the lassoed plastic water bottle, ready for casting over the brink. Alison the observer (whom I had only met that morning), ate her first sandwich of the day, balancing her notebook on her knee. So far so good. So far no sharks.

'You ready?' Alan shouted, the breeze whipping his voice up and over the starboard side. Earplugs cushioned all but the arterial thumping of blood, but

I could still just about hear shouts (wind direction depending) and Alan's whistle. Desi launched the bottle into the air, landing it just beyond reach before dragging it bouncing back towards me. I unscrewed the top like I had practised a million times during training swims, relaxed my throat and tipped my head back, swallowing all the Maxim (a sickly-sweet sports drink) in less than forty seconds, my record during training. Desi blew a kiss and lugged the empty bottle back on board.

'What if I need a poo, or worse, get the squits?' I'd been plagued by scatologic apprehension since booking my crossing slot. 'All that adrenaline might light a stick of dynamite down there. You know what my dodgy tummy's like.'

'I wouldn't worry,' Alan had reassured me at the time, 'that part of your body shuts down. It's super important to urinate and if you do need a poo, just do it; it'll make you swim faster escaping a floater!'

*Boudica*'s engine roared. Rapidly resuming front crawl, I sprinted for twenty metres, outrunning the cold eager to crampon its way into my bones. *I am warm, I am warm, I am warm.* I'd read on a smug self-help influencer's Instagram post one ought to articulate exactly what one wanted rather than what one didn't. We should have been taught mindfulness at school; it might have helped ease the anxiety regarding Tracey Bates and her nest of vipers. *Tracey is dead, Tracey is dead, Tracey is dead...*

'You can't risk obsessing about failure,' Desi had said last year once I'd accepted his challenge.

'Well, that's like a red rag to a bull!'

'One of the open-swimming podcasts suggests keeping a list next to the bed of what you are to remind yourself you're more than just the swim. If the swim doesn't go your way, it can mean a big blow to one's self-esteem if you're attaching too much to it.'

'An almost forty-eight-year-old spinster with night sweats and an atrophied vagina is what I am. Bring it on.'

'You're an animal lover and dog mummy too! Don't forget about poor Kevin!'

'Bloody hell, Desi, it's not my sodding Tinder profile!'

'No, that would read GSOH, keen cinephile, likes sex on first dates, red wine, and being taken from behind, not in that order.'

'Be specific – a Pinot Noir or a Malbec – not all red wine is created equal.'

*Head down, four strokes, breathe out. Bubbles.*

# 4

## PATTERN OFF A PLATE

The day Mum handed us 'Dad's' letter coincided with friends being unwelcome at home and a subsequent ban on playdates elsewhere. Mum's deafness in the face of all protests forced me to hammer home my feelings by slamming my bedroom door so hard that the gilt-framed print of Constable's *The Hay Wain* smashed on to the landing, the frame cracking on the right hand corner. Mum ordered the permanently idle chip pan to be scraped out and cleaned as atonement. The lard had been squatting in there since Lady Di married old big ears.

A month later, my best friend, Lydia, moved to Scotland with her family, leaving me rudderless, making it difficult to forge new friendships after Mum's unreasonable clampdown. At school, adrift in a sea of kids without my own bestie, I unwittingly fell prey to Tracey Bates, who ruled our year with a mixture of fear and inane superiority due to her precocious prettiness.

'Why you all sad? Is it cos your dad's run off?' She feigned concern one breaktime as I skirted the edge of the playground, keeping out of harm's way.

'He's not run off; he's away with work. He'll be back soon.'

Tracey pursed her lips and tilted her head to one side in a jejune presaging of her future gossip-peddling self. 'That's not what *my* mum said. She said *your* mum and—'

But the bell rang and she pretended to zip her lip and waltzed back to her gang.

'What did you mean about my mum?' I asked, following her into the classroom.

'Did someone say something?' She exaggerated looking round, pretending not to see me while her admirers giggled.

'You know nothing about my family,' I said in a fit of misplaced bravery, nerves fluttering like a sparrow trapped in a chimney. 'Keep your nose out of my business.'

'Or you'll do what?' she said, spinning round to face me. 'I know more than you ever will.'

'No you don't.'

She stepped on my shoe and ground the ball of her foot into my toes. 'Your mum isn't as squeaky clean as you think she is.'

'Seats please,' Mr Hazelwood shouted. 'Stop chatting.'

Every day after that, she greeted me with, 'How's your mum?' or 'Heard any rumours?' or 'Do you wanna know what I know?' before cackling like a hyena. Ignoring her became an Olympic sport.

The summer holidays couldn't come quick enough.

\* \* \*

'You've had your tea then?' Mum said, letting me and Stephen back in, reaching for our empty chip wrappers. 'Saves me a job. Your dad and I have something to say.'

After leaving the house, we had headed two roads over to Marino's, a famous purveyor of the finest fish and chips and deep-fried battered sausages. Trouping into the living room, dusty light fought its way through the smeared front bay windows, catching twirling motes on their way to smother the TV screen. Dad sat at the table in what was considered the dining room, separated from the living area by flimsy wooden louvre doors in a late-seventies identity-crisis refurb. He pulled out two chairs either side of him and Mum sat opposite.

'Kids, your mum and I have decided to separate.'

I *knew* we should've stayed behind! Stephen let out a howl; Dad put his arms loosely around his shoulder. 'But your mum—' Mum cleared her throat, '*both* of us want to keep it quiet. Grandma and Grandpa will be sad, and... people talk. Let's keep it between us.'

Mum nodded firmly.

'What if people ask where you are?' I said, tears creeping up my throat.

'Have they so far?' Mum replied knowingly.

'No, oh, right—' No one comes to the house and we were forbidden to visit anyone. Mum could have plugged leaks for MI5.

'Exactly. It's not that hard to *not* talk about it, is it?' Mum said triumphantly.

An old news story popped into my head. A local airline pilot had murdered his wife and dropped her body in a lake wrapped in an old roll of carpet, telling their only son she had gone to live with another man (*in Australia?*). No one questioned it, until her body was discovered by accident decades later when divers were searching for another missing person. I'd been fascinated that you could murder someone and no one would know. *God would know. He knew everything.*

Stephen sniffled into his hands, setting me off – Dad was leaving for real! Tracey had been right! Mum got up and brought in the kitchen roll, ripping off a square for each of us, kissing the top of our heads before sitting back down.

'What if I don't want you to be separated?' Stephen said quietly, wiping his eyes with it.

'Well, pretend that we aren't,' Mum said almost cheerily. 'It's just a word and it's not final, like divorce. We still... *care* about each other. Dad's still your dad and you'll still see him – he's going to live in a flat nearby instead. But for now, he's in Australia, OK? You mustn't forget that part. I'll take you to see him every week.'

'Isn't that lying?' Stephen asked. 'I thought that was one of the sins.'

'Not really,' Mum swiftly replied. 'I don't want to upset Grandpa and Grandma. They're happy as long as they think Dad's in Australia and we're still together, which we are, just not in the same house. I've said he comes home once a month, so it's plausible.'

'Can Dad stay for tea?' Stephen asked.

'You've already eaten,' Mum said.

'Can he stay for pudding then?' I suggested, hoping for some long-lost Neapolitan ice cream hibernating in the freezer. As well as ITV, Mum lobbied against sugar but we were sometimes allowed that or Arctic Roll. 'What is there?'

'Don't be greedy, Cordelia; you don't need pudding,' she snipped. 'Haven't you eaten enough already today? Honestly, you'd lick the pattern off a plate.'

# 5

## THE CHANNEL

I couldn't risk despair if the cliffs continued dictating the horizon, and if they'd shrunk to the depth of a loop pile carpet, with nothing but endless sea before me, the swim might escalate into a Sisyphean task depending on other factors I had no control over: weather, tidal currents, seasickness, jellyfish. All I could do was keep going, one stroke at a time. *How many hours though? Three? Four?*

I'd studied the Channel's nautical charts like I'd been cramming for an exam and gathered we must be edging the Southwest Shipping Lane. The constant influx of lolly-stick-sized tankers, cargo ships and ferries sloping across the distant horizon now arose from the left as bright and as large as floating cities, funnels belching clouds of smoke like fire-breathing dragons. The wash produced from some scooped me into cresting just below *Boudica*'s fly bridge before throwing me down a water slide, my stomach slapping the back of my throat.

It had taken this long to pin down the perfect rhythm and win the latest skirmish between body and sea. So far, I'd battled the cold, winning by a negligible margin, distraction proving to be the key there. But swimming into the choppy shipping lane, my hard-earned groove slid away as easily as everyday words and people's names. I dipped into the roster, lining up the next film – it was a good one (they all were, but this one was special). Desi had introduced me to *Roman Holiday*, though technically it had been his mum, only because it was Desi's all-time favourite. But before I could summon up sylph-like Audrey Hepburn as Princess Ann, burnt out from her extensive European tour, *Kramer vs Kramer* queue-barged – it wasn't even on the list! Had I watched this before or after *Roman Holiday*? Was this even allowed? I foolishly chuckled, almost taking in a lungful of water, rotating sideways to breathe before facing down into the yawning depths; the seabed had disappeared quite some time ago.

*No sharks, no sharks, no sharks.*

STOP! Before I could block it, *Jaws* snapped its way into my head with the clip of impudent Hooper standing on Amity Island's quayside squaring up to a complacent Chief Brody. Ecstatic after bounty hunters catch an impressively large shark (but not *the* shark), Brody wrongly thinks his troubles are all over at roughly only a quarter of the way through the film. What did he think was going to fill the remaining hour and a half? Mermaids showcasing synchronised swimming skills with singing crabs bringing up the rear?

Hooper knows otherwise. Of course the shark was still out there, somewhere...

Shadows played tricks below. I closed my eyes, the dull fleshy glare from the sun's blazing halo radiating out in triplicate against my irises.

*Head down, four strokes, breathe out. Bubbles.*

# 6

## THE LUGE

The summer of The Secret (so all-encompassing, it was anointed with the definite article), we visited our grandparents, dreading Stephen might slip up no matter how much he was coached.

'Selling books out of a suitcase, I presume?' Grandpa had sniffed, his only enquiry about Dad the entire visit.

'Yes, in Australia!' Stephen had cried proudly.

I honestly wished they'd died instead of Dad's parents. My enduring memories of Granny and Grandad Franks were two faint grey ghosts and a tin of Foxes Glacier Mints on a dark wood sideboard inside a gloomy cottage, windows as small as jam jars. Stephen and I pressed our dislike of Mum's parents deep into our bones. It was a blessing we only visited twice a year whilst the gardener was on his holidays, staying in his modern two-bed bungalow built at the bottom of their one-acre garden. No one was allowed to stay in the Big House because it was stuffed with an endless conveyor belt of precious antiques from Grandpa's dubious house-clearing business.

'When are you going to get that girl's ears pinned back?' Grandma habitually asked before I'd even left the room. *All the better to hear you with, Grandma-ma.*

'Stop sucking your thumb, boy, or you'll end up with a mouth full of tombstones.'

'How are the children coping at *state* school?'

But they loved their racehorse more than they loved their own daughter. Lady Madonna (who had yet to win a race) could have trampled through the house shitting on the Persian rugs, chomping the Aspidistras while they watched indulgently, cooing at her like she was their monstrous baby.

'I suppose they need one daughter to be proud of,' Mum had said when Grandma had rung to boast that Lester Piggott had patted the horse's flanks in the parade ring.

Grandma unfailingly served stewed-to-death food (made by the home help), doling out measly portions to me and Mum. 'A woman shouldn't let herself go.' Guests *never* helped themselves. 'Stephen's finally grown. We were dreading he was going to turn out to be a dwarf like old Uncle Geoffrey. Shame his nose overtook his face.' Every visit, we walked barefoot over broken mirror.

Whenever Grandpa and Grandma Simpson deigned to visit Eastbourne, rather than stay at 17 Villiers Road, they took a suite in the Grand Hotel along the seafront, arriving during term time, spending no more than the requisite three hours with us. Grandma and Grandpa always returned to the hotel the second Dad strolled through the door from work. After The Secret was in place, the wedding photo remained on the sideboard and Dad kindly donated a couple of old suits to hang in his side of the wardrobe, *just in case*. There were no friends to ask where he was, no visitors to feign that everything was as normal.

'Can we get a pet now Dad's left?' I asked a few weeks into our new living arrangements, hoping the guilt of our broken home would somehow manifest into us being allowed to have some gerbils.

'No chance,' Mum said. 'Terry was more than enough of an experience for me, thank you very much.' Terry had been our first and only pet, a yellow and blue parrot, plugging the hole that I had previously filled by rescuing injured birds savaged by next door's cat and adopting worms, plopping them on the back garden swing and gently pushing them in lieu of any furry creatures. The flowerbed was accordingly littered with tiny crosses fashioned from twigs and garden twine, marking several dead thrushes lovingly nursed inside old shoe boxes until they lay stiff and lifeless, eyes unblinking.

Mum had inherited Terry from Grandpa after one of his piratical house clearances when the owner disappeared off to a care home. 'He's going to the knackers yard otherwise,' Mum had obliquely explained. 'A parrot can't be any harder than a baby...' Terry quickly settled into the lounge area in his brass cage like he'd always been holding court. At first, he'd try and scratch anyone in his vicinity, shoving his gnarly claws in visitors' faces from between the bars. Regardless, I was fond of him, striking up a rapport that revolved around administering snacks and tickling his downy blue head. Anticipating Mum would eventually agree to a gerbil, I volunteered to clean his cage and feed and water him. It was a two-person job anyway, Mum grabbing him in a towel to prevent him blindly flying round the living room seeking an open window.

The first morning we took his cage cover off, he greeted us. 'Hello, you ugly cunt!'

'Terry!' Mum scolded him like a recalcitrant child. 'You can't say that.' And so it came to pass Terry taught me the meatiest (and some might say the best) swear word at age eight. He squawked it every morning and during *John Craven's Newsround* on the TV, and each time I fed him treats between the bars, tenderly nibbling my fingers in a show of affection. Unfortunately, Mum had refused to divulge the word's meaning. 'Just ignore him and he'll stop, he doesn't mean it...' Until she found herself called into school after I had drawn a picture of Terry screeching it in a speech bubble.

'Where's Terry?' I cried after school the following afternoon, his cage conspicuously absent.

'Ah yes, he, er... died. I think he missed old Mr Humphrey. The vet said it was a broken heart. I'm sorry, darling. By the way, Cordelia, you can't ever say that word again. It's the rudest, most dreadful word on the planet referring to a lady's foo foo. OK?'

I nodded, tears streaming, filing 'cunt' away for future use.

\* \* \*

Every Saturday and the occasional Wednesday, Mum dropped us off at Dad's small, two-bed flat in Pevensey. We'd never had Dad all to ourselves before. The minute we arrived, he'd be ready with a packed lunch and we'd head out on an adventure. Drusilla's Animal Park, Hastings Castle or Eastbourne beach where he would use a garden shovel to dig holes so expansive, they would draw a crowd.

'Why do you keep the shovel in the boot?' Stephen asked once.

'In case I ever need to bury a body.' This was not the Dad we were used to. He let us stay late on the beach, never dragging us out of the water threatening we wouldn't be allowed back if we Didn't Come Now!

I'd mess around for hours in the surf, diving into waves with goggles on watching as the breakers collapsed over themselves, froth curling like butter on the stony shore. The sea was *always* ready to play, and there was no need for anyone else; that was the beauty of it.

Lying in the narrow single bed back at Dad's, happily tired from a whole day outside, I realised something that felt inherently against the very nature of life as I knew it.

'What would you do if Dad moved back home?' I asked Stephen in the twilight of our tiny room.

'He's not going to, is he?' Stephen said, suddenly distraught, his camp bed squeaking as he turned to look at me.

'I know, I feel like that too. It's weird, when he lived with us, it was like he wasn't here, but now he's gone, we see more of him and he's... better. I prefer it. I think all parents should live in separate houses... I don't want them to divorce, though; they might meet other people. I just want it to stay like this forever.'

Stephen had nodded enthusiastically. 'Me too.'

\* \* \*

In a house where the air was stuffed with secrets, I couldn't help but snoop. When Mum was at work and if I wasn't watching TV with Stephen, I'd dig. Not too much because we'd seen an episode of *Murder She Wrote* where Angela Lansbury had detected an extraneous sheet of paper upon her desk within one second after a baddie had been prying. I'd already carefully rooted through Mum's chest of drawers in her bedroom to no avail. Her room smelled different after Dad had finally moved out: more floral, less of feet. Bored one afternoon, I opened the wardrobe for the first time with my detective head on. After moving a pair of leather boots and a spare blanket, I spotted an ancient Clarks duck-egg-blue shoe box, a sketch of Runabout lace-up shoes on the side while on the top, three 1950s stiff-looking children posed jauntily. 'Liz' was written in Mum's loopy script next to the figure of a girl walking a dog. Gingerly lifting off the lid, I discovered a stash of airmail letters and photos crammed in envelopes. I pulled out a black and white picture – a chubby baby with black curly hair and solemn dark eyes. Turning it over, *Derek six months* was printed in unfamiliar handwriting.

'What are you doing?' Stephen asked, the photo slipping from my fingers and down a crack in the wardrobe, trapped between the base and the back.

'Looking for the blanket. We could have a picnic?'

When I next looked, the box and photo had vanished.

\* \* \*

In August, Dad unexpectedly 'flew' back from Australia to live with us while Mum took part in a church retreat. She'd been unable to elaborate on her exact destination, other than it was a few days with another church group in Penzance. 'I'll ring you once I'm there.'

'Is Pastor Michael's wife going?' I asked, a rancorous volcano ready to erupt any second.

'No, Vanessa has to stay and look after their children.' Mum had bitten her lip and narrowed her eyes.

'Is anyone else going?' I asked airily, smiling, cheeks aching from the effort.

'A few others...'

'Who?'

Mum pretended not to hear and disappeared off to load the washing machine.

By the time Dad arrived on the Wednesday before Mum's lunchtime pick up, I just wanted her to go and refused to wave her off.

'Be good for your dad. No staying up late!'

'There was no one else in the van,' Stephen reported when he wandered back in.

'I think they were picking people up on the way,' Dad said, clearing his throat, leafing through the *Radio Times*. I wanted to scream at him to do something, stop her going in case she wrecked our cosy, separate-parent set up, but I didn't. Instead, I stomped upstairs and scrubbed under the rim of the toilet with his new toothbrush before being consumed by guilt, swilling it in Dettol to recompense. I pushed Tracey Bates' jibes out of my head. Mum was away with the church, not a singles club.

That Friday lunchtime, Dad had meetings in Brighton. 'Maybe don't mention to your mum I was out from eleven.' Stephen and I agreed to stay at home same as when Mum worked her half days at the Spar. Loaded up with Tesco own brand ready salted crisps and spaghetti hoops, we were frothing at the mouth for an unsupervised day. Stephen had seen a TV show about the Winter Olympic luge the day before and was keen to recreate it using Mum's black metal tea tray decorated with red roses. Sliding on the kitchen lino while I pushed wasn't quite the adrenaline rush he had been hankering after. Not even Vaseline along the bottom increased the speed.

'How about we try the stairs, but just start on step three,' I suggested sensibly. 'Nothing can go wrong from step three.'

Stephen immediately took it to step five; I waited with the sofa cushions at the bottom. After picking up some speed, Stephen made the giant leap to the top of the stairs, a vertiginous fourteen steps. He pushed himself off and skidded down the slope in a dignified manner, landing on cushions, slamming into my open hands before he could bounce any further.

'I'm going to do it properly now, like they do on the luge.'

In retrospect, I had no idea why I didn't stop him. What I *could* remember was watching helplessly as he careered out of control, slamming into the wall, the tea tray crumpling like tin foil, before smashing into the bannisters, the snapping sound more terrifying than the action itself. There was a moment's calm before the hallway filled with Stephen's high-pitched screaming. I scrambled to the third step where his head and shoulders were pinioned between two shattered spindles, his arm crushed beneath him. I knew enough from watching *Blue Peter* not to move him.

'Stephen, shush, shush, listen, I'm going next door to see if they can help.'

His howls rang out into the road as I jumped over the low garden fence and cut straight to the Bingham's front door, fruitlessly banging. They were out. The family on the other side, the Hills, were on holiday in Benidorm – Mr Hills had asked Mum to water the garden twice a week. Benidorm was their Mecca and they reliably stayed in the same high-rise hotel, returning home with blistered skin and T-shirt tan marks that lasted until November.

Stephen's wailing increased in volume and I ran back inside. With only a succession of elderly neighbours in the remaining houses and strangers towards the very bottom of the street, I tried not to panic. There was a boy two years above at school at number twelve, but I'd rather break my own arm than knock there.

I wished I hadn't hated Brownies – I'd stuck it for just three months, leaving with a useless Hostess badge. If only I'd bothered with the First Aid badge instead; tea-making skills were of no help in an emergency... Luckily, a policeman had given a talk at school before the holidays, all about Stranger Danger and how to call the emergency services if anyone dodgy approached you in the park asking if you wanted to see their puppies. I remembered wondering if gerbils were considered less threatening?

By the time I got off the phone, Stephen had wound himself down to a sheep-like baahing having turned the colour of watery blue skimmed milk.

'I feel sick,' he whispered in between bleats.

'Are you going to puke?'

He shook his head, then promptly vomited all over himself. Thankfully, we hadn't had lunch so it was only Ribena and a mulched up Granny Smith.

'I'm sorry.' He started to cry.

By the time the ambulance arrived, I'd soaked his Airwolf T-shirt with Dettol and dabbed it as much as I could.

Lord Baden Powell would have been impressed.

'Remember, you tripped and fell,' I hissed before opening the door. I wasn't going to prison for this.

'Where are your parents?' Barry the paramedic asked after establishing our names. He cast his eyes around the hallway before kneeling on the second step to examine Stephen, who whimpered when he gently prodded his arm.

'Mum's on a trip with the church and Dad's at work.'

'He's in Australia!' Stephen automatically piped up, groaning from the effort.

'He isn't, Stephen, that's only what we have to tell Grandma and Grandpa when he's not actually here, but he's here this week.'

'So you have no parents here?'

We shook our heads.

'When are they due back?'

'Dad's home at six-thirty, I think.' By now, another man had joined us, a moustachioed Ronald McDonald with curly ginger hair.

'Hello, I'm Alex. It looks like we're going to have to take you both in.'

'We're not supposed to leave the house,' I chipped in. 'Can you fix him here?'

'I'm afraid not. He needs an X-Ray and probably a cast.'

'Oh no.'

'How did it happen again?' Alex asked doubtfully, eyeing us suspiciously.

'He fell.'

'I want Stephen to tell me in his own words...'

I held my breath, sweeping my eyes up the wall, Stephen's erratic descent boldly scraped into the peach paintwork.

'I tripped and fell.'

'How exactly?'

'I was running, we were playing a game.'

'I see, OK.' That seemed to satisfy them both. 'Is there anyone else we can call? You mentioned grand-parents. Where are they?'

'In Leicester. Please don't call them; we'll get in trouble.' I changed tack. 'Would you like a cup of tea?' My Hostess badge skills were itching to create a diversion. 'There's custard creams too...'

'No thanks. We have to call someone and let them know what's happened. I'm sure everything will be fine.'

Everything was about to be the exact opposite of fine.

# 7

## THE SECRET'S OUT

Stephen was asleep on a sea of painkillers with his arm in a cast when Grandpa and Grandma arrived to collect us from Eastbourne's overflowing A&E department. 'Your brother has a clean break on his radius here,' the criminally young doctor had explained, pointing halfway up his forearm. We had been left in a cubicle with nurses occasionally poking their heads in. I passed the time by counting up to sixty in bananas and then checking the clock above the nurses' station every five minutes to see if my method was accurate. The first five minutes had been slightly too fast, so I slowed down and switched to elephants. By half an hour, I was on a roll.

'Home time!' a nurse sang, whipping the blue

curtain open, clapping her hands to wake Stephen up. 'Your ride has arrived!'

'Thank you, Nurse. So sorry you've had to look after them for us.' Grandma's deferential tone instantly set me on edge. 'What *are* you wearing, Cordelia? Aren't those shorts a bit too tight? Your foo foo's on show.'

I picked at the white trim on the navy terry towelling beach shorts. I probably had outgrown them, but they were my absolute favourite. I'd dragged them out of the dustbin twice after Mum had consigned them there. They were a carbon copy of George Michael's shorts in the poster I'd bought in Brighton HMV. I only preferred George over Andrew because he was the real talent behind the duo, *everyone* knew that, though if Andrew had asked me on a date, no way would I have turned him down despite its unlawfulness.

'So your father's back from Australia?' Grandma's enquiry strictly perfunctory, snapping me away from George and Andrew. Her main concern lay with holding a hankie against her nose. 'Herpes is rife in places like these.'

'Yes, he is,' I squeaked.

'How long is he home for this time?' Grandpa asked.

'Until Mum gets back.'

'He's flying back Sunday night?' Grandma was incredulous. 'That's rather a short trip with all that jet lag.'

I shrugged.

'Well, let's get you home and in to some more suitable clothes... Has your mother told you about deodorant?'

\* \* \*

'What happened to this?' Grandma appeared in the living-room doorway clasping the tray, a steely glint in her eyes. From the moment we'd returned from the hospital, she'd been banging pots around in the kitchen in an unprecedented display of domesticity.

I clamped my hand over my mouth. I'd hidden the bashed-up thing by the bin, intending to throw it out later. I frantically tried to think of a brilliant lie but low blood sugar tripped me up. They'd offered us Bourbon biscuits in A&E with a cup of sweet tea each, but that had been hours ago.

'What on earth!' Grandpa gasped, tearing his attention away from the TV and a news story about the Eurotunnel. 'I gave that to your mother when she left home. It's a genuine Russian antique from the Romanov family vaults, worth a bleeding fortune!'

We should have sold it to buy a VHS player! But then I recalled Dad ranting last Christmas through the kitchen door when we'd all opened our annual collection of mini shampoos filched from hotels and the twice-yearly cruises: 'Your dad's so tight, he'd skin a fart!' Grandpa had probably swiped the tray from a hotel too.

'Who ruined it?' Grandma snapped, eyes swivelling between me and Stephen.

Stephen immediately started to cry, snivelling into his good elbow. He would have been hopeless in *The Great Escape*, choking out the locations of all three tunnels in under two minutes of limp questioning. Grandpa was about to join all the dots when...

'Mum and Dad are separated!' I shouted, nerves shredded.

'What?' Grandma yelped. 'What do you mean "separated"?'

'Dad's in Australia,' Stephen said, tears pouring from his eyes.

'So your dad isn't here at all?' Grandpa was almost gleeful, clapping his hands together. 'He's in Australia, ran off and left you all for good this time?'

'No!' I cried, trying to reign in the truth.

'What do you mean, girl? Spit it out!' Grandpa instructed.

A key turned in the door at exactly the same time as burning hit my nostrils.

'Whose is that brand-new Jaguar in the street?' Dad called, opening the front door. 'Has Prince Charles come to visit? Whoa, something's burning!' He dropped his leather book bag in the hallway and ran into the kitchen where I met him amid the smoke clouds billowing from under the grill and spiralling from the pan on top of the stove.

'Oh, dearie me, I forgot all about their dinner!' Grandma cried, rushing into the kitchen, almost bashing into Dad who turned off the grill, yanking out the tray, and as he did, the two pieces of charred toast instantly caught fire like a couple of crêpe flambés. He threw the whole thing and the spaghetti-hoop pan in the sink, blasting them with the taps, steam violently hissing. Wafting the smoke away from his face, he scrabbled about for the key on the side by the back door and opened it, gulping in fresh air.

'Grandma and Grandpa are here!' I managed to wheeze in between coughs.

'I can see that. Hello, Beatrice, how are you?' Dad's eyebrows arched.

Grandma appeared momentarily flummoxed while Grandpa strode into the room on a cloud of testosterone, leading with his pink-shirted barrel chest, everything escalating in double time. 'I think we need to have a chat, man to man,' he growled, his shirt buttons straining, nodding at Grandma.

'Can someone tell me what's going on?' Dad asked, ignoring the pugilistic invite.

Before I could say a word, Grandma bustled me out of the kitchen, then darted back in, shutting the door in my face. Pressing my ear against the wood panel above the brass handle, all I could hear was the low rumble of Grandpa's baritone in the farthest corner of the kitchen. *Lois, loser, cut out of, made her bed, didn't listen, flighty, like Elizabeth...* As soon as the tap blasted, indicating the kettle was probably being filled, I scuttled back to the sofa. The kitchen door swung open and Dad joined us in the living room, giving Stephen a big hug. Of course it made him cry.

'Well, the S H one T is about to hit the fan.'

'I'm sorry,' I mumbled. 'It just slipped out.'

'They would have found out sooner or later.'

'What?' Stephen asked. 'Find out what?'

I stared at him sat on the sofa, resting his cast on a pillow. Did he not listen to anything?

Grandpa and Grandma left soon after, filling

their tartan flask with tea for the homeward journey, excited about 'getting back to civilisation'. Apparently, there was going to be a phone call. Or a solicitor's letter, I was too tired to remember.

\* \* \*

Mum was in the front of the transit van next to Pastor Michael; they were alone. The pastor had parked opposite our house but further down nearer number twelve. I'd decided to await Mum's grand return inside the bay tree which was really a bush, spilling up and over the low front wall. Pastor Michael suddenly grabbed Mum's face, holding it between his hands like an actor, then kissed her. Mum immediately pushed him away vehemently shaking her head before opening the door, yanking out a bag from the footwell. I strained my ears but could only hear a magpie's machine-gun rattle, far-off traffic on the main road, and the rustling of the branches every time I moved. Mum stood staring through the open van door when the pastor stretched his hands towards her. 'Please, Lois, I'm begging you...' I *definitely* heard that. Mum just slammed the door, swinging her bag over her shoulder and made a beeline for the house. As she opened the garden gate and walked slowly up the path, she turned round to wave away the van like a nuisance pigeon then rummaged in her bag for keys.

'Just go, will you? Pathetic.'

As soon as she disappeared inside, I hastily wriggled out, branches scraping my arms. Propelled by powerful wings of injustice, I ran down the side alley at the end and round to the back gate which I'd unbolted earlier. Creeping up the grass, undetectable from the house, I opened the back door to the sound of conversation floating from the living room.

'But I don't understand how you fell.' Mum's voice stretched dog-whistle thin.

'We were playing upstairs and I just fell.'

'But what's the massive gouge down the wall? I spotted that before the smashed spindles. It's like you chiselled it out with a knife.'

'I hadn't even noticed it until you pointed it out,' Dad said.

'Of course you didn't,' Mum sighed. 'You don't notice anything.'

I hurtled through the kitchen in a storm of white-hot fury. 'Why are you being so mean?'

'Cordelia! I'm only asking what happened! Nice to see you too.' She leaned in for a kiss but I backed away. How had a pious church retreat turned into a hot bed of sin? What was going to happen to our radical family arrangement now? 'I got you a present.' She proffered a white paper carrier bag with *Visit Cornwall* stamped on the side. I took it despite the rage; a present was still a present. Stephen was already wearing his cool yellow T-shirt, emblazoned with a red surf board. *Surfers do it in the waves.*

'I think we need to talk.' Dad's sober tone hinted at no children present.

'I'd love to,' Mum cooed. 'Let me just go and powder my nose and I'll meet you in *our* bedroom.' She jumped up and swanned into the hallway like she knew the room was watching. Dad shrugged at us before doggedly following her upstairs. Peering into the paper bag, I pulled out a small fake-leather jewellery box; inside was a delicate gold-plated chain bracelet with a mother-of-pearl bead strung in the centre. It was the most beautiful thing I had ever owned.

I headed towards the door.

'Where are you going?' Stephen asked, pulling a face.

'To say thank you for this and sorry for shouting. Maybe I didn't see what I saw...'

'What are you on about?'

'Nothing. Won't be a minute.'

# 8

## THE CHANNEL

'Gross!' My hand plunged into a corpulent mop of bladder wrack, ropes of plump nodules catching between my fingers. So much for sharks; the terror of the Channel revealed itself as a gargantuan floating bank of flocculant seaweed, something I hadn't yet encountered off Eastbourne beach, but had been warned about. Pockets of raw sewage another potential impediment. Lifting my neck while continuing to swim like a nana anxious about a shampoo and set, I glanced to *Boudica's* port side for guidance, taking out an earplug. To my left, the bladder wrack stretched about the length of two white vans but maybe only one to the right, its length indeterminate.

'Swim through it; it'll be quicker than going round!' Desi instructed. 'It's not huge!'

A wave cuffed the back of my head, the gentle swell rippling the russet carpet like an autumn breeze ruffling rotting leaves on a woodland floor. A hulking tanker muscled through the water roughly six hundred metres behind.

'You're doing so well!' Desi called encouragingly. 'Keep going! Have you been for a pee yet?'

'Just giving the fish a golden shower now!'

'They'll love that, the kinky things!'

Temporary warmth flooded my thighs, blunting the cold's knife edge. I'd resigned to operating with numb extremities so dipped my hands into the wee stream. No time to stop, I popped the earplug back in and struck my leading arm straight through the matted weed, its pungent smell coating the back of my throat. I managed to pick my way through in less time than it took to re-establish my train of thought.

Our parents had been so comfortable within their dysfunctional marriage that neither Stephen nor I had noticed until it reached the tipping point panning out like a farcical storyline from Texan oil-baron soap, *Dallas*.

Prolonged training swims had naturally led to navel gazing, vignettes from childhood and more recently, the dating battlefield of middle age, filtering up from the vaults. Sinking into a trough of shared interests, shared living arrangements, holidays, meeting family members and introducing friends, ignited an anxiety-induced spiral that I couldn't rationally explain. Or rather, I didn't want to, though I did enjoy connection. I am by no means a nun. However, not everyone was keen for a relationship within such limiting parameters; compromise remained a foreign concept. So it was by complete default that I was a perfect candidate for casual dating apps and all the 'interesting' encounters they bred.

Ian, forty-one, divorced (Bumble, sixth attempt), had been a memorable date. By our second rendezvous in Bibendum, having already dispensed with niceties, he proceeded to scrape his teeth with the olive-bowl toothpick, wiping the gluck on his finger (licking it clean!), then replaced said toothpick in the dish with the olives. Pretty standard behaviour after a few months of dating, or in a long-term relationship, but read the room on a second date. I escaped to the 'toilet' via the front door, in the knowledge I was wholly imperfect myself. I hoped at least I had never instilled anyone with 'the ick', a word I'd recently gleaned from Instagram (who knew there were so many posts about 'the dating ick'?). I just thought it was the perfect umbrella term covering so many unsavoury habits.

One of my own dating howlers involved my short-term memory, so stunted I'd be unable to pick anyone out of a line-up if they'd shot me at close range and I lived to tell the tale. I was on a date with James, forty, (Hinge, first ever app date!) when I returned from the toilet just after I'd introduced myself. Faced with a busy bar packed with identical tables and a few single men sat at them, I panicked. I couldn't remember his face; it was like losing your car in a car park. I'd left my phone inside my bag on the ledge behind his chair, so I couldn't check his picture. I didn't recall his outfit, then when I tried to think of his name, it evaporated. John? Jack? Jake? George? Fuck. Forced to nonchalantly wander from table to table where all the men were scrolling on phones, heads bent, I hazarded a guess and sat at the nearest one, praying he was George/James/Jack. I *thought* he was blond. He smiled expectantly.

I was in the middle of a passable conversation about the benefits of cactuses versus succulents (they were dotted all over the bar) when the genuine James waved me over from two tables away just as that gentleman's date arrived. From that day on, I never left the table without my phone, not even if it was a third date – rookie error. Trust no one, not even yourself. Thankfully, I'd never been caught picking my nose and flicking it on the floor like another nameless Hinge date. Everyone loves a good nasal passage rummage but not on a first date and certainly not before you've had sex. At least he hadn't popped it in his mouth.

I tried to imagine Mum let loose on dating apps back in her pomp. Strings of broken hearts as far as the eye could see. These days, it was a different story.

'I'm far too busy, Cordelia, no time to waste mothering some sad sack of a man baby who can't boil an egg. *Golden Years* won't produce itself.' Oh yes, my mother, queen of the septuagenarian podcasts.

*Head down, four strokes, breathe out. Bubbles.*

# 9

## SURPRISE SURPRISE!

'The kids want us to live in the same house. Ask them.' Mum's syrupy tone had been replaced by an urgent, pleading lilt. I'd fully intended on knocking to thank her for the gorgeous bracelet, but my parents' conversation poured salt on that. Instead, I huddled on the threshold of my room, listening through the gap in their door.

'Do they, Lois?'

'What's that supposed to mean?'

'You've kidded yourself it's about what the children want, but you're really concerned with what *you* want. I'm not a fucking paper-doll husband here for your amusement – thought I made that clear last time. I'm just here for the kids, plain and simple.'

'No need to swear.'

'It's time we started being more truthful, for us and the kids. They'll be fine, just ask them, we have a great time at the weekends. Go off and make yourself happy.'

Wow, Mum and Dad never swore! Not even a 'bloody', which I'd pounced on at school, brazenly informing anyone who would listen it was safe to do so: 'Bloody's in the Bible, bloody's in the book. If you don't bloody believe me, take a bloody look!' That shut most people up.

'They're kids, Philip. They don't know what they want,' Mum said distractedly.

'You mean like you?'

'Funny... I want you to live here with us, to be a family again. It'll be different this time. I feel different.'

'Gone off him, have you?'

'It's not like that.'

'It can't all be roses and rebellion, Lois. The sooner you accept life's mostly dull, painful and repetitive, ending in death, the sooner you'll get over whatever it is you're chasing. Rainbows aren't permanent. Life's the same whomever you're with.'

'Listen to you,' Mum said sadly. 'The tortured young writer's still in there somewhere.'

'You must think I'm a complete idiot. You're like a cat with a bird. I'm surprised you dug in deep this time and actually went full Jesus creeper. That's real method seduction.'

'How many times...? Nothing happened!'

'Whatever you say. I never saw the point of this charade in the first place. Your parents know we're separated now so we can just get on with it.'

'What? How?'

Bloody hell, I was for the high jump now.

'I told them.'

*Phew!*

'You know how your dad gets, all thumb screws and blinding spotlight. We couldn't play along forever. We're not reconciling, not this time; let's just call it a day.'

'Philip! You've no idea what you've done.'

'Told them what they've been waiting to hear ever since we got married?'

'Yes, but... Honestly, it's the end.'

'Cake and eating it, Lois? I wasn't going to wait in the wings for eternity.'

'Don't say that. This isn't how we work.' Mum sounded like Stephen when he wasn't allowed to stay up past his bedtime. 'I'll have a flip out, need some space, you let me have it to make up for what happened, then we fall back together... It's what we do, have *always* done.'

'Until now. You wanted the moon on a sodding stick.' Dad got up, the bed springs squeaking. He was a prolific fiddler; Stephen was equally unable to sit still for long. 'Why on earth did you insist on the separation in the first place if it's not what you really want?' Dad snapped.

'A little break, to make sure I stuck it to the end, until they died.'

'*Stuck it to the end*?'

'That came out wrong.'

I imagined Dad covering his face with his palms and shaking his head in disbelief like he did when I called a spade a club during Pontoon.

'I was never going to leave, Philip. I can't. But... I dunno... I got married so young. You'd already lived a life, sewn those oats left right and centre.'

'I think you're imagining someone else.'

The official mandate of their union was well worn. Dad had been a poverty-stricken writer on a tiny, under-funded, arts-review magazine based in Brighton. Mum had caught the train down in 1969 to visit a secretarial college while staying with a friend, declaring she needed to escape the landlocked Midlands, see the sea. But she'd met Dad in a pub in the

Lanes on the first night of her stay, dazzled by his coolness, his long hair, his flamboyant musician and artist friends. They'd fallen madly in love and eloped at Brighton registry office with two strangers bearing witness. So romantic. I was born five years later.

'Lizzie didn't seem to think so.'

'Your sister's a bloody lesbian, what does she know?'

*Sister?* Mum was an only child.

'A lot more than you think. She's slept with a few boys too.'

This was more scandalous than an episode of *Surprise Surprise* on ITV, not that I'd been allowed to watch it.

'Remember Dad said if I kept in contact with Lizzie, they'd cut me off like her? The fall out about her and Sarah – throwing her out on the drive...' I could well imagine Grandpa's reaction to lesbians. 'They still think we have no contact, even now. I couldn't let them win; one of us had to inherit their ill-gotten gains so the sodding horse didn't get it.'

'It's not like they're the Rockefellers; they've probably already spanked it all on Lady Madonna.'

'Dad's the Donald Trump of the Midlands! There's bound to be something worth having at the end. All that money scammed from those poor old people.'

'Habits formed during the war, Lois. A hell of a lot of looting went on from both sides... House clearing old dears' antiques for peanuts before they go into a care home is pecuniary deception, no different to Nazi's "liberating" Jewish gold.' He cleared his throat. 'No matter, what's all this got to do with us?'

'Everything.'

I rocked my bum sideways; it was starting to tingle.

'After the wedding, they sent me a solicitors letter saying if we split up, they'd cut me off.'

'Yeah, he ranted along those lines. I just assumed he was bluffing.'

'No! He meant every word!'

'Nice to know you'd have legged it had they forced the handcuffs on beforehand.'

'They never mentioned it; we eloped, remember... Anyway, you're forgetting I was four months pregnant – how could I run away? But *that* didn't work out, did it? By then it was too late; we were already married.'

'Hey! I was—'

'Don't pretend it was a love-conquers-all scenario; you were just doing the right thing.'

'We were in love, once. You make it sound like
you've had the most awful time.'

'I haven't always, I just feel...' Her sentence glided
into an abyss.

No one spoke for a whole minute.

'Why didn't you ever tell me instead of all this
byzantine cloak and dagger?' Dad asked eventually.

Mum failed to reply.

'Jesus, Lois, you really are something!'

'What?'

'Don't "what" me. You were always going to divorce me as soon as they died.'

'That's ridiculous. We might still have another
twenty years of them in dotage... though with Dad's
smoking, I'm not confident.'

'He'll outwit death in an iron lung, just you see.'

The bed springs squeaked again and Mum must
have joined him standing at the window. 'I didn't tell
you because how would it look? We'd just got married, then May died, I went a bit – sorry, a *lot* loopy,
then oh, guess what, you're trapped with me forever
because I prefer money more than anything. I actually thought they'd eventually come round, accept
you, especially now you're doing great guns at work.'

'I think we both know your dad's a stubborn old bastard who'll never admit when he's wrong.' How could an innocent tea tray betray so much secret history? 'Do you really need that cash?'

'It's not just mine, is it? It's the kids' and Lizzy's and Derek's. We both agreed I'd split it with her. She needs it; Jeremy's care bills have stripped them.'

Jeremy, Lizzy, May? Derek – the baby in the photo?

'But meanwhile, I'm expected to what? Watch you do whatever the fuck you like, all the while thinking it's helping you from going doolally again, but really it's to keep the fortune in sight. That's all I ever was, a Golden Goose?'

'No! I'll try harder. I'll leave the church, the Spar. I know they're looking for a secretary at Cavendish School. I can finally use my training.' Blind desperation seeped through the gap in the door.

'It's too late.'

'I *know* I can change their minds. I'll say it was a mistake, that all marriages go through ups and downs – we're making a go of it.' Mum's voice cracked in places. 'I can't let them win, not after all this time.'

'No, Lois, I'm sorry. You were right; we were flogging a dead horse.'

'Have you met someone else? You're different.'

A deep silence threatened the already precarious status quo.

'I'm forty-four, Lois. I'm sick of the drama. I just want to enjoy my time with the kids and have some fun.'

My chest flooded with relief. Dad was still ours.

'But it's life or death.'

'It isn't, it's money procured from swindling! There's a Faustian price tag attached.'

'But Lizzy—'

'Lizzy's a grown up. She chose to move over the pond.'

'Philip, Jeremy's terminal.'

'Cordy, what are you doing?' Stephen hissed through the landing bannisters. 'You've been ages.'

I sprung like a cat, stepping over the treacherous floorboards and met him at the top of the stairs.

'Go!' I whispered just as the doorknob turned. We skidded down the stairs, mindful of Stephen's cast, and bolted into the living room. 'Put the telly on!'

# 10

## THE CHANNEL

Half an hour of elephants trampled past before the whistle blew, heralding the next feed; *Boudica*'s engine petered out, the yellow rib bumping her stern like an eager puppy. The horizon's brink drifted below the rising cerulean haze, a brisk breeze rippling the placid surface. The sun had yet to reach peak arc; it must be morning still. *Or was it?* I cast around for Cathy's simple sun trajectory explanation; predictably it dissolved like names, faces and every random reason for nipping upstairs. I couldn't be the only one with a giant stock room hunched at the back of my mind holding all that misplaced information ready to download in a final moment of deathbed clarity. *It was Tim Sullivan, in the bedroom, looking for the love eggs.*

I removed an earplug and popped it into the tiny pocket just beneath my left strap. Handy.

Alan waved from the deck, bottle in hand.

Breath flowed easily; that was never going to be a problem – this wasn't a sprint. I'd since been schooled to not shun strength, a potent word synonymous with over-developed, East-German female shot putters whose barrel thighs collided when they walked. I'd pushed myself to deadlift eighty-six kilograms – how about that for strength? Watch your back, Arnie. How had the unattainable thigh gap ever been my lodestar? Thanks to bicep curls, my wrists no longer crumbled while emptying pans of pasta water down the sink. Dylan, thirty-eight, (Tinder, fourth attempt) would be screaming, 'I told you so'. Hadn't it been obvious that after almost a year of dating I didn't relish unsolicited advice?

'You know you should try lifting weights instead of cycling on your spin bike all the time – you don't *need* to lose weight. Once you get past a certain age, women are supposed to build muscle, not try and outrun it. It's better for you.'

'I appreciate your concern but it's probably better for *you* if you don't comment on women's bodies.'

Dylan had managed all that time without ruining the post-coital glow; why had he decided to start now?

'All OK?' Alison called out between mouthfuls of yet another sandwich, yanking her long grey hair out of the way. 'You're doing really well.'

I shot her a thumbs up and necked the sickly Maxim, in awe of anyone able to eat in sight of an undulating horizon.

Desi stood gazing out from the stern, all pensive pout, Simon Le Bon in the *Rio* video, a flash of neon-pink nails as he dragged his hand through his Afro. The tone matched his T-shirt. Desi never abandoned his post – style over substance every time.

'Dad would love to have been here, see you do this. He'd be so proud.'

'Maybe he's on day release?' I shouted back.

'I wish! You've got a boat to catch home, don't want to miss it. Love you!' Desi wiped his eyes and dramatically flicked tears into the sea, stomping over to Alan to give him a big kiss.

'Love you too. Where am I, by the way? And don't say the middle aisle in Aldi!'

'In the Channel, you numb nut. We're not falling for that trick! Keep swimming!'

*Head down, four strokes, breathe out. Bubbles.*

# 11

## THE SHOE BOX

Stephen and I longed for Dad to remain single in perpetuity. 'Nothing will change,' he'd promised us after the divorce announcement. Which was a great relief. Mum could do what she liked, as long as we still had Dad's undivided attention to escape to – a good job because Mum appeared to be in the grip of a major crisis. She'd resigned from the Spar (Wednesday Slimnastics remained at the Tin Pot Cathedral), and had forsaken Jesus entirely, meaning she was at home all the time, leaving unfinished cups of tea dotted around the house like discarded Eucharist. I'd even found one in the empty bath.

'Children, I've something to tell you.' Mum appeared spectre-like, her face more wan than her beloved skimmed milk. We were in the middle of erecting the tent for an epic sleep out in the back garden. She beckoned us inside, arms wrapped around herself as if winter had unexpectedly dropped by. Once in the living room, I spotted the old Clarks' shoe box from Mum's wardrobe sitting incongruously on the coffee table. *Oh, God. Here we go...*

'Mum, I'm sorry, I didn't mean to—'

'I had a letter today from your grandparents—' Mum spoke over the top of me, patting the sofa. Stephen sat on the red foot stool. 'What's wrong, Cordy?'

'Nothing.'

'OK, I don't think we're going to see them any more.'

'Why?' Stephen asked, reassuringly clueless.

'Because they're angry that Dad and I are getting divorced.' Mum's full beam cut straight to the section of my brain where I'd stuffed the truth. She knew! Grandpa must have dobbed me in. Was I in for a slow painful punishment or a swift, sharp stab in the back? Both, it turned out.

'Will we have to sell the house?' I asked, recollecting the part about not inheriting the family fortune. 'Are we poor now?'

'No, we should be OK, as long as I get another

job. It just means no more visits to Leicester, which is no bad thing.'

'We're never going to see them again?' Stephen asked, unsure whether he was supposed to be upset.

'I don't know.' She paused. 'When one door closes, another opens up.' Mum inhaled sharply. 'I have a sister...'

Stephen smirked and subtly kicked me. Normally I would have returned the favour, but was too concerned with Mum's revelation. 1983, the ABC Cinema, *Return of the Jedi*, Stephen cried, 'Ewwww, Luke kissed his sister! Gross!' Leia had just come to the same crashing conclusion.

'I haven't talked about her because I had to keep her a secret all this time.' Resemblances with Leia continued.

'Why?' Stephen asked.

'Because she and your grandparents massively fell out and they wanted me to cut ties with her as well.'

'Why?'

'Is that all you can say, Stephen?'

He nodded.

'They were, *are* very old fashioned with strange ideas and are champion grudge holders.' She reached over and picked up the shoe box, lifting the lid, drawing out the uneven pile of photos and letters. 'Aunty Liz lives in Chicago; she moved there when I was nearly twenty.' She shuffled out a black-and-white picture of her much younger teenage self with a girl whose angular face was buried under a long fringe skirting a dark beehive hairstyle creating the illusion she was moderately taller than Mum. 'She married a man called Jeremy to get what's called a green card.'

'What's that?' Stephen asked.

'An official document that allows you to live and work in America. You can get one by marrying an American citizen.'

'Why did she move all that way?' I asked. Was it something to do with being a lesbian? I didn't know any confirmed lesbians. Everyone teased Vicky Wentworth because she wore turn-up jeans and polo shirts outside of school. Dean Hitchens had even called her a lezzer in the dinner queue when she refused the lamb hot pot. Despite Mum's warning about radioactive lamb in the wake of the Chernobyl disaster, I chose it in case he picked on me too. I only ate the potatoes.

'To be with... someone.'

'Uncle Jeremy?' Stephen asked, delighted about the added prefix.

'Yes, and no, someone else, but that part doesn't matter; it didn't last.'

I knew who Aunty Liz was from stealth eavesdropping and had relayed the facts to Stephen, who promptly forgot, like he did with everything unless it involved a car. He memorised makes and models of every vehicle in existence if they featured on his Top Trumps cards.

'So, Aunty Liz married Jeremy, and they had a son called Derek. He was born before Cordelia.' She handed out another few black and white photos of an older Aunty Liz with a pageboy haircut, now holding a little baby with dark curly hair. *Derek six months.*

'He's American?' Stephen gasped in awe.

'Yes. He's also half caste.'

'What's that?'

'It means his dad, Jeremy, has black skin and Aunty Liz has white, like you. Derek is in between.'

A more recent picture filed at the back showed a young Derek in all his colourful glory wearing red shorts, paddling in a lake, waving at the camera.

'So... he's brown?' Stephen marvelled.

'Yes! Derek is brown, but he's still your cousin.'

'Wow.'

'Here, this is Jeremy.'

I studied the picture carefully. He blissfully cradled Derek, his hooded eyes holding stories he'd not told a soul. Stephen kept trying to grab it but I elbowed him. The string of beads poking from between the collar of his shirt was the most bohemian thing I'd ever seen. I tried to imagine Dad wearing some. No.

'When was the last time you saw Aunty Liz?' How could anyone hide they had a sister? I couldn't hide Stephen if I tried.

Mum bit her lip and gazed meaningfully out of the window. 'She last visited the UK about nine years ago, when you were little. I met her in London overnight; you stayed with your dad.'

'Can we go and visit them, in America?' Stephen asked hopefully.

Mum slowly shook her head.

'I think they might come over next year, after...' Mum looked down at her lap and tightly clasped her hands. 'Jeremy isn't well. I'm not sure you'll get to... see him before... he...' A lone tear trickled down her cheek. She gracefully stood and wandered into the kitchen as if seeking the rest of the sentence.

'Why did you have to ask that?' I snapped before trailing after her, finding her at the sink getting a glass of water. 'Are you OK, Mum?'

'I'll be fine.' She sniffed and wiped her cheek with the back of her hand before combing her eyes over me. 'I thought I asked you to throw those shorts away. They make your legs look like tree trunks.'

*Oof!* I touched my face, convinced she'd slapped me. Mum narrowed her eyes and for a split second I was confronted by Grandma's flinty glare capable of cutting sheet metal. I fled upstairs, slamming the bedroom door, ripping off the offending shorts, throwing them across the room so they hit the back of the door with a dull thud. Bursting into tears, I curled into a ball in just my kickers and A-ha T-shirt. I didn't hear the gentle knocking at first.

'Cordy? Cordy? I didn't mean it. I'm just upset. I'll buy you some new shorts. We can even go to Topshop?'

'Go away.' I buried my head in the pillow.

The incident drew my love affair with shorts to a close. I still had to wear mandatory PE ones, but even then, I permanently wore a size too big.

# 12

## THE CHANNEL

Isn't it amazing what your brain can disinter given enough time to reflect? I'd not thought about the shorts for decades. Breath constricted, I forced my head above water. I took a moment, swimming upright, face drenched in glorious sunlight. Should someone have the temerity to body shame me now, the words wouldn't find the chance to germinate into something more insidious. The shorts had snatched carefree sea swimming from me. I'd since insisted on wearing baggy T-shirts to my knees before dipping a toe in the water, a prudish Victorian swimmer weighed down by a crinoline skirt and umbrella. Eventually, I stopped swimming in the sea altogether, but that was after everything else...

If I'd never worn the shorts, if I hadn't snitched to Grandpa, if Stephen hadn't skidded on the tea tray, if only I'd stopped him. *If we'd chosen Dad.* If, such a small word with incredibly broad shoulders. Yet I wouldn't be swimming the Channel *if* none of that had happened.

*Head down, four strokes, breathe out. Bubbles.*

# 13

## THE PINK PALACE

A few nights before school resumed, there was a knock on the front door just as Mum eased a tray of Findus pizza fingers out of the oven.

'Can you get that?' she cried to no one in particular so that Stephen and I lingered where we were playing Monopoly. When no one answered, the doorbell rang instead. Mum strode into the hallway. 'Thank you for listening,' she grumped passing the living room. I heard the front door open before the scream. We jumped up and skidded into the hallway to find Mum splattered in broken eggs, her face dripping in yolk. Mrs French, Pastor Michael's wife, stood on the front step, an open egg box in her hand, three missing, two having hit their target, the third ready to

launch. Thank goodness for wipe-clean carpet pro-
tectors.

'Be thankful I'm not a violent person and didn't
take the Bible literally,' she choked out. 'I chose eggs
instead of stones. It's symbolic.' Mrs French was a
diminutive woman with wiry brown hair and sides of
ham poking out of her sleeveless white blouse.

'What on earth are you doing?' Mum eventually
spluttered, wiping albumen out of her mouth. That
was the first food I'd seen near her lips in days.

'Letting you know you chose the wrong marriage
to wreck.'

'Vanessa—'

'You're worse than Jezebel.'

'Believe me, I'm not interested in Michael.'

'No, not any more, he told me how you dropped
him – he's broken. He's not just for your amusement.'

Mum turned round and ushered us back towards
the living room. We hid behind the door frame,
catching every word.

'It's your family I feel sorry for. Your daughter
especially – how can she look to you for moral guidance? She'll end up—'

'Enough! It takes two to wreck a marriage; perhaps look in the mirror and wonder why his eyes
wandered.' Mum slammed the door in her face as an

egg splattered the glass panel. The rest of the eggs followed suit.

The letter box flap flipped open from the outside. 'And forget about your Fatnastics classes,' Mrs French hissed, viper-like. 'We don't need your custom any more.'

'You owe me my deposit!'

But the flap had already snapped shut. I dashed to the bay window, catching a furious Mrs French barrelling down the path and into the street, the empty egg box lying face down on the step. She'd bought the cheap ones from Tesco. No one mentioned the egg incident again; regrettably, it wasn't the end of it.

Day three at Cavendish senior school, I had managed to make two new friends: Sarah Williams (wavy brown hair like me, no freckles) and Michelle Savage (sleek blonde hair and understatedly pretty). They'd joined from St Barts middle school; thank the senior school overlords, Tracey Bates was in a completely different class to me.

'I'm Cordelia, but everyone calls me Cordy for short.' Not true, only my family did. I boldly shook off boringly average, middle-school Cordelia: new name, new me.

'Oh my God, I love Madonna's "True Blue" album and Cadbury's Boost Bars too.'

'Wham! or Duran Duran?'

'Wham! all the way! George is the best!' We had *everything* in common; we even found farts unbearably funny. Sarah could also burp to G in the alphabet. We were definitely not cool.

Meanwhile, in the changing room after Games, our whole year had been instructed to strip naked and shower after hockey. I think I would have preferred prison.

'You don't want to go back to class and smell, do you?' Mrs James, the PE teacher, bellowed like a drill sergeant, swinging her whistle on its ribbon, eager to take someone's eye out. A few of the girls showered in their knickers while everyone else shimmied in and out with towels round them. I waited until everyone had finished before dashing in, becoming the last to leave the communal stalls. Shivering, desperately hoping no one had noticed my embarrassingly patchy cloud of fresh pubes, I stumbled to a halt just before returning to my peg; the unmistakable voice of Tracey Bates recruiting potential acolytes brayed from the far reaches of the benches. Michelle and Sarah were agog.

'And then she threw a box of twelve eggs at her,

screaming the place down so all the neighbours came out to watch – they were all cheering, Mum said so anyway. Her dad left ages ago, that's when it all started really, but Mum said it was only a matter of time. That the Spar manager's wife was on to her. They've cancelled her Slimnastics classes; Mum used to go. Must be so embarrassing for *her* mum though, not only the whole adultery thing, but being a fitness instructor and having a daughter with—'

Icy fingers slid around my heart. Blind fury propelled me towards them, ramming fists in Tracey's hair, yanking out chunks whilst kicking her in the groin. Only last week I'd seen Daisy deliver that kind of justice on *The Dukes of Hazard*. Without warning, a splash of blue and yellow feathers flapped through my mind's eye.

'You ugly cunt!' I hissed just before a whistle splintered my ear, Mrs James bundling me over to the other side of the changing room completely starkers.

It. Was. The. End.

Later in the headmaster's office, fully clothed and brimming with hostility, both of us refused to crack.

'So neither of you can tell me what happened? You must have said something, Tracey?'

'No, sir.'

Mr Kilburn steepled his hands, before touching them to his chin like a Bond villain.

'I have no choice but to put you both in detention for the rest of the week.'

'This isn't over, Streaker,' Tracey hissed in the corridor afterwards, shoving me into the wall. 'Things are only just getting started.'

Detention was a slap on the wrist compared to Tracey's threat, school swiftly becoming an endurance test until Mum played her trump card.

'I've got some good news,' Mum delivered rather smugly once we'd all sat down to dinner that evening. 'I got the job as Cavendish School secretary. I start after half term.'

'What? Nooooooooo!' I shot upstairs, abandoning my fish fingers. Mum was going to be the person you reported to if you got caught by a heavy period and needed to borrow a spare skirt from lost property, if you had to see the nurse, or ring your parents. The gatekeeper to so many arenas, wielding an impressive slice of power. It wasn't quite as bad as being an actual Godforsaken teacher, but still, senior school wasn't dispensing the fresh start I'd prayed for. So far, the only person who acknowledged me after the entire year had been treated to Tracey's twisted version of Streakergate, was David Plimpton. We weren't exactly friends, though I had voluntarily chatted to him in the lunch queue during the first week, bathing in my new-friend ambrosial bubble, dispensing kindness like Jesus offering alms to the poor.

'Don't lose this.' I'd tapped him on the shoulder and handed over a brown pocket envelope clinking with coins. I'd watched it drop from his school bag. 'Someone'll spend it all on chips!'

He'd mutely taken it, nodding a silent thanks.

David was of small stature with a sandy, brutal, dictator haircut that showcased his dimples and round freckled cheeks, making him look like he'd hopped straight from an Enid Blyton novel. On the first day of senior school, he'd turned up in a perfectly pressed pair of grey shorts. He lasted a week before the name calling and piss-taking preceded him everywhere until it was passed round that his mum had died just before the summer holidays. No one felt right teasing him after that.

'It will get better, you know. They'll all forget what happened in a few weeks,' he said, claiming the adjacent spare seat as I stared listlessly at my cheese and pickle sandwiches. 'D'you want a chip?'

I was too upset even for chips. Unheard of. But every lunchtime, he saved a seat next to him. We didn't talk, just ate lunch in silence while the chaos of the dinner hall exploded around us. If I arrived first, I made sure to seek out a table with a spare seat, certain no one but him would dare to sit next to Streaker.

\* \* \*

'I want you all to memorise a famous poem or a short piece of prose that you'll then recite out loud during our next lesson,' Mrs Merritt announced in the fourth week, our English class collectively slumping. The dreaded day rolled round way too fast. My roiling guts had me bent double on the toilet during the entirety of morning break, desperately unable to recall any of 'How doth the little crocodile', a short verse from our childhood poetry book that I could reliably deliver word perfect under any other circumstances. After sweating through my jumper and leaving a considerable wet patch on the seat, it was my turn. Nearly forty years later, I could recite the poem flawlessly, but that morning, it took leave of absence.

'Sit!' Mrs Merritt barked. I was too insignificant to garner any reaction, possibly the biggest insult of them all. There was no sweet relief of having completed the task, just confirmation that I, Cordelia, was shit at everything. 'Where are my Romeos and my Rosalinds?' Mrs Merritt lamented.

When David stood to recite his piece, Mrs Merritt raised her eyebrows, as if expecting yet another fiasco.

> *'But, soft! what light through yonder*
> *window breaks?*
> *It is the east, and Juliet is the sun.'*

David proceeded to recite something I half recognised as Shakespeare, later identified as a soliloquy from *Romeo and Juliet* no less. He set his jaw with passion and determination, glazed eyes trained on the top right-hand corner of the classroom, our entire class open-mouthed at the sheer balls of trying so hard in the fourth week of school, showing us all up. Mrs Merritt appeared to be having a stroke, shaking then clapping in places, pressing her hands to her heart in others and throwing her eyes to the ceiling as if searching for the Bard himself. The performance was impressive, but ultimately, a curse. As he brought the short speech to a close (thank God he was wearing a pair of trousers or he would have been skinned alive, dead mother or no dead mother), he gently brought his hand to his cheek, eyes momentarily catching mine, igniting my face.

> '*See how she leans her cheek upon her*
>     *hand!*
> *O, that I were a glove upon that hand,*
> *That I might touch that cheek!*'

Stunned silence rang through the classroom, save for the sound of Mrs Merritt sniffling into her hankie. David immediately sat down; his own cheeks florid from the sheer effort it must have taken hammering out every single word.

'I will get you on the stage, just you see, dear boy,' Mrs Merritt eventually said. 'That was simply wonderful.'

From that day on, 'Touch that cheek' usurped any mention of shorts, the epithet shortened to 'Cheeks' within days. It wasn't technically bullying, simply a way of distinguishing David from all the other quiet boys who kept their own counsel. I never called him Cheeks, it was blatantly against the code of outcasts, but I did start eating lunch in the north playground.

* * *

'I've got a surprise for you!' Dad gleefully announced, collecting us in half term. I wished I'd been made aware that bad things generally arrived in threes. We drove in silence away from the seafront, passing the turning for his road, flying beyond Pevensey high street. Dad eventually pulled up outside a large semi-detached mock Tudor house at the bottom of a 1960s cul-de-sac. The first thing I noted was its egg-yolk yellow front door. Yellow is my favourite colour. The neat front garden's perfectly square lawn was embellished with a small grey stone fountain (a beatific cherub balancing a wide dish in its chubby hands), classically installed in palazzos all over Tuscany.

'We're just going to nip inside for a moment. I want you to meet someone.'

'Is this one of our adventures?' Stephen asked.

'Maybe.'

As Stephen and I scrambled out of the car, the front door opened and a lady in a red dress stood on the step watching, arms folded across her chest. Blonde hair piled in a messy top knot revealed dangly gold earrings drooping either side of her cheeks, almost touching her shoulders. She looked like a glamorous actress proselytising about the health benefits of Special K cereal on the back of the box. *Can you pinch more than an inch?*

'Annette, this is Cordelia and Stephen. Children, this is my *friend*, Annette.'

Sometimes, Dad's work friends stayed overnight when there had been a publisher away day in Brighton – Stephen had had to sleep in with me on the camp bed and complained about the iron bar digging in his back. We had *never* met anyone like Annette before.

'Hello there,' she said, smiling, revealing an even set of pearly white teeth. 'It's lovely to meet you. Do you like Tizer?'

'We're not allowed Tizer,' Stephen said, receiving a vicious arm pinch. Fizzy drinks were another of Mum's capricious rules along with no ITV, no children's magazines, no burping or farting, as little sugar as possible and looking presentable at all times.

'Not even as a treat?' Annette asked innocently, eyeing Dad as if awaiting a cue.

'As a treat is fine.' Dad grinned widely.

'Great, two glasses coming right up.' She beckoned us inside through to a cavernous living space of the type I had only seen on television. Every single wall had been knocked through so the living room, dining room and kitchen flowed into each other, wooden parquet stretching towards a tree-filled garden at the back, visible through the floor-to-ceiling sliding glass doors.

'Wow!' Stephen sighed in awe. 'It's like James Bond's house.' It looked like a bomb had gone off in Land of Leather while they were shooting Wham!'s 'Last Christmas' video, but in a good way. A stupidly grandiose Tibetan carved cabinet housed a TV the size of our bath at home, dwarfing the white marble fireplace behind it. Overwhelmed by the Viking-longboat inspired wooden table in the kitchen area, I almost didn't spot the cut-glass chandelier dangling overhead, even more breathtaking than the one hanging above Southfork Ranch's grand entry hall in *Dallas*. I glanced, dumbfounded, at the glossy space-age kitchen displaying the apex of modern gadgets right next to the chrome four-slice toaster.

'You've got a Soda Stream!' Stephen screeched, his face lighting up as if he had just won a penny slots landslide on the pier amusements.

'I certainly do. Now if you prefer, I have Coke, lemonade, ginger ale and cream soda.'

'Tizer, please!' we both chimed. That was when I noticed the bowls of crisps, nuts, jelly babies and two magazines (*Jackie* and *The Eagle*) all laid out on an occasional glass table near the TV.

'Are they for us?' I asked uncertainly, knowing Mum would disapprove of such an audacious question. Mum wasn't here.

'How did you guess?' Annette laughed like wind chimes tinkling in a gentle breeze.

Dad beamed – his smiles usually fell short. A warm glow radiated from my belly up through my throat. I wanted to hug him for bringing us to this stupendous place with the Soda Stream and the magazines. But hugs were reserved for when we injured ourselves.

'Thank you, Annette,' I said instead. 'You have a beautiful home.' I'd seen a character compliment Valene Ewing in *Knotts Landing* about her extremely modest house, when they were clearly just being polite. It hadn't even got a Soda Stream.

'That's very kind,' Annette choked. 'Please help yourself to the snacks and magazines.'

Before Stephen could announce magazines were also the work of Satan, I intercepted with a second arm pinch. He deserved it.

'Did you two want to see upstairs?' Annette asked a bit later. 'I have two bedrooms already made up.

Your dad was saying you may come and stay one night if that's OK with you?'

'Do you have children?' I asked, curious. She didn't look like a mum.

'I do, yes, but they're grown up. Lisa's an accountant and Charlotte's an air hostess. They have their own flats in Horsham – and boyfriends.' Lisa and Charlotte – I would gladly trade my virgin librarian married to a cat name for either of those crowning glories.

'So, what did you think of Annette?' Dad asked afterwards in the car on the way to his flat. Both bedrooms, each as pink as the other, had been so utterly captivating with their white venetian blinds and luxurious cream carpets, the pile so deep I lost my toes.

'She was nice,' Stephen butted in. He usually awaited my opinion on all matters before submitting his own.

'Yes, she was,' I agreed, my guard down. 'I liked her house.'

Yet Annette sunk without a trace until a few days later after an entire day in Brighton shopping for new trainers for Stephen and a coat for me. I had unprecedently been allowed to venture into Topshop by myself without anyone steering me towards Marks and Spencer's duffle coats. Sitting on the floor in

Dad's living room eating fish and chips out of the paper with greasy fingers watching *Top of the Pops*, the price tag swung into view.

'What would you think of me moving in with Annette?'

Cyndi Lauper was miming her new hit, 'True Colours', in the studio in front of a swaying audience. I joined in the swaying, a spear through my heart.

'Mum's the same age as Cyndi Lauper,' I informed him. *Please don't move in with Annette.*

'I know,' Dad said wearily, hinting at countless years of being fed the same fact. 'Did you hear what I said?'

'Yes,' I answered for both of us.

'And?'

'Are those bedrooms going to be for us?' I fielded another question. 'You wouldn't be here any more?'

'Yes, you can have a bedroom each. In fact, I could ask to share your time with Mum, spend half a month with me and then half with her. School is near enough on the bus so it would be—'

'But they're pink!' Stephen cried in anguish. 'I hate pink.'

'I could ask if we can paint your room blue?' Dad suggested, clearly not anticipating this kind of reaction.

Jealousy sluiced through my guts, eating the happy memory of the brief time we'd spent with Annette and how mesmerising her James Bond house had been.

'I don't want you to live there!' Stephen yelled. 'I don't like pink. You can't make us go there!' He ran into our tiny shared bedroom and threw himself onto his camp bed, which collapsed, snapping in half like a clam shell, trapping him inside its jaws. Sobbing, he furiously wriggled unable to force his way out before Dad prised the bed apart. It hadn't been funny at the time, but we had laughed about it since.

On returning home, echoes of *Kramer vs Kramer* tolled loudly as Stephen and I sat at the top of the stairs unable to do anything else but listen as Dad's shared custody proposal garnered a similar reaction from Mum. I gripped Stephen's hand in mine as a tear slid down his cheek.

'They'll stop soon,' I whispered, giving it a squeeze. 'It'll be OK.'

With no high-court judge to moderate their plea bargains, Mum and Dad faced each other without gloves.

'They can hear, Lois! Keep your voice down!' Dad cried from the living room.

'I'm beyond caring. You just want them because it

means paying me less money, meanwhile, Annette, who *doesn't* have to work, will bring up *our* children while you carry on with your glittering career.' Dad had just been promoted to Regional Sales Manager. If only Grandpa could see him now with his own office, name etched on a stick-on gold plaque.

'I don't get what the problem is; it's not like I'm asking to sell the house. And Annette does work; she's an Avon Lady!' he snapped. 'Eastbourne and Pevensey saleswoman of the year 1984!'

'Good for her. She won't have time to look after them then.'

'They don't need looking after like that any more; they're not babies!'

'They're ten and twelve, Phil! I chose this job because it fits round them so they're not left alone at home in the holidays. I know, why don't we send them down the mines and then they can earn their own money.'

'Now you're just being ridiculous.'

'Am I? It would all be so convenient for you, wouldn't it? I bet Annette planted the seed, her empty nest tugging at her heart strings, not quite ready for grandchildren, but happy to take on her lover's kids in the meantime, give her a bigger sense of purpose instead of flogging lipstick to bored housewives.'

'God, you're a bitch sometimes.'

I was about to hurtle downstairs and beg them to stop, that we didn't want to live at Annette's, when the phone rang in the hallway. Mum answered it.

'Hello? Hi, is everything OK?... Oh no!'

Dad stepped into the hallway. Mum turned round, pain etched across her face. 'Oh, Liz, I'm so sorry.' She put her hand over the mouthpiece and looked at Dad, tears streaming. 'Jeremy's died.'

Joint custody was never mentioned again.

# 14

## THE CHANNEL

The sea had plunged to unapparelled depths of cold. I must have entered the Separation Zone – a vessel-free expanse of water signalling the approximate halfway mark. My hands ached as if I'd been gripping a metal bar for hours, my shoulders throbbed and yet my feet remained strangely detached. With lips like a couple of cured fish, I scraped at the crusted salt with the back of my hand on the next stroke, catching the corner of my mouth, tasting blood. Sharks could smell blood from four hundred metres away.

Cringing at the host of micro-aggressions I'd hurled at Annette throughout the tumultuous teenage years, the guilt stung as fresh now as it had then. It didn't matter that I'd subsequently redressed the situation by religiously sending her Mother's Day presents in appreciation of her unwavering support and retrospectively apologising for my constant stream of passive-aggressive insults.

'Cordelia, you don't need to feel bad; you had your own mental health battle going on. I'm just glad you're OK.'

Being older now than Annette had been when she met Dad, I couldn't understand how she had never retaliated. If Finn and Evie nosedived into a meltdown during a visit, or displayed an inch of entitlement, I sneaked into the kitchen to prevent shooting my mouth off. And I loved Finn and Evie, Stephen's kids, more than my menagerie of pets. More than Stephen. No, not more than Stephen. As much as Stephen. Perhaps Annette had an effigy of me that she'd stabbed each time Dad dropped us back home?

It was time for *Roman Holiday* – its joyfulness always reminded me of Desi finally accepting my hand of friendship. Conversely, hadn't it also played a bit part in my own self-persecution?

*Boudica*'s horn sounded, jolting me back to the cold where Desi jumped up and down, waving his rainbow pompoms like a cheerleading Teletubby speeding its nuts off. I pulled out an earplug.

'It's treat time!' He announced my arrival in the Separation Zone – chocolate rewards had been promised for reaching this juncture. 'Are you ready?'

'Hit me up!' My belly grumbled for the first time since leaving Shakespeare beach. With adrenaline killing what little appetite I had, I'd forced down previous feeds, but the Channel had finally hollowed me out. I teased my costume away from my armpits, it had begun to nip. *Stop thinking this is easy; how are you still swimming?* The voices found space to twist my ear between deep dives into the past. I felt like Tracey Bates was stalking me in the sea. A couple of times I'd lurched out of rhythm, convinced a figure was shadowing me stroke for stroke. Treading water also chiselled into the distractions, allowing horror to intrude at the water's true depth, at the potential of colossal creatures skulking in the tar-black depths waiting to pounce in a flash of fins and fangs. *Keep swimming, just keep swimming...*

Alan flung a lassoed goggle case as far as he could then dragged it towards me like an inert fish. I grabbed at it, flipping open the end, tipping out ten giant Cadbury's chocolate buttons, smashing them between my teeth. No time to savour their distinct velvety smoothness; they were merely functional. Calories in, calories out.

'Remember when we first met, Cordy?' Desi called as I sent the case on its way. 'I had chocolate buttons for the first time then. They were like crack to a kid raised on Hershey's!'

*Head down, four strokes, breathe out. Bubbles.*

# 15

## COUSINS

Gossip whipped round our year that the new school secretary was actually Streaker's mum. Mum's innate attractiveness and fondness for knee-length denim skirts somehow negated the unfaithful slag reputation Tracey had been fiercely peddling, yet she persistently tortured me, purposely smashing my shins in hockey or poking fun out of my new coat, despite its Topshop provenance. I kept my head as low as possible, forever balanced on a narrow ledge of anxiety, praying today would be OK, she'd just leave me alone. Most of the time she did and I'd since accrued a few people to sit with at lunch or pass time with in the playground and they were nice enough, but they weren't Michelle and Sarah, who had now been assimilated into Tracey's gang. No one else had managed to hit the sweet spot like Michelle and Sarah. No one else found farts as amusing, or shared an enduring love of George Michael. Almost everyone had migrated towards Jon Bon Jovi – apparently he had better hair.

I still sat next to Michelle in French; seats had been set in stone once chosen at the beginning of term. After Tracey turned her, Michelle would spend the entire lesson with her head inclined away from me, one bum cheek hanging over the edge of the seat, avoiding all eye contact. But lately, she had decided to sit face forward and occasionally smiled, especially if we had to test each other on verbs. Once, she shared a packet of strawberry Chewits under the desk when we were supposed to be revising for a vocab test. Sarah had moved her seat from next to me in tutor time but she was never mean; she just didn't speak to me.

'Don't stand too close to Streaker; her breath stinks. She licks her own armpits instead of showering.' One more insult to add to the collection.

I vainly checked my breath a million times a day, using the theoretically reliable cupped hand method

*Jackie* magazine swore by. The magazine's seminal article on how to correctly brush one's teeth gaining maximum whiteness using Aquafresh toothpaste couldn't have been timed better. I cited the promotional puff piece daily until Mum finally caved. 'Fine, I'll buy Aquafresh! And this is why we don't have children's magazines.' *White equals healthy, equals better, equals a happier life.*

These self-improvement pages were the ones I unfailingly flicked to first. Some articles were as innocuous as braiding the perfect French plait, but the most recent edition dedicated a double-page spread to how to tone muscles in your arms and legs using baked bean cans as weights (suspended in plastic bags from your ankles). I spent an entire hour after school in my bedroom scrutinising my arms for signs of definition after completing five press ups and ruthlessly comparing myself to the flawless blonde teenage girl posing in her crop top and cycling shorts, flexing limbs like an oiled-up Mr Universe. Did she really do all those exercises to look like *that*? Was I the only one who *wasn't* born to wear shorts? Standing on my bed, peering down towards my thighs in the small circular mirror above my desk, was fraught with anxiety as from certain angles, my thighs appeared disconsolately inflated beyond all recognition.

'What on earth are you doing?' Stephen barged in, catching me in the act of wobbling on one leg in the middle of the bed, school skirt pushed up round my neck.

'Knock before entering!' I yanked my skirt down, face incandescent with shame. There was no spitting out the apple after *Jackie* magazine had been introduced.

\* \* \*

'You haven't changed at all,' Liz kept repeating in a transatlantic drawl, each vowel stretched to capacity then flattened with a hammer. Derek had stayed glued to her side from the minute they arrived dragging two brand-new suitcases behind them. He was the same height as me, quite small for fourteen and slight, like his limbs had yet to catch up with his hands and feet which were uncommonly large. He wore an oversized black sweatshirt with the word *Bulls* emblazoned across the chest in a bold red typeface. Baggy blue jeans belied his stick-thin legs but his neat Afro added an inch to his diminutive stature. Stephen couldn't stop staring.

Aunty Liz wore her brown hair dramatically shorn save for a white-blonde quiff springing from the crown of her head like a ship's figurehead, held in place by inordinate layers of hairspray.

'I can't smoke when I've just fixed this,' she joked. 'I'll go up in flames.' She matched her bright-red-framed glasses to her scarlet lips, the embodiment of self-caricature. Liz's be-zipped cargo pants (as she called them) made her look like an army deserter. She spent all her time patting every pocket to find where she had hidden a lighter when it was time to smoke, which was every five minutes. I searched her face but the dark-haired woman with the beehive from the black and white photo had checked out long ago.

'Do you want to come and play Monopoly?' Stephen bashfully asked Derek when he hadn't left the kitchen for half an hour, not even to go to the toilet. 'We've set it up on the dining-room table. We've also got Kerplunk, Connect Four, Cluedo and Operation.'

'And Hungry Hippos, but that's a bit babyish,' I added. 'Stephen likes it.'

'Hey!'

Derek pulled a face like he had no idea what we were talking about and looked up at his mum. She nodded and pushed her hand out in a move-along gesture.

'Mom, no! I'm tired.'

Stephen's mouth dropped open.

'He's still in shock after, you know... We all are.' Liz smiled at Stephen and me, trying to get us on side.

'Mom!' Derek remonstrated. 'Stop!'

'Why don't you lie down on the sofa? You barely slept on the red-eye,' Liz said. 'I'll come with you.'

When I peered in the living room five minutes later, I found them both asleep at opposite ends, Liz upright, head lolling back, mouth open and Derek curled in a ball like a cat. He was beautiful and fragile; long lashes fringed his dark eyes that most girls would kill for. Stephen sneaked in to stare at him like he was an exotic creature hiding from visitors in the zoo.

When they woke up, Derek's mood hadn't improved and the day had crept over the floor.

'Do you want to see your room?' I asked, desperate to spark a smile. Mum had taken the suitcases up earlier. 'You're in my one.'

Derek shrugged noncommittedly.

'Or you could come to mine instead,' Stephen asked hopefully. 'I've got a Hornby trainset and

Scalextric we can get out. One of the cars is a Ferrari. It always wins, just like in real life.'

Derek shook his head and sloped off into the kitchen.

'Why don't you three go and watch TV. Is anything on?' Mum asked after ten minutes of us silently listening to her and Aunty Liz ridiculing Grandma's obsession with monogrammed towels. Mum had furtively mentioned yesterday that we would be permitted to watch ITV for the next few weeks *and* use the remote control.

Seven p.m. on a Thursday meant *Top of the Pops*. As soon as the credits rolled and the synth-heavy theme tune exploded throughout the living room, Derek started jigging his feet, alive for the first time since he'd arrived. He remained mostly mute but swayed his shoulders and hands in an elaborate body-popping move before jumping up. Stephen ended up missing A-ha perform 'Cry Wolf'– so mesmerised was he by Derek's interpretative dance. As soon as the camera panned away from the House Martins crooning the 'Caravan of Love' and Steve Wright bid the audience goodnight, Derek sharply turned round.

'What?! It's the end?' It was the most he had spoken in two hours.

'Yes, it's *EastEnders* now,' I informed him. What would he make of *that*?

'Where's MTV?'

'What's that?' I asked, intrigued. 'Is that from America?'

'You mean you don't have it here? What was that we just watched?'

'*Top of the Pops*.'

'You don't have Vanna either?'

I shrugged at Stephen while Derek snatched the remote from his hand where he'd been gently cradling it. He pressed number two and a wildlife documentary flicked on. Three was *Murder She Wrote* and four was the end of the news.

'There's only four channels? Mom watches Vanna; don't you have her on here? We watch her when we have our dinner, every day! Mom loves her.'

'What's Vanna?' Stephen asked.

'Vanna isn't a *what*, she's a *she*!' Derek stormed off, clearly distressed. 'Mom, they don't have Vanna!'

We followed him into the kitchen where Mum was leaning against the sink and Liz the oven.

'There's only four channels, no MTV and no Vanna! It's shit here!' Derek clenched his fists.

Mum almost swallowed her own head in an effort not to scold Derek for his bad language. I silently fumed at his ignorance of the honour bestowed upon him. Had we not tuned in ITV, there would have only been three paltry channels to choose from! Then I felt mean because his dad had just died.

'I told you, sweetie, when we set off, that it's very different to Chicago.' She turned to Mum and explained in a *sotto voce*, except we could hear every word. 'Vanna is the hostess on the *Wheel of Fortune*; we used to watch it with his dad at dinnertime. It was "our thing".'

Derek narrowed his eyes and crossed his arms. 'I just wanna go home.' The fight drained out of him as a giant yawn overtook his face.

Taking this as a sign, Liz shepherded him to bed, leaving us to start dinner without her.

* * *

School had ended the day before and in the last period, Miss Fairbrass, our form tutor, had handed out all the cards from the school Christmas post box. Astonishingly I had ten, having only sent two – one to Michelle and one to Sarah in an attempt to rekindle the magic of the first week. All but two of the cards were actually for Mum.

*Dear Miss Franks,*
  *I think you're fit...*

*Dear Miss Franks,*
  *Are you single?*

*Dear Miss Franks,*
  *I want to kiss you.*

*Dear Miss Franks,*
  *Will you go out with me...?*

All pointlessly anonymous, though one boy had scrawled *Keith*; however, Cavendish was awash with Keiths. The first card solely meant for me was from David Plimpton. Had he posted it in solidarity as a fellow outlier? Or because we still occasionally sat next to each other at lunchtime, book-ended with a brisk 'Hello' and a 'See you later'? I scrutinised the card for a veiled message other than the sign-off David had scrawled beneath the ubiquitous pre-printed *Have a happy Christmas: with Best wishes for the new year, David P* and one kiss. I turned it over and over before assuming he'd sent the whole form a card. The only other envelope genuinely addressed

to me was equally puzzling, the cheery Frosty the
Snowman card a complete contradiction.

*Streaker*
   *Just because your mum's fucking Mr Klin-*
*gon, doesn't mean your cool. I've got my eye*
*on you. I'll be waiting for you next year ready*
*to make your life hell. Happy Christmas.*

# 16

## THE CHANNEL

'I can't believe you didn't thump me that Christmas,'
Desi called from his port-side position. 'I was such a
little bitch!'

Alan laughed, hauling in the goggles case.

'You don't have to answer; I know you shouldn't
waste your breath. Get on and swim! You're halfway
to heaven!' He blew a kiss, I reached up and caught
it, then pressed my earplug back in.

I clippered through startlingly clear water. Visible shoals of black-scaled fish shimmered far below,
sunlight refracting, deceiving me they were touch-
able. I'd reached the Channel's deepest stretch: vast
open water, miles from either coast, at the mercy of
the tides, currents and my punitive training plan. I'd

allowed myself a backwards glance and if I hadn't been under the aegis of *Boudica,* I could so easily have swum off in the wrong direction.

As tired and cold as I was, peace seeped into hairline cracks of doubt. 'You never finish anything, Cordy,' Mum's voice reverbed inside my head. Even in her seventies, she could flay bone and sinew with casual comments. *Whatever it takes, Cordelia,* I muttered silently. I *had* to finish this and so far, it felt within reach. I wasn't just a spinster with an atrophied vagina. I was so much more.

Earthly boundaries blurred and instead of carving my path, I became the path, limbs merging with the water, deadened from the icy sea, lungs breathing in life-giving oxygen like battered leather bellows stoking a fire. Oh, to flip onto my back and float gazing skywards, feeling held, integrated, understood, but time and currents would not wait. Gliding towards the Northeast Shipping Lane, only a nautical mile away, my heart fluttered in my chest; contentment swirled. I remembered Desi's smile that landed like an early Christmas gift, with Audrey Hepburn as the fairy on the top of the tree.

*Head down, four strokes, breathe out. Bubbles.*

# 17

## ROMAN HOLIDAY

We drove in silence to Brighton, Stephen in the back staring at leafless Beech hedges whipping past while I kept a close eye on Mum. She slammed the Mini Cooper through the gears like she was snapping limbs. So far, the visit wasn't paying the dividends we'd all been excited for. At least the drama distracted from the sinister Christmas card shoved under my bed. There had been words that morning.

'Lois, I told you on the phone, Derek's in a bad way.'

The sisters had retreated to the kitchen while Derek skulked off to my room to plug into his boundless supply of pop music tapes after branding our beloved Brighton Christmas lights 'lame'.

'He's not even seen them!' I'd huffed to Stephen.

We visited the lights every Christmas, each year as magical and wondrous as the previous. This would be the first time without Dad.

'I completely understand he's sad and I honestly don't care about not wanting to come to Brighton, but he's behaving like a...' Mum's voice faded into her cup of tea.

'Go on, say it!' Liz said evenly. 'I've been waiting for this.'

'No.'

'You think he's an American brat. Well guess what, you're sounding just like Mum, especially after joining that religious cult – don't they condemn homosexuals?'

I inhaled sharply from behind the door jamb.

'It wasn't a cult and I'm *not* like our mother!'

'You are... At least you saw sense and left.'

'I never heard Pastor Michael mention homosexuality was a sin. Not once.'

'No, you probably closed your ears to that cherry-picking judgement. Just like you're criticising Derek for how he's offloading his inconvenient grief. I warned you, I said he won't fit in with what we want to do, that he's angry, that he's confused about all sorts of things, not just his dad's death: about family, about how to have a relationship with Edward and what that means going forward. His world has blown up. Not to mention the unmentionable, but one day he'll know what his dad really died of, because *he* has to be safe too. We all do... It's getting worse.'

*Who was Edward?*

Mum sniffed before replying. 'I just think it would be nice if you both joined us for the Christmas lights. It might help him.'

'I didn't bring him up to do "nice". I hate that fucking word. I can't believe you're still trapped in that whole paradigm.'

'There's no need to swear!' Mum snapped, wounded.

'Sorry... Look, I'm not about to force Derek into something he doesn't want to do. I spent my entire childhood trying to meet our parents' unattainable expectations and then failing spectacularly. I don't want the same for him. He's not even sure what he *is* yet. At least I *knew* I fancied Julie Andrews when I was fourteen. Derek still hasn't got a clue.'

'Hasn't he? He seems pretty... flamboyant to me.'

'Yes, but he doesn't *know* he is. Anyway, let's not do this. We can't both be Mum.'

I'd slipped away when Mum playfully threw a tea towel at Aunty Liz.

As we pulled into the multi-story car park just off the seafront, Mum turned to me.

'Do you think I'm like Grandma?'

'No! Not at all,' I lied, fingers crossed inside my mittens.

'Good. Right, let's go and see the lights; it'll be dark soon.'

We actually had a lovely time and I spotted a giant tube of festive Cadbury's buttons in Debenhams and bought them for Derek to cheer him up. Chocolate had always been my steadfast panacea.

\* \* \*

'Cordelia, have your heard of Audrey Hepburn?' Aunty Liz asked as she flicked through the *Radio Times*. Hadn't she been in *African Queen*? 'I think you might like her. She's Derek's favourite. Go and get him, would you? *Roman Holiday*'s on in fifteen minutes. We could all watch together.'

Earlier that morning, Mum had requisitioned Aunty Liz to help wedge the tree from Hillier's Garden Centre in its rusting stand by the front windows. Derek hadn't even bothered to investigate, let alone help decorate. In protest, I held back the chocolate buttons.

'We're going to watch a film; do you want to join us?'

Derek leaned against the pink padded head-board, eyes closed. *Papa Don't Preach.* He couldn't hear, incensing me tenfold. He'd checked out of existence, something I was never allowed to do! I strode over and pulled the headphones away from his ears.

'Oi!' he yelled.

'I was asking you a question!' He really was an American brat!

'Cut it out! You didn't have to do that, did you?'

Standing still, heart on fire, I wrestled with the urge to shout that our father had been pushed out of our home and now lived in the Pink Palace with Annette.

'Cordelia, Stephen, I was wondering if you could call me Netty instead of Annette. It's a lot more informal,' she had requested the previous weekend at the dinner table.

'As in net curtains?' I'd responded, all calculated naivety.

*So, yes, Derek, we all have shit things happen to us, but it doesn't mean we can act like a total knob head!* Hands on hips, I practised it briefly in my head.

'What?!' he snapped, glowering. 'Spit it out; you obviously want to say something.'

'My dad left,' I wheezed, voice wobbling on the edge of tears.

'At least you still have a dad.'

Infuriatingly, death trumped everything. I turned on my heels and stalked out but annoyingly had to poke my head back in, stealing my own thunder. 'Oh, your mum said *Roman Holiday* is on downstairs in a minute if you want to come. We're all going to watch it.'

'Really?' For the first time since he had given us a peak of the true Derek during *Top of the Pops*, his precautionary scowl softened. 'That's my favourite film of all time. They have things like that over here?'

I couldn't help giggling.

'What's so funny?'

'We have films and everything. We just don't have a video player.'

'Why not?' he asked as if we had no running water.

'Mum won't let us, says it rots our brains. So having you here is a treat because we're allowed to watch as much TV as we like.'

'Wow! Dad used to say TV rotted your brain. He didn't really watch it apart from Vanna – because that was educational.'

Understanding seeded between us.

'I'm so sorry about your dad,' I said, breaking the lull. 'That must be truly awful.'

'It is. I miss him. So much.' Derek remained sitting on the bed and I hovered by the door, torn between getting him to watch the film and wanting to stay and fire off questions.

'You two, are you coming or what?' Aunty Liz yelled up the stairs. 'It's on in five minutes and we need to get some movie snacks ready.'

'Movie snacks?' I asked, awestruck.

'You don't have them here?' Derek asked.

I shook my head.

'Mom makes the best popcorn with cinnamon sugar. She brought a load of microwave stuff with her.'

'Coming!' I called down. 'I have something for you too.'

We galloped downstairs where I grabbed the Cadbury's buttons from the kitchen; Aunty Liz was indeed making microwave popcorn. Wonders would never cease from America. As we shuffled into places for the BBC Two afternoon film, I handed over my gift.

'I thought these might, you know...' I smiled, lips pressed together like *Jackie* magazine advised if one hadn't yet brushed one's teeth, even though I had. Aquafresh had yet to improve my life.

Already warmed up by our previous encounter, Derek took the present and granted me a beatific smile, his glittering white teeth an instant lifelong envy.

'Why, thank you, Cuz.'

My neck burned. Majestic oaks grew from small acorns.

Derek cracked open the Cadbury's buttons. 'Oh my Jesus God – what are these? They're delicious! Mom! Have you had these?'

The whole room burst out laughing.

'It's just chocolate,' Stephen said.

'No, it isn't!' Derek cried. 'I feel like Charlie Bucket in Wonka's factory! I'm taking a suitcase of them home!'

*Roman Holiday*'s black-and-white opening credits infused a sprinkling of much-needed festive cheer, despite its summer setting. No matter, my heart swelled with Christmas Eve expectancy, the tree lights twinkling against the darkening windows while outside, the dull overcast sky gave way to dusk. The film's rousing Hollywood score teamed with insightfully shot Roman locations lent the family participation a grand sense of occasion. Audrey mesmerised as ingenuous Princess Ann on a state visit reluctant to shoulder the responsibilities of her role. I could relate. Life happened whether you were prepared or not; that was the danger of it. I'd thought I could handle my parents' divorce but Dad had found a new life, replacing us all with Netty Curtains. He was supposed to have remained in his little Pevensey flat, go to work every day, then spend weekends having adventures until we flew the nest and had our own adventures. Wasn't that the whole point of parents? Evidently not. They selfishly wanted their own lives too. Just like Princess Ann.

A tale as old as time, *Roman Holiday* was strewn with haphazard capers, venal journalistic subplots and the loss of innocence as Ann wishes to live the life of an ordinary 'Joe', and eventually falls in love with undercover reporter 'Joe' (pensively handsome Gregory Peck). Completely spellbound, I forgot to shovel in the accompanying bowl of buttery American cinnamon sugar popcorn.

Audrey's elfin beauty transcended the black and white film reel, as relevant thirty-three years later in 1980s Eastbourne. She effortlessly sashayed her way across the screen, taking up so little space while demanding the attention of everyone. If only I could harness a fingernail full of her star quality, boasting

perfect cheekbones off which I could hang my entire
future, then Tracey wouldn't hate me, no one would,
least of all myself. Maybe even one year, I'd receive
Christmas cards from all the Keiths at school, ex-
pressing in romantic iambic pentameters how truly
fit I was. Instead, I'd been graced with footballers'
thighs and wonky ears; desperate measures included
taping the right one down in anticipation of it
growing closer to my head. It didn't. The Sellotape
ripped out a clump of hair, leaving a noticeable bald
patch for months which I coloured in with permanent marker until it grew back. As if those imperfections weren't bad enough, I also had to contend with
freckles and limp hair unsalvageable even after a
giant can of Elnett Mega Hold.

'Look at that waist,' Mum lamented. 'I would literally kill to be that thin.'

'Lois! Don't say stuff like that,' Liz admonished.
'It's not feminist!'

'I'm not feminist,' Mum retorted. 'All that burn
your bra rubbish.'

'It's not good for Cordelia to hear those words.
You don't eat enough as it is.'

'Do you mind? Some of us are watching this!'
Derek intervened before the testy discourse slid into
a full-blown argument.

I snivelled into my pile of popcorn while martyr-like Princess Ann innocently shook hands with smouldering Joe at the close of the film, my heart throbbing for her, totally short changed because in the end, love did *not* conquer all. Prince Charming married a skivvy; why couldn't Princess Ann marry a journalist? As the credits rolled and everyone eased themselves up from the sofa and armchairs, stretching, chatting about dinner, I remained on the beanbag, mind ticking over.

'Did you love it?' Derek asked, jumping up from the sofa. 'Wasn't she beautiful? When I get married, it has to be to someone like her.'

I nodded, still not ready to surrender my abject sadness towards the film's unsatisfying conclusion.

'Do you want to play Connect Four?' Stephen asked, emboldened by Derek's dramatic personality change. 'Do you have that in America?'

'Durr, yes. We also have the electric chair.'

* * *

I didn't mean to scream, but I'd never seen a boy in girls' clothes before. Stephen and I had just returned to a quiet house from the Pink Palace and I'd charged into my room to find Derek riffling through my wardrobe wearing one of my old puffball skirts – he was slim enough to fit it, I no longer was. He'd teamed it with a lace-trimmed white blouse and a pair of white lace gloves, looking every inch a glamorous pop star. An irrational flame of jealousy singed my breast.

'Derek! Put your clothes on,' Mum cried, aghast, standing in the doorway. Stephen joined us, instantly bursting out laughing.

'What's going on?' Aunty Liz called from the bathroom, water sloshing. 'I'm in the bath. Is every-thing OK?'

'Derek's wearing Cordelia's clothes.'

Derek's face froze in a mask of defiance.

'And?' Aunty Liz replied unruffled.

'He should take them off!'

I quickly recovered from the shock of seeing my cousin looking better than I ever could in my own clothes.

'I don't mind Derek dressing up. That wasn't why I screamed,' I said nonchalantly. 'It's only the same as being in the pantomime.'

'What are you getting your knickers in a twist about?' Liz called. 'Do you need me to get out?'

'I haven't got my knickers in a twist. It's fine, finish your bath. Cordelia, let Derek... get dressed.'

'It's OK, she can stay.'

Flummoxed, Mum pursed her lips and dragged Stephen out.

'Keep the door OPEN!' she instructed.

Derek and I looked at each other and burst out laughing. *What did she think we were going to do?*

As soon as she'd disappeared downstairs, Derek spoke.

'Thank you.'

'What for?'

'For having my back.'

I nodded dumbly, baffled by his turn of phrase.

'I don't fit in that skirt any more. You can keep it if you want.'

His eyes lit up. 'Nah, I was trying for an Audrey Hepburn look, don't think it worked. You should have a go. I noticed you've a full skirt in there. The yellow one.'

'It makes me look ugly.'

He frowned and reached into the wardrobe and pulled it out.

'Do you dress in girls' clothes at home?'

He shrugged. 'Not really, there aren't any. Mom is hardly into those kinda things.'

'If you could, would you?'

'Maybe. Here, try this with that little crop top I saw in your drawer, the pink one.'

'You've been going through my drawers?'

'No... Perhaps. Sorry, I was bored when you guys were away. I wanted to watch *Breakfast at Tiffany's*, but you've no video player then we could have rented it. Dressing up was the next best thing.' He proffered the clothes, raising his eyebrows expectantly. 'It's OK, I won't look until you're dressed.'

Five minutes later, I stood on the bed in my lemon-yellow cotton summer skirt, the one with pockets, and swayed in the mirror. A roll of flesh bulged in between the gap where the crop top finished and the skirt began. I pinched it, immediately ashamed. Audrey didn't have a roll protruding over her waistband.

'We need some make-up to finish the look. I can't believe you haven't got any – I searched everywhere. Let's go shopping tomorrow. You have make-up stores here, right?'

I threw a pillow at him.

# 18

## THE CHANNEL

Tracey's shrill voice perforated my head while cramp concurrently seized my right foot, daggers pinioning the arch, muscles contorting like a drowning fish. Even with numb toes, the pain was acute. I stopped swimming; Alison noticed immediately, calling to Desi, who was helming the boat with Cathy.

'What's wrong?' he called. Alan joined him, peering through binoculars for a clearer view.

'Cramp!' Blanket numbness hampered my weak attempts at wriggling my toes. 'Foot!'

'You need fluids,' Alan shouted. 'I'll throw some over.'

'It's Tracey's fault! She popped into my head,' I

called as a ripple smacked my cheek just like one of her insults. 'Then – ouch!'

'What a bitch!' Desi cried delightedly. 'That'll go down as one of my all-time greatest character assassinations.'

I grabbed my foot, momentarily dipping below the surface to pull on my splayed toes, stretching them out. *It's not cold, it's not cold, it's not cold...* Why does the cold frighten us so much? Consistently listed as most Channel swimmers' zenith of fear, maybe humans' reptilian brains couldn't shake the congenital terror of freezing to death. Hypothermia was a real threat, but apparently quite a peaceful, painless death.

I tensed my stomach against the shakes, eager to outswim the rattling. A water bottle landed a metre in front and I swam to collect it, Tracey's startled face flashing before my eyes. I couldn't help smiling – the infamous confrontation had been precisely like a scene from a John Hughes film, the kind of high-octane, gossipy incident I'd been desperate for Derek to deliver about teen life in America. The scrappy titbits he *did* feed me were insufficient: 'It's boring, not like the movies.' Yet I had starred in this real-life occurrence as the heroine, possibly Molly Ringwald but shorter with lank brown hair. I relished the memory like salty crumbs in a crisp packet – it even surpassed the theatrical teenage pressure cooker, the *Breakfast Club*, up next after *The Godfather*.

*Head down, four strokes, breathe out. Bubbles.*

# 19

## TRACEY BATES LOSES MATES

'What have we here?'

I froze next to the Boots Number 17 make-up range. Mum had banned make-up 'Until you're older', so I'd been reduced to dabbing the dreg ends of her rose-scented roll-on lip gloss that I'd swiped out of the bin. *Jackie* magazine offered picture tutorials on how to apply mascara without clumping and the perfect technique for a smouldering eye. But a whole new world opened up before me with Derek here.

Skulking underneath his Bulls baseball cap, Derek checked out Max Factor further down the aisle, but that reminded me too much of hairy-chinned old ladies, Grandma in particular.

Tracey's mordent voice jostled me away from the

extensive lipstick range. Twilight Teaser had topped my wish list for the last twelve months, the shimmering lilac shade transforming all complexions into a pallid, two-day-old corpse pulled from the morgue's chiller drawer. I revered it nonetheless. Wearing brand-new, stone-washed Levis and an oversized suit jacket, the shoulder pads plump enough to dive off, Tracey stood, arms folded across her chest, head cocked, oozing supremacy like a newly launched Impulse body spray. Michelle squirmed behind her with Ashley Taylor, a member of the cool boys, who couldn't have been less interested in make-up if he tried. He barely gave me a glance, so entranced was he with his own reflection smeared in the narrow mirror above the face-powder section.

'Hello, Tracey.' My stomach plummeted into my grey suede, Dolcis pixie boots, a Christmas present from Dad and Netty.

'What are you doing here, Streaker? You don't know how to dress; why you bothering with make-up?'

Curiously, instead of expiring on the spot, it was as if a personal coach began whispering directives in my ear. What would Audrey do? *Don't show fear, kill with kindness.*

'Hello Michelle.' I ignored Tracey entirely. Michelle's awkwardness wafted off her in waves. 'Hope you had a good Christmas.'

'Yeah, you too,' Michelle mumbled, ears burning beneath her rock-hard Frisby fringe.

Before Tracey could lob another putdown, Derek appeared at my elbow.

'Hey, Cuz, who's this?'

Tracey gawped, awestruck. Michelle's neck caught fire and Ashley snatched his eyes away from his reflection, cowed by the presence of superior coolness.

'This is Tracey Bates from school.'

'Wow,' Tracey said dreamily. 'Hi.'

Ashley puffed out his chest, his pole position eclipsed.

'...And Michelle and Ashley,' I added as an afterthought.

'Hi,' Derek drawled in an exaggerated accent. 'I'm Derek, so buzzed to meet some of Cordy's friends.'

'Oh yes, we *love* Cordy,' Tracey simpered.

*Cordy?*

I held my breath; where was he taking this?

'Yeah, well, she's a true sweetheart, aren't you, Cuz?'

I shrugged, embarrassed.

'She *really* is.' Tracey grinned. Was she flirting? She flicked the side of her hair that wasn't cemented with hairspray and shook her head coquettishly, her preposterous fringe bouncing like an extra limb. 'Are you going to be here for New Year?'

Ashley shuffled like he wished to speak but had been rendered mute, his balls in a vice.

'Sure am.' Derek winked; what was he playing at?

'Well, I'm having a party and only the cool people are invited, which obviously means you and... *Cordy.*' Tracey's face momentarily flinched; perhaps she'd swallowed sick.

Derek linked arms with me. 'I'll give you our formal answer now. Cordy and I won't be able to attend your bash. We're going to a party in London. In fact, Tracey, before you call my cousin Streaker again, check your outfit choices. I mean, for God's sake, that jacket is too *Miami Vice*, so last season, and your hair?' He leaned over and prodded her sprayed helmet whilst grimacing. 'I don't even know where to begin. You should take a leaf out of Cordy's book; au naturel is all the rage in the US. She's well ahead of the curve.'

Tracey's face burst into flames while Michelle's eyes gunned the floor, avoiding a slaying.

'I-I-I...' Tracey stuttered, evidently unused to being the butt of anyone's jokes.

'Oh, a quiet word?' Derek leaned towards Tracey, who recoiled, her neck disappearing into her shoulders like Stretch Armstrong. 'Sending anonymous Christmas cards, not cool. If I hear you've made life hell for my cousin, you'll have *me* to deal with. Understood?'

Tracey managed to nod, eyes wide, terror coursing through them.

Derek patted her shoulder gently. 'Glad we cleared that up. Now you guys enjoy the rest of the holidays, ya hear? Hope New Year's a success. I'm sure we'll meet again.' He waved and dragged me away towards the hairspray section at the rear of the shop. I glanced over my shoulder, just catching Tracey scrambling out of the door ordering the others to follow. Transfixed, Michelle smiled before reluctantly trailing Tracey outside.

'Derek, what on earth?' We'd ground to a halt in front of the Elnett.

'What?' he asked, smiling. 'Don't tell me she was really a friend?'

'No, but how did you know all that?'

'I'm psychic.'

'Are you?'

'No, are you kidding?'

'What? How then?'

'I found your Christmas cards when I was looking for a secret make-up stash.'

'What made you think Tracey sent the nasty one?'

'I heard how she spoke to you. She called you Streaker in the card too. She's got a bad vibe.'

'I mean, it probably was her who sent it.'

'It doesn't matter who sent it.' He shrugged. 'She'll leave you alone now.'

'Thank you.' I reached over and hugged him awkwardly.

'I got your back.'

I nodded, understanding this time.

'Who was the David guy? His card was cute.'

'Someone in my form group. No one really.'

'I was getting "in like" vibes from him.' He eyed me carefully.

'What? No! I barely talk to him – he's nice I suppose, has a posh voice, always volunteering to read in class.'

'I'm telling you now, boys don't send cards unless they have to get a message across. He likes you.'

'He doesn't! Anyway, I don't fancy him. I don't fancy anyone!'

'OK, whatever you say.' Derek laughed. 'Come on, we still need hairspray and make-up.'

'I thought you said au naturel was in fashion.'

He burst out laughing. 'I lied; we gotta do something with your limp locks.'

I hit him playfully on the arm as he grabbed two cans of Mega Hold and some mousse. Derek wasn't like other boys.

\* \* \*

'How do you know what to do?' I stared at my reflection in wonder. Derek had transformed me into a teenager: back-combed hair doused in hairspray and an application of subtle make-up. I blazed as bright as Audrey and twirled on the bed before we set off for the pantomime, *Cinderella*. In stumbling Cordelia's place stood a graceful swan, thighs under wraps beneath the yellow maxi skirt. This was the transformation *Jackie* magazine couldn't deliver; such a pity no one from school would bear witness.

'Edward showed me.'

'Who's Edward?'

Derek stepped away from the bed where he had been straightening my skirt. He tilted his head to one side, eyeing me cautiously.

'Dad's... my dad's best friend.'

'How does *he* know?'

'He's a stylist, and a make-up artist. He works in theatres all over.'

'Wow, that's wicked.'

'Wicked?' Derek smiled. 'You Brits say some weird shit.'

Downstairs, Mum miraculously gave me a nod of approval.

'You look pretty,' Stephen said genuinely. 'I like your hair.'

\* \* \*

'What do you think about me walking you to school?' Derek asked the day before term started.

'I'd love it!'

But on the Monday morning, a cloak of ambiguity descended. I curiously became an observer in my own life, disconnected from reality, *all the world's a stage...* An unbidden anticipation rumbled through my chest and the edges of my vision fizzed with a surreal, deeply plumbed feeling of serenity. For the first time ever, something was going to go my way, yet I couldn't discern exactly what. Derek winked from across the table before biting into a piece of Marmite toast.

'This stuff is unreal! Is it even legal?'

In the hallway, I jabbed my arms through my Topshop coat, disquietude rumbling like background music while stepping into my narrative. I was Bobbie (Jenny Agutter) in *The Railway Children*, on the way to the station to meet a mysterious passenger, tension cranking up as she glides in a dreamlike state along the platform, every character ever encountered wishing her good day, asking her how she's feeling about the news (*what news?*). Emotive music underscores the scene, the audience holds its breath as smoke clears from around the open carriage door and Bobbie's exonerated father steps into the frame. I scooped up my school bag from the bottom of the stairs, tears streaking my cheeks. What on earth? I laughed at my own ridiculousness.

'Hey, Cuz, I'll be back in a few days. You know Mom's desperate to show me Buckingham Palace,' Derek said apologetically as he slipped on his baseball cap, topping off another knock-out ensemble of Bulls hoodie, baggy jeans and a bright-red life preserver, twinning with Michael J Fox in *Back to the Future*. We were writing our own script.

'That's not why I'm crying,' I sniffed. 'You wouldn't understand; I barely do.'

'Wouldn't I? Try me.'

'I can't explain. Life's been... but now it's...' I sighed. 'I don't really know. You don't need my crap. You've enough of your own.'

Derek stepped towards me and touched my hair, smoothing it down. He'd given a detailed tutorial on how to lift roots to make the most of it; I'd practised all Sunday afternoon with Mum's hairdryer until peak hair satisfaction had been achieved.

'All you need to know is your hair looks great. Great hair equals a great day. Let's go. You got this.'

As we reached the school gates under a low-slung dishwater sky, Michelle and Sarah wandered into view among a throng of other kids. They waved in my direction; I turned round in shock to establish they'd meant me. They had.

'Act cool,' Derek hissed. 'Don't wave back. Just smile.' I followed his prompts, wishing he could stay and gently guide me through the intricate diplomacies of pre-teenage game play. 'Don't jump into bed with anyone today. They're gonna be courting you, so play it down, OK?'

I nodded.

'That Tracey bitch will try and get you on side. Just be yourself. You don't need her in your back pocket. She's nasty.'

I glanced at him anxiously.

'You'll get the hang of it.' He stopped at the gate, hands in his life preserver, cap pulled low over his eyes. 'This is me. I'll be gone when you get back. But I'll see you on Friday. Have a good week.' We stood staring at each other as kids streamed past and into the grounds. Out of the corner of my eye, I spotted Tracey, whose aeroplane-wing fringe visibly drooped at the sight of us together. Derek chose that exact moment to grab me into a hug before kissing my cheek. I hugged him back, the kiss rather startling. I ran off into the melee, looking back to find Derek waving; he blew a kiss. I laughed, walking straight into fit Keith Doyle in the year above.

# 20

## THE CHANNEL

Jesus could have effortlessly glided over the Separation Zone without a misstep, gentle ripples ruffling its slick surface, the occasional dazzle of a sparkler on bonfire night. I swam through my golden era, a gloriously burnished few years of childhood before darkness snuffed out an almost-carefree existence. I'm nothing special. Most people could reflect back on a time where they were truly unhindered by life's nonsense. My own age of innocence just happened to be squeezed into a three-year period between the divorce and my boobs bursting forth like mounds of fermenting dough. If I'd been blessed with lemons like Mum instead of preposterous cantaloupes, life could have taken a very different turn, and if the Channel was indeed a mirror, then the Separation Zone was my golden era. I ought to enjoy it while I could, before the sea gods rose up to throw down the gauntlet. If, if, if – there it was again! *If* I counted back to reason zero for swimming the Channel, my tits were responsible – they'd started all this. But *if* I was going to apply meta-analysis, genetics had a lot to answer for, namely my parents. It was *always* the fucking parents' fault. Smug old me existed knowing that none of my progeny were currently in therapy citing my parenting as *the* major offender their lives were a shitstorm.

Alan's whistle slashed through this lively debate, turning me towards *Boudica*. Both Desi and Alan were yelling, pointing excitedly towards the horizon. I stopped swimming in time to witness two large grey dorsal fins curl into the water. I almost expelled the last feed, my heart wedged like a brick in the base of my throat. Spurred on by terror, I madly began thrashing towards the boat's port side.

*Sharks.*

## 21

## A BIG DISEASE WITH A LITTLE NAME

'It happened exactly like you said it would!' I regaled Derek on his return from London. 'Michelle, Sarah and I are friends again, and I didn't even have to fight Tracey!'

Derek burst out laughing, 'Cordy, you kill me.'

'What?'

'You? Fighting? Are you kidding me? She'd eat you for breakfast.'

'I could do it, now I know how to do my hair. It's given me strength, like Samson.'

Later that evening after dinner, Aunty Liz waltzed into the living room hefting a giant gift-wrapped box.

'Derek and I have a thank-you present for letting us stay. And Lois, you're to accept it gracefully!'

Mum rolled her eyes theatrically, letting slip this was no surprise.

Stephen and I were given the go ahead and eagerly tore at the paper, revealing the contents on two mighty rips.

'A VHS player!' Stephen cried ardently.

'Oh wow, thank you so much!' I enthused. This had been the best week of my life; future ones would be hard-pressed to beat it.

'We can rent *Breakfast at Tiffany's* tomorrow before I leave,' Derek said happily, handing me a three pack of blank video tapes to kick-start our recording journey.

As Liz and Derek connected the wires, they switched on the TV; the end of *'Allo 'Allo!* played out. The second the theme tune finished, the screen briefly blanked then a sinister rumbling volcano appeared before dramatically exploding, accompanied by the voice of John Hurt booming across the room. 'There is now a danger that has become a threat to us all...'

'Switch it off!' Mum cried. 'I'd heard about this, but didn't know it was going to be now! Kids are watching!'

Derek leapt up to press the off button; Liz stopped him.

'It's important, Lois. Everyone needs to see it, even children.'

'No they don't! Kids, out, now!'

Liz shook her head in disappointment. 'You're just delaying the inevitable. Better we watch it now and then explain. You can't police the TV; it'll only be shown again. It's not going away! There's going to be a leaflet drop too.'

Mum jumped up from the sofa and grabbed Stephen's hand, but he resisted.

'I haven't officially explained the facts of life yet!' she hissed at her sister.

'No time like the present!'

'I want to watch!' Stephen cried, drawn in by the gloomy, post-apocalyptic, cinematic aesthetic.

By the time an anonymous hand chiselled the monolithic gravestone we'd missed half of John Hurt's doom-laden monologue. When the AIDS tombstone smacked the floor in tempo with a sinister bong of a church bell, silence rang through the room. Derek glanced back at his mum who'd blanched considerably, her hand covering her mouth. He jumped up and ran into the hallway, taking the stairs two at a time. Ten seconds later my bedroom door slammed. Aunty Liz breathed deeply, biting her closed fist as the theme tune for *The Colbys* played in the background.

'Is he OK?' Mum asked uncertainly. 'I didn't think he knew... I told you we should have turned it off.'

'Lois!'

Mum bowed her head; she'd overstepped the mark.

'What's AIDS?' Stephen asked tremulously. 'Are we going to get it?'

'No, you're not,' Mum explained weakly. 'It's... it's nothing you need to worry about.'

I already knew about sex – Mum had handed over a cartoon book when I was almost ten called *How a Baby is Made*. 'If you have any questions, just ask.' Then she'd scurried off, evading further lines of enquiry. I'd shown it to Stephen who had laughed at the cartoon man's priapic willy poking the air.

'What's a virginga?' he'd asked; he'd only been seven.

How HIV was transmitted through sex wasn't clear – *could you get it from kissing*? I'd yet to receive my first official kiss, having pinned hopes on senior school opening the door to snogging, something *Jackie* magazine naturally gave lessons on.

'I'll just go and check on him.' Aunty Liz stood

before disappearing upstairs, only to return a few minutes later. 'He said he wants Cordelia.'

I'd never been requested as a support by anyone. Blushing with pride, I knocked gently on the bedroom door before pushing it open. Derek sat on my bed, fiercely hugging his knees, his face pressed into them.

'Hello... Your mum said you wanted me?'

'I just didn't want *her*.'

'Oh.' Crushing disappointment. 'Shall I go?'

'No.' He raised his head; his cheeks slick with tears. 'That's not what I meant. I wish Edward were here.'

I perched at the foot of the bed, desperately wanting to help but not sure how.

'Dad... Dad... died of AIDS.'

My stomach lurched. *HOW?!* I wanted to scream, but refrained. 'Oh, I'm so... sorry, that's... rubbish.' I winced at my own inadequacy, longing to grab Derek's hands currently clenched into tight fists.

'No one told me. Mom said he had pneumonia, and skin cancer, that he was really sick. We visited him every day in the hospital at the end – he was too sick to be at home. But I could see what was happening – I heard people talking. I'm not stupid! Kids at school got wind of it and said my dad was dying of the "gay plague". That he deserved it, that I'd be next.'

'That's so mean!' My breast beat with anger. I wanted to punch those children until they grovelled on the floor, noses bleeding in the dirt.

'Oh, Cordy, you don't know the half of it...' He stretched his legs out, feet dangling over the edge of the bed. 'I don't really have any friends at school.'

'Why? You're so cool! I'd want to be your friend straight away! Just look at how you squashed Tracey. If you came to my school, you'd be the most popular boy there!'

'Would I?' he said doubtfully. 'Really? When they find out the truth, I'd be back to square one.'

'You wouldn't have to tell them anything.'

'As soon as they found out I had two dads, I'd be fish food.'

I gawped. 'How do you have two dads?'

'Well, I don't any more, but Edward's still alive.' He paused, briefly glancing at me. 'Edward was, is more than my dad's best friend, he was his... boyfriend.'

I nodded.

'And Mom got pregnant with me using Dad's... sperm – they were married, but not like other people are married. Dad sometimes lived with me and Mom and sometimes with Edward down the block.'

'Will Edward move in with you now?'

Derek shook his head.

'This is truly... *shit*.' My fingers tingling with delight. I'd never sworn out loud in my life. *Shit* was a righteous improvement on limp-wristed *rubbish*.

'Thanks, Cuz. It is shit.'

'Why didn't you say anything? You go home on Sunday.' He'd bared his soul at the eleventh hour before flying three thousand miles away; who knew when we would see each other again.

'Cordy – I didn't even wanna come here. Mom made it sound like we were visiting Mars. The last thing I wanted to do was talk about Dad, about what he died of. I didn't want to meet cousins or explore my British roots! I just wanted to be at home with Edward and have Christmas there.'

'Why didn't Edward come too?'

'He was working.'

'How do you feel now?'

'Of course I'm glad we came. At least you're not gonna get bullied any more.'

'I wasn't being bullied!'

'Well, what would you call it then?'

We sighed in unison, smiling at each other.

'I'm going to miss you,' felt the most natural thing to say, even though no one admitted things like that in our family. 'I wish you lived nearer.'

'Me too. But I don't mind writing. We can be pen pals?'

'I'd like that. But if you need to ring me, honestly do, any time. I won't care what you need to talk about; if it's upsetting you, you should tell me.'

Derek leaned over and gave me a clumsy hug. 'Thank you, that means a lot.'

When Aunty Liz found us, we were clearing out the wardrobe, or *closet* as Derek called it, piling up clothes that no longer fitted, which was most of them. Derek took the puffball skirt and a few crop tops in the end.

'You never know when a crop-top emergency is going to leap out at you!'

I had no recollection of Derek leaving, if we had a tearful farewell, or what happened after. One minute he was there and the next he wasn't. Life returned to normal, but he'd left an indelible imprint on my life.

## 22

## THE CHANNEL

'Cordy, stop!' I was one arm's length from touching *Boudica*'s hull. I looked up, terror slashing the length of my stroke, panic binding my chest. Desi and Alan were laughing. 'Over there!'

I glanced to where I'd spotted the fins and two dolphins broke the surface, jumping high into the air. Another two joined in the leaping further behind, drawing arcs with their bodies.

'Aren't they incredible?' Desi cried in wonder. 'They're cheerleading you.' He was taking pictures with his phone. It was like watching a firework display, rockets bursting across a night sky, blasts of intense red and electric orange fading to black. Panic defused, I oohed and ahhed at the dolphins' indefatigable springing, happiness and awe flooding my limbs. I could have watched all day. 'Come on, play-time's over!'

I resumed my stroke, buoyed up by the unadulterated beauty of nature. Animals were a blessing; I was so grateful to witness them. Until...

'Motherfucker!' *Jellyfish*. I'd driven my arm right into a floss of diaphanous tentacles; I'd been too entranced by the sodding dolphins. Story of my life.

Swimming with my head clear of the water, I removed an earplug to receive instructions. I detected another creature a few metres ahead. My whole hand throbbed but it wasn't a hindrance. I laughed at the vast dissimilitude of the animal kingdom. Ever since moving into the flat during my twenties, animals had sought me out – Terry the parrot's legacy burning bright. Injured birds, mangey foxes, lost cats all found their way into my postage-stamp back garden, cluttered with bird feeders, two bird baths, a raised bed bursting with bee-friendly perennials and a hedgehog house constructed with a sheet of plywood and some old bricks I'd unearthed from behind the dilapidated shed. I shared rescue dog, Kevin, an energetic mongrel (Jack Russell crossed with a nutty Poodle – a Roodle!) with Desi and his partner, Tim, while Nimrod, my sixth Syrian hamster, lived beneath the aquarium where Finneas and Snook, two angel fish, observed life from their eyrie set on the living-room bookshelf. Mince (chocolate brown) and Pie (golden agouti), two Mongolian gerbils, were recent additions to the kitchen. I'd only ventured into Pets at Home to buy Nimrod a new ball when they charmed me from the adoption enclosure, pressing their tiny paws against the glass. Powerless against such cuteness, I adopted them on the spot, their gerbilarium taking pride of place in the chimney breast above the knife drawer.

'Boys, I'm home!' Knowing creatures with delicate hearts and intelligent eyes awaited my return at the end of the day or after a disappointing date beat the solitude of my one-bedroom flat into submission. They each had their own personalities, especially Nimrod, a cheeky little nipper who followed my every move round the flat once ensconced in his ball. But more than anything, they relied on me for, well, *everything*.

'There's a few of the buggers dotted here and there,' Alan called across the water. 'It's not a whole bloom, so you're OK; swim with your head above the surface until we're sure. Do you need painkillers?'

I gave a thumbs down and ploughed on in a cloud of undimmed optimism. *Jellyfish, you're not in the way, I am in the way, this is your habitat. Thank you for letting me pass.* I let Alan guide me while Desi kept lookout for more. *I feel you,* I spoke to the dull ache in my shoulders. *But you're a result of achievement. Pain means we're still going forward. Pain means I'm alive.* Of course there was the hellish period when I'd acted like I didn't want to be alive, but that had only been a reflective observation. I'd just been trying to remain afloat before reaching that mythical time when I would be content with myself, with my body, with the person I actually was rather than bullying an exhausted body into being what I unrealistically believed I *should* be.

That was then, this is now, the past and present swimming cheek to cheek. Far in the distance, the moving cities sailed from the right across the horizon in a steady stream. I would be swimming among them, but not yet. This very moment was all there was. The vessels before me were in a world as un-knowable as tomorrow, next week. Next year. This was my life now. How had it taken over forty years to realise this?

'Everyone gets it eventually. Some wait until their deathbed, but it comes; you can't fight it,' Aunty Liz had said on the quay side.

*Head down, four strokes, breathe out. Bubbles.*

## 23

# THE GODFATHER

At age fifteen, the sudden appearance of sizeable breasts deposed my thighs from the top spot as most loathsome body part. Instead of cradling two fried eggs inside my training bra, I was consciously squashing pockets of flesh under my armpits to fit inside school blouses. I began wearing jumpers over everything, shirts gaping in seclusion. Then one evening, Mum unceremoniously shoved a leaflet in my face.

'It's Duke of Edinburgh season. Thought you should sign up for it. All that fresh air will do you good. You could do with the exercise, Cordelia. Your brother's signed up for football.' She judiciously eyed my roomy school jumper that I'd begged for last month. When I refused, she tutted.

'I'm not being mean, Cordy, but you need to do some exercise. You don't want to go to seed before you've even blossomed.'

The following day at school, Keith Philips, with whom I'd experienced my ill-fated first kiss at Michelle's birthday party, declared open season on me in the French corridor. I'd spent years awaiting the perfect set of lips with which to experience this first snog, turning down Neil Tuck, Garry Speight and Mark Winkler in quick succession at various parties until I was considered long in the tooth. According to the toilet wall, almost all my contemporaries had been fingered; I had a lot of catching up to do.

'Streaker used to be fit before she got fat,' Keith announced from the lofty podium of third most good-looking boy in our year. The jibe felt more caustic than anything Tracey Bates could have hurled at me. Had this anything to do with the pernicious rumours that followed our syncopated clashing of gums, none substantiated by me? I'd complained profusely to Michelle about the whole anticlimactic experience Monday morning.

'It was so disappointing, like a sloppy washing

machine on a slow spin. Then he had the cheek to slip two fingers in my knickers. I was so shocked; I didn't have time to stop him before he jammed them up there! They were freezing, like being stabbed by two ice popsicles! I really liked him too.' This blow-by-blow account mysteriously escaped the confines of the far corner of the north playground, and winged its way to the south playground, reaching Keith's ears to the hyperbolic tune that his rudimentary technique caused my subsequent consumptive-like collapse and ensuing vomcano.

'I'm fat!' I hissed that lunchtime.

'You're not fat!' Sarah faithfully reassured. 'You've just "developed" a bit later than everyone else. I wish I had tits.' She prodded her own two Scotch pancakes.

'Do not wish for tits. That's exactly what I did, now look at me!'

'You could go on a diet?' Michelle suggested, nibbling a Ryvita loaded with an inch of snowmen's brains (cottage cheese). 'Not that you need to, but it might make your boobs smaller.' Watery white whey dripped into her packed lunch box, splattering a Granny Smith's apple. 'My mum's always on one. She suggested Ryvita instead of bread, said I would thank her for it later.'

'A diet? How do you know what to do?' I'd observed Mum's various food crazes but saw no sane reason to apply them to my own life.

'Just cut down, I think?' Michelle shrugged.

'Cut down what?'

'Meals. Don't eat lots. That's what I do.'

'Aren't you always hungry?'

'Yes, but you get used to it.'

'I don't think I will though. I like food too much.'

\* \* \*

The VHS player meant films could now be watched at any time of day or night as long as they met Mum's stringent age requirement. It would have been impossible to sneak *The Godfather* past her, so we watched it at Dad's when he and Netty met friends in Eastbourne.

On the brink of teenagerhood, Stephen had enjoyed the countless guns, mindless killing and the testosterone-fuelled storyline. In later years, he would appreciate its layered Shakespearian artistry. For me, the fascination lay with Michael Corleone (enigmatic Al Pacino). Here was a man trying (and failing) to stay on the straight and narrow path diverging from his crime-riddled family who thought

nothing of executing anyone for insulting their belli-
cose patriarch. It was impossible not to compare
notes. A lesbian (still uncorroborated) sister flees to
America where she marries a gay man and produces
a baby; a bitter father who cuts his daughters out of
his ill-gotten fortune; and an estranged, telly-ob-
sessed Grandma who still secretly rings every month
to discuss her favourite shows that she gorges on like
a gavage-fed goose, while endlessly boasting about
Lady Madonna (her real love) winning the Holsten
Cup. Of course, there was also Dad, the waster done
good (but too late for Grandpa), now shacked up
with Avon super sales lady, Netty Curtains. The Corleone family's psychopathy didn't feel so far out of
reach sat next to Stephen in the Pink Palace.

'Do you think if Michael had never given in, not
murdered Sollozzo and McCluskey in the restaurant
and stayed true to himself, he would have been
happy? Just led a normal life?' I asked after the film
was over.

'What do you mean?' Stephen looked quizzical.

Unable to grapple the appropriate words to fully
explain, I let it go. But deep in my belly, cement set,
and I reconsidered Keith's brutal remark and
Michelle's solution. The next mealtime, I left a fish
finger and only ate a quarter of the chips.

'Are you feeling OK, Cordelia?' Netty asked when faced with unprecedented leftovers.

'I only like the way Mum cooks fish fingers.'

My stomach grumbled like a dyspeptic old man for the rest of the evening, but I was so giddy with expectation, I just accepted the cramps as a badge of honour. Michelle's sagacious words ran on a loop: *You get used to it.*

The trouble was, I just couldn't.

Peering at the numbers spinning past the tiny glass window on Mum's scales was like pulling the lever on a one-armed bandit. Eight stone eight pounds: *congratulations, you have won a bag of McCain Oven Chips.* From that day forth, every waking moment was fraught with thinking about food. After a week of half portions, gnawing hunger pains waking me at night and donating one cheese and lettuce sandwich to David Plimpton each lunchtime, I was curious to discover my weight loss.

'You need to eat more,' he insisted, having learned it would otherwise go to waste. 'I can't eat your lunch every day!'

Racing home after school, I dragged the scales out from under Mum's bed. As the roulette began, I feverishly prayed the sacrifice had worked and life could return to normal.

'Half a stone, please, God, half a stone.'

A pound. A pitiful, pathetic pound. I balanced on one leg, but the needle stubbornly refused to budge. I was so hungry, my head had filled with air, my brain having eaten itself in despair.

'You're doing it all wrong,' Michelle advised before French. She had since claimed the position of guru for Operation Titless. 'You weigh yourself in the morning, naked, before you've eaten Ryvita or whatever you're having. That's your true weight. If you want to lose more than a few pounds a week, do some exercise. You could join your mum's classes?'

'Absolutely not. I can't leap around; my boobs'll give me black eyes.'

'OK, swimming? Cycling?' I'd outgrown my pink Raleigh bike some years ago.

'Have you been weighing yourself on my scales?' Mum asked one Saturday.

'No.'

'They keep moving from under my bed. I don't like anyone else using them. It messes up the calibration.'

I started walking the long way to school while skipping breakfast because, why not? I pushed hunger pains until breaktime, eating just two plain Ryvita to prevent a blackout. Inching my way into daily discomfort, I found a perverse consolation in the pain. One day closer to having whittled away flesh until I existed solely inside a tight circle.

In the meantime, after a dearth of animated phone calls or airmail letters, a postcard arrived from Derek bearing the iconic film poster of Audrey Hepburn smoking a cigarillo. With her miniscule waist and waif-like arms, I still upheld her as the paragon of perfection. On the back, in Derek's childish writing was a succinct update. He and Mom were moving, Aunty L would ring with the new address. The big news was that Derek had a girlfriend. She had a beautiful tush (*bum to you!*) and was called Jodie. He was besotted. *Derek had a girlfriend?* Maybe not, he could be exaggerating a basic friend. But when I quizzed Mum, she confirmed it.

'Apparently, she's like Madonna while Derek looks like a model! He finally had a growth spurt.'

But he liked women's clothes. This didn't feel quite right.

## 24

### THE CHANNEL

Fat – such a divisive word across the board (unless applied to a banker's bonus), mostly negative depending on its grammatical position, or indeed, its place in history. In the time of Rubens, one would have been hailed a great beauty possessing such curves and enormous boobs. Muscles, flesh, strength, were now my watchwords. I was liberated in the Channel, just me in my body, one stroke at a time, no more fear keeping me safe, my world small. Now was my chance to ruffle those feathers, contradict my own limited expectations. Fear was there, it never went away, you had to feel it and do it anyway. How else had the human race survived?

Fortified by a sweet milky coffee and a square of

Battenberg cake, my arms efficiently sliced through the rich saltwater, wasting very little energy. Well within a groove, this robotic stroke, refined by monotonous pool drills, freed my mind to prudently pick over the carcass of the past, transporting me away from numb feet and chafing shoulders. Leaving behind aching fingers and a sunburned nose, I was a finely tuned machine, carrying inside the flame that Desi had relit when he'd suggested this odyssey.

'Jodie's physical perfection. Honestly, Cordy, you should see her, she's so pretty. I find myself staring at her constantly instead of finishing essays in class.' After the postcard, Derek had rung, eager to gush. How was this Marlboro Man voice associated with my idiosyncratic cousin? Wasn't he still prancing around in a puffball skirt, more stylish than I'd ever be? Even in photos, I'd noted his physical transformation, but it was as if he were a *Jackie* magazine photo story, not Derek. Whilst he reached towards the sun, desperate to grow, I had begun to shrink into the shade, ravenous for perfection. It was impossible to join in his conversation – Derek talked at me, but I had nothing to add even if he'd given me space. His sumptuous descriptions of Jodie cut like glass, leaving me feeling lumpy and ugly. I would never be *that* beautiful, *that* perfect and so I pretended to be out when he subsequently rang, so that in the end he stopped altogether. Of course I felt guilty, I missed him, but we were different people now, with an ocean between us, the distance growing wider every year. What on earth would we have in common?

*Head down, four strokes, breathe out. Bubbles.*

## 25

### TV-AM

'Sandra Willis bought her sister-in-law to a class when they were staying during the Easter holidays. Her husband's a producer on *TV-am*. Said he was looking for someone to stand-in while their regular fitness lady goes off on maternity leave. Everyone they interviewed so far was too boring or ugly.' Mum beamed like she'd delivered the mathematical equation underpinning the moon landing.

'*Trish's Tone and Tease*?' I asked, shocked. 'Isn't that on ITV?'

'Yes, that's the one.' Mum paused thoughtfully, ignoring my ITV dig. 'They're calling the slot *Miss Slimnastic*. I've resigned from school; I start in two weeks. James wasn't happy... Oh well. Upwards! I get my hair and make-up done every morning!' My skin always prickled whenever Mum called Mr Klingon by his first name. Teachers' first names and baby seagulls were synonymous in that they didn't exist.

Stephen abandoned his Findus Crispy Pancake mid-air, the cheese sauce globbing the peas from his suspended fork.

'Will we have to move in with Dad?' he asked, unimpressed.

'No. A car will arrive at four in the morning and drive me to London in time for hair and make-up. You'll be OK here on your own, won't you?'

Stephen was now nearing thirteen, yet still shared his bed with Ned, Squashy the penguin and a gaggle of other cuddlies scattered over his *Muppets* duvet. His bottom lip wobbled.

'We'll be fine!' I grabbed Stephen's hand under the table and squeezed it. 'Wow, Mum, that's amazing. Are you going to be famous?'

'We'll have to wait and see.' She caught her reflection in the kitchen window and fluffed her hair.

I was about to gain unobserved free rein over the scales first thing every morning – the timing couldn't have been more perfect.

* * *

'Hello, I'm Lois and I'm here to show you ten minutes of something called Slimnastics. You don't need any equipment, just your own body weight. And if that's something you'd like to reduce, then I'm here to help you do that and get fit!' Mum gleamed from the TV screen in a royal-blue unitard, painted, blow dried, manicured and pedicured into a glossy hard shell of her former self. If only the viewers had been party to the previous week's Slimfast marathon and daily facials at Tina's Beauty Emporium in Eastbourne. *Television adds ten pounds!* had been scrawled in permanent marker on a plain postcard and stuck to the fridge door under a wooden pig-shaped magnet inscribed with the 'thinspirational' message: *A fridge pig stays big.*

We sat in our school uniforms on the sofa, Stephen eating Marmite toast minus a plate while I sipped tea with a splash of skimmed milk. I'd lost an impressive half a stone in four weeks, yet nevertheless, my boobs had the audacity to enter a room before me and my thighs still dared to touch. The anticipated euphoria had failed to land while standing too quickly often resulted in a virtual blackout.

'When do I stop?' I complained in the north playground the week before Mum's TV debut. 'I miss chips.'

'Not until your boobs are smaller,' Michelle cautioned, counting out her grapes to make sure there were exactly six in her packed lunch.

'When will that be?'

'After a few more pounds?' Michelle suggested. 'Though, I've been eating like this since Christmas now. You can't ever go back to eating "normally" if you want to stay thin! Mum's eaten Ryvita and cottage cheese every day for as long as I can remember. I only let myself have chips or chocolate on a weekend now.' Michelle had never been fat as far as I could recall. However, being fat and going on a diet weren't mutually exclusive.

'Why hasn't anyone invented calorie-free chips?' I moaned, wondering if that was my calling in life. 'My mum never eats chips.'

'She can't now!' Michelle said reverently. 'TV adds ten pounds.'

'How do you even know that?' *What did real life add?*

'Everyone knows that. All the film stars say so. How do you think they stay so skinny? They probably vom it all back up.'

'What? That's gross. Of course they don't.' Not Saint Audrey, surely?

'Jane Fonda did it to stay slim,' Michelle replied. 'The Romans installed vomitoriums outside banquet halls so they could scoff loads of food then chuck it back up before starting all over again.'

'Chelle! Stop!' Sarah jabbed her with a crusty ham baguette. 'I'm eating!'

*  *  *

'Do you think she's nervous?' Stephen asked, dusting toast crumbs from his fingertips. Mum launched into a quick warm up, her blue unitard popping against the pale-pink studio background, hair bouncing, set in solid Renaissance curls. For added ambience, a pair of exotic potted palms were arranged either side of her like security guards.

'Mum, nervous?' The fact had never crossed my mind.

Stephen shrugged.

'No, she's loving it.' Despite her rictus grin, I refused to believe Mum would be nervous about anything. 'Do you think Dad's watching?'

'Doubt it.'

I would have bet a thigh gap that Netty Curtains

was studying her every move. Maybe she was kitted out in her leggings, ready to go.

When Mum had bent her body, squeezed her buttocks and toned her stomach so that 'you too can enjoy flexibility and strength, no more sucking that saggy tummy in', she waved the camera off and it panned out to a politely clapping Anne Diamond on the studio sofa, while co-host, Nick Owen, smiled benevolently, as if fundamentally appreciating the plight of the nation's wobbly bits.

'Thank you, Lois,' Anne said demurely. 'That was just what the country needed today, to get us ready to bare all in our bikinis.'

'I don't think you'll be seeing me in a bikini any time soon,' Nick joked drolly.

'Give me six weeks, and you'll be beach-body ready!' Mum quipped off screen, her mic already switched off, her voice tinny and flat. Nick's eyebrows wormed across his brow. *How dare the hired help chip in?* I half expected a board rubber to fly across the studio any moment. Stephen started laughing, almost dying when a piece of toast lodged in his throat. I thumped him on the back until it shot out, hitting the coffee table.

'Now there's a challenge!' Anne joshed, covering for Nick's rising hackles.

The phone in the hallway started ringing. Stephen glanced at me, my ranking indisputable.

'Hello, dear. Is your mother there?' Grandma's reedy voice faltered in the earpiece. She still rung on the sly ever since Grandpa had cut Mum off. 'I don't know why she bothers,' Mum had said. 'She's not once asked how anyone is, just wants to talk about *The Colbys* and *Coronation Street*.'

'No, she's at work.'

'Tell her well done from me, dear.' Abruptly switching to a whisper, 'I've got to go; I thought he'd gone to get a *Telegraph*.' The line went dead.

* * *

'To celebrate my first week,' Mum said proudly, clutching a cellophaned bunch of cobalt-blue flowers. 'My dressing room was rammed when I arrived this morning. Ironic as I won't eat any of it. Don't go mad and scoff the lot in one go. I'm going to ration you both.'

This was not helpful. My iron resolve instantly pressed against the fence confronted with an Aladdin's cave of Belgian chocolates, tins of Fortnums' biscuits and a splendiferous cake in the shape of a woman sporting a blue unitard. The sodding cake immediately assumed control of my brain; nothing sweet had passed these lips for weeks. I deserved a modest slice – I'd lost half a stone, for God's sake, the equivalent of chopping off an arm!

After a Lean Cuisine vegetarian cannelloni (two hundred and fifty calories), any genuine nutrition sacrificed upon the altar of low-fat, food-additive heaven, Stephen plonked a skinny slice of cake in front of me. I cautiously chopped it into tiny squares and nibbled it like cheese; stars burst behind my eyes. It took all the restraint in the world not to stack up the sections and wolf them in one bite. Predictably, I wanted another slice. I *needed* another slice. Life depended on another slice. Stephen routinely polished off his block of cake and licked his fingers.

'Can I have some more?' he asked casually.

'A small bit.'

He cut himself a slice larger than mine, sinking his teeth into it, the calories not even registering. Resentment simmered.

'Do you want another slice?' Mum asked me.

'No thank you, I'm full.'

'Good girl.'

Five hours later, my soul screaming, tummy empty and my head bursting with scenarios where

my thighs and boobs begged me not to devour another thing, I tossed and turned in bed, unable to
sleep. The cake was every bad boyfriend who didn't
ring, snogged your best friend, before getting so
drunk at a party, they face planted in a flower bed.
*How did anyone stop dieting once they had started?* I was
going to stop right there and then – I'd had enough.
Once the decision crystallised, a tidal wave of relief
propelled me onto the landing where I floated downstairs like a sleepwalker.

In the kitchen, knife poised, I whipped out the
protective piece of foil and cut through the blue and
white icing figure, slicing through the layers,
squashing them into each other, the caramel-soaked
sponge relinquishing its integrity, crumbs scattering
onto the table. I shovelled the crumbs with my other
hand and heaped them into my mouth before the
knife had touched the silver cake board. Ecstasy
burst across my tongue. In three bites, the slice was
gone. I hadn't breathed the entire time and gulped
down air, surveying the cake: it could afford to lose
another inch. Planting the knife alongside the gap, I
sliced a rectangle and jiggled it away from the
mother cake, chopping it into three biteable chunks,
relishing every mouthful. If I'd been mown down by

a run-away bin lorry there and then, I would have died happy.

I glanced at the kitchen clock (quarter past midnight), mutinous and dizzy with not giving a shit – oh what freedom. If Michelle was here, she'd be horrified. Should I have another slice? I stopped chewing. No, I'd go to bed, get some proper sleep and see what the morning brought.

'I'm not dieting any more,' I declared at the lunch table on Monday. 'It made me crazy. And I can't bear never eating cake again for the rest of my life.'

'You could chew and spit?' Michelle suggested, desperate for an ally. 'The weight will creep back on eventually. And you've done so well. Operation Titless is finally working – don't give up now!'

'Welcome back to the land of the living!' Sarah said, offering me a Hobnob. 'Life's too short – eat the cake!'

# 26

## THE CHANNEL

'Treat time!' Desi yelled across the water, shaking a giant packet of Cadbury's buttons like a purple maraca. The current had teased me away from the boat, forcing me to swim closer in order to hear clearly.

'Don't stop to talk, don't waste time on the food breaks, down in less than forty seconds and do not, whatever you do, stop to chat. I know what you two are like!' Alan had chastised us the week before.

'Us, chat? Whatever are you insinuating?' Desi had laughed. 'I'll be as quiet as a church mouse during evensong.'

'Jesus, Desi, evensong?' I'd groaned.

'Yes! You know how I like to imagine that I live in

a quaint, English country theme park circa 1952 – all scones, strawberries, old ladies, knitting circles and whatnot.'

'Whatnot? I'm afraid you'd be in prison for being gay!'

'Well, I'd remain in the closet, like every other man until the time was right.'

'Can you give me a pin drop?' I shouted, pulling the goggle case towards me. 'An estimate at least, so I know how far.'

Alan and Desi glanced at each other, then at Alison, the observer. The other traffic had grown in stature, sailing from the right as ships headed into the North Sea up towards northern Europe and Scandinavia.

'You're just about to hit the Northeast Shipping Lane.' Alison confirmed my estimate: well over halfway.

The fire-breathing sun hung directly above, battering my skull. Sparkles skittered along the ripples etched by the north-easterly wind currently caressing my right cheek. I inhaled the chocolate buttons, sending the empty case on its way. Numb feet, crusty lips, burnt nose – an indisputable swipe right on Bumble. I must have been in the water for at least an eight-hour work day. I made a rambling attempt to count back feeds to gauge a more accurate measure, but lost track, the elasticity of time unspooling from its centre. Einstein should have swum the Channel to test his theories.

Even though the swim had overtaken my life, it was not my life. I'd never shied away from pain – that was a kind of warped superpower. Yet in the past, running towards it had cost me dearly.

'What film are you on now?' Desi called as I reinserted an earplug.

'I'm about to start the *Breakfast Club*.'

'Oh, God help us!' Desi pressed his hands to his sweatshirt-clad chest. 'Those were the lost years for both of us. Good luck out there. Keep in mind I was only eighteen and such a little shit! Love you! Keep swimming!'

I rolled my neck before resuming my stroke. It seemed inconceivable now that Desi hadn't always been in my life. Before he cracked open my humdrum existence, I'd been hovering on the starting line, waiting for something to happen. Maybe I'd always loved him, those familial bonds formed before we knew we were linked by DNA. *Derek six months...* But I'd turned my back too, forcing the stream of our connection deep underground until it sought the perfect occasion to burst forth and rekindle.

I massaged the space below my heart, the solar plexus, where my iron resolve roosted. This stubborn, determined streak that had been my undoing had been persuaded to dance to a different drum. The thump of the first beat hit and I squared my shoulders, curling my arms over my left ear, driving it into the water. As I kicked towards an oil tanker cleaving its way to the northern tip of the globe, I summoned the *Breakfast Club*, basking in the aura of John Bender's (menacing Judd Nelson) vulnerable hostility; it had taken just one of his molten glares to reduce my teenage insides to Swiss fondue.

*Head down, four strokes, breathe out. Bubbles.*

## 27

## THE BREAKFAST CLUB

To British teenagers in the eighties, the *Breakfast Club* was as exotic and unattainable as spray cheese. Touted as the quintessential dissection of American high school life, the film is set during a nine-hour Saturday detention – even *that* was cooler than litter picking or sorting out lost property (a pair of skid-marked Y fronts *always* lurking). While boundaries between hard-line cliques temporarily crumble, ex-posing a web of similarities that bind them all, namely fucked-up parents – the flies in everyone's ointment – not everyone thought the film was a true representation.

'Yeah, there's bullying, that always happens,' Derek had conceded when I asked if it was like his school. 'But it's not real in that movie. Those kids are just stereotypes with white-bread gripes. Show me someone with brown skin, with Afro hair, someone who's scared to walk home at night in case they get jumped. That's *my* reality.'

I agreed, but that wasn't *my* reality. Mine involved constant judgement from peers and worse – myself.

When we had watched it at Sarah's, Michelle had sniggered at the infamously cutting words of John Bender to school princess, Claire (Molly Ringwald), accusing her of having a fat girl's name.

'How can a *name* be fat?' I'd complained while squashing down my boobs.

'It's America, the land of opportunity; anything's possible,' Sarah said dryly, absently munching a Twix.

'Michelle's a fat girl's name. Or it would be if I let myself eat chips like I want to!' Michelle milked virtue out of suffering, gnawing on one of her fatless, flavourless, colourless crackers baked as hard as floor tiles. 'You want one?' she offered.

'They make me guff.'

'Me too, but they fill you up against the evils of biscuits.'

Sarah shook her head and waved her Twix at us.

I had to sit on my hands so I didn't grab the other chocolate-dipped finger.

Michelle had tediously been right. The weight jumped back up as if I had hewn papier-mâché flesh and slapped it on myself. After two weeks in Greece with Netty and Dad, drowning in delicious cheeses, a cornucopia of ice-cream flavours and the crispiest of chips, my body had indeed revolted. Moderation had become an impossibility, a voracious hole required constant filling.

'Who do we think *we* are?' Michelle asked, pausing the *Breakfast Club*, Molly Ringwald freeze framed, mouth provocatively half open. 'Choose your character – criminal, basket case, princess, brain or jock.'

'The criminal,' Sarah said proudly. 'Cos I don't give a shit.'

'I think you're more like the brain,' Michelle said. 'You're always doing your homework.'

'I'm the basket case,' I said quietly. Neither one disputed it.

'I'm the princess,' Michelle said, sighing against one of life's forgone conclusions. 'But I have shades of the brain too.'

'How are we friends if we're all different?' Sarah asked.

'We can't all be princesses!' Michelle said, biting sarcasm outstripping her pragmatism.

'Who's Cheeks?' Sarah asked. 'He's one of them too.'

If I'd been casting a classic leading man, David Plimpton would *not* have graced the top of the pile. Johnny Depp, Kiefer Sutherland or even a journeyman like Richard Gere would have sprung to mind first. David was not even as tall as me and had spent the last few years teasing Michelle, me and Sarah about PMT, our pathetic crushes on George Michael, Mags from A-ha, and being 'on the blob'. He'd edged his way into our orbit, cashing in his heart-searing motherless ace from up his sleeve, operating under the banner of 'just friends'. Being part of our gang certainly didn't immunise him against constant ribbing. Me and Michelle would run fingers down his inside leg beneath the desk in English in a stab at triggering a fun-sized Mars Bar. As his knees smacked the table from below, Mrs Darwish would whip round from the blackboard and hurl chalk in his general direction, often smacking the window behind. 'Again, Mr Plimpton? You can hardly be accused of being too big to fit under the desk now, can you?'

'I think Cheeks is the geek. But one day, he might

be the criminal,' Michelle said suggestively. 'Don't you think he's hiding something underneath that innocent "just friends" façade?'

'Listen to her, just because you accidentally snogged him at Neil Tuck's party,' Sarah scoffed.

'I'd no idea it was him in the under-stairs cupboard,' Michelle pouted, blushing. But by all accounts, he'd been well versed in tongue sarnies. 'It was a one-off! Anyway, it's Cheeks! Who would purposely snog him? He's a Borrower.'

Michelle pressed play, Molly Ringwald bursting into life. Was it possible to break out of the archetype you were slotted into at school? Once a basket case, doomed forever a basket case? And who decided who was what in the first place? What if you didn't want to be a basket case any more, refused to play the game?

At the end of the *Breakfast Club*, we were left hanging. Would the kids all still be tentative friends on Monday morning after smashing the social norms? Or would all the barriers slip straight back into their well-worn grooves? Ever the idealist, I longed for them to walk into school Monday morning, linking arms, defying convention, but it's hard to break a pattern in more ways than one.

\* \* \*

'We get a makeover and new clothes and we need to spruce up the house!' Mum chatted in overdrive. 'They want you two featured as well.'

I automatically sucked in my tummy.

'I was thinking, and don't take this the wrong way, I'm just trying to help,' Mum said, carefully eyeing me up, 'maybe you'd like to try Slimfast, just for the photoshoot?' Surely I'd misheard: *Mum* was doing Slimfast for the photoshoot. 'Cordy, did you hear me?'

'What?'

'You need to get fit.'

'Why?'

'Because we're going to be in a national magazine!' Mum's agent, Alvin, had rung. *TV Times* had offered an entire five-page spread about Miss Slimnastic's world, in return for a Banish the Bloat diet plan rolling out after Christmas.

'I've ordered a new sofa, painters are coming in to decorate the whole of downstairs – we've a month until the shoot. I thought you might want to look... your best.' She paused and gave me a desultory once-over. 'You were almost as thin as Michelle before

Greece.' She smiled professionally (teeth together, lips stretched). 'Unfortunately, Grandma's boobs and sluggish metabolism must have skipped a generation.' She sighed like I'd deliberately foxed the genetics myself. 'People have expectations. If it was up to me, I'd just say sod it, but we need to set an example to everyone, how to be healthy, that kind of thing. We're a family others look up to. If I can't make my children stay healthy then how am I going to wield any power over the rest of the country?' Mum had slipped into a Thatcherite style rhetoric as if Slimnastics upheld the bedrock of decent British society.

I shook my head. 'I am healthy. What about Stephen – what does he have to do?'

'Have a haircut.'

'A haircut?' Stephen moaned, running his hands through his brown mullet. 'What's wrong with this?'

'It needs to be neat and tidy. We *all* need to be neat and tidy. The whole of the United Kingdom will be looking at us. You'll be on every newsstand and in all the shops.'

Fuck. *I didn't choose the diet life; the diet life chose me.* This was an emergency.

* * *

I curled over the toilet bowl, pressing my left fist deep into my stomach.

This was not fun. And it wasn't easy. But I couldn't endure another crash diet.

'How long are you going to be?' Stephen asked impatiently through the locked door. 'I need a poo.' With the absence of a convenient *Make Yourself Sick For Dummies* book offering shortcuts and handy tips, I was reduced to trial and error. I'd blithely assumed I'd just ram my fingers down my throat and out my lunch would pop in a neat little pile – not so. With an aching jaw and watery eyes and mouth, I relinquished the toilet as if nothing had taken place. I hated being sick, but it offered a short-term solution to a long-term problem. A simple experiment: I'd eat 'normally' as soon as the photo shoot was in the can.

'You sounded like you were choking. Are you OK?' he asked, face riddled with concern.

'I'm fine. Don't listen at toilet doors, it's rude.' I stormed into my bedroom, brushing off Stephen's raised eyebrows, ears scorching ignominiously. Waiting for him to traipse downstairs, I inspected my imperfections in the mirror. If only I looked like Michelle, I just *knew* I'd be happy.

When it was time, I sloped into the bathroom

and shoved a towel under the gap in the door. I'd drunk a pint of water, hoping to loosen things up.

After almost half an hour of forced dry heaving, water surged up my throat, spurting like a fountain, the Lean Cuisine lasagne and four custard creams infuriatingly absent. Oh, Jesus Christ – the mess! I used half a roll of toilet paper to wipe away splatters on the wall, rim, seat and floor. It took two flushes to clear my conscience, but the sour stench lingered. I sprayed Mum's deodorant like air freshener, noting I'd better buy some Glade if this was going to continue.

Two weeks of covert bathroom manoeuvres and I'd graduated into a seasoned pro: plenty of water, tea, Diet Coke, finishing strong with chocolate, drawing the evacuation to its conclusion. Now master of the ceremony, I didn't see why I had to stop at flushing away just lunch or dinner. Why not treat myself to all the colours of the beige rainbow? The sinful snacks I'd blackballed now became open to me (Cadbury's Boost Bars the absolute pinnacle of the forbidden snack triangle). I was a child let loose in a sweet shop with unlimited reign, as long as I could throw it up sharpish. If I was going to the effort of secret eating before silently vomiting, I may as well splurge in style, raiding the breadbin for rounds of delicious buttery jam toast and gulping down Dairylea Cheese Triangles like jellied sweets. It wasn't like I was going to keep doing it forever.

By the time the photoshoot was upon us, Mum clucked around me like an indulgent mother hen. 'Cordelia, you're unrecognisable. Well done, you'll shine in the photographs. I'm so proud of you.' She even bought me a new set of lilac short dungarees from Topshop, handing them over wordlessly, pecking me on the cheek with a Judas kiss.

*  *  *

'Smile, love, you're going to be in one of the biggest-selling magazines in the country,' the photographer cajoled from behind his tripod. Journalists brandished Dictaphones, make-up artists powdered and painted, curled and preened. An off-limits beige bounty was delivered from a local eatery: Danish pastries, a platter of squashy tray-baked pizza, tuna pasta salad and a whole cream-cheese frosted carrot cake crowned with miniature confectionary carrots. I chewed on an actual carrot to keep my mind away from the forbidden fruit.

'You've got a beautiful figure, Cordelia,' the stylist complimented at the same time as pulling a pink puff-sleeved blouse tight at my waist, securing it at the back with a bulldog clip. 'I would kill for your perky boobs and skinny legs. I bet you can eat whatever you want and not gain a pound!'

I gave her a Mona Lisa smile.

As Mum waved everyone off at the end of the day, I eyed the sad vestiges of the buffet laid out on the kitchen counter: just a quarter of carrot cake and a pitiful portion of pasta salad that wouldn't have satiated a mouse. I sighed. No more reckless eating. From now on, I was on my best behaviour.

The carrot cake had other ideas.

## 28

### THELMA AND LOUISE PART ONE

'Are you finally ready to listen?' Derek awaited the Kettle For One's watery crescendo before looking at me. A utilitarian metal desk lamp cast a warm halo across the shiny cream wall, the communist chic halls of residence's yawning ceilings giving a false impression of space. I lay on my side in the narrow metal bed; it squeaked when I wrapped my arms round my middle, afraid to let go. Four pairs of hand-washed knickers lay draped over the cast iron radiator like creased dish cloths. I'd not bothered to pimp my room with pictures, plants, scatter cushions or an ubiquitous Indian scarf draped over a chair. It was the same as the day I arrived, save for the lone poster of Kurt Cobain Blu-Tacked above the bed, and my panoply of videos, two cases deep, lining the wall on top of the desk, as well as running the entire length of the skirting board towards the sink. My portable TV and VHS player were balanced on a wooden chair at the end of the bed. 'You can't go on, like this, Cordy. You'll kill yourself.'

I pressed my face into the dented pillow, inhaling the stale smell of grubby hair. I hadn't washed the bedding yet this term; it was nearly the end of February. I rarely cried, but a tsunami tested the blockade in my throat.

'I think you should go home early, see how you feel after Easter.' That was pretty much the last place I wanted to go. Why couldn't I just hide here?

'Stephen's coming to stay this weekend,' I muffled into the pillow.

'I told him not to. Unless he's coming to help you pack everything up and go home. You're in no state. I can't believe you haven't told your mom what's happened.'

Since becoming a household name, Mum had started dating *TV-am* weatherman, Bill Fisher. They'd morphed into a hybrid D-list celebrity invited to the opening of envelopes at the back of W H Smiths. Bill suffered from a receding hairline that Make Up patted down with a temporary mixture of face powder and cream eye shadow before he appeared on camera. He'd stayed a few times over Christmas – he was divorced with two grown-up children. Simultaneously, Trish never returned from maternity leave to reclaim *Tone and Tease*, so Mum had made the spot her own with a solid fan-base and a glut of endorsement deals, using the money to refurbish the entire house, gifting herself an en-suite bathroom and a downstairs utility room.

'Maternity cover's usually like being the brides-maid, never the bride. At least they realised! They could hardly call it *Tone and Tease* now,' Mum had slyly observed. 'You would have thought she gave birth to twins. I lost all my baby weight in two months, both times. She's had almost a year.'

'My mom said to drag you back home by force if necessary,' Derek said quietly. 'She's ringing your mom tonight to order her to come and get you. Your dad too.'

I swivelled my head, briefly catching Derek's apologetic eyes. 'Dad? I haven't seen him for months. I don't want him to come. I don't want Netty to either.'

'She isn't coming.' Derek sighed. 'Look, I feel so bad.'

I shivered. The heating was on but ice water coursed through my veins.

'I had to tell Mom, Cordy. I had to tell someone sensible.'

Recovery meant talking but I couldn't pinpoint why I'd been unable to step off the purging merry-go-round. Not even the force majeure of three fillings in six months, persistent exhaustion and a bloated, rag doll face, cheeks stuccoed with broken capillaries, had been enough to make me sit on my hands.

'Do you want tea?' Derek asked.

I shook my head.

'I thought tea made everything better with you Brits?'

'I've... gone off it. Can I have an instant coffee instead? No sugar. There's a jar somewhere for guests.' I waved towards the shelf housing the kettle and mugs. 'The milk's out there.' I pointed at the window where a Tesco plastic bag was tied to the handle and suspended outside.

Painkillers had dulled the cramps, but shock clung to every waking moment. The last time we had seen each other, Derek had been eighteen, feverishly straight, with token appendage, Jodie, in tow.

'I thought we could watch this?' He produced a

video – *Thelma and Louise*. 'Just sit for a bit, chill. This is so good.'

'It is. We're going to study it next. Our lecturer wants us to dedicate a whole term on the female gaze.'

When Derek looked nonplussed, I tried to explain, but ran out of steam.

'Sounds great.' Derek had settled into his first year at Brighton University reading Fashion and Business. An inimitable presence in his wacky, multi-coloured, baggy rave trousers, a neon-yellow string vest and a battered biker jacket slung over the top as a protective shell, he'd bagged a place based on his dual nationality and immense talent for throwing together spectacular outfits from others' discarded tat. He handed over my coffee, having made himself a black one, ever suspicious of the taste of British milk. He unboxed the video and slipped it into the player, switching on the TV at the same time before settling on the end of the bed near my feet. He knew better than to have invested in movie snacks.

I'd felt stunned after watching *Thelma and Louise* for the first time at the back of the multiplex. I'd never seen a film where such flawed female leads commanded complete control of the narrative. Hadn't that been what I'd been aiming for? Total control? It felt more convincing that I'd driven off a cliff and survived than been in control of anything. It was safe to say my eating disorder had taken me hostage.

I caught Derek side-eyeing me.

'I'm sorry, Derek.'

'Desi.'

'What?'

'I'm Desi now. Have been for over a year. Ever since I came out. Derek was the old me.'

'Oh, right. OK. I'm sorry, Desi. I couldn't put Mum down as my next of kin. I didn't know it would go wrong.'

He leaned over and gently patted my foot. 'S'OK. What's family for?'

I'd thought I was tripping from the anaesthetic when he walked onto the ward. He'd been a name on a form; he wasn't supposed to appear like a genie, despite his uncanny resemblance.

'I'm sorry too,' he said. 'I wasn't ready to hear what you had to say back then.'

'I could have worded it better.'

'We both could have.'

# 29

## SUMMER 1990

Within my travelling circus, I'd been completely capable of operating rationally, like a part had splintered off to solely manage the underbelly of my psyche. This dark half would walk in a fugue state to a shop or the kitchen, stockpiling feast foods triggered by an unstoppable urge to satisfy blood-sugar receptors, so utterly mangled that I had no control over neurons firing up, warning me when my tank was full. I was either starving or bursting at the seams like a pig's bladder football. The dark half didn't examine motives, or emotions thickly layered beneath the craving; it was an automaton following a narrative that wasn't bedded in anything remotely logical.

However, the shadow of the beast couldn't block

all the light; a sliver of sangfroid persevered. I still attended school, laughed with friends, sought out genuine pockets of joy that temporarily side lined the dark half, making life bearable. The purge represented a reset, a clean slate, a chance for a whole new me, one who ate without inventory and could push aside my plate when full and not obsess over an abandoned slice of pizza. I could last two whole days without a clear out, eating within the realms of normality without my abdomen straining against my waistband.

I'd begun to leave lengthier and lengthier gaps before tickling my tonsils, allowing calories to slip through the cracks. A true disciple would have headed straight up those stairs the minute they'd finished revelling in the last mouthful. Gradual weight gain performed a sleight of hand – only a cadaver duly caused concern. The deliciously sweet relief of feeling completely hollow, rinsed of all burdens, gradually lost its allure. In its place, a small voice pleaded at the very base of my throat, *please let that be the last time.*

Distraction was key to limiting opportunity for these episodes and watching films played a huge part of this trickery and rather unsurprisingly so did sex. When I'd been eight, Mum washed all our clothes in chemical-riddled Daz instead of the usual Fairy Non Bio – big mistake, though not for me. While my knickers irritated my genitals, frantic itching un-veiled a whole world of pleasure, one I dipped into fervently despite the inevitable side order of shame. Little did I know I would develop into a sandwich board carrier for the word.

Bored? Have a wank. Horny? Have a wank. About to eat ten Mini Rolls, two packets of Walkers Ready Salted and a Boost? Have a wank instead. Masturba-tion possibly saved my front teeth from crumbling. It certainly held me in good stead for the bedroom.

\* \* \*

'Please can you come round?' Michelle rang during Easter break. 'It's an emergency. Bring bleach.' Michelle had started dating a boy from the local sixth form college. They'd met on the beach when she'd been walking Pickles, the family spaniel. He'd cocked his leg on Scott smoking among a group of friends by the pier. 'Imagine in twenty years' time our kids ask how we met,' she'd mooned. 'Pickles' golden shower!'

I arrived, half a bottle of Domestos in tow. 'Oh my God, I've got about two hours till Mum comes home.

Quick, upstairs!' She led me straight to the bathroom, pointing towards bed sheets wallowing in a
biblical blood bath. 'Do you know how to use a
washing machine?' She promptly burst into tears.

'You poor thing, did it hurt?' I hugged her. If this
was a typical first time, then I was joining a convent.
What a twat running off and leaving her. 'Why didn't
Scott stay and help?'

'It was him!' she cried. 'That's not *my* blood. His
banjo snapped.'

'What you on about?'

'His foreskin tore.'

'Jesus Christ. Haven't we got enough to worry
about with VD, AIDS and getting pregnant. Now
this? There's no such thing as safe sex!'

'It was soooooo embarrassing. He was crying – it
wouldn't stop bleeding. I thought I was going to have
to call an ambulance!' Michelle sobbed, probably the
only time I've ever seen her look remotely ugly.
'What if he dumps me?'

'He'll be too scared you'd tell everyone you broke
his penis.'

Silence dropped before we simultaneously
launched into hysteria, Michelle crossing her legs,
bent double, shoulders shaking. Once the howling

subsided, we heaved the bleached sheets into the utility room inside a black bin bag.

'It's like getting rid of a body.'

'It wasn't like I thought it was going to be,' Michelle reflected as the machine filled with water. 'I mean, I've obviously... seen *it* before, but it was as hard as this!' She gripped one of the thick, black, metal bars holding the utility room shelves together. 'I can't believe I'll have to do it again!'

Solo bean flicking had never looked more attractive.

We silently watched the machine turn, sipping tea.

'Thanks for coming, you totally saved me. Don't tell Sarah; she can be a bit... soap boxy. Bollock me for not waiting six months like we'd discussed.'

The sudden urge to unburden myself of my own dark secret materialised out of thin air. *I couldn't, could I?*

'Michelle, I need to tell you something; you promise you won't...' *Won't what, Cordelia? Think you're gross? Stop being your friend when she realises what you get up to?*

'What? What is it?' Michelle grabbed my hand, immediately understanding the significance. The workings of her head were stapled to her sleeve. Mine lived on the sole of my shoe.

'I-I, er, you see, for a while now, I've been…' Tears surged at the back of my throat. I caught sight of my grazed right forefingers in her hands. Unnerved, the dark half muscled in. 'No, nothing, it's OK.'

'Tell me, you're upset. I can help? I promise I won't say a word.'

Sighing, I waved my first genuine cry for help goodbye. 'I'm just worried… I'll die a virgin.'

Michelle burst out laughing, then looked stricken. 'I thought you were joking.'

'Nope.' It wasn't that removed from the truth.

'My advice? Go older. The boys at our school probably bash the bishop in record time; they've no idea what to do. It's all in the hips.' Like a phoenix from the flames of a broken banjo, Michelle the Sexpert had been born and after that pivotal day, she spent most weekends practising with Scott while Sarah decided to bed down with her books and study hard for the upcoming GCSEs. That left David Plimpton; our inevitable union formed on the cutting-room floor. He had sprung up over the Easter holidays, making it hard to slot him in a *Breakfast Club* pigeonhole.

'Cheeks has finally stopped looking like a Borrower,' Michelle declared quietly in GCSE French. 'And he's lost his hamster cheeks. Shame, I liked them.'

'*Je peux t'entendre!*' David hissed from the row in front. 'I'm not deaf.'

'*Monsieur Plimpton, vous parlez toujours!*' Miss Rayner barked across the first four rows, fingers itching to hurl chalk.

I had noted the growth spurt and the potential man couched behind his boyish charm, but for now, couldn't see beyond motherless David who'd worn shorts. But after a drunken fumble fuelled by Woodpecker cider and Thunderbird at a post GCSE bash, I'd inexplicably wound up in a dark bedroom with him when we were searching for the hoover to clean up a crisp avalanche from the kitchen floor. *What light through yonder window breaks...*

'Is this weird?' he kept asking as we snogged with abandon.

Of course it was weird; it was David! Bloody hell though – the kisses were the most arousing I'd ever encountered, even though my playbook was a tad limited. David wiped the floor with robo-tongued Keith Philips.

What cautiously started out as friends sharing a sexual awakening became something else, though I shied away from staking any wild emotional claims. That entire summer, we furtively explored what buttons worked on whom and how to press them under the heavy disguise of 'just being mates'.

'Can I touch your chest?' he asked politely on one occasion after skirting the perimeter of my bra for an hour. 'Properly?' Unaccountably, as long as we remained under the duvet, I was strangely immune from my own body fascism, parking all concerns at the bedroom door.

'My dad keeps asking if we're going out!' David gleefully declared later in July after we'd writhed around in just our underwear.

'You told your dad?' This was *not* in the guidelines.

'No!'

'Then how the flip does he know anything? It's supposed to be secret.'

'Jonah.'

Jonah was David's eight-year-old brother whom he was supposed to babysit while his dad was at work. We had clearly not done a good enough job of sneaking me into the house.

However, our encounters weren't all exclusively gropes and dry humping; we talked too, similar conversations to ones I had with Michelle and Sarah.

'Do you miss your mum?' I'd asked on the first visit, spotting a framed photo on his desk of a laughing blonde woman in large sunglasses hugging what could only be a younger David, his dimples an exact mirror of hers.

His eyebrows had shot into his floppy hair. 'No one's ever asked me that before.'

'Sorry, I didn't mean it.'

'No, it's OK.' He glanced at the picture. 'I do miss her, but it's getting harder and harder to remember her clearly. I know who she is but I can't smell her any more. This sounds pathetic... I used to be able to feel her sometimes, like she was standing next to me, but now she's gone.'

I slid my hand along the bed and gripped his fingers, my eyes prickling.

'It was awful after she died. Dad cried all the time. Nanny and Grandad had to move in. I feel worse for Jonah; he really won't remember how amazing she was. He was only five.'

David had bought me tampons when I unexpectedly got my period at his house (he had worn a bobble-hat disguise to the Spar), and he'd cooked us vegetarian burgers with salad for lunch once, all on his own without help. I'd eaten everything and not given it a second thought. I'd find myself daydreaming about him when I was at home, wondering if he'd also seen *Naked Gun*. I don't think we ever stumbled across an awkward silence. It was... easy. Like being with Michelle except we were snogging almost naked.

'David, can I ask you something?' I accidentally caught the eyes of Damon from Blur within the frieze of *Smash Hits* centrefolds yanked from the magazine and papered round the bed. As well as Blur, Kurt Cobain, the Stone Roses and the Happy Mondays, Julia Roberts was pinned in my direct eye-line on the opposite wall. *Oh, how original.*

'What's wrong?' David asked, concerned.

'Does my fanny smell?'

'What?! No!'

'Are you sure? Because I think it does.' Unconvinced, I probed further. 'How many other fannies have you got to compare it with?'

David's face clouded as he calculated the grotesquely large number he'd been exposed to. 'Three.'

'Was one of them Michelle's?'

David's face contorted. 'Cordy! That's gross. I only snogged Michelle!'

'Sorry... So you're sure it's OK down there?' I'd driven myself insane, positive that in conjunction with my legion of disfigurements, my vagina harboured a mysterious pong that afflicted no one else.

'It's perfect, I can assure you.' It wasn't long after that we surrendered our virginities, which turned out not to be the gothic horror story Michelle's had been. Whilst so utterly preposterous that I'd just had sex with David of all people, it had at the same time been... promising, with only a modicum of pain. His hip action had been in sync with mine but I would have preferred it to have lasted a bit longer. He came faster than when I had a risky danger wank on the sofa.

I'd expected some kind of epiphany, to feel like a proper grown-up, to instantly understand what the FTSE index was at the end of the news, or to maybe have a hankering for olives, the one adult-type food I couldn't fathom. Lamentably, it was business as usual.

'Are you my girlfriend now?' he asked as we lay half-undressed on his bed while Jonah watched endless digger videos downstairs eating bags of beef Monster Munch, their artificial bovine reek floating as far as the landing.

'I don't know if I can do boyfriend stuff at the moment.' A seed of panic sprouted in my belly.

'Oh.' He dipped his brows. 'I just thought...'

'Look, sorry.' I gave him a doleful smile. 'Can we just stay friends? I really like you.'

'Friends-friends?'

'Well, we could continue this, if you want?'

'Yes!'

I didn't suffer butterflies with David; 'friends with benefits' was self-explanatory. But when he disappeared on holiday with his dad for a month touring the UK, I unaccountably missed the comforting soap smell of the back of his neck. Emptiness throbbed in my chest; the dark half leaped into the gap. By the time Derek and Jodie landed on their European tour, I was permanently sluggish, mouth poised to yawn any given moment, bloodshot eyes and bulimia bloom (hastily disguised with Boots cover-up) upon cheeks puffy from overstimulated saliva glands. Thankfully, Mum was oblivious; Stephen had also lulled me into a false sense of security.

In the interim, Derek had transformed – so tall and angular, he could have passed for a dancer in Madonna's 'Like a Prayer' video. He'd breezed out of the station like he was flouncing down a runway, his growth spurt thrusting him towards manhood, making him a stranger – we'd not spoken for a year. I shrunk against the back seat of the car as Mum opened the boot and shoved the two rucksacks inside.

'Hey! Cordy! Meet Jodie!' A Madonna lookalike poured into the seat next to me, bleached hair and pale skin substantiating the illusion.

'Hi,' I breathed in a voice I imagined more husky and sensual than my reviled trademark nasal blurt.

'Hi, Derek's told me so much about you all.' Jodie dazzled with a smile so utterly Hollywood, it commanded a bubbly theme tune. *How did Americans have such great teeth?* I poked a throbbing molar with my tongue. I dragged my feet telling Mum – our sadistic dentist regularly filled teeth without anaesthesia.

'In the Vietnamese jungle, we plucked out incisors with pliers – no time for anaesthetic then, too busy dodging bullets.'

I'd been ten.

Day two of the Derek and Jodie Show, Derek delivered a nauseating public display of affection towards a bikini-clad Jodie on the beach while she screeched theatrically in the surf, a well-choreographed cri de coeur. I mourned the loss of my sweet, crop-top-wearing cousin.

Later, he knocked on my bedroom door, my nose still running from waving off lasagne.

'Cordy, is everything OK?' he asked, pushing the door open, quietly closing it behind him.

My stomach tied in a slipknot. I stared above my desk at the poster of Winona Ryder ripped from *Just Seventeen* magazine as thinspiration. *Jackie* had long since been traded up.

'I'm fine.'

'You don't seem it, that's all.'

'Well, I am,' I assured him, wiping my nose on my arm, heat crawling up the back of my neck.

'Listen, if there's anything—'

'Honestly, there's nothing.'

'It's just Jodie feels there is.' Perfect fucking Jodie. '*Both* of us think something's wrong. You look different... Your Mom isn't—'

'Please stop,' I said quietly. 'How does Jodie know anything? The last time *you* saw me was three years ago.'

Derek seemed to carefully consider his next move. 'Jodie's sister had bulimia...'

'Don't... You've been here five days, that's all. You know *nothing* about me.'

'If there's nothing to worry about, why are you so uptight?'

'Because you're making shit up.'

'I'm just showing concern, that's all.'

'Jodie should be worrying about what's going on under *her* nose.'

'What're you getting at?'

'Don't have a go at me when you're living a complete lie.'

Derek's face froze, betraying nothing. 'Like you, you mean?'

My chest heaved with indignation.

'Pretending that you're not making yourself sick. This is serious; we heard you! Your mom and Stephen might be deaf, but we're not!'

'And I'm not blind. Jodie hasn't even noticed you're gay!'

'I'm not!' Derek's eyes narrowed.

'The last time I saw you, you were dressing in my clothes and took all my crop tops.'

'I'm not gay! It was a phase... Sort yourself out before spreading lies!'

'Same to you. I don't need sorting out. I never asked for your help. Maybe I should tell Jodie about who you *really* are?'

Derek shoved his face right into mine, his garlic breath warming my nose. 'You speak one word of this and I'm telling your mom *exactly* what's going on. I'm only flagging this cos you need help.'

'So do you.' I conceded no ground but my face hummed with humiliation.

# 30

## THELMA AND LOUISE CONTINUED…

With my feet resting on Desi's lap, I'd never felt safer. So far, rock bottom had been peculiarly peaceful, the unravelling not so much. I decided to let the film perform its distraction instead of indulging in self-examination.

Running from shooting a would-be rapist, Thelma (Geena Davis – wish-list cheekbones) and Louise (sassy Susan Sarandon) hole up in a grungy motel with seductive matinee idol hitchhiker, JD (Brad Pitt in his break-out role), concealing a six pack and a nefarious past. Among other themes, I adored *Thelma and Louise*'s nod to the Great American Road Trip, challenging *Easy Rider* for the counter-culture crown. The distinct lack of space for diehard romance elevated it above and beyond every Cinderella-complex film I'd encountered. Regardless of the film tending to wounds, I still blundered down a rabbit hole when Louise rings her boyfriend, Jimmy (brooding Michael Madsen), asking him to wire her his life savings. Bugger it, Jimmy was a dark-haired David bloody Plimpton. I'd stake money on him also arriving in person unannounced with the cash despite an express order for him not to. Like Jimmy, David was a good egg.

*'You're the closest I ever came to knowing what falling in love might feel like.'* If I hadn't been in so much pain, I'd have winced at the memory of David's hangdog face when I turned down his offer to graduate from friends with benefits once we reached sixth form. Like every bump in the road, I only had myself to blame, though as unfair as it was, I'd have loved to have to hung this current mischance on Michelle.

'The pill's so convenient. No more slippery con-doms,' Michelle, the group sexpert, had lorded over me and Sarah, the ostensible virgins.

'Aren't you worried about AIDS though? It's not gone away,' Sarah asked, genuinely concerned. 'We're still advised to use condoms.'

The shadow cast by HIV had definitely informed my decision to experiment with nebbish David; after all, virginity, a greatly coveted commodity, had been traded for millennia.

'Nah, I'll be fine; Scott's not gay! Anyway, we're not shagging around. We're in love.'

Sarah had rolled her eyes at me. I kept my broken hymen to myself. However, I had taken Michelle's sagely advice and gone on the pill.

\* \* \*

I'd loathed sixth form, reserving special judgement for students siphoned off from surrounding purple-pleated private schools. The sheer volume of hege-monic, flicky-haired girls commandeering corridors in Benetton jumpers, brightly coloured pashminas and Levi 501s was a swarm of flies in need of swat-ting. I almost flung myself off the Seven Sisters when David started dating one of them, shucking off his Cheeks soubriquet, reborn as a cool kid, smoking and drinking, swanning round college wearing a brown leather jacket. The black pit of self-loathing refused to be filled – my thighs had run amok and my boobs had burst their banks. The dark half tight-ened its grip as the net closed in. Never mind Claire, Cordelia was a fat girl's name.

I'd started working Saturdays at the local cinema, but the pick and mix proved problematic.

'So, you're allowed to eat as many sweets as you want,' Reggie, the charismatic manager, explained on my first shift. 'None of us can touch fizzy strawberry laces any more.' They had not bargained on me emptying them out in one fell swoop during a slow evening.

When Aunty Liz visited during the summer of A Levels, she brought news of Derek's successful application to Brighton University.

'What happened between you two?' she asked. 'He said you'd drifted apart. It'd be so nice for you to have each other when he's here studying.'

'I'll be in Manchester anyway, if I get in.'

'Stephen and I will be here,' Mum assured her.

'He finally admitted he's gay,' Liz divulged. 'Better than hiding in that dusty old closet.'

My fingers itched to ring him, to hear his voice, to tell him well done for being his authentic self, but we'd parted without so much as a goodbye.

Then one afternoon, I arrived home from college to find Netty in the kitchen with Mum.

'Would you sit down, Cordelia?' Mum asked, her voice raspy with dried tears.

'No, not until you tell me what's going on? Is Dad dead?'

'No!' Netty cried. 'Gosh, absolutely not. He's at a sales conference.'

'Death's probably preferable in that case,' Mum muttered darkly.

'Why are you here then?' I asked sharply, suspicious of Netty's motives.

'Annette thinks you have *bulimia*.' Mum's obvious distaste was proportionate to me contracting genital warts. 'I said that's complete nonsense. You'd be all skin and bone.'

Netty's shoulders sagged in disbelief.

'People make themselves sick to lose weight, not put it on.'

I ran upstairs and slammed my bedroom door. Voices floated upstairs from the hallway. I poked my head out before creeping along the landing.

'I asked you to be gentle,' Netty pleaded. 'She'll be sensitive about it. Of course Philip doesn't believe me either—'

'Philip wouldn't notice if you grew two heads, Annette. But I'd know if my own daughter was doing something as disgusting as that!'

I clenched my fists.

'She's very secretive,' Netty persisted. 'But I've

noticed food going missing. Whole packets of biscuits, tubs of ice cream, crisps—'

'I can't believe you have all those terrible things in your house. Don't buy them and maybe set an example—'

'Lois!' Placid Netty disappeared in a puff of L'Air du Temps. 'You're not listening to me. She needs to see a doctor. You should talk to her.'

'Don't you think you're imagining it? Too much time on your hands?' I recognised verbal jousting when I heard it. 'I haven't got the headspace to deal with this today; I've a meeting to prep for tomorrow. Another bid for a low-calorie food replacement product.'

'No wonder...' Netty jiggled her car keys.

'What's that supposed to mean?' Mum's voice hardened like Mint Chocolate Ice Magic.

'Nothing. Please talk to her.'

'I'm not sure it'll make any difference.'

'It might, just try...'

The door banged; Netty left. I sat back on my bed and wrapped my arms tightly around my knees. I could stop, I would stop. Right now. I sucked in my tummy and pinched my muffin top above my jeans.

Mum knocked on the door.

'Go away.'

'I'm sorry about Annette barging in,' she said through the gap in the door. 'I told her you're fine. You are, aren't you, Cordy? You seem fine to me.'

Tears sprung from nowhere. I stood in front of the mirror and studied myself, blocking my raw knuckles from view. When was the last time Mum had looked at me properly? She was too involved with her own life since *TV-am* had lured her away with its glitz and glamour and her own range of satin unitards.

'OK in there? Do you want me to make you a tea?'

'No! I'm OK. I'll be down in a bit. I'm fine, Mum. You don't need to worry, I promise.'

But she began hovering at mealtimes, sitting with me and Stephen when she hadn't previously, a strained look on her face, chasing a small salad round her plate.

'Stop being weird,' Stephen said in the coming weeks when I refused to visit the Pink Palace for the third weekend in a row. 'Dad's really upset.'

'He should have stopped Netty interfering and making up lies then. She's not my mum!'

'She didn't make up lies.'

I couldn't look at him and feigned fascination with Ace of Base on *Top of the Pops*.

* * *

'Do you think they were scared when they drove over the cliff?' Desi asked as the credits rolled.

'No. I think being in a US prison or waiting on Death Row would be even scarier. They ended on a high, on their terms. Going out with a bang like Butch Cassidy and the Sundance Kid. What choice did they have?'

'Is that how you feel?' he asked after a minute. 'Like you have no choice? I've read about... you know. It becomes automatic. You eventually can't keep anything down because your gag reflex is screwed.'

'Desi, I can't talk about it now.' I turned my face to the wall.

After rejecting David, I'd fallen into an on-off work-related casual fling with Simon, another student, and carried on taking the pill, pushing my AIDS deathbed scenario to the back of my mind. Getting pregnant was far scarier. Approaching the first term at Manchester university, common sense (proof I did have some) leaned towards remaining on the pill, just in case. I made a few friends on my film studies course, their names having since evaporated but decent enough girls, and there was Paula, an English graduate in the room next door. Once home for Christmas, I ended up in jittery, multiplex pick and mix, chaotic binge cycles succeeded by copious pints of cider. I bumped into David at the Hart on a night out with Michelle and Sarah a few days before New Year's Eve – he was newly single; Flicky Fiona had dumped him after her first term at Edinburgh.

'She probably hooked up with a posh wanker called Archie during Freshers Week,' I scorned, before hastily back peddling. 'Sorry, I'm sure she didn't. I'm being unfair.'

Placing his pint on the wonky table between us, he just about caught it with his hand before it slid to its death. 'You're probably right,' he agreed. 'I'm going away anyway in February, perhaps for the best.' David worked in office-furniture hire (Desks R Us), a small local business, and had since bought a rusting, canary-yellow Golf that leaked oil. 'I'd love to see Machu Picchu before I give my life up for *the man*. What would I learn at university?' This bravado was probably more driven by the fact he'd scraped through seven GCSEs and two A Levels despite his obvious oratory talents and ability to memorise entire tomes of Shakespeare. *Friends, Romans, countrymen, lend me your Bisley steel filing cabinets with four lockable drawers.*

After taking me for a night dancing, 'for old

times' sake', we snogged up against a speaker and I awoke alone (deaf in my right ear) in his childhood bedroom (David had left for work) while the new Mrs Plimpton hoovered downstairs. The jury was still out on her matriculation from his mum's younger sister's best friend to his step mum. I cringed at my performative bedroom display bolstered by five pints of cider and two flaming Sambucas. The walls had better be robust. Many a night at home, I'd rammed my head under the duvet after being awoken by Bill Fisher crying 'Lois' into a pillow.

The brief yet touching encounter dented my heart, leaving me wondering if that was the last time I'd ever see David. I had an inkling he was destined for a life more urbane than one set in Eastbourne.

Back in Manchester, the second term ploughed into the winter of discontent. There were several signs, but I chose to ignore them. It might go away, mightn't it? When I voluntarily threw up before eating, three positive pregnancy tests confirmed the worst. *How had this happened on the pill?* I ignored the voices telling me to ring David, that he would murmur the perfect platitudes and hold my hand. This was something no one need know about, just a blot on the landscape. Rinsed through with shame, I hunted down a clinic in leafy Didsbury, paying for it with my savings – in and out in a day. Simple.

On the morning itself, sweat greasing my sides, I wiped my palms on my jeans, walking down the surprisingly suburban street edged with silver birch trees in narrow grassy verges, rows of monied, red-bricked detached houses set back from the pavement. Just before I reached the entrance, two middle-aged male protestors jumped from behind the gatepost. They could have been members of the Tin Pot Cathedral's congregation, they had that 'look'. Self-righteous, as if they had pre-booked a cloud in Heaven.

'Do you know what happens when they murder your baby? Look!' The bald one shoved dog-eared graphic pictures in my face.

'You gonna adopt the baby for me?' I hissed, nerves frayed. 'No? Thought not!'

I had to lie about having no immediate family and put Derek down as my advocate, scrabbling around for his halls of residence telephone number in my address book, foisted upon me by Aunty Liz.

'He's coming to pick me up, said he'd wait outside in the car.'

Astoundingly the receptionist believed me, or rather, she wanted to.

Back in halls, groggy from the anaesthetic, I crawled into bed, sincerely hoping life could continue as if nothing had happened. But stabbing pains dragged like a blunt knife through my abdomen, persisting into the night; eventually, breathing hurt. Paracetamol helped, like the nurse said it would, but only briefly. I felt marginally better two days later and decided to shower. Whether I washed was immaterial because the next thing I knew, I was speeding along in an ambulance on my way to A&E – Paula from next door holding my hand. She had discovered me crumpled against the wall in the communal showers, bleeding. As they wheeled me into surgery to scrape away the infection, removing the remaining cells carelessly left behind, I gave Derek's details as my next of kin, not believing for one second that they would need to contact him.

\* \* \*

'But you're ready to admit there's a problem?' Desi turned to look at me as he switched the TV off, poised to deliver more home truths. 'Your body couldn't absorb the pill, you know that, right? Mom said if you're in constant digestive flux, no medication will ever work. I—' He paused.

Tears ran silently down my cheeks.

'I'm sorry, I just want to help... You had such a close call.'

'Yes, I know that now. I want to get better,' I replied hoarsely. 'Can you promise me something?'

'Yes, anything.'

'If I ever end up in a coma, can you be in charge?'

Desi laughed, nodding enthusiastically.

'Pluck my brows – they'll grow into a mono-slug. And if left to their own devices, my leg hairs plait themselves; I look like a yeti. Maybe a bit of make-up and do my hair just in case the doctor's fit. You never know.'

'Same for me too – I think we need to get it in writing. If I don't shave every few days, my chin looks like it's wearing a merkin!'

'It's a deal.'

'So we're good?' he asked. 'You'll get help? Promise?'

'Of course, you numpty. We're good.' I changed the subject. 'Tell me what happened about coming out.'

'Never underestimate the damage of seeing your father die of AIDS,' he said, washing up the mugs in my clutch-bag-sized sink. 'It's enough to propel you so far into a closet, you're prepared to live in Narnia.'

'I'm not surprised. I can't believe I didn't under-stand that at the time. I was just angry at you, for, you know…'

'I know, doll. I get it. Bite or be bitten,' he smiled. 'Being gay felt like a death sentence. Everywhere we looked, friends were dying and no one cared – Reagan acted like it wasn't even happening. Dad's health insurance was cancelled, so Mom had to work two jobs along with Edward.'

'That must have been awful.'

'Mom only told me recently. They shielded me from most of it.'

'Did Jodie ever realise?' I asked.

'Of course she did. That's why we split up. I was still in denial for ages. Then Edward sat me down and asked if I was ready to talk. He and Mom totally knew, as did you.'

I sat up on the bed to listen properly.

'I thought if I could just ignore the one thing in my life that might kill me, I'd be safe. Jodie was per-fect because she was so pretty, she also boosted life in general, the haters couldn't touch me cos of her. Other kids began to include me, we even got short-listed for prom King and Queen.'

'No way! I can't believe you didn't mention this when you stayed.'

'If you remember, you barely spoke.'

'I'm sorry...' I shrugged apologetically. 'It seemed so obvious you were hiding who you were. You have a gay family – it made no sense. Now it does.'

'And you come from a home where your famous mom's constantly on a fucking diet or criticising you. She doesn't pick on Stephen. I told Mom that she—'

'Hey!' I bristled. 'You've no idea what happens at ours. Mum didn't stick my fingers down my throat – I did that all by myself. Mum didn't force me to go on a diet.'

'Didn't she?' Desi was unrepentant. 'I guess you're not ready to face that yet.'

'Face what? What do I need to face?' My belly griped, forcing me to gingerly recline onto the bed.

'I overstepped; I'm sorry. I think dealing with my own stuff in therapy has made me a bit of an eager beaver. I love Aunty Lois, but she's a piece of work. Forget what I said.'

But the toothpaste was already out of the tube.

# 31

## THE CHANNEL

If there were gulls, I couldn't hear their satanic war cries, in a small part because of the earplugs, but mostly because I was swimming amongst the past embroidered with sounds and sensations long since boxed away. In life, there was never pure silence, even with noise-cancelling headphones. You still brought along your bodily vibrations: beating hearts, clicking joints, gurgling bellies and throats, hissing ears, breathing, all the rumblings a still house generates while its occupants sleep.

I'd already spent years circumventing life, ignoring gut instincts, dodging challenging situations rather than face failure, pain, disappointment. I found most things could be finished or started later, whether that was an awkward phone call or that coffee catch up you'd been planning for six months. Later had the potential to proliferate into a year, stretching into eight years of infinity and beyond. My entire life gradually sifted into 'later'. Then I woke up and everyone had left. Most of them still lived within Facebook, growing older on screen, accruing families, new jobs, bigger houses. *Hashtag blessed.* Desi, my family, a tiny cluster of locals and of course the boyfriend du jour (there had been many) were the constants. But I finally felt ready to stage a mini revolution.

The irony of working at the Journal Co wasn't lost on me. Marking time in a multitude of ways: *A Journal For Every Reason* had been my sparkling marketing pitch that had made it as the main strapline across the website home page. Why use a plain notebook when you could record your activities in a journal specifically tailored for your exact needs? Manifesting, gratitude, baby's first year, my wedding, our house refurb, first year at school, my gap year: a stark reminder of many milestones not reached let alone aimed for. Diaries and fancy moleskin notebooks were also part of the paper-backed merchandise. My yearly diary gifted by Joan, the Journal Co's

founder, gathered dust and empty months in a
drawer under the bed.

*** * ***

Every joint sang in pain. My right shoulder had
suddenly decided to click every other stroke, my toes
ached from persistently pressing against the heft of
water, my hands throbbed from shovelling vast
quantities of sea behind like a snow plough. With yet
more sea to conquer, I clenched my fists every ten
strokes, sanctioning temporary relief. *You can do this,
Cordelia.* I rode multiple trains of waves generated by
an oil tanker just shy of four hundred metres astern,
calling on the very same calcified iron will that had
seen me ignore hunger pains so severe, I imagined
my stomach cannibalising my internal organs. *Come
on Cordelia, mind over matter.* If only I'd utilised that
laser-focused stubbornness for something worthwhile – a meaningful career or laying down tangible
roots together with the expected societal accou-
trements, instead of gaining a first-class degree in
self-sabotage. I couldn't fail at this, absolutely not.
My mother had been right – it really would be the
only thing I had ever achieved.

The sea lurched unpredictably, waves eddying a

few metres high before petering out, only to return, fanning out from a vessel's choppy wake. Trying to bolt down four tiny squares of buttered malt loaf amid a swollen sea, whitecaps smacking my cheeks, triggered a gush of nausea so intense the creatures of the deep were gifted a rare malty treat. Seasickness on a Channel swim was of course a common occurrence, but not one I'd seriously considered after bargaining with the sea gods for a safe passage having paid my dues following a misspent youth with my head down the bog.

'I'm coming in!' Desi shouted as he hauled back the empty goggles case. 'Get ready to race me!'

My heart sang.

*Head down, four strokes, breathe out. Bubbles.*

## 32

# PAULINE DENTON IS FUCKED UP

'Mum's doing my head in,' I hissed in the dark, Desi curled in the foetal position on the gifted, brand-new tartan sofa bed butted in the narrow chimney recess. Mum had recently starred in a TV advert for new sofa superstore, DFS (rechristened Dick Fucks Shit). 'She won't let me go to the toilet on my own "in case I get the urge". She's pre-recorded all her workouts so she can stay home. Believe me, the urge has gone. Though it was never really an urge in the first place.'

'How do you know it's gone? What if you can't stop and something else happens?'

'But I have stopped! I ate dinner and was OK.' Apart from crippling tummy pains but the less said about them, the better. Regardless of the dire circumstances reuniting us, I was overcome with joy that Desi was once more a fixture in my life. This time, I was determined not to fuck it up.

'You only had a bowl of soup. How are you not hungry?'

I rolled on to my back and stared at the ceiling, casting around for the right words, but they slipped over the edge of the bed.

Gallingly Desi was right – how did I know I wouldn't mislead myself, starting off slow (like on so many occasions) with one insufficient round of molten cheese on toast, its savoury, burnt, salty, bubbling crust laminating the air with greasy anticipation. When the toast lit the touch paper, I'd immediately make another round then crack open a family packet of Walkers Ready Salted, crunching fistfuls at a time just because I could. Momentum gathered usually with four French Fancies (the pink and lemon ones), then I'd controversially switch back to savoury with three Dairylea Cheese Triangles squeezed straight from their foil wrappers like plump pimples, scraping out the creamy flecks trapped in the creases with my nails. Maybe I'd push the boat out eating half a pack of Melba Toasts, finishing strong with a chaser of tea, sinking a small bar of Cadbury's Dairy Milk, dipping it in the hot liquid before sucking it down so it glazed the back of my throat. At no point did I ever stop and think: *What am I doing? How will I feel when I can't breathe?* The dark half consistently overrode logic. What was the point of examining this rush of sanity? I'd stopped, wasn't that enough?

Nonetheless, what *did* make this moment the *right* time? Why not after the raw chocolate cake batter incident when Mum disappeared to answer the phone halfway through making Stephen's thirteenth birthday cake? Unable to resist, I'd guzzled nearly all of it and had to lie I'd accidentally knocked the bowl, smashing it on the floor; Mum had to start again. Or Michelle's sixteenth birthday after eating an indecent amount of pizza and strawberry gateaux, belly straining so hard, I'd not had to implement force, almost blocking the toilet. That was a night I vowed NEVER AGAIN.

There were of course, countless other occasions, shame and revulsion slinking in sideways when I was least prepared. What happened away from the bathroom mirror occurred with impunity. How else could I treat myself as a garbage disposal unit? By the time I washed my hands, I'd blanked it out, presumably like a mother dismissing childbirth. Surely, recalling contraction for contraction was the definition of insanity?

*So why stop now?*

Was it because of the baby? The innocent sacrifice on the pyre of puke shocking me away from behaviour I had no means of understanding.

*God, Cordelia, you're disgusting.*

I was just so grateful no one had asked about the father...

Directing my reply towards the sofa bed, I addressed Desi in the shadows.

'I can't explain how I feel. I just know I don't want to go there any more. I don't want to do *that* again. I'm done with looking like a fucking Cabbage Patch doll. You're going to have to trust me on this.'

'I think you should go and see someone. Mom talked to your mom about it.'

'Desi – why? This is no one's business.'

'You made it our business when you almost died of blood poisoning.'

'I didn't nearly die.'

'As good as!' The springs strained as Desi shifted position. 'When are you going to realise people actually care about you? You're the closest I have to a sister. When Dad died, you made it OK. Being here with you guys made me feel part of something again, even if I was a little shit. You didn't judge me, my gay mom or dad – it made no difference to you. When we told that bitch to fuck off in the drug store, it felt great helping you. No one's ever needed my help before.'

Desi's words clipped onto my heart like a smiley-face pin badge. I rubbed my eyes. 'Thank you.'

'Mom said it's all very well stopping making yourself sick, but if you're not looking at the why, then are you really better?'

\* \* \*

I sat in the waiting room at a specialist psychiatric unit in Brighton General Hospital. Disinfectant smacked the air and squeaking footsteps hushed down shiny white corridors where an inordinate amount of arrows pointed out fire exits. Maybe they dealt with pyromaniacs here too.

I'd met a brown-suited psychiatrist six weeks previously, for an initial assessment in a small, grey-walled room. The incinerator chimney, visible through the venetian blinds, belched out spindling smoke in a crooked line. *What did that mean on the Beaufort scale?* Behind the plain Formica-clad desk,

Brown Suit was flanked by two student doctors, obvious coevals of mine, cranking up the humiliation.

'So you dropped out of university? Any plans to return?'

'No, not yet.'

'Good, good.'

No it wasn't.

'Are you working?'

'At the multiplex in Eastbourne...'

*Scribble scribble.*

'So tell me what you want to change. Why are you here? In your own words.'

What was this? Play school?

'Well, I've been making myself sick since I was fifteen—'

'And you're' – he checked his notes – 'nearly nineteen now?'

I nodded.

'How are your teeth?'

'They have a lot of fillings.'

More note taking.

'Good, good.' He looked up at me. 'Sorry, carry on.'

'And I don't want to do it any more.'

'That's great. First step to recovery is admitting

there's a problem in the first place.' He smiled encouragingly.

'I haven't done it for a few months now, but—'
Oh perfidious tears. Where had they come from?

Brown Suit stared, his brows knitting together in
well-rehearsed concern; the students took hurried
notes. *Patient crying.*

'Are you worried you might start again?' The
clock ticked loudly like something from a Stanley
Kubrick film. I imagined the camera on a dolly
closing in on my face then a sharp cutaway to the
clock on the wall, maybe a sinister zither.

'I don't know,' I sobbed. Not even Stanley could
stop the tears. I dug my fingernails into my palms,
driving them deep, waiting for the skin to yield. It
didn't.

'OK. Tell me about your childhood.'

I burst out laughing. 'Sorry... So sorry.' *Jesus
Christ!*

'Don't apologise. Why are you laughing? You
don't have to say, I'm just curious.'

'I feel like I'm in a Peter Sellers film, that's all.'

Brown Suit wiped away the ghost of a smile with
the back of his hand.

I took a big breath and then relayed my childhood in concise bullet points. This was like a school assembly.

'So, do you think the vomiting was triggered by your father leaving the family home, meeting someone else and moving on with his life?'

'No!'

After that, the consultation drew a blank consisting mostly of a treatment path forward and who would be a suitable match as a therapist.

Today, I had returned to meet with the female eating disorders specialist, who beckoned me into a different grey room. They could have made it more homely by adding some beanbags and a few pictures, create a bit of a lounge space instead of leaving it glaringly sterile. There was a table and two patchy blue armchairs, the style Grandpa swindled off elderly dowagers. The woman indicated with a flourish the one she'd chosen for me; conversely, I wanted to pick the other one. I didn't. Pauline Denton sat opposite as angular as a Picasso in a long, shapeless, black tunic, a whiff of stale cigarettes wafting off her, hair a mass of black frizz with a crop of white roots bursting from her scalp. Her face looked as if all the laughter had bled out under anaesthetic without her knowledge. Age indeterminate, she could have equally been thirty or sixty; her skin was creased but bizarrely no crows' feet. After introductions, a precis of my illness, the length of time she anticipated it would take to treat me and how she was qualified, Pauline surprised me.

'I'm in recovery from an eating disorder.'

I was pretty sure she wasn't supposed to reveal such infallibility, just like teachers weren't supposed to admit they had their own lives and didn't sleep in the stationery cupboard overnight. Pauline didn't look like she was in recovery from anything. In practice, she could have stood in for Keith Richards after a seven-day bender in Amsterdam.

'So I've been where you're sitting right now. Not in this very hospital, but in your situation.' She attempted a smile, but her heart wasn't in it. Maybe she needed to hide her teeth. 'So I have a unique insight in to your particular condition. Please tell me about what kind of foods you'd choose and how you feel when they're inside your stomach.'

I listed my poison while Pauline nodded along, taking notes. When I'd finished, I paused. *How did I feel?*

'I'm always relieved when the food's gone.' I trained my eyes on my lap.

'But how is it before that? When you know you have a job to do, to get rid of it?'

I wriggled in the seat. A young Michael Corleone flashed across the back of my mind; tingles cascaded like a waterfall down my spine. The seminal scene in *The Godfather*, set in Louis' restaurant, the scene that had spoken to me aged fifteen, returned to finish its job. Michael waged a battle within at the dinner table, conscious that if he disappeared to the bathroom to retrieve the gun stashed behind the cistern, his peripheral dovish existence would, for all intents and purposes, be over.

'OK, we'll try something. So I made a shopping list of all the foods you just mentioned. I'm going to buy them for next week's session. You're going to eat them and record your emotions while they sit in your stomach.'

'What, all of them? Sit where?'

'Here. You'll eat them in front of me and then we wait.'

'For what?'

'To see how you feel, knowing you can't purge. If necessary, you'll be forced to sit here. You won't be allowed to go to the toilet.'

'But I'm only here for an hour.'

'We'll stay as long as it takes. I can clear my appointments.'

I checked Pauline's deadpan face; unfortunately,

it appeared she wasn't joking. The long arm ticked towards the fifty-minute therapy hour on the clock next to the window. We had ten minutes left.

'Do you mind if I go to the bathroom? I'm desperate.'

'Be my guest.'

I felt anything but. Sweeping my bag up from the floor, I headed out of the door. There was no receptionist to sneak past, just a clump of orange plastic chairs bordering an empty antechamber leading to a long shiny corridor, reminiscent of *The Shining*. But it was *The Godfather* that catapulted me past the lift, running from shooting Pauline Denton in the skull. I skidded through the fire doors (thank you, informative arrows) and down the stairs, shoving my way through the glass door at the bottom and into the car park. I looked up to the window of the room I'd just fled from. If anyone needed to be force fed a bag of chips and some Mr Kipling Apple Pies, it was Pauline Denton. Maybe that was a one-session wonder? Some innovative new technique designed to shock patients out of negative behavioural patterns?

'No!' I cried out loud, startling a woman shepherding an elderly man into the front of her car, accidentally banging his head on the door. 'I don't buy that. She was mental.' At least I wasn't as fucked up as Pauline Denton.

# 33

## DESI

'Shiiiiiit!' It didn't matter how many times Desi threw himself into deep water, it always hit him like an ice cream truck. After eleven hours at sea, how was Cordelia continuing to swim without a wetsuit? Not that this insanity had happened out of the blue – they had been carefully preparing for well over twelve months, but this was the longest stretch of cold water she'd tackled by far. Weight training; total body confusion training; endless lengths at the Sovereign; swimming in a giant loop on the seafront; technique tweaking; monastic ice baths; Lutheran cold showers; sleeping with windows open; leaving the heating off; spending time outside without a coat, even in sub-zero temperatures; gaining half a stone (that had been surprisingly easy) – Cordelia had tackled them all to strengthen her immunity against the cruel sea. But nothing really prepared you for the grinding cold of deep open water.

Desi had overseen coaching like a benevolent dictator, feeling the heavy weight of responsibility having provoked her into this in the first place.

'Swim the Channel?' Cordelia had repeated back at him on the seafront after their Sunday morning group swim, her face scrunched into a fist. She had recently joined Eastbourne Egrets after yet another ghosting by the latest in a shopping list of much younger men, a dating trend transcending sexual preferences currently cutting through society's stratum. Desi had noticed it amongst his cohorts, young cubs chasing after daddies and the more grizzly bear types. He'd suggested cold-water swimming as a sharpener, help shake off post break-up blues. It was how he and Tim had met.

'Yes, swim the Channel,' he replied. 'You're always bleating on about how fifty's gonna hit and what have you got to show for it.'

She narrowed her eyes. 'That's a bit extreme though. Swimming the Channel, just to prove a point?'

'A massive point, stick the finger to the haters.'

'I don't know that many people, unless you're aware of a gang of haters I'm oblivious to. No idea why they'd hate me though.' She side-eyed him then. 'For rejecting a scatological journal to record one's daily dumps in, perhaps?'

'Hey! I still think that'd be a best seller if you got it illustrated too, highlighting the danger poos and whatnot. Bowel cancer is one of the biggest killers.'

'Joan was never going to go for *My Little Book of Poo: a Journal.*'

'Missed a trick. Cross over from all the Winnie the Pooh fans who'd buy it by mistake. Earn you guys millions. Millions, I tell you!'

Desi considered himself half British having been soldered from the egg of an English mother. It drove him to seek dual citizenship after living in nineties Brighton, unleashing the dormant Englishman within. He began speaking in an exaggerated English accent, classically referred to as received pronunciation.

'The English twat stage,' Cordelia named it recently. 'You sounded like you lived in an English theme park run by Dick Van Dyke eating crumpets whilst drinking Earl Grey tea. You were insufferable.'

Uncle Phil had originally orchestrated an internship at his publishers post-graduation when Desi had expressed a wish to stay in the UK. He only lasted two months – staid textbooks smelled too much like school. He preferred serving donuts on the pier while chasing the fashion disco express, applying for every entry-level job there was. He regularly questioned his sanity when he returned from work to sleep in the poky cubbyhole in the even pokier Brighton flat he rented with two other postgraduates above a Chinese takeaway, all navigating bottom-feeder positions in the world of work. He didn't want to return to Chicago not having 'made it'. It took six months of living and breathing donuts (brilliant rocket fuel) before Desi struck gold securing a very junior stylist job on the now defunct *B* magazine (steaming clothes in the fashion cupboard). He escaped the seaside to share a flat in Brixton with Anthony, a city trader, who weighed out his chicken breasts every day for maximum gains and set an alarm every hour to remind himself to drink a glass of water. In the six months they cohabited, they only went out once for a beer to a nondescript pub in Stockwell. So convinced was he that Anthony was gay, he scatter-gunned hints about Fire, the Vauxhall Tavern, cruising, even scraping the barrel with the royal family.

'I suppose you love Princess Diana,' was his

parting shot as he stood to walk to the bar for his round just as Anthony's Casio watch beeped.

'Not really, she's nuts, mate.' He swigged down a half litre of Evian in an impressive five seconds. Maybe Desi's gaydar needed rebooting if Anthony didn't like Saint Diana. 'Not much of a rack on her either,' he'd added as a smokescreen.

The following week, Desi spotted a half-naked David Hasselhoff poster stuck on the inside of Anthony's wardrobe door.

\* \* \*

Even though Cordelia had side-swept the Channel swim idea, Desi wasn't done with it.

'I think the challenge would be good,' he reiterated. 'For many things.' Aunty Lois the tacit pinnacle of his list. He'd suggested therapy on countless occasions to smooth things out, but Cordelia ran from that idea like it was a burning building.

'Your aunt is a complicated person,' his own mom had said once when he'd asked about their dynamics. 'On one hand, she deals out a conveyor belt of judgement while on the other, grace and favour. We'd be in massive debt without her.' A fact he was certain his cousins were in the dark about. 'She cleared all the credit cards we'd maxed out for Dad's care.' She'd also waved her generous wand in his direction the summer he'd stayed with Jodie.

'I hear you're not going to go to Rome,' she'd said while they were walking along Eastbourne beach in search of the perfect picnic spot.

'Yeah, we had to choose between Paris and Rome – we couldn't afford both. Jodie chose Paris.'

'But you've wanted to go to Rome since you were a little boy.'

He'd shrugged.

Two mornings later, while a star-jumping Aunty Lois was beamed into the nation's living rooms, he'd found an envelope addressed to him propped up against the kettle. Inside was five hundred pounds in twenties and fifties, a yellow Post-it note stuck on the centre of the cash's clear plastic slip.

*Make sure you go to Rome xx*

He'd grabbed every ungodly shift at Burger King to fund the European tour, scribbling down High School English essays in the cramped staff area while people smoked over the top of his head through the window. He'd fall asleep in lessons with his eyes open and jerk awake when the bell rang, drool crusting the corners of his gaping mouth. His hair permanently reeked of burger grease, enough to turn him temporarily vegetarian, like Edward. The week before he bought his ticket, Edward sat him down in the living room where he used to play chess with his dad, the board permanently set up on the small side table by Dad's Chesterfield armchair. He'd gradually folded into the creased leather as he fought his fate, until sitting was no longer an option. Watching the world pass his window from his beloved chair had made him feel like king of the castle instead of a man grasping at life's straws. The end came quickly after that.

'Is there anything you need to talk about before you head off into the big wide world?' Edward hinted at meaningfully.

'No, I don't think so.'

'I don't need to remind you to be safe.' Edward preferred the direct approach; Mom had placed five packs of condoms on his bed without saying a word. 'Always use a condom – the extra-thick ones. Safety before pleasure at all times.'

'I'm with Jodie; I don't need to worry.'

Edward had arched his eyebrows as if this was news to him.

'You're a handsome young man jetting off to Amsterdam. It's a place of... sexual experimentation. You might, I don't know, want to join in.'

'I won't!'

He'd never kissed a boy, not properly. Jacob Ericson behind the sandpit at kindergarten barely counted, though if he remembered rightly, Desi had been keen to give it another stab. Jacob less so. He'd peed his pants in protest. Jodie proved to be a brilliant distraction, her resemblance to Madonna blasting away Desi's embryonic exploration of his true self. Everyone loved Madonna – *Truth or Dare* bore witness to all her gay dancers garrotting each other to win the coveted spot as her latest plaything.

Jodie had picked him out of the hole he'd been hiding in after he'd grown over a foot the previous summer, when his voice had dropped into his Air Jordans, when his razor-sharp cheekbones had fought their way out of his babyface. She asked him to join her on a trip to the movies to see *Dead Poet's Society* then proceeded to sob all over him; she sat with him in the lunchroom when he had previously sat alone, occasionally finding himself pelted with Twinkies from a neighbouring table – *Plague Boy*. She hung out during recess and shared her Doritos with him, asking him what music he liked and whether it was true he was half English. She taught him how to French kiss. She basically saved his life at high school.

'We make a cute couple!' she'd said. 'People notice us!'

She wasn't wrong. Instead of having his head rammed down the john to 'clean his hair', kids began respecting him. It became addictive. In turn, he couldn't help but fall under Jodie's spell. Her bouncy hair entranced him, as did her unique fashion style, her exceptional ironic sense of humour (lacking in so many), her ability to crush with an icy put down. If she'd looked like Audrey Hepburn, he may have actually asked her to marry him. Eyes closed, she could be anyone he wanted her to be: Bruce Willis in *Die Hard* or Philip Michael Thomas in *Miami Vice*. But that was unfair. He tried so hard not to think of boys and it helped to imagine Derek and Jodie as picture-perfect lead characters he watched from his other life, the one that Cordelia had tried to pin on him. He and Cordelia had more in common than he cared to think about.

In the end, it wasn't Amsterdam, the city of sin, that forced open his eyes; it was Paris, the city of love, a place Jodie had passionately begged to visit ever since Desi had introduced her to Audrey Hepburn's lesser film, *Funny Face*.

During an exorbitant trip to iconic Moulin Rouge, sharing a solitary beer because they could legally drink in Europe, but also terrified of bankrupting themselves despite Aunty Lois's benefaction, Desi found himself bewitched by the half-naked male circus performers. He swore he saw one of them winking, sparking a stampede in his nether regions. He didn't imagine the bottle of champagne arriving at their table, courtesy of Henri, the cute acrobat who had been spurred on by Desi's undivided attention. Jodie didn't say a word, even when the keen young man sent a discreet note inviting him backstage; he regrettably declined. Back at the crowded hostel in Montmartre, Jodie asked for the truth.

'I love *you*, Jodie,' Desi had cried earnestly. A world without Jodie filled him with existential dread. He was nothing without her.

'I didn't ask if you loved me. I asked if you like boys. I mean, it wouldn't surprise me. Look at your parents.' Spoken without malintent, Jodie was a realist. 'You were like a kid on Christmas Day when you read that note. That's the truth right there.'

'I only like you!' Desi pleaded, grabbing her hand which flopped in his.

By the time they'd reached Rome, the spark had

been snuffed out by a week of Jodie retrospectively following breadcrumbs. They may as well have stayed home to admire the Clarence Buckingham Memorial Fountain in Grant Park instead of staring dolefully at the Baroque spectacle that was the Trevi Fountain. Regardless of his misery, Desi couldn't help but admire Triton's impeccably chiselled torso.

\* \* \*

'I need to do something,' Cordelia had said a few months before another birthday thrust her closer to fifty. 'I just don't know what it is. Look at me, Des – I'll die never having *been* anyone.'

'I'm not anyone!' he'd cried, deep down knowing his own comfort zone would have suffocated him.

'You are. You came over here from Chicago, travelled Europe, leaped out the closet, got a degree, lived in London, had a brilliant job, then freelanced, now you're here, all happy and settled with Tim. What did I do? Err, I worked in a cinema, then a bookshop, then a design agency, then a doctors' surgery and now I work for Joan who wants me to buy into her journal business and that scares the crap out of me because I still don't know what I really want to do with my life. I'm almost forty-eight, never lived with anyone. I need something *to happen*. If you pushed me through a sieve, all you'd have left is fucking Dr Doolittle, a criminally abnormal knowledge of the calorific table, and the *Which? Guide* to sex aids,' she said rather bluntly.

'Come on, your cheeseboards are unrivalled! Tim told everyone about that Stinking Bishop from Christmas.'

She punched him in the arm, laughing dolefully.

* * *

'So?' Desi asked, pulling Cordelia up to standing from the seafront bench they had been sitting on. 'It's three and a half grand to swim the Channel, all in.'

'How on earth do you know all this?'

'I asked Alan, that older dude down there, the one walking up the beach now. He's already done it. Said it was the best decision he ever made.'

'If you're that interested, why don't *you* do it?'

It was a considered question, but not one he was willing to share the honest answer for. His cousin's misplaced dogged determination, the obsessiveness, the tenacious tunnel vision had always shone its spotlight wide of the mark. Despite this, she was his favourite person in the entire world (apart from Tim), and all he wanted to do was help. She talked non-stop about doing something with her life, yet had operated from her comfort zone for as long as he had known her. If for one minute he believed she was happy, he would have let her be.

'I'm too scared. I don't think I have the mindset. But I know you do,' he admitted.

'Er, hello. Have you met me?'

At least she knew what she was.

However, six months later, he found himself drowning under elaborate training plans, listening to open-water-swimming podcasts, and reading every book on Amazon about famous swimmers past and present. He couldn't be certain what eventually flipped the switch but he'd anticipated that by planting a seed, a feverish obsession might sprout, because she would never have thought of this by herself.

On the day itself, they had decided that he would join her in the water as soon as the French Inshore Traffic Zone was in sight. With no discernible border it was only visible on charts and *Boudica*'s navigational system.

'You're not wearing your wetsuit when you join me!' Cordelia had ordered. 'I'll be expecting red budgie smugglers. You didn't want children, did you?!'

\* \* \*

Desi set off from *Boudica*'s port side before treading water, waves striking his cheeks as he awaited Cordelia to reach their approximate two metre exclusion zone.

Buggering hell, his balls had ziplined back inside his abdomen. The middle of the Channel was considerably colder than the relative shallows hugging Eastbourne's stony shore. He struggled to acclimatise, teeth chattering so badly, he clamped his jaw shut. He was no stranger to swimming in mid-winter, though he only braved it in a wetsuit and woolly hat from December until the end of April.

'You still feeling nauseous?' he checked as she bobbed closer, pausing her stroke to grin at him. She popped out her right earplug, slipping it in a hidden pocket.

'Yep, sight of your ugly mug's not helping.' She jokingly crossed her eyes. 'You look like one of those shrunken heads.' Cramming his recalcitrant Afro inside an extremely snug swim hat was more troublesome than mismatching a 'grower' with the wrong sized condom. Needs must – wet hair was a sure fire way of inviting cold into your bones. They had an hour's window to swim together before Desi was required to clamber back on board. He could return for the final push – instinct told him she would need it. They were about to cross the threshold of what most swimmers and pilots portentously regarded as the Swimmers' Graveyard. This home stretch of the Channel unspooled many swims, either terminated on the orders of the pilot due to inclement weather, an inhospitable current, or the swimmer's crumbling fortitude.

'Cathy thinks aiming for the Cap is a tad optimistic. The tide's against us. Alan said Wissant's an easier landing anyway. No slippery rocks.'

Her lack of reply made it hard to discern if she was disappointed or just plain exhausted. You had to swim over sixty strokes per minute to reach the Cap on the relevant tide. Her stroke had fallen below forty-eight in the last hour. She'd need to sprint to cross the Graveyard.

'I'll swim slightly ahead; you need something to aim for,' Desi had proposed the week before, finalising plans after the Eastbourne Egrets Sunday meet up. As good as his word, Desi managed to improve Cordelia's strokes per minute by cutting a steady pace. In the meantime, his mind wandered faced with infinite sky. What would have happened if his grandparents never had the wool ripped from their eyes about Aunty Lois's divorce? He most certainly would have stayed in the US; he may have lingered in the closet. But most importantly, he wouldn't have met Stephen and Cordelia – he'd no idea he had cousins until Mom broke it to him before Dad died. The day he 'suggested' all three of them surprise their grandparents had gone down in family lore. Deep water must run in their blood...

# 34

## THE CHANNEL

'You need to keep the pace Desi set or drifting's a reality!' Alan bellowed as *Boudica*'s engines coughed into life. I attacked the water with renewed brio, a subtle spring in my stroke. Having reached the Graveyard, I'd saved my most ambitious film until now: *The Shawshank Redemption*. I was impressed with my inner fire restoking itself on just sweet tea and milky coffee. Desi's encouraging pacesetting coupled with *Shawshank*'s storied plot, the single-minded determination of one man pitted against wrongful incarceration and his Gordian journey to freedom, planted a much-needed rousing flag in my threadbare attention span.

Less than three years ago, I hadn't swum in the

sea since being a child, just the odd plunge or paddle on an unbearably hot day. I'm not a fan of swimming pools, apart from when abroad. Goose-pimpled flesh, cellulite on show and pinching more than a wobbly inch: no thanks. The slippery changing rooms and shivering shimmying out of a sodden costume were also a turn off. Yet the effect open-water swimming had on Desi after just a month was astounding. The shackles of his big break-up visibly loosened.

'It's just the water,' he insisted when I probed about therapy. 'It's like a drug. The cold shocks the pain away. The sea holds the space while you swim and then the rest is up to you. Either you drag all the crap out of the sea with you, or you let the water carry it away. It's magic.'

When Desi met Tim, the kindest, loveliest man, an illustrator and musician, a few months after, I took it as a sign to give open-water swimming a whirl. Tim had joined the Egrets during an extensive period of creative block.

'I swear, after a month of swimming, it sharpened my brain; I was able to look at the project with different eyes and find what the client needed from me. Open-water swimming returned myself to me.'

I'd forgotten the deliciousness of slipping beneath the silken surface, to be free, to have my body firmly held in place by a magnificent mass of water. To roll with the punches, to lie on my back and stare at rice-pudding clouds, focusing on how to breathe up from my toes while the cold crushed my lungs. To be playful again, to be a child, to wave off my cynicism, the salty sanctuary taking care of business. The sea filled in the cracks, leaving my heart whole each time I stepped from the water and into my Dry Robe, skin ablaze. I had fallen in love and there was no going back.

I pushed against an unchartered spectrum of pain; this was my chance to find the grit in the oyster. Desi had been back on board *Boudica* for as long as it had taken to summon the opening scenes of *The Shawshank Redemption*, when my right hand slammed into a slimy slick of flotsam.

I'd drifted a fair bit from *Boudica* and missed the approaching trailing tributaries of garbage marshalling my passage into a floating mass of bags and bottles tangled in knots with discarded fishing nets. No one noticed until I shouted.

'Swim back out of it, Cordy,' Desi yelled, pacing

from the stern and along the port side, his urgency piercing my earplugs. But plastic wrapped itself around both arms, dragging me under as I tried to yank them free, swallowing mouthfuls of water.

'I can't get it off!' As soon as I escaped one bag, another limpet suctioned my forearms, bags circling like sharks. In less time than it took to do a wee, I was surrounded by coagulated rubbish clinging to my legs, everything rinsed of logos by the unremitting elements. Chunks of debris swung round, splintered by my thrashing, latching on to the trail, building a barricade against a rear-ended escape. I poked out an earplug to take instructions.

'Stop!' Alan ordered. 'Take your time, slowly tread water. Breathe. That's it, calm... Now turn around and see if you can swim under it then back towards the boat?'

Swell had built up yet again from shipping-lane traffic, small white crests crowning, forcing the island of crap into and around me. A hefty clump of nets laced with faded pink and yellow floats made a break for it and coiled round like a comforting arm, further trapping me. Desi headed to *Boudica*'s bow, diving into the cockpit on the way, grabbing binoculars. Scanning the horizon, he shouted back.

'Fuck. It's a carpet! How did we miss it? It's long,

but it tapers off out the front. One thing I can see –
France! Cordy, France is in sight!'

I squinted into the sun as an oscillating shard of
coast slunk beneath the rippling junk before being
thrown a childhood memory. Stephen and I
watching *Star Wars: A New Hope*, God knows what
year. Han, Leia, Chewbacca and Luke all entombed
in the garbage compactor as the walls closed in,
mashing the Death Star's waste (and possibly them)
to a more manageable pulp. I surveyed the shape-
shifting rubbish raring to claim me as its own.

'Swim away from us! Underneath it all,' Alan
suggested, his voice lifted up like a gull on a
sudden gust. A cargo ship was about to eclipse the
horizon, white, blue and green sea containers
stacked four high, six along, in no particular pattern. The ship's surging surf chopped the plastic
into spikes and valleys. Cathy cut *Boudica*'s engine
and she drifted diagonally towards the midst of the
matted pollution. *What if my foot caught in
something?*

I'd been prewarned about this eventuality by
Cathy. 'The plastic can be a hundred metres long,
like a giant twisted sea snake. Bottles, ghost nets,
bags – trapping birds, fish – they all die... We'll keep
our eyes out, but if you've drifted a bit too far from

the boat, you'll see it before we do. Sometimes, you're in it before you know it.'

I stopped swimming, goosebumps springing up like spines.

'Cordy, there are other options,' Alan called. 'Your safety is the first priority.'

The plastic writhed like bladder wrack, a fishy, pond-like aroma wafting off the mottled surface, eerie sounds leaking like a creaking shipwreck. Having withstood irrational fear of sharks and other monsters of the deep, this manmade serpent surpassed them all. Sun beams sparked off dented drinks bottles, intense flashes penetrating my tinted goggles. An overactive imagination breathed life into gruesome scenarios involving dead sailors ensnared beneath the knotted web as well as killer barracuda waiting to rip me limb from limb, drawn in by nets dripping with carrion. Logically, they didn't populate the busy Channel, but who knew what dolphins were capable of if poisoned by a rogue can of Red Bull. Tripping their tits off, they could easily mistake me for a giant squid, one of the more humiliating deaths, tantamount to being flattened by a drunk pensioner on an out-of-control mobility scooter.

Caged within the floating dystopian garbage heap, I tried and failed to rein in the fear. Cathy left the cockpit and stepped out onto the port side, tightening her ponytail. *Boudica* dipped in the cargo ship's swell. A seagull skimmed over the top of the fly bridge, screeching into the sky.

'Cordelia, if you can't clear this, I'm going to have to call off the swim.'

I violently shook my head, giving the thumbs down. For the first time since I'd jumped from the concrete steps, tears gathered.

'We've no choice, Cordelia!' Cathy shouted again. 'Unless you can clear it – there's no way of swimming through it. You could drown. You need to clear it in the next few minutes. You should be able to – just be mindful of what's beneath. You never know if there are fish hooks in the nets, or rods that could catch you. It could be a metre thick in places.'

I pulled up my goggles and rubbed my eyes. I'd considered the reality of failure due to exhaustion, or an unexpected squall delivering treacherous conditions, perhaps a sudden tidal surge pulling me off course, missing the opening for the French coast, a resulting dangerous drift towards Belgium.

'Pleath can I have a hot drink?' I lisped, all furry tongue and kippered lips.

Alan sent Desi off to the galley to decant some tea. Minutes later, I squashed the bottle between my hands, easing the white pain in my fingers. Builders' tea had been my tipple of choice during a binge; I'd been unable to drink it for three years into recovery. Tossing the empty bottle towards *Boudica*, I refitted my goggles, snapped my costume out of my bum and eased away the chafing straps. Desi, Alan, Alison and Cathy, now reinstated on the flybridge, all waited. I practised deep breaths, my diaphragm grazing my ribs. Surely swimming under this mountain of crap was no match for the trauma of taking Desi to visit our toxic grandparents?

## 35

### GET OFF OUR LAND

'So you were last here 1986?' Desi asked as we watched a hovering taxi emptying out passengers in front of Leicester station's remarkably Baroque entrance. I held my hand out to request it.

'I think I was eleven, nearly twelve? It was before we met you.'

'It was the time we came without Dad,' Stephen piped up, digging his fists into his Levis, the turn-ups deep enough to catch an inch of rain. 'And I was terrified I was going to give the game away.' Stephen had just started his final year studying Geography at London School of Economics; his digs were round the corner from Desi in Brixton behind the Ritzy Cinema. His flat also hosted a family of mice amid the damp walls. I'd only stayed once last term even though Stephen had offered up his bed. However, this term, he'd inherited a camp bed from Dad, a brother to the one that had almost severed his limbs years before.

I'd taken Friday to Monday off work for our first weekend together since Desi had absconded to London five months ago, the stars not in alignment before now. Having worked at the multiplex on and off since I was sixteen, girl and woman, I was axiomatically the longest-serving employee (apart from Reggie) and had by default, been promoted (against my will) to Assistant Manager of the Ticket Booth, a title conceived just for me. Reggie had implemented it as a favour to Mum, a fact I only found out when she had drunk the equivalent of two thimbles of rosé the previous weekend after a whole bowl of lettuce dressed with fresh air. This was a peculiar juncture – simultaneously being treated as Mum's confidant whilst she attempted to parent like she always had despite my official adult status at twenty-two.

'You know Reggie fancies me,' Mum had slurred while *Blind Date* filled the Saturday-night void. 'Also Cilla tried the Deflate Plan and lost a stone. She sent me a massive bouquet from Fortnums.' Deflate was her latest endorsement deal, aimed at the 'more mature' person who found that 'mid-life bulge hard to budge'. Mum had come up with that strapline all by herself. Genius. Sweeteners whitewashed any traces of flavour, leaving it smelling disconcertingly cheesy. I'd squeezed out relentless eggy wind for three successive hours after one snack bar.

'Reggie's gay, Mum.'

'Doesn't stop them. I'm a gay icon!'

Jesus wept. She'd performed a small part in *Aladdin* last Christmas at the Hippodrome. Christopher Biggins had starred as the Genie and Miss Slimnastics as Wishy Washy was billed under a puppet elephant from a loo-roll advert playing Aladdin's sidekick.

'I've seen less wood in a forest,' the snippy lady behind hissed when Mum had finished her first scene. 'That woman gets everywhere.'

'I didn't need a promotion, Mum. It's embarrassing,' I said while Cilla crowed, 'What's yer name, where d'ya come from?'. Reggie's fascination with Mum wasn't the sole reason for an assisted promotion; he had also recently lost two stone on the Deflate Plan.

'You could have said no or left. You're a bright girl, Cordy, wasted there. Can't have Miss Slimnastics' fans thinking her children have no ambition.

You can be anything you want to be if you just put your mind to it… Look at me!'

The trouble was I had no idea what I wanted, spending life in a permanent dither. Mum didn't bother shoring up her disapproval with niceties any more, not since I'd been cured of all that 'bulimia trouble' by Pauline Denton. Little did she know I used to sneak in to Desi's history of fashion lectures, bypassing Pauline completely. In the dark of Brighton University lecture theatre, I discovered that women had been physically abusing their bodies for centuries under various guises of 'fashion'. Men got off very lightly with powdered wigs and cod pieces.

I'd nipped purging in the bud, vowing daily not to list calories consumed in an attempt to keep track of my arbitrary limit (that fluctuated depending on my mood). But the sneaky bastards just appeared in speech bubbles outside my head, like a *Jackie* magazine photo love story. Satsuma: twenty calories. Fresh air: forty calories. Calorie Tourette's. The daily cross-examination in the mirror persevered, legs touching, punishment for not achieving the Holy Grail thigh gap, tummy sucked in until I'd achieved my unrealistic childhood waist. I ignored my boobs, plastered to my chest under a minimising bra. Balanced eating was lost amongst the forest of fad diets, juice detoxes, binary choices.

I wished I could escape food, just take a pill and be done with it. Food was the comfort blanket or the cruel dictator depending on the day, racking up an onerous burn count. Sit ups, squats, an hour on Mum's exercise bike. I never sat still, but when I did, it was to crash and eat chocolate while engaging in dizzy heights of self-loathing, firing synapses refusing to forget the signals they'd been transmitting.

'You need to leave here, get out and see the world,' Stephen loftily suggested after his first term at London School of Economics. 'It's not good for you to stay here.'

'You've been in catered halls for three months, not to fucking war!'

He'd shaken his head and walked out of the room, my position on the pedestal in question.

But here we were, the three of us in a taxi bombing towards the Big House with no discernible plan. It had been Desi's idea, of course – he'd a bee in his bonnet about tracing his English roots, fixating on all things British.

'I want to see them in the flesh, just once. I need to look them in the eye and see where I came from.'

'But you have your mum – why d'you need to go

there? Your mum would say the same.' I'd tried to dissuade him. 'Mum said she thinks Grandma's got dementia. She never calls any more and if Mum calls the Big House, the phone just rings off. She's done with it.' We'd been inhaling Brixton Riots with abandon tucked up inside the Brixtonian rum bar when Desi dropped the bombshell.

'Look, I don't expect you to get it, but it feels important. My dad's parents threw him out when he was seventeen. Same as Mom's. The difference is, I know exactly where Mom's parents are. I have no easy links back to Dad's family. I'd get lost under mounds of paperwork. All I know is they came from Milwaukee further up the lake. Grandma and Grandpa Simpson live up the road.'

'Leicester's not up the road!' Stephen protested, erroneous geographical knowledge his bugbear.

'It is compared to the US! Everything's fucking decades away there.'

The taxi dropped us outside the rusting, double wrought-iron gates on the northern side of the picturesque village of Warningham. Desi's hangover faded driving through the chocolate-box hamlet, even more quaint and Englishy than the elaborate fantasy theme park he'd dreamt up. The house had weathered away from the stately residence of my childhood. It seemed smaller, the front garden not quite the rambling, flower-filled meadow I'd played hide and seek in with Stephen. The gate was jammed open a few inches on the weed-pocked, pea gravel drive, numerous concentric arcs revealing mud beneath. Tyre marks cut tramlines towards the red-bricked house, where Grandpa's Jaguar sat, guarding the black front door, the sentinel greying pillars in decline. I pushed the protesting gates and slipped between them.

'Come on! Let's get this over with.' This was unquestionably out of my comfort zone and I'd been hoping the entire venture would be called off any moment. But when Desi hesitated, instead of relief, I found something else. 'You can't back out now! Not after all this effort. We're in this shit together.' When he refused to move, I reached through the slim gap and dragged him in, Stephen bringing up the rear. We traipsed in unison, loud crunching announcing our approach.

My heart thrummed in my throat, sweat beaded in my armpits; a curtain twitched in the drawing room. When we reached the bay trees lining the top of the drive, their once sleek topiary sadly in need of trimming, the front door opened. Grandpa stepped onto the front step, clutching the rifle he used for shooting rabbits. His hair had thinned considerably at the temples, now completely white, while his nose had fought for prominence, leaving his beady eyes and thin lips behind. People say babies grow into their faces, so it only made sense that the elderly out-grow theirs.

'I'm armed; we don't want your sort round here,' he wheezed, the effort triggering a coughing fit, dangerous when furnished with a gun.

'Grandpa, it's us, Stephen and Cordelia,' I called over the car roof once he'd recovered. 'Your grandchildren.'

His body had coiled in on itself like a cowrie shell.

'We don't have grandchildren.' He narrowed his eyes, shifting the gun into a wavering pose, aiming it in our general direction. Desi ducked.

'You do. You have three!' I poked Desi. 'Come on,' I encouraged him. 'I'm right next to you.'

He slowly unfurled and smiled theatrically.

'Leave the grounds or suffer the consequences.' Grandpa jabbed the gun at us again as a warning. 'It'd be self-defence.'

'Jack?' a reedy voice whimpered from the bowels of the house. 'Who's there?'

Grandpa looked over his shoulder into the hallway, the gun momentarily grazing the sky. 'No one, Beatrice, go back to your telly.'

'Grandma! It's us!' I shouted urgently. 'Stephen and Cordelia, we've brought someone to see you.'

Grandma shuffled to the doorway, her demise clearly manifest without the place-setting, frosted pink lipstick, her bloodless mouth set adrift on a patch of saggy pale flesh. The same could be said of her sunken eyes just detectible above her nose, no visible eyebrows tethering them in place. Navy nylon trousers, tartan slippers and a beige polo neck jumper sat in direct contrast with her impeccable twin sets of old. Her helmet of hair usually set like a whipped ice cream flopped limply on top of her head, in need of a good wash.

'Jesus,' Stephen whispered under his breath. 'Have they just been dug up?'

I waved at Grandma who swivelled her head between her husband and the three of us in bleak confusion.

'Grandma, this is Derek, Liz's son,' I introduced Desi with a flourish of the wrist like his beloved Vanna on *Wheel of Fortune*. 'Your other grandson.'

'I said we don't have grandchildren,' Grandpa bellowed, the gun juddering precariously, 'especially not a darkie one.'

'Let's go,' Stephen said defeatedly. 'They're awful.'

'Hang on,' Desi reasoned. 'I've come all this way.' He crept round the car so as not to startle them. 'I just want you to know that your daughter, Liz, is well and living in Chicago. I'm her son and she's a great mom. You should be proud of her and Lois, who's looked after both of us since my dad died. We would have been in the gutter if it hadn't been for her.' He paused, awaiting a reaction. They just stared blankly. 'It's a shame you cast Mom out of your family. All she ever wanted was to love who she chose without condemnation. I'm going to—'

Grandpa suddenly aimed the gun scarcely above Desi's head and pulled the trigger. The blast split the air, the sound detonating in my chest. We cupped our ears.

'Is that Lois?' Grandma's voice faltered, a glimmer of recognition in her rheumy eyes.

'Lois is dead,' Grandpa spat then turned back to us. 'Go on, be off with you! There's nothing here for you. Bloody Yanks.'

'Leg it,' Stephen urged. 'Before he shoots that thing again. I don't trust him not to kill us.'

We ran down the drive, death snapping at our heels, gravel spraying up behind like bullets. When we were through the gate, we turned back towards the house. Grandpa peered myopically, cutting a lonely figure under the portico, the gun held loosely by his side. Grandma was nowhere to be seen.

'Fuck him,' Desi growled, and pulled down his jeans and mooned his bare arse at the gates, slapping his left cheek with his hand. 'Kiss my ass, Grandpa!'

We didn't wait to get a response and hustled Desi past the gate post in lieu of a bullet in the bum.

'I think I'm deaf,' Stephen announced as Desi pulled up his trousers.

'What did you say?' I asked, smirking.

# 36

## THE CHANNEL

'You got this, Cordy. It's not even a length at the Sovereign!'

*Not helping, Desi.* I could easily cruise a length underwater if I dived in. A static start under considerable pressure in the open sea, swimming against the current a possible ten or eleven hours after battling the unpredictable Channel, was like comparing sharks with dolphins. I poked my face below the surface, then relaxed, sinking while keeping one arm above, marking my bolthole. The rippling scrim cast ominous silhouettes into the water. Fish darted in and out of shadows playing follow my leader, the sun blasting the first few metres before being swallowed into the inky depths. I glanced around, appalled at the gaping nylon ghost nets ready to snare unlucky creatures, fish carcasses entwined in every one alongside decomposing birds and myriad plastic bottles, a sinister Rogues gallery. I'd need to dive down a few metres to clear it before safely heading aft to breach the surface.

Thrust unwillingly into this crepuscular world, Richard Dreyfuss returned, this time suspended in the flimsy-looking shark cage, the sinewy apex predator slipping like silk between shafts of light in the closing scenes from *Jaws*. Something spikey lightly scuffed my foot, catapulting me upwards. 'Get a grip!' I gasped after clawing my way into fresh air. Alan wouldn't think twice about hauling me out of the Channel if I didn't calm down. I steadied my breathing. 'I am safe, I am well.' I gave the boat a solid thumbs up; *Boudica*'s engine restarted. Alan had stationed himself on the stern, ready to jump into the rib if necessary. I'd be swimming backwards, not for the first time in my life...

\* \* \*

Thank the Lord Desi had temporarily stowed Claud and the other two vibrators at his. '*They better be anti-bacced!*' I'd also spring cleaned both phone and laptop, deleting any glossed-over degenerate pictures from would-be past situationships. Dating in the twenty-first century was fraught with digital man-holes ready to take you down.

'Make sure you get here before Mum in case of my death,' I'd instructed Desi a week before the swim.

'Cordy! You're not going to die!'

'I know that, but in case I do. I don't want her finding out about my sex life.'

'Aunty Lois was hardly a nun! She'd understand.'

I pulled out my second desk drawer.

'That unmarked brown envelope there, burn it, OK?'

'Jesus, Cordy. Are you a serial killer or something?'

'No! Naked photos of David when we were young.'

'Throw them if you don't want them.'

'I do want them.'

Desi thwacked my arm. 'You perv.'

'Back at ya. Oh, there's a tube of lube in the bed-side drawer, don't let her find that either.'

'I'll take it, always useful.'

\* \* \*

Along with over a year of gruelling preparation, this was the first time in my life I'd not taken the easy road. I inhaled deeply through my nose, distending my abdomen, creating space. I'd wasted so much time trying to take up as little space as possible, flattening my stomach, my chest, myself to fit in. But the dichotomy of the easy road was it was capable of turning you inside out then spitting you on to the hard shoulder, leaving you scrabbling for the pieces of your life, time and time again.

'Fuck you, easy road,' I whispered. 'I'll see you in hell.' Taking a final breath, I sunk well below the surface, glancing up before fiercely kicking my legs, thrusting forward.

Richard Dreyfuss would have been proud.

## 37

### DISCO DAVE

'Where is he?' Stephen asked, competing with the bass as if expecting the Saturday night crowd to hold the answer. Desi had slipped off to meet a DJ he had styled for a photoshoot, a quick 'cocktail' before joining us at the back of the Dog Star in Brixton on a sticky leather sofa that had seen better decades. Condensation trickled down the windows as the venue geared up for an evening of Ibiza anthems crossed with a sneaky whirl of techno trance. This was the pre-evening warm up before swapping one den of iniquity for Love Muscle at the Fridge, a packed arena of men coiled like springs ready to launch into the rest of the weekend. Poor Stephen wasn't quite sure what he was letting himself in for.

'D'you think Desi's OK?' he asked. 'I mean, what happened today was awful. I'm not sure I'd be OK. It was bad enough Grandpa denying our existence and trying to kill us, but he was so racist.'

'I don't know is the honest answer,' I said. 'Our grandfather is a bigot. I knew he was dreadful before, just didn't realise the depths of nastiness dwelling there.' I'd turned it over all the way home even though Desi assured us he was fine.

'I've been called worse than a darkie,' Desi had said lightly, staring out of the train window, the passing countryside smeared into thick green stripes. 'I'll live.'

I'd silently taken his hand and squeezed it.

'We may as well have another drink if he's going to be properly late,' I added, checking my watch for the millionth time. 'He's probably getting off with that DJ as we speak. What do you want?'

I fought through the boisterous crowd, each person desperate to grab the bartenders' attention. When someone tapped me on the shoulder, I disregarded it as an accident of the scrum. But no, a more insistent prod.

'Cordelia Franks, is that you?' The music thumped louder by the bar but I definitely heard that. I reluctantly turned round, certain the red-haired lad was going to serve me next.

'David? David Plimpton?' I was hit with an unholy wave of déjà vu. 'Oh my God, it's you!' A glitter ball cast spells above our heads.

'Ta daaah!' He grinned over the shoulders of the man crushed between us who was single-mindedly forcing his way past without any grace at all.

'Do you want me to get you a drink?' I asked as the man jabbed an elbow in my ribs, levering himself past. 'I'm in pole position.'

David laughed as I crashed into his chest, spat out of the running by the ruthless horde. He gripped my arms, steadying me. 'I think you just got ousted.'

It was unbearable to meet his eyes, so I focused on his mouth. I'd forgotten about his dimples. He dropped his hands to his sides.

'I didn't know you lived in London,' he said, leaning into my ear, his warm breath prickling my neck. A subtle waft of Acqua Di Gio tickled my nostrils; Reggie bathed in it daily. I pulled away and glanced over at the door just in case Desi made an entrance.

'I don't; I'm visiting Stephen and my cousin, you remember Derek?'

He shook his head.

'No, I don't think you met him actually. Well, he and Stephen live here and we're on a night out.'

'Where'd you dump your coats?' He wriggled his Schott bomber jacket off his shoulders, swinging it round into his hands.

'In the back. What are you doing here?'

'A friend's birthday, private party upstairs. Thought I'd take a drink up. Never been up there before – I think there's a bar?'

'No idea. This is my first time.'

He smiled properly. 'What are the chances of that? I normally go out in Clapham.'

David was more man than boy now, his shoulders broader, his sandy hair styled with some blokey wax product flogged by footballers. Why oh why did my brain choose that exact moment to silently stream footage of us having frantic teenage sex in his bedroom, Damon Albarn turning a blind eye? God, we'd known how to turn each other on with just a look some days. No one else since had quite measured up. I flinched. *Could he read my mind?* It was disconcerting when the past annexed the present without my consent.

'Do you want to come and say hello to Stephen? If you remember him?' I asked hastily, pushing back towards where we'd camped, his reply drowned out under the music. Stephen jumped up, excited, his face dropping the minute he realised David wasn't our cousin.

'Have you seen him?' he asked, distrustfully eyeing David.

'Nope. This is David Plimpton from school. Do you remember him?'

'Vaguely.' Stephen paused. 'Were you the one that wore shorts?'

'I see I'll never live that one down,' David said good naturedly. 'Let me get you guys a drink. I'll pop upstairs and be right back – think it'll be quicker than getting served down here.' He eyed our empty Amstel bottles. 'The same again?'

'We should go,' Stephen said as soon as David disappeared. 'Go back to the flat in case he's left a message.'

'David's getting us a drink.'

'He was just being polite – couldn't get away quick enough.'

'Only because you mentioned the shorts!'

'Be thankful I didn't say is he the one you lost your virginity to!'

'Stephen! You're annoying when you've had a few beers.'

'You're just annoying.'

'At least I didn't lose mine on the bread rolls out the back of Zippins on my lunch break. Doesn't Laura have two kids now? Just think, that could have been you.'

'Ha, no, thank fuck. The smell of fresh bread's been ruined for life.'

I playfully punched him. We waited five minutes and when it appeared David really wasn't returning, we surrendered our pitch to a group of circling girls in matching baggy jeans and neon crop tops, each pierced with a silver belly-button ring. I coveted their confidence.

David's surprise entrance didn't immediately land. The botched abortion lay hidden beneath an assortment of unexciting crap. Other people (Sarah and Michelle) would have worked towards something more robust than a tenuous job in the local cinema to paper over such trauma. In reverse, I sat at the back of Screen One on quiet Monday afternoons, sinking into a comforting romcom, or a thrilling heist film, or an indie flick starring some unknown actors on the cusp of greatness. I wasn't delusional, the stories didn't mirror my life, but digging deep into any film narrative, there was generally a tiny kernel of truth you could bundle up as your own. I found that a consolation of sorts.

I jostled my way through the Dog Star's writhing crowd, shoving people out of the way to reach the door. Once outside, I gulped down mouthfuls of London air before bending over, hands on knees as if I'd just run a marathon.

'Bloody hell, you almost flattened some woman,' Stephen said moments later as he joined me on the corner, a fat full moon throwing dramatic shadows down sly alleyways where anything could happen. 'What's wrong?'

'Nothing, let's go. I'm worried about Desi.' I waited for Stephen to take the lead; I was born without a compass in my head. We were halfway down the adjacent backstreet before I heard him.

'Cordelia! Wait! I got you some beers.'

Stephen stopped.

'Keep going,' I hissed.

'But it's David. Don't you want to say goodbye?'

'Not really. I changed my mind.'

Stephen carried on walking, but a third set of footsteps echoed along the pavement.

'Hey, wait up.'

Stephen stopped and glared at me, giving me no choice but to grind to a halt.

'You ran off. I don't blame you; I got trapped talking to some dullard upstairs.'

I bit my lip. 'Sorry, David, we really need to go. Our cousin might be in trouble and we need to make sure he's OK.' An amber street lamp illuminated his hair like stage lights. *Arise, fair sun, and kill the envious moon...*

'Is there anything I can do to help? Do you want me to come with you?'

'Yes tha—' Stephen began.

'No, we're OK. You're in the middle of a party.'

'They're just people from work. I don't really know them that well. Another friend was supposed to meet me but he bailed. Any excuse to leave to be honest.'

'Sorry, David, but we need to get on,' I said firmly.

His face drooped. 'Fair dos. I guess I won't see you around if you don't live up here.'

'No, I guess not.'

'I'm down all the time to visit my dad. You still there?'

'Yes.'

'Might be nice to meet up for a drink?'

'Sure.'

'I'll let you get on. Hope your cousin's OK.'

'Thanks, bye, David.'

Stephen waved as he headed back up the street. I turned on my heel, shot through with shame.

'That was a bit harsh,' Stephen hissed as we turned up another side road running parallel to the Ritzy. The flat lay up ahead within a wonky, Victorian, red-bricked terrace straight out of a Roald Dahl story. Stephen let us in and we took the stairs two at a time to the top-floor flat where empty beer cans and a giant pizza box balanced on the coffee table. His flatmates were out.

Stephen dialled 1571.

'There's five messages. We never have messages!'

## 38

---

# THE CHANNEL

My chest seared as I cleaved my way beneath the bricolage of crap. I glanced only once into the sepulchre depths. Anticipating an imminent break in the relentless canopy, I'd counted in elephants, clawing my way towards a promising shaft of light. So far, I'd swum for sixty of the beasts, arms spread wide, scooping my passage through the water. As I initiated a new round of elephants, I glimpsed to the left; *Boudica*'s hull drew level twenty or so metres away, the rib smacking along the surface behind, a trail of fizzing water in her wake. Face forward, twenty-five elephants. Burning. I expelled the last of the bubbles. This was it; I had to breathe – churchly light penetrated the gloom up ahead. There were no sharps or ghost nets, just a loose tail of bags fringing the dregs of the plastic clot; I could clear it.

Almost.

As my fingers broke the surface, I surged face first into a white bag. I couldn't even scream because it melded to my lips, suctioning my airway shut before I grappled it away, inhaling a huge breath, promptly vomiting tea all down my chin.

I swam towards *Boudica*, Desi jubilantly jumping up and down on deck, waving his hands. I focused on my own rasping breath, on the blood hammering between my ears; my body throbbed in ways it hadn't half an hour ago. Stress carved up muscles, cramping them, restricting the lungs, speeding up the heart – a perfect storm for death by drowning. I whipped out an earplug.

'You did it! Are you OK?' Desi called, his face searching mine. *Boudica* began her gradual U-turn towards France, guiding me past the remnants of the plastic island and back on course across the Northeast Shipping Lane. Another floating citadel loomed in front, this time with yellow, red and blue sea containers, a cheerier colour combination. Its waves rolled like hills, scooping me up and away from

*Boudica*'s trail. With no energy to answer, my fragility was almost on a par with the time Desi had rescued me from my first year at university.

I repaid the favour three years later, by rescuing the fuckwit right back...

*Head down, four strokes, breathe out. Bubbles.*

## 39

## OPERATION BREAKOUT

The taxi slowed to a crawl; we peered owlishly towards the house numbers, tricky to decipher in the dark.

'I think it's here, thank you!' I called from the back seat. Number seven Shamrock Street, as expressed to BT 1571 answering service in escalating panic over five successive phone calls. We hopped out onto the pavement; the cab drove off. It had just begun to drizzle. As the rest of the street slept (it was way past midnight) I gingerly pushed open the front gate, stoically hanging on by a lone hinge.

'Desi!' I called up to the top floor front window. 'DESI!? We're here!'

The net curtains twitched before a hand scrabbled them aside, revealing Desi helplessly pressing his palms on the glass, a ghost in the attic.

'You need to open the window.' He signalled that he hadn't the faintest idea how. 'They're sash windows. You have to slide them up?' I gestured with my hands. 'Fuck, how are we going to get him out? He can't work this out. He's going to be trapped there for the whole bloody night.'

'Is that such a bad thing?' Stephen genuinely asked.

'Stephen! What if the guy's taken something and never wakes up, and Desi gets embroiled in some kind of murder investigation? We need to get him out of there now.'

'Then we call the police, wake up the neighbours?'

'No way! It's too dramatic... Think, Cordelia, think!'

Desi banged on the window, cupping a hand to his ear, then shouted through the glass. 'The frame's warped – it won't open.' His voice struggled against the noise from the high street a few roads away, sirens and horns contending with each other in a wall-to-wall urban symphony.

'Shit, he really is trapped. Maybe he could try the

window above the doorway, assuming that's in the same flat?'

'You could climb up and talk to him clearly, work something out?' Stephen suggested.

'Climb up how?'

'The tree.' A mature tree in next-door's garden leaned eagerly towards number seven from across the fence, its sturdy branches brushing the narrow window ledge. 'How exactly did you think he was going to get down in the first place? Jump all that way? It's quite a drop.'

'OK, you climb up and talk to him.'

'Fuck off, no way. You know I hate heights.' Stephen pulled a face.

'I haven't climbed a tree since I was a kid.'

'And I have?'

'Fucks sake.' I shrugged off my fake fur jacket. 'Hold this.' I waved at Rapunzel in his tower. 'I'm coming up!'

Fifteen minutes later, instead of moving closer to freeing Desi, we now had another problem.

'I can't get any higher, it feels like the branches'll snap, it's too slippy.' I was wedged a third of the way up a major branch that had opted to grow towards number seven.

'They won't, you don't weigh very much; it can take it.'

'Now is not the time to try and boost my self-esteem!'

Desi banged on the glass. 'I'm not climbing a tree!'

'You may have to!' I shouted back at him. 'How else you gonna escape?'

'All this for a fumble on the sofa!' Stephen mocked.

'Go and shake him awake!' I urged. 'He might have come round now?'

'I just did; he's dead to the world.' Desi pawed the glass like a cat.

'He's not actually dead, is he?'

'I don't know. I don't want to find out.'

'Shouldn't you check?'

'I found an empty packet of Xanax in his pocket – explains a lot.'

'We could wake the neighbours? See if they have a key?'

'Are you kidding me? Black male locked in white guy's flat while he's comatose. The cops'll be here in seconds, bang me up.'

'I'm assuming you've looked everywhere for the

keys, even the bread bin? Mum always puts them there.'

'Yes, Cordy, they're nowhere.' Distress stretched Desi's eyes to the far corners of his face.

'Can you open the window in the room next door?'

'Have you seen the drop?'

I nodded. It was worth a try. As I fruitlessly flicked through fantastical getaways (stealing a ladder, borrowing a trampoline) a car abruptly stopped in the street below.

'Stephen?' a familiar voice called as someone climbed out of the car. 'Where's Cordelia?'

'David?' An irrational rush of relief surged through my chest.

'Where are you?' he shouted, swivelling his head.

'She's up the tree,' Stephen said, jabbing a finger in my direction.

Desi knocked on the glass. 'What's going on?'

'David's here!' I cried.

Desi shrugged – *who*?

'What are you doing here?'

'I live round the corner: Clapham Manor Street. Stephen here was looking very shifty.'

Stephen relayed our current predicament in succinct detail. 'We've yet to work out a rescue plan.'

'Have you tried waking up the neighbours? They might have a spare key.'

'We'd rather not.'

David strode over to the parched bay tree in a cracked terracotta pot standing guard to the left of the front door and tipped it up to one side.

'Thought there might be a key underneath. We sometimes leave one there if we've gone out and don't want to lose it.' His eyes crinkled in concentration before an idea unfolded. 'I think you just need to smash the glass.'

After I hung out of the tree, then slipped into David's open arms a few metres below, Desi bashed the windowpane with the bathroom steel peddle bin like *Buffy the Vampire Slayer* smashing her way out of danger. However, Buffy wouldn't have screwed her eyes tightly shut, screaming like the teenage girl she was. She was as hard as nails.

Desi scrambled onto the interior window ledge, squeaking, 'Oh my God, oh my God,' on repeat for a solid two minutes while bashing all the remaining shards of glass into the garden, where they tinkled like caustic snowflakes.

'Bend over like you're rowing and grab the nearest branch as if it's an oar, then launch yourself off, swinging like a gymnast,' David calmly instructed. 'You can drop down – I'll catch you... It'll be OK.'

'Who the fuck's this guy?' Desi asked, his eyebrows kissing each other.

'David, from school. Now just do as he says,' I called up, panic boiling my throat. 'Hurry, Desi, I think the neighbours have noticed.' Lights had started flicking on in surrounding houses, and a bleary face poked from behind a closed curtain at number nine before disappearing again.

'I don't think I can. It's too far down.'

'You're using the branch as a bar to swing down from, just like when you were a kid in the playground,' David assured him, his unruffled delivery spot on.

'What sort of fucking playground did you go to?'

'Desi!' I pleaded. 'Just do it.'

'I'm not a fucking Nike advert.' Desi balanced, leaning over twice, then immediately withdrew. 'I can't reach.'

'Crouch lower,' David suggested, 'then tilt forward and rest your hands on the branch below, gripping it hard, then let the rest of your body follow.'

'I can't.'

'Fucks sake.' I wished I could do it for him.

'Breathe in and then—' David stopped mid-sentence.

'Sirens,' Stephen said frankly. 'It's now or—'

Desi tipped forward like a novice facing the parallel bars and grabbed the branch below his feet, jumping a little bit too enthusiastically from the ledge, his propulsion coupled with his weight snapping the branch so he hit the one underneath, breaking his fall, all the while still gripping the first branch that had now lodged itself in the foliage, leaving him hanging like a bird feeder four metres above the ground.

'Let go!' David shouted. 'I've got you!'

His hands slipped off and David caught him, both of them tumbling over backwards into a bush. David clambered up, hauling Desi to standing.

'Follow me!' David sprinted out of the garden, the sirens ricocheting off the houses as they drew closer. Just as we turned the corner, the whole street illuminated like a prison break. We ran, chests on fire until we reached David's house which really was just around the corner.

* * *

'Do you want neat rum? That's all I have.' David rummaged about in the back of a kitchen cupboard, bottles clinking. Considering three boys lived in the house, it wasn't Satan's armpit. Stephen's flat had crossed the borders of acceptable basic health and safety levels with daily mouse droppings audaciously plopped along the kitchen counters and the brazen appearance of the chief mouse baiting the house-mates by running the gauntlet across the TV cabinet during *EastEnders*. It was a wonder none of them had caught the plague.

'We'll have whatever you've got,' Stephen answered for everyone, Desi and I still in shock.

'And you don't think the police saw us?' Desi asked. 'I can't get pinned for something I didn't do. I'll get thrown out of the country.'

'You won't, Desi; you're a British citizen,' I assured him. 'Anyway, he wasn't dead. You were trapped in his flat. If anyone's to blame, it's him for kidnapping you against your will!'

'I can't believe I jumped out of a window,' he said dreamily, in awe of his own achievements.

'I can't believe you went back to someone's house who'd taken a load of sleeping pills,' Stephen said. 'What did you think was going to happen?'

'I didn't know he'd taken Xanax. He'd done back-to-back nights DJing with no sleep when I met him at the Ku Bar. He looked fine.'

'*You* look like a scarecrow.' I leaned over the table and picked leaves from his hair. 'Did he at least suck the salami?'

'Cordy,' Stephen gasped, 'don't be gross!'

'It's OK, I'm used to it,' Desi laughed. 'No, Cordelia, I was stranded with my pants down when he passed out in the gusset.'

I spat rum across the table, hitting Stephen in the face.

\* \* \*

'Here's my number,' Stephen said, handing it to David scribbled on a Chinese takeaway menu, the cab waiting in the road, engine ticking over. 'Ring tomorrow. We're around.'

'Thanks.'

'No, thank you,' Desi cooed. 'I'm taking you for lunch, my treat. Just call Stephen in the morning so we can arrange.' He hugged David tightly. 'You saved my life!'

'I don't—'

'Zip it, you did! See you tomorrow!'

'Bye,' I said, uncertain how I felt. Not unhappy,

I'd go with that. 'Thanks, David. You're a complete star.'

We shuffled into the back seat; I waved.

'Right, if he isn't your boyfriend after this, then I'm disowning you,' Desi said.

'What? No!'

'Don't "what no" me. David from school. I remember him. He sent that Christmas card. I told you he liked you back then. He's a fucking legend after tonight.'

'Agreed,' Stephen said.

'I don't want a boyfriend.'

'Whatever.' Desi waved his hand in dismissal. 'Just be friends with him then. We need him in our lives!'

'It's complicated,' I eventually admitted as we pulled out onto Clapham High Street, drunks all but throwing themselves under the wheels of the cab.

'Still think you should give him a chaaaaance,' Desi said, yawning at the same time.

'He hasn't aaaaasked for one.' The yawns were contagious.

'I think he did,' Stephen said, losing the battle of the yawns, 'and he just paaaaaaassed the test.'

# 40

## THE CHANNEL

Even with fatigue restricting my stroke and lungs burning from the underwater diversion, I smiled magnanimously at the many faces fear projected, desperate to trap me in permanent stasis.

'It'll take over my life; I won't be able to do anything else. It's such a massive undertaking and it takes so long to train for,' I'd complained when Desi prodded me yet again about the Channel challenge. 'Never mind that I'm scared, it'll be exhausting, and er, hello – SHARKS!'

'There are no sharks in the English Channel. Not killer ones.'

'I don't have time.'

Desi had pressed his lips together and raised his eyebrows, but didn't say another word.

The truth was, I couldn't stop thinking about The Swim. Fantasies swirled in idle moments of staggering ashore exhausted to rousing applause, someone slipping a wreath around my neck (it's *my* daydream – wreaths are permissible!), until the thrill ricocheting through my chest every time I entertained the idea had become as addictive as that one womb-jangling shag you'd exchange your dog for. *Sorry, Kev*. David's 5 a.m. knee trembler just beneath the sea wall still topped the leader board even now, the jeopardy factor scoring high on the orgasmic Richter scale.

When I eventually folded, the shove came from a surprising source.

'I got you this.' Mum handed me a purple box, an electric shaver on the front.

'Is it another vibrator?'

'Cordelia! Why do you always have to be so crude? It's a jumper debobbler.'

'Why?'

'So you can have bobble-free jumpers.'

'I like the bobbles.'

'No one likes the bobbles, don't be ridiculous.'

Mum sighed. 'Look, if you're going to buy into the Journal Co and become a director, you need to be smart at all times.'

'Jesus Christ.'

One Saturday afternoon, hours before a Bumble date with a man called Christopher (roasted his own coffee beans bought wholesale from Peru), I found myself elbow-deep in a pile of snaggled, bobbly jumpers with old favourite, *The Shawshank Redemption,* on the TV. A fitting backdrop for such a laborious task. Tackling my second jumper, the bobbles resisting like tenacious dandelions rooted in a bowling green, I was suddenly thrown off track when erudite Andy Dufresne (dependable Tim Robbins) reminded me I'd better get busy living or get busy dying – his sure-fire way of surviving prison.

I looked up from my Zara pink and orange striped cardigan, one arm practically bobble-free, the debobbler impatiently buzzing, eager to guzzle more fluff.

'What the fuck am I doing?' I hurled the debobbler across the room where it hit the wall. The back pinged off, pink fuzz exploding all over the carpet. I texted Desi.

CORDELIA

Fuck it, I'm in.

DESI

That's good cos I've already worked out your training plan.

CORDELIA

How did you know?

DESI

Because I know you, Cordelia Francesca Franks. Better than you know yourself.

\* \* \*

I'd made good progress across the Swimmers' Graveyard, a hint of French coastline bobbing on the hazy horizon. I forced myself back to *The Shawshank Redemption* and away from my creaking body. I punched every other stroke through the water with clenched fists, overthrowing the technique police cracking the whip at the back of my mind. As well as all the swimming and running, every pull up, bicep curl, press up, every relentlessly executed Bulgarian split squat distilled into this moment underpinning my resolve. The thorniest of all the battles had in reality required the least amount of effort.

'Cordy, you know you'll have to put on a bit of weight to swim the Channel.' Desi had pulled his wide-mouthed frog expression that preceded awkward exchanges.

'So, you've left it until after I booked my crossing to tell me?'

'I didn't want anything to put you off.'

I'd stared over the road from the café towards the beach. Day trippers, babies in buggies, dogs on leads, the standard Saturday-morning crowd.

'You don't *have to* put on any weight – it's not in the rules! It's supposed to make the swim more bearable. The cold is one of the biggest obstacles and the more...' he winced, 'insulation you have... the warmer you'll stay and potentially have a better chance of finishing. It's also good to be able to pull on reserves.'

Through the window, a young mum hitched a baby up her hip while pushing a toddler on a scooter, its helmet so bulky, the child's neck looked in danger of snapping. I'd seen Michelle one of these Saturdays, walking along the prom with her mum, who must be in her seventies now, same as my own mum, both still engaged in a perennial battle of the bulge.

'Just because I'm in my autumn years doesn't mean I should take my foot of the gas, Cordelia. You stay on top of your appearance and weight, you stay on top of life... No one *needs* to eat cake; it's just pure greed.' But castigatory denial had begun hollowing out Mum's cheeks like sunken Victoria sponges, meatless twig arms protruding from her Boden Breton striped T-shirt. Thankfully, Aunty Liz arrived in time.

Two willowy teenage girls dawdled behind Michelle and her mother, phones in hand, ignoring the beautiful sunny day, their attention likely focused on some unattainable ideal of physical perfection subliminally streamed on Instagram or TikTok via innocuous posts about knitting your own disco wig from plastic bags, how to make body scrub out of cat litter or untold baking soda beauty hacks claiming to transform one's life (they don't, I've tried them all). Either that or they were hooked into videos of cats riding robot vacuums. I'd wanted to hop across the road, snatch the phones from the girls' hands and throw them into the sea. But who was I to judge? I didn't have children, so was completely unqualified. All I knew was that things may have been very different if...

'OK.' I hit the café table with my hand.

'OK, what?' Desi asked, his eyes engaged in a smile his lips were uncertain about.

'I'll do whatever it takes.' I picked up the café menu, scanning it. I'd already had an oat milk latte and a round of wholegrain sourdough toast with a regimental scraping of butter, my Saturday-morning ritual while Tim was at the gym and Desi and I took Kevin for a walk. 'I'll have a scone with jam, but no cream, only because I don't actually like cream. And another coffee, please.'

Desi bent over the table and kissed my cheek, his eyes glittering. 'Whatever madam wants, madam shall have.'

Kevin barked; I bent down and tickled his ears.

* * *

My clicking shoulders heaved me through the Channel, the comfortable half a stone carrying me past exhaustion in a meditative state. 1997, the new flat in Brixton, David had rented *The Shawshank Redemption* from Blockbusters – he still hadn't seen it. This would be my fourth viewing – Desi and I were obsessed. The film's plodding narrative and bleakness sang to my own eternally cached battle. It plucked strings I didn't realise I had, serving up tears and a pledge to be more adventurous once the credits rolled. But a week later, tentative plans to enrol on the Brighton Met film studies course would have been invariably filed away, unease creeping with its own voice: *you'll just fail again.*

*Head down, four strokes, breathe out. Bubbles.*

## 41

### 1997 AND THE SHAWSHANK REDEMPTION

'I can't believe you're going out with David. Cheeks!' Michelle said when we met up at the BFI along the Southbank, conveniently midway between Brixton and Notting Hill where Michelle lived in a basement flat with Sarah and two other girls.

'I know. I'm as shocked as you,' I laughed along.

I topped up Michelle's Rioja while people milled around in scarf-tangled groups, awaiting the next showing of *It's a Wonderful Life*. I was bringing David tomorrow, another film I could introduce as a cherished family member; meanwhile, he'd yet to meet my actual parents.

Life's mundanity transformed because of David. Boring job? No worries, fall in love and you too will enthusiastically scrape chewing gum from swirly nylon carpets without stabbing your boss. Still living at home with a domineering mother? Swipe aside that concern by falling in love – even Joan Crawford's coat hangers won't sting when she belts them across your naked back.

I hadn't socialised with Michelle and Sarah since they'd graduated university; our lives had swerved in opposite directions. Namely, I'd stayed in East-bourne, they had not. If they visited the multiplex, we always exchanged banter and more often than not, they'd gallantly ask me to join them for a drink. My rebuffs eventually hit home.

Michelle's cheeks were now a tad fuller, thighs thicker – no doubt the toll of surviving weekly hang-overs with intravenous takeaways. Just like the calorie bubbles, unbidden observations about oth-ers' appearances burst their way into my head on a regular basis, like an ungracious aunty who had set-tled down with a bowl of popcorn, passing judge-ment. *That extra roast potato will inflate those bingo wings... Sarah's arse wasn't the size of a small caravan last time you saw her...* I was literally powerless to stop it.

'How did you and David come about?' Michelle asked.

'I bumped into him when I was up visiting Stephen at uni and then he asked me out. I said no. We stayed in touch as friends, having the odd drink whenever he visited his dad. Then he turned up at my house in December on my day off and took me to Brighton. I don't know, something clicked, we had such a laugh and ended up snogging on the pier next to the rollercoaster. We've been together ever since.'

'Wow, a year.' Michelle whistled through her teeth. 'What's he doing now?'

'Sales and Marketing for Vodafone. Does pretty well for himself – he never went to uni either. Bought a flat in Brixton six months ago. It's inspired me to sort my bloody life out, apply for uni again.'

'That's great, when are you doing that?'

'Now, if I want to start next September. Part time at UCL and work at the same time. It was David's idea.'

'So you'll move in together?'

I wanted to spend every waking moment in his bed; our bodies clicked together like a Barbara Hepworth sculpture I'd seen in the Tate. But if I moved in? The very concept furred up my throat like the bad case of tonsillitis I'd caught last month.

'I don't know. We'll have to wait and see.'

'Well, I'm happy for you,' Michelle said, smiling.

'Tracey Bates got married to someone in the year above during the summer. You could be next!'

'It's a bit early for that!' Hadn't we only just finished school?

'Well, it was a happy coincidence bumping into you in Paperchase. I'm sorry we lost touch.'

'No, don't be silly, it was me. I found everything a bit too much back then, dropping out... It was easier to just not... you know.'

'I get it. But you're on the up now! David's obviously making you very happy. Sarah was gutted she was away this weekend. Let's do this again, the three of us!'

'I'll drink to that!' By the second glass, the tannins typically peppered my taste buds, the wine slipping down like velvet. Peculiarly not this time. Red was usually my favourite – it was David's too. He'd taken me to a wine tasting in Clapham Oddbins and instead of spitting in the bucket alongside everyone else, we had swallowed every mouthful, discounting grape variety and soil acidity. We rolled home drunk and if it hadn't been for upstairs' pizza delivery, we would have almost certainly ended up in a threesome with the tatty fire blanket hanging in the communal hallway.

* * *

Andy Dufresne, a new inmate, paces the yard at Shawshank State Prison, observed by Red (reverential Morgan Freeman), an old hand lifer, the same as Andy. Red's the prison 'fixer': if you want it, he can source it. Andy enquires about a Rita Hayworth poster and a small rock hammer, with which to carve a chess set from small stones scavenged from the prison yard. Red's success drives the two to become firm friends, Red narrating Andy's harrowing journey from the violent early years of his incarceration. Drifting slowly on the chronicle of their interminable prison sentences, the characters flourish like latent images in a developer bath, drawing us in to the minutiae of their world.

I held my breath, even with the outcome no surprise.

'Do you like it?' I leant over, pressing my hand on David's thigh while he spooned Häagen-Dazs Cookies and Cream into his mouth straight from the carton. I opened mine wide and he curled up an impressive scoop, scooting closer so it didn't drip on the sofa.

'Brain freeze!' I pressed my tongue to the roof of my mouth.

'I don't like it, I love it, almost as much as you.' David tapped my nose with the spoon, leaving a cold splodge which he dutifully licked off before kissing my lips.

'I love you too.' My stomach backflipped at words I'd never thought myself capable of saying, least of all feeling. After cynicism pinned me down during my latter teenage years, I believed that all the romance films I'd devoured at the back of the Multiplex touted lies and no one really experienced love. It was merely a mythical construct to keep people in their place, a commodity to be traded in, to be gambled with, to coerce people to do your bidding. I mistrusted the concept of true love eliminating anxiety or turning you into a hero willing to walk over broken glass for the object of your affection. Or that it could jam open your heart like a ruptured dam, love flooding the plains of your being, affecting everyone you encountered. My parents had *never* felt this.

Meanwhile, innocent ex-accountant Andy Dufresne played the long game, creating a life on his terms within the oppressive walls of Shawshank. He increased meaning in his snail-paced existence, seeking pockets of joy not just for him, but for the prison population at large. He made lemonade when life doled out a knuckle full of dirt.

Revisiting *Shawshank* with David reframed the story; previously overlooked narrative nuances magically burst from the screen. Being In Love meant I was able to fully interpret the world. But watching unteachable old dog, Brooks, hang himself after release on parole, the fear of inchoate freedom skinning him alive, my scalp pricked as if someone had walked on my grave, and I turned away, unable to witness his body jerking from the light fitting. Not long after, Andy Dufresne makes his decades-in-the-orchestration escape inside the prison sewer pipe after diligently chiselling a hole (concealed behind his Hollywood starlet poster that shifted with the seasons) through his cell wall with his blunted rock hammer. Turns out anything is possible with enough determination and a bar of soap.

\* \* \*

Time spent with David burst the incipient calorie bubbles. Life shifted, wandering hand in hand through Hyde Park or visiting Chinatown indulging in previously cordoned off deep-fried blowouts.

'I love it when we're out with Desi and I'll look at

you across the pub and know exactly what you're thinking,' David said on more than one occasion.

'What am I thinking, apart from everyone's a fuck-boring Womble and you're the only man for me?'

'That you'd like to disappear into the toilet and shag me up against the cubical door.'

'Is that right?' Inevitably, we would tumble into a knot of limbs and recreate the bathroom scenario to my exact specifications. We'd once had a quickie in a phone box on Clapham Common, knocking the receiver from its cradle, coming to the stabbing of the disconnected beeps. Nowhere, it seemed, was off limits, not even David's desk at work. I wallowed in our shared puerility, relieved he still found farts hilarious because it was physically impossible holding them in for a whole weekend.

We didn't automatically pick up where we had left off, for one, we were older, but we melted into each other's inner worlds as easily as if we'd shared a womb (or a prison cell), the shorthand of communal schooldays coming almost as close. I could be my inane self with David like I could with Desi and Stephen. Some mornings, we'd lie in bed playing our version of *Call My Bluff* with his ancient Oxford Medical Dictionary. It was his mum's (she had been a nurse). Her name graced the title page: Helen Reynolds. 'Her maiden name,' David explained, drawing his finger over the faded ink. 'I like knowing she used it all the time. Her finger-prints will be all over the pages.' Mum would most likely bequeath me a lifetime's supply of nause-ating weight-loss bars and her collection of dodgy Lycra unitards, the gussets not stretching past my knees.

'Don't you think it's funny that most of the weirder words either sound like cars or women's names?' I observed. 'Fibula? Aureole?'

'I've just seen a Ford Clitoris for sale, one careful lady owner and only ten thousand miles on the clock.' David joined in.

'I've just met a woman called Epiglottis; she was choking on a biscuit crumb. I had to do the Heimlich manoeuvre. Saved her life,' I batted back.

David chuckled, carefully leafing through the Bs, so as not to tear the flimsy pages.

'I just met a woman called Bulimia, ew no, gross, anyway—'

I jumped up from the bed.

'What's wrong?'

'I don't want to play any more.' I wrapped a towel around my naked body and headed straight for the bathroom, locking the door. It was all too easy to forget that I was actually somebody else.

'I love that you're not always obsessing about diets like every bloody girl in my office. Honestly, it's so boring!'

Shame gripped me in its teeth like a dog with an old bone. David loved all of me, but what about the parts he couldn't see? The minute I stepped on that Eastbourne train, heart heavy with longing watching grey concrete blossom into trees and fields, calorie bubbles emerged in an artful deception as if they'd never disappeared at all.

'I still think you should do that film studies degree,' David said as *Shawshank*'s credits rolled, stroking my hair. 'You're wasted working in the multiplex.'

\* \* \*

I wiped my mouth with a fistful of bunched-up toilet paper and walked back to my post in the ticket office, legs wobbling.

'You OK?' Sunita asked as she opened the office door. 'You're awfully pale.'

'I think I ate something dodgy for breakfast. It didn't agree with me.'

'Oh, I get like that after fish fingers. If you don't cook them past the watery stage, my stomach turns. They have to be super crispy.'

'I hear you. I hate being sick,' I replied, my badge of honour pinned firmly to my chest, a reassurance that no matter what had gone before, I'd transcended the past. Nonetheless, unscheduled puking was peculiar.

\* \* \*

'Right, our mum's strange, just so you know.' I chewed my lip. David had driven down Christmas Eve and we'd met at the Lamb on Eastbourne high street.

'The build up's been impressive – I'll be disappointed if she's completely normal. Will she make me do an endurance plank? I've been practicing.'

'She's the Devil in a lace dress,' Stephen said, picking up his cider.

'I love that!' Desi laughed. 'I know she's got her issues but she's not as bad as you think she is.'

'She is,' Stephen said flatly. 'Now I've left home, I can see I had Stockholm Syndrome. She's not right. She contributed to—'

'OK, Stephen, that's enough,' I warned. 'I'm sorry

it's taken so long to meet her, David. But I think it's safe to say she would have mentioned something on the radio if I hadn't asked you to come round.'

'She'll ask if you want to see her do the splits,' Stephen said, uncowed. 'She's still not recovered from GMTV jilting her for being too old.'

'Right, let's get this over with.' Dad and Netty were on their way. 'Mum's doing a whole let's pretend we're all friends when we know she hates Annette. We've never all been in the same room at once,' I explained. 'Why, God, why?' Mum was definitely exploiting David's introduction. Something was afoot.

'Because it makes her look good!' Stephen said. 'Why else does she do anything?'

'You two! At least your parents are here. Mom's on holiday in Mexico with her new squeeze! Er hello, how about a family reunion with your only son? Thank God for Aunty Lois I say!'

# 42

## LOIS

'Hello! You must be David. I can't believe Cordelia's been hiding you for a year. I thought she'd given up and become a lesbian like my sister.' Lois shuffled backwards behind the front door, theatrically waving everyone through like the Dorchester doorman. Lois adored the Dorchester; its jaw-dropping glamour and discreet service could not be beaten, apart from maybe Claridge's. Alvin, her agent, took her there whenever he had good news to deliver, his booming baritone assuring a captive audience; drama pulsed through his veins. At ninety-five calories a glass, she allowed herself three champagnes, if she only ordered the garden salad and overlooked the Devil's breadbasket. Alvin loyally polished off the remains of anything she didn't manage. She'd received the inside track at the Dorchester about TV-am having their licence revoked, Alvin gleefully announcing successor, GMTV's silver lining.

'Their words were they want to continue with the nation's favourite workout queen busting flab across the country. It's a golden handcuff deal.' He'd then lowered his voice. 'Gavin, the series producer, suggested a visit to Dr Sebagh on Harley Street. Apparently, he can inject your face with botulism to make you look younger.'

'Botulism? That's poison!' A step too far even for Lois.

'It's completely safe; everyone's been doing it for years. How do you think Joanna Lumley still looks twenty-nine? Anyway, it's part of your contract; they've agreed to pay for all procedures... Might give it a whirl myself!' Alvin had helped himself to a sizeable wedge of artisan bread as he topped up Lois's champagne before slapping on a paving-slab of butter, eating the entire hunk in three bites.

When it came to it, Lois didn't need to be told the end was coming. The fact had been cemented after Alvin had asked to meet at the Groucho on Dean Street one April morning last year. Earlier in the studio, she'd executed a particularly strenuous workout involving planking at the same time as touching nose to alternate knee ten times in a row whilst fighting to restrain from breaking wind. Lois detested bodily functions. She imagined herself on a par with the Queen. She had never seen her own mother so much as cough when she'd been younger.

'Bodily functions are for the lower classes, girls,' her mother preached to her and Liz one afternoon before deportment lessons in the drawing room. 'We keep them to ourselves. Better still, we ignore them. Breaking wind and belching are not necessary, unlike breathing. Just because they may want to come out, doesn't mean they should.'

Lois and Liz had dutifully nodded.

What class her parents determined themselves from was never fully clear. Money could certainly buy you the trappings of the upper class, but breeding and status remained as elusive as unconditional love. Lois wagered she'd been about six before deciding that from then onwards, she would deny herself the relief of letting anything apart from the absolutely necessary exit her body. The punishment for any slip ups was a sharp, hard clip around the ear. They soon learned. Of course it meant living with trapped wind sometimes almost as eviscerating as labour pains.

So that morning before her meeting with Alvin, as her rock-hard abs steered her through her punishing plank under the boiling studio lights, traitorous wind rumbled deep in her bowels. As her buttocks parted to complete the final move of right knee touching her nose, out it slipped, loud and proud walloping against the restrictive Lycra. There wasn't a day afterwards when she didn't receive fan mail from grannies to schoolgirls thanking her for farting live on television and normalising it.

'Normalising, my arse,' she'd muttered to Alvin on the phone. 'It's disgusting. I don't want to be remembered as the woman who broke wind on live TV.' But the public and the gutter press felt differently. Hosting her own mid-morning show on BBC Radio Sussex, *Your Coffee Break with Lois Franks,* callers occasionally mentioned it, and she had to laugh, though it pained her to. In the future, though Lois wouldn't yet know that, she would become an infamous internet meme. If only she could have copyrighted her own fart, she would have become a millionaire and none of this would have had to happen.

* * *

'Mum! I haven't been hiding him!' Cordelia snapped, her face alight. She'd always been dramatic, unlike Stephen who just got on with life. Just as well really – he was going to have to be a breadwinner one day and needed a level head.

'Hello, Mrs, er, Lois,' David bumbled. Honestly, had no one briefed the poor boy that she wasn't a Mrs but a Ms? And she'd kept Philip's name; it was better than reverting back to Simpson.

'Lois is fine, David. So pleased to meet you.' She leaned in to kiss him on both cheeks and caught a whiff of some young, trendy aftershave. Personally, she preferred Penhaligon's Blenheim Bouquet on a man. She'd unsuccessfully suggested that Phil wear it but he'd insisted on that football manager stench, Brut, from Boots. Funny how he'd changed since marrying Annette; it was like she'd rebooted him, switching him on and off, like Lois's blasted computer upstairs. She almost fancied him again with his groomed hair, tasteful aftershave, pressed shirts and dark suits. His silver Mercedes was an additional attraction, testament to his big promotion to the board as Sales Director. She'd fallen for the tortured, long-haired writer who could make her knickers fall to the floor with one smouldering glance. She'd loved waking up in his tiny Brighton bedsit that first year, before it went wrong, to find him clicking away on his knackered Olivetti, the keys jamming together when he was in frenzied focused flow, fingers flying, blind to everything apart from the words spilling from his head. She'd watch him for an hour against the backdrop of the window before he even noticed, his face in shadow.

Lois had not anticipated Phil remarrying; she herself was dead against the idea, not since she'd secured her own future. Why did she need a man? Her own father had cut her free in the wake of their separation. She'd known instantly it wasn't Phil who'd slipped up, of course it was Cordelia, testing the boundary. At the time, Lois had been terrified they would become destitute. She'd been siphoning off money to send to Liz as soon as Jeremy got sick in early eighty-two. Phil never asked why they had no money for fancy holidays or why the kids only had one pair of shoes. He knew where it went, Liz had been his friend first, but it was as if he didn't look past the end of his own nose. He never even blinked at all the time she spent at the blasted church. Then there was epicene Michael – wanted to leave his plain wife, abandon Jesus. That had never been the point! He'd been a filler, though she'd quite enjoyed the benign monotony of church, and the urgent fumbles in the cramped vestry next to the bins and his office at the Spar. They'd never had actual sex though. Michael had classed that as gold-plated adultery! Phil assumed she ran after men because she couldn't help herself. She was doing it for both of them, to keep the fizzling flame alive and the fortune in reach! She'd spent her entire childhood hiding, and then her entire marriage fighting to get noticed. They barely had sex after May passed; it was a miracle that Cordelia and Stephen were born at all.

Phil had offered to marry her, not even a murmur of abortion. She hadn't known what she wanted. To escape her family mostly, and how better to do that than by creating a new one? Her dad had played his ace in the end, trapping them both, with no get-out clause. Of course she could have walked away, washed her hands of her parents, and been free to be with whomever she wanted after she lost the baby. It wasn't the sixties any more, the eighties had rumbled along to the tune of freedom for all and greed is good. She knew Phil would take care of Cordelia and Stephen, but who was going to look after her sister and nephew in the long run with Jeremy's health declining and the US government acting like there wasn't a health crisis, cancelling people's medical insurance, tarring people with a brush they didn't deserve? Edward did his best, but he didn't earn enough to cover spiralling hospital bills and Liz was already working as a cleaner three evenings and a PA to some city slicker lawyer, burying her true self in case she got sacked, concealing Jeremy's illness for the exact same reason. The hope was one day, their parents would die and the inheritance would save them all. That ridiculously massive house, the horse, the house-clearance business, the antique hoard, all of that should keep everyone afloat for the rest of their lives.

As an only child, of course Phil didn't understand the sisters' dynamics or Lois' inherent desire to keep her sister from going under. It ran deeper than filial duty. He'd no idea what life had been like in Leicester, how they were paraded as the picture-perfect family to the entire village every Christmas when the Big House opened up to the locals, Cook making mulled wine and mince pies, while the sisters smiled and handed out cheap presents to all the children from under the magnificent tree.

The sisters shared a room because everywhere else was stuffed to bursting with a collection of rotating antiques filched from beneath the elderly's noses. In the school holidays, they slept in the same single bed until they were eleven and thirteen. Liz reading bedtime stories from the *Hamlyn Book of Fairy Tales* because no one else was going to. They had all the books, all the clothes, all the sugar and spice and all things nice, but no one to bear witness apart from the au pairs (so many the faces melded into one fleshy blob).

Dad sent them to private boarding once they reached eight ('You're a big girl now.'), then the plan was to marry them off to rich husbands. 'Someone else can take you on,' he'd said when Lois turned eighteen, as if he had been grafting at the parental coal face for the last two decades. Unpicking boarding school with Matron's liberal use of the steel ruler, the sub-zero isolation room, and the feudal hierarchy within the dog-eat-dog world would have kept a psychiatrist busy for years, had Lois not sunk it deep into her skeleton where not even she could recall what had been real and what felt like a harrowing film she'd watched with Liz one Christmas.

She had no idea why her parents had children at all – they were so besotted with each other, horses, Mum with her TV shows, and Dad with making money, leaving no scope for anything else. Had they been expecting sons? It was as if they'd lain in wait for her and Liz to snag the invisible tripwires so they could wash their hands of them once and for all. Of course if anyone had asked, they'd have a valid excuse: 'Those girls behaved like they'd been brought up in a brothel. We gave them the finest education and they threw it back in our faces.' She'd never make that mistake with her own kids.

Tidemarks remained from the panic that engulfed her when Liz announced she was following Sarah back to Chicago.

'There's a friend of hers, Jeremy, who needs a beard for work. I can marry him, get my green card. He asked me about having a baby too. Not sure what I think about that, but we could see how we get along with a turkey baster!'

Lois had feigned happiness, yet abandonment ate away at her. Liz had been her sister and mother rolled into one. She'd eventually only got pregnant again to fill the glaring gap Liz had left. She remained behind, tending the connection with their parents, keeping it to a bare minimum in order to pass Go, hoping to collect a bit more than two hundred pounds. Dad cutting her off was actually the best thing he could have done. Look at her now, reliant on no one. If she wanted sex, she could just ring one of the names in her little black book. Bill Fisher was still keen even after she'd brought their liaison to a close a few years ago. He'd kept asking her to marry him, putting a dampener on things. But since he'd finally lost the last remnants of hair (and his TV weatherman job), she'd gone off him completely, despite his generous manhood. He sold double glazing windows now in Sutton, trading on his weatherman status. *'Keep the cold at bay, every day.'* He'd even opened a village fete in Epsom last summer, rang to invite her along, they'd throw in a free cream tea and a Waitrose bottle of cava. Oh, how the mighty had fallen. She'd declined.

'What about dinner instead, just friends; I've got a property investment you might be interested in, just the right thing for someone with a bit of spare cash. We're doing the windows.'

\*\*\*

'You OK, Cordelia? You look a bit peaky,' Annette asked as Lois brought in the bottle of Moet she'd chilled in the fridge earlier. Annette had handed out the glasses from the silver tray on the dining-room table and passed round side plates and holly-print paper napkins for the Marks and Spencer mince pies, vegetarian mini quiches and pigs in blankets all laid out on two china serving platters next to the glasses.

'I'm OK, Netty. Thank you.'

'I've been asking her the same thing,' David said. 'She's not been feeling her best the last few weeks.'

Lois pursed her lips. She had her own ideas about what was going on with Cordelia. She was possibly about to fly the nest, move in with David, she knew the signs, but also knew her daughter. She had suspected Cordelia was up to something when she'd said she was visiting Stephen and Desi far too many times. She rang Stephen and asked to speak to Cordelia one evening, her cover immediately blown.

'Mum, I just want to keep David for me for a bit longer.'

'Are you embarrassed of him, Cordelia? You know I'm not like Grandma; you won't be in trouble for being with someone poor and unambitious.'

'Not at all! David's from school. His dad lives round the corner. And he's doing just fine. Lives in London, has a good job.'

'If you like him then I'm sure we all will.' Pity, she'd hoped he had been unambitious, keep Cordelia at home for a few years longer now Stephen was probably never coming back. She enjoyed them more now they were adults. The small-children years had been like trench warfare without the sweet relief of death.

'I'd like to do a cheers,' Lois said, quelling the chatter with a little cough. 'It's lovely to finally meet David; we've all heard so much about you. And wonderful to have the family all together in one place to celebrate Christmas.' She caught Phil poking Annette in the lower back and wanted to jab him in the eye with his bloody Parker pen he kept on the inside of his jacket pocket. 'Here's to Christmas and family.'

Stephen yawned inexplicably instigating a lump in her throat.

'Cheers!' everyone cried, clinking glasses and smiling madly. Cordelia's face momentarily flinched as she took a sip of champagne. 'Help yourself to the nibbles.' Of course Lois wasn't having any of them, perhaps one mini quiche; it was Christmas after all.

'Thank you for hosting,' Annette said. 'We should do this more often. The kids are going to be off and away before you know it. Strike while the iron is hot.'

'Well, yes quite,' Lois said, not entirely sure how to slip into conversation the real reason she was hosting. Phil joined them at the table, his hand hovering above the platters, indecisive about what to go for first, while David and Stephen sat with Desi on the sofa, plates of food balanced on their knees. Cordelia was nowhere to be seen. Perry Como tinkled in the background; it could almost be fifteen years ago.

'We have the grandchildren visiting this Christmas,' Annette continued. 'It doesn't seem five minutes since my girls were that age.'

'How lovely,' Lois answered. There was no way she was ready to be a grandparent, but she might have no say in the matter.

'How's the show?' Phil asked, popping a sausage in his mouth and chewing as if his life depended on it. 'You seem to be enjoying yourself.'

'Yes, it's OK, can't believe it's been six months. Not the same pay as TV.' No it certainly wasn't, and losing her slot on GMTV had automatically cancelled all her diet supplement endorsement contracts which were actually what brought in the serious money. She was working just one job for the first time since she could remember. She had thought about starting up Slimnastics again, but was hoping she wouldn't have to if she could pull this off.

'Well, it doesn't look like you're having to economise,' Phil said, then instantly paled; he never made digs.

'Well, you say that...' She took in a big breath. 'I needed to talk to all of you today about a new venture.' She coughed again. Where was Cordelia? The living-room door moved and Cordelia slipped into the room as if she'd never left.

'Did I miss something?' she asked innocently.

'Mum was about to make an announcement,' Stephen said listlessly as if she were about to read out a shopping list.

*Fuck*, Lois never swore, not even in her head, but with all eyes on her, she had sudden prescient insight into how this was going to land and it wasn't to her advantage. She almost balked but then Alvin's words lifted her up.

'You have nothing to lose by asking them, Lois. You've already lost everything. Think of this as a business deal that the whole family can benefit from. They get a percentage, don't forget to hammer that home, and it's up to you to negotiate the package with them. It will also be determined by how much of the limelight they take up compared to you, the star. But all that's in the future. All you have to do now is pose the question.'

With all eyes trained on Lois, her guts swirled with loose ball bearings.

'I was approached by MTV last week. Well, Alvin was approached. They're looking for a family to film. There's a format of television that's popular in the US called reality TV?' She paused as Phil and Annette drew blanks but the others nodded. 'They're after filming a British family for six months of the year with a rolling contract that can be renewed if the viewing figures are big enough.'

'And you want us to be filmed too?' Stephen asked incredulously, shooting Cordelia a sideways glance. She continued staring at the floor.

'That was the idea, yes.'

'But I don't even live here,' Stephen said.

'They'd post a camera crew in London to cover you and Desi.'

'I'm involved too?' Desi cried, unable to quash his obvious delight.

'And us?' Annette squeaked. 'Why us?'

'Apparently, we are the quintessential modern nineties family. Split but together, very bohemian, just what MTV are looking for.'

'This's the first time we've ever had a "family" gathering,' Phil scoffed. 'It's hardly like we spend Christmas together or even send Christmas cards.'

'Well, I actually wrote you one this year. And got you both a present,' Lois said unashamedly. 'It's under the tree.' He'd better take it; she'd never use a fondue set.

Cordelia didn't say a word. By the slope of her

shoulders, Lois already knew her answer. Unde-
terred, her spiel continued.

'It's planned to coincide with me releasing another fitness DVD for the over-forties.' She'd signed
a three-tape deal with Environ Ltd six years ago; she
had to honour the last one, even if the production
budget had been slashed, reducing them into using
the producer's garage as the 'gym' with nothing spare
for hair and make-up. 'You'll all get paid on a sliding
scale, which we can negotiate. No one's expecting
you to do this for free.'

'Who on earth would be interested in watching
us?' Stephen said. 'For a start, we're all ordinary and
pretty dull.'

'Speak for yourself,' Desi said. 'I know I'd set the
screen alight.'

'We don't do anything together, we'd have no privacy,' Stephen continued. 'Do they film you on the
loo?'

'No! We'd work out a schedule to fit around
everyone. Then they edit all the footage together into
half-hour episodes once a week for six weeks. What
do you say?'

'Have you run out of money?' Phil asked, toying
with a lone pig in a blanket. 'Because I don't believe
even you would put yourself through this otherwise.'

## 43

---

## THE CHANNEL

I lingered inside the final frames of *The Shawshank Redemption*, Red trudging along a golden tongue of sand towards Andy on Zihuatanejo beach, both of them free men. I'd not fully considered what would happen after I finished the swim, and what that meant. Who would I be?

An injection of Hollywood hope was needed right now. I'd been swimming in a long-distance tour of the French coastline, studded with shimmering buildings and concrete bunkers, hangovers from World War Two, the current tugging at me like an irritating toddler. Nausea had returned tenfold; I'd vomited up three warm sweet teas in quick succession. An unruffled horizon prevailed, no white crests, just gentle undulation, so the sickness was puzzling. I carried the surface of the moon on each fingertip, certain corresponding waterlogged craters pruned my toes but I couldn't see them, much less feel them. Now would be the perfect time for an out-of-body experience, watch from above while my limbs whirred without me. Only replaying films had managed that deflection thus far but I'd reached the end of the rota. I'd dug out back-up films: *It's a Wonderful Life*, *Tootsie*, *La Femme Nikita* and re-watched them all in preparation, but my brain struggled retaining too much information. The same affliction hit me like anyone this age: the plots wander off after a day or two alongside all the books I've recently read and the TV shows I've watched, swiftly fading into the melee of emails, to-do lists, dating profiles, and recipe ideas.

'You're exhausted, Cordy. Your body's just re-acting how it knows best. It's clearing you out for the final push. Alan said you need to sprint in order to break this stalemate. It's the only way you'll make it. Big strokes! I'm coming back in.'

'Can you imagine crawling through a river of shit to freedom?' David had asked twenty-six years ago after we had finished watching *The Shawshank Redemption*. 'I'd do it for you, in a heartbeat!'

'No! Ewww.' I'd thrown a cushion at him.

Nonetheless, I had swum through one, I still was. David had asked that question when I'd still been imprisoned. I was living the answer now.

I burrowed into my epidermis, letting *Shawshank* go. The films had shielded me from the sea's immediacy, from icy tendrils slithering into my marrow, from the sheer tedium that accompanies a marathon of any persuasion. Now it was just me and the water.

And the past.

As another wave of roiling biliousness broke inside me, I lifted my head in time to catch Desi break the surface by *Boudica*. I poked out an earplug.

'Come on, Cordelia Franks, Cross Channel Swimmer, you got this. Follow me!'

*Head down, four strokes, breathe out. Bubbles.*

## 44

### MORE BLUE LINES

'Cordelia, I'm going to have to sell the house.' Mum squinted uneasily from across the dinner table. I paused cutting a Quorn sausage. Mum bit her lips and pushed a salad round her plate with her fork like she was mixing a cake.

'This house?'

'We have no other houses.'

'Where are we going to live?'

'I was thinking... round here. Small flat, maybe two bedroomed if I can afford it. Hopefully one with a garden.'

'Why?' We had yet to address the debacle of the TV showdown. Mum and I had brushed it into a corner and covered it with another rug. 'Is this to do with no one wanting to do the TV show?'

Mum sighed, pushing out a shallow groan. 'Yes.'

'So Dad was right; you've run out of money? Why didn't you say?'

'Because if we'd all agreed to the TV show then I never would have had to say anything at all.'

'Maybe people would have been more sympathetic if you'd admitted the truth. Though no way I wanted in.' I studied Mum's face, used to this loose-tongued version since it had just been the two of us. Many secrets bubbled up under the influence of two glasses of rosé on a Friday night:

'James was a wonderful lover. People shouldn't knock anal sex; it's very under-rated. The gays know what they're talking about.'

'Mum! I'll never get minging Mr Klingon out of my mind now.'

'Kilburn! If you're going to insult him, at least use his real name.'

Stephen had graduated last year, moving back for a scant few months before taking a temp job in Wandsworth Council's housing department, escaping 'small-town syndrome', something Stephen had decided Eastbourne would poleaxe you with whether you believed it or not. I suspected I suffered from it but reskinned it as big-fish-in-a-small-town syndrome.

'Why don't you move to London too? We could get a flat together near Desi? I could leave the dump I'm in. You'd be nearer David. It'd be like living at home but better cos Mum wouldn't be there! We could have parties without her trying to steal the limelight.'

When Mum had trashed what was essentially the first official Franks cross marital family Christmas party, Netty and Dad only stayed for a further ten minutes.

'What were you thinking?' Dad had spat. 'It's a huge invasion of privacy for a derisory fifteen minutes of fame with barely the recompense for being publicly ridiculed at the bloody Circus Maximus!'

'Oh, Phil, stop being so dramatic. It's a sleeping income – you just live your life and they film it. Unless you two have something to hide?'

'Pah! I told Netty this so-called olive branch get-together would be a sodding pre-Christmas Trojan horse, though she fought your corner like she always does.'

'I'm sorry, Lois, I just don't want to air my laundry in public,' Netty had said more tactfully.

'Well, Aunty Lois, I'm all for it!' Desi had enthused. 'Maybe we could do our own series "*Desi and Lois on the town*"? A gay Chicagoan and his crazy divorcee aunty ripping stereotypes to shreds?'

'Less of the crazy,' Mum had replied, watching her dreams smash at the foot of the Christmas tree.

\* \* \*

'What happened? I thought everything was going OK with work,' I asked. 'Honestly, you should have just said if anything was wrong.'

'There was no way I was publicly admitting to your father that I gambled the house, and all my ISAs in a property scam. At least I still have a job. Bill's lost everything.'

'Bloody hell, Bill Fisher? You're very calm for someone who's lost everything. Are we destitute?'

'No! I haven't exactly lost everything. Not yet. I borrowed against the house and dissolved my ISAs. I don't have a pension – this investment was supposed to be it; we were told we'd make millions, was a sure thing, Irish property tycoon with a solid track record that turned out to be as solid as Bill's hairline. Work associate of Bill's; funnily enough, he's gone AWOL. Bill's business's been liquidated, filed for bankruptcy, and he's living in a caravan in the yard while they sort the paperwork. I'm in a better state than he is. I've the house still, but the mortgage is crippling after years of not having one, interest rates are still shooting up, not that I expect you to know any of this.'

'Ask Grandpa for a loan?'

'I'd rather live in a skip.' Mum toyed with half a cherry tomato before spearing it and popping it in her mouth. 'I honestly thought you'd all jump at the chance to be on MTV. Free money for living your lives. You wouldn't have had to learn any lines or anything. They just wanted a fly on the wall of a modern British family. You wouldn't know they were there.'

'Annette was never going to go for it. Dad neither. We're different to you.'

'Desi was keen,' she sulked. 'Annette could have had a new wardrobe. We all could. They'd offered to throw everything at it. You never know where something like that's going to lead you. One minute you're a nobody, the next, Cilla Black's got you on speed dial.'

'You don't even like Annette, Mum.'

'I do!'

'What? Then how come that was the first time you've ever invited them round?'

'They've never invited *me* round.'

'Because they knew you'd say no.' I bit into the sausage. It was like chewing a mattress. Mum drummed her fingers on the tabletop, her face softening, putting me on high alert.

'Is the baby what's stopping you from doing the TV show? I thought you would have jumped at the chance, what with you loving films.'

'What did you say?' My cutlery clattered onto the plate.

'Your pregnancy. You're pregnant, aren't you?' She smiled. 'I'm sorry I guessed before you were ready to tell me. Do you know when you're due yet?'

'Mum!' Abruptly standing, I smashed the back of the chair into the wall, squeezing past the edge of the table before bolting into the hallway, taking the stairs two at a time. By the time I reached my door, I was out of breath. I banged my fist on the light switch, the room snapping into focus: the duvet scrunched in a ball at the bottom of my Dick Fucks Shit freebie double bed. Apart from the lack of Kurt Cobain posters, my room had remained pretty much untouched since the teenage years. I'd become an observer of my own prosaic story. Instead of living it, I was marking the days until real life began, whenever that was going to be. The only thrilling aspect was David, but he lived in London.

'Why don't you move in here when you start uni?' he'd asked on Boxing Day when we lay in his bed. 'I could have a word with the landlord, ask him not to charge any rent. Maybe the odd sexual favour instead?'

I'd hit him in the arm before wrestling him flat and straddling him, unease wriggling in my belly like rats in a sack. We'd not spent this much time together since a week in Cornwall during the summer. I'd been reduced to doing sit ups and squats in the bed and breakfast shower to mitigate the daily cooked breakfasts. Sharing a flat would be like living in a goldfish bowl.

'I don't know, David; I need to get in first.'

'Why don't you move in anyway? Find a temp job up here until then. Stephen escaped. You're the last one standing – what are you waiting for?'

Instead of answering, I'd leaned down to kiss him and soon we were scrabbling at T-shirts and underwear.

Mum's question coiled itself round my guts, squeezing so hard that I ran to the toilet, only just managing to flip the seat up as dinner made a swift exit. Her concerned face haunted me from the mirror above the sink.

'If you're not pregnant then you need to see someone. This isn't normal. I thought you'd got over the bulimia.'

'I didn't make myself do... *that*.' I flushed the chain. 'It came from nowhere.'

'When was your last period?'

'Mum, I'm not pregnant! I've just had a weird bug, probably from eating too much crap over the last month.'

'But—'

'Stop! I'm on the mini pill. I don't get periods.'

'But that's how you got pregnant last time. Throwing up the pill.'

'I haven't got an eating disorder! I'm fine.'

Mum pursed her lips. 'I know what being pregnant looks like. Your boobs have grown.'

'How do you even know that?'

'I can see with my own eyes. And you had antibiotics at the end of October. They disable the pill.'

'What?' My heart flew to my throat. I jammed my fingers into the soft dip at the base of my neck to prevent its escape.

'Did the doctor not tell you that when you went?'

'No!'

'Are you sure?'

'I'd remember that. I'm not a child.'

'Then stop acting like one. Do a test to rule it out.'

'Where would I get a test? Everywhere's shut.'

'No, it isn't.'

* * *

We stared at the prognostic stick, the thin blue line emerging in the tiny window.

'Fuck.' I sat down heavily on the toilet seat, hands slapped over my open mouth.

Mum had driven us to the giant Tesco – it had a section stuffed with pregnancy tests and condoms, Creation's diametric opposites.

'Do you want a drink?' she asked in earnest.

'Yes please.' How the effing Jeff was I here again so soon? I was no more ready now than I was then.

Mum returned holding two tumblers each with an inch of clear liquid.

'Vodka. Best thing really: low calorie compared to wine.' We didn't clink, just knocked it back in sync. The warmth landed in my tummy, stifling the burgeoning horror.

'I don't know what to do.' I looked to Mum,

knowing she wouldn't really have the answer, but there wasn't anyone else available. Michelle? Our fledging reconnection might snap under this. I wanted to ring Desi but my mouth had seized up, words collecting round my tonsils, the chief culprit in this bloody shit show.

'I would say maybe don't tell David.' Mum sighed slowly, emptying her lungs. 'I told your father and it changed everything.'

'You were married, that's different.'

'No, we weren't. This was before that.' Mum straightened the towel on the rail after I had wiped my hands.

'You had an abortion?'

'No, late miscarriage, stillbirth really. Little girl, May.' Mum explained the sorry story while I twisted sheets of loo roll until they were as tight as rope.

'I wasn't the first baby?'

Mum shook her head sadly. 'No, there was an accident. We were madly in love – forbidden love because he had no real prospects. I was younger than you are now: nineteen. Grandpa didn't approve, thought it would fizzle out once I realised a lawyer would be a better option. Ha.'

I suddenly recalled eavesdropping outside my

parents' bedroom. Had she alluded to a baby back then?

'I'd never been in love before. I wasn't prepared for the madness. No one had explained that part to me. Life was a complete mystery... Liz and I hadn't even been informed about periods; I thought I was dying when I got "my curse".' She shook her head. 'Your dad proposed on the spot, didn't even mention the A word. It had been legal for a few years but you had to prove you were going to suffer mentally if you didn't want to pay. And we had no money. We got married without telling our parents and a few months later, the baby inexplicably died. I went a bit crazy after that... I think your dad was scared to touch me, thought I might break.'

'I'm sorry, Mum, that's awful.' I patted her arm. We weren't really a hugging type of family. Maybe life would have been different if we were.

'I think what I'm trying to say is, does David need to know?'

I shrugged. 'It would be my second... one. I feel so bad.'

'You'd feel worse bringing a child into the world that you aren't ready for. You'd be lumbered with David forever.'

'I love David!'

'Right now you do. I was besotted with your father – that's the magic of first love; it's so powerful, you think you'll never feel like that again. You never forget it. But that feeling doesn't last forever; things change. You still haven't done anything with your life, Cordelia. Don't get trapped.'

'I'm not trapped – I'm applying for university in London!'

'You never said! That's good. He need never know then?'

'I can't not tell him. He has a right to know.'

'He doesn't; it's your life.'

I pushed past Mum and headed to my room to sit on the unmade bed. The bottom of the door brushed the carpet as Mum poked her head round.

'So I guess a mother-daughter housemates show is out of the question then? I could ask MTV. You might have to wear a leotard.'

'Jesus, Mum!'

'I'll call the estate agents tomorrow.'

## 45

---

## THE CHANNEL

*Cold, I'm not cold, I'm warm. Super warm. Look at that sun. It's toasty, my head's warm, it's hot, too hot. Breathe. Where are my fingers?* I scrunched them, pressing the nails into my palms as I drove them into the water, dragging them underneath me, the cycle beginning again.

Desi swam in front just out of reach, his presence as comforting as an electric blanket. What I wouldn't do for mine right now cranked up to Gates of Hell burrowed like a hedgehog in the back garden hibernacula. Better than sex any day – a fact I'd struggled to come to terms with. Sex had always been my forte.

'Low libido afflicts us all eventually,' Desi had commiserated. 'Tim and I watch porn with a cup of tea and some shortbread instead of actually doing it every night. Makes you feel like you've still got skin in the game.'

I estimated it was about four o'clock, the sun having joined me on *Boudica*'s starboard side. Cathy had switched position, using the boat as a bulwark to discourage drifting. I had been swimming for a possible twelve hours. I'd never persevered with any task for longer than twelve hours.

I decided to rekindle the elephants.

After one thousand and two hundred elephants, the French coast was no nearer. Determination leaked like a slow puncture as I hamster-wheeled in the sea. I stopped swimming. Alan blew his whistle, cutting through the cumbersome earplugs.

'What's wrong?' he yelled. Desi stopped and turned round, then swam back, treading water a few metres away.

'Cordy?'

'I can't cross this current. We'll end up in Belgium.'

'Uh oh. No way. We're not giving in now.' Desi wagged his finger.

'We? It's just me in here.'

'Cordelia,' Alan yelled, 'I'm throwing you some

chocolate and some coffee. Try and force it down. You need the calories. That's an order.'

I caught the goggles case and tipped the buttons in my mouth. I'd never had to force chocolate down in my life. If anything, I tried to resist it. Desi handed over the coffee, careful not to touch me.

'Yes it's you doing the donkey work, but I'm here too. I love you. We all want you to finish. Don't give up now; you can practically touch the beach.'

I just wanted a little rest.

'There's no time to rest,' Desi pleaded, reading my mind. 'You have to sprint. Can you find the grit in the oyster?'

I swallowed a mouthful of seawater, choking it down.

'Cordy? You've been through worse. It's time now. Come on. Do this...'

A little rest, an electric blanket, Kevin snuggling in my lap, Nimrod zooming round the floor inside his ball. From the depths, a dagger struck my right leg. White-hot pain tore through my shin, another piercing my thigh. I howled from the base of my soul.

'Jellyfish!'

# 46

# FLEE THE SCENE

David's face matched the exact colour swatch for under-ripe brie. 'How pregnant are you?'

'The doctor thinks eight weeks.'

I'd broken the news during *London Tonight*, hoping the TV would act as a buffer.

'And what do you want to do?'

'Not have it.'

'You're sure about that? I have a spare room.' David smiled cautiously.

'Don't joke.'

'I'm not. I'm deadly serious. I'll do whatever you want.'

'David, we only left school five minutes ago. My life hasn't even started yet.'

'Er, I take offence at that.'

'It's not about you! You know I love you, but I haven't done anything. You've travelled, bought a flat, have a good job, live in London. I still live at home with my bloody mum. Who's mental.' Mental she may be, but her words hung round my neck like worry beads.

'This could be your chance?' he suggested weakly.

'Being a mum? I meant a career, university or travelling, something exciting – not *that*.' *Travelling?* The very thought terrified me, but wasn't it what people did so they could say they had actually been somewhere? Honestly? I'd rather have a cavity search.

'OK.' David turned his eyes back to the TV – a news story about an unexploded World War Two bomb discovered in a Soho basement. How could you not know there was an unexploded bomb in your basement? *How could you not know you were pregnant for the second time?*

'Do you want kids?' I asked. We'd never actually had this conversation; twenty-three feeling far too young to even float the subject.

'Hell, yeah. One day... or now, if needs be.' He leaned over and cupped his warm hands round my

ice-cold ones. 'Look, I completely understand everything you're saying. I don't want you to feel alone
with this. Whatever you really want, I will want too.'
He squeezed all the joints on the fingers of my left
hand in turn. 'I'm petrified, I can't pretend I'm not,
but I think I've loved you since you handed me my
lunch money in the dinner hall. I see a future with
you... Fuck, it's all kind of crystallised right this
second.'

'You see *us* having a family?' Did our progeny realise it was an uninvited squatter? A memory
slammed into me: winter 1993, Paula, the girl in the
next room, holding my hand on the gurney in the
back of the ambulance, gently massaging it. 'It'll be
OK, Cordelia,' she'd soothed in her thick scouse accent as the lights flashed like the union bar's
Wednesday-night disco.

My throat closed up; I sprung from the sofa, the
front door four leaps away. Swinging it open, I darted
into the brightly lit communal hallway, clashing
down two flights of tiled stairs, slipping on the last
three pooled with rainwater. I bashed the button on
the wall, releasing the heavy main door, and stepped
outside, street lights reflecting onto glistening pave-
ments. If only I could jump into a puddle with Dick
Van Dyke and escape. Though, being a film buff, it

had been the rain that had washed away the beautiful chalk-drawn *Mary Poppins* Utopia where cartoon penguins danced and turtles talked.

Panic snuffed out the sirens, the pattering of rain, car horns, the whooshing of buses as they pulled up outside the flats, their opening doors sighing. I had to get away; he couldn't find me. I needed to think. He'd be here any second.

\* \* \*

'What the hell? You're soaking wet!' Stephen cried, dragging me over the threshold downstairs. 'I was just about to go out. Did you lose your keys?'

'I can't do it; I can't have a baby. I'll go mad. I can't do it, Stephen.'

'Come upstairs.' He took my hand, guiding me back to his flat like a lost child. Malachi and Coren where eating beans straight from cans next to the coffee table opposite the TV while fish fingers had been laid out like gourmet canapés on a baking tray plonked on top of a magazine (*Loaded*, most likely). *TFI Friday* blared from the screen like a boisterous stag do haemorrhaging testosterone, Chris Evans leering at the camera before it pulled back and panned across the jeering crowd towards sneering Liam Gallagher strutting the stage. Lad culture in its purest manifestation. Stephen steered me past the boys and into his bedroom, positioning me on the unkempt bed.

'Shall I ring Desi?'

'Don't leave me. Something's gone wrong, but I don't know what.'

'You're not making any sense,' Stephen said gently.

I took several deep breaths, my heart refusing to slow down. My mouth filled with fur as if I'd burned it on a steaming baked potato.

'I can't be here; I need to go home.'

'Back to David's?'

'No, home.'

'There's the heartbeat,' the sonographer announced from her stool, tapping the screen. I turned my cheek and stared at the glossy beige wall, four greasy splodges marking the corners of a ghost poster. Perhaps it had advertised condoms. A small potted fern cowered in the corner of the room, lack of life scorching it brown. Why did they scan you? Here's the human you will be extinguishing because you are too vain to get fat.

Pregnancy was not a land I'd considered visiting, not even in my wildest dreams where I liberally ate cake and pizza without compunction. How did people eat five consecutive biscuits and then not visualise them shoring up their waist like sandbags? Everything I put in my mouth had a price. But growing another person would shove that into freefall. I shook my head. No. I wasn't ready... *Would I ever be?*

'So you're about nine weeks.'

Mum squeezed my hand, giving me a thin-lipped smile. We'd had a chat last night while sorting through some of my old clothes to go to charity. Mum was hell bent on getting the house in some kind of saleable state and that meant ridding it of clutter. Stephen had given her permission to chuck everything in his room. 'I don't need any of it; I'm never going to live there again,' he'd said on the phone.

'Cordelia, if there's a part of you that wants to keep the baby, I can help,' Mum had offered.

'How? You're selling the house. I'd have to live with David in London. You're not there. I'd be on my own with a baby in a city where I only know three people. I don't even know if I like Brixton. It's so... grey.'

'Five people. Michelle and Sarah live there too. That's more than most people know in a place like London.'

'They live miles away and they'd be at work, so would Desi and Stephen. It's not like living in Pole-gate just down the road. London's so—' I'd shrugged; London's sprawl was overwhelming; being with David offered an anchor point amid the metropolis. With no beach to make a break for when you needed to breathe, how did people live their whole lives there?

'OK, I was just checking. I agree with you, by the way. You're doing the right thing. And if keeping David at arm's length is what you need to get through this, then that's what has to happen. You know what I think about getting trapped. It doesn't always work out. One in four—'

'Mum! I know, don't remind me.'

A week later, I lay on the sofa like I used to when I'd been sick as a child, the TV on, watching brain-numbing fodder with the volume turned down. I'd evicted the squatter. *Just a bunch of cells*, I silently re-peated; my heart told a different story. The cells had also been a perfect mix of me and David and he had seen them as the future, sending conciliatory flowers and chocolates.

I had killed a family; I deserved neither.

'David's rung again,' Mum said. 'I told him you loved the flowers. I also said you'd ring him back at some point this week. I think it's only fair.'

I nodded. But when faced with the phone hand-set, a swarm of angry, buzzing bees clustered behind my eyes.

'David, it's me.'

'I know it's you! Are you OK? I've rung a few times. Did your mum say?'

'Yes.' A bomb ticked in the background.

'Are you in tomorrow? I've got something coming for you: a present. It means we can talk to each other all the time.'

'What? Why?'

'Well, then I don't have to get past your mum when I want to speak to you, do I? If you have a mobile phone then it cuts out the middle mum!' He laughed nervously.

'I don't need a mobile.' Why the rage?

'Everyone has them. You can't stay analogue for-ever, you know.'

'What if I want to stay analogue and speak on a rotary phone and use a typewriter?'

'You don't use a typewriter!'

'But what if I did?'

'No one's stopping you but eventually it would get harder and harder.' David sighed down the phone. 'What's really going on? You've been avoiding me since the... procedure. Before it, actually. I'm not angry with you – it's your body. So please don't think that.'

'I don't think that.' I twisted the phone cord round my left index finger, drawing it tight until the fingertip turned white. I pulled it harder still, causing my finger to sting. I bit it to see if I could feel my teeth digging into the flesh. It was dead.

'Then what is it? I know you must be feeling awful—'

'I don't, I feel perfectly fine.'

'You don't sound fine.'

'Well, I am. And please cancel the phone; I don't want it.'

'Too late, it's being delivered tomorrow by a courier.'

'I'll send it back.'

'Don't do that. Just put it somewhere safe and when you're thinking straight you might find you want it after all.'

'Thinking straight? You think I'm mad?'

'No! Just that you've been through something traumatic.'

'I'll tell you what's wrong,' I snapped at him, the bees' buzzing now intolerable. 'I don't want children. Ever! They ruin your life.'

'I'm not asking you to have children. In fact, you've just done the complete opposite.'

'So you wished I hadn't had an abortion? You wished that I had got fat and tired and given you a baby even though we hardly know each other?'

'Cordelia! Stop it!' David's voice cracked, two breaths away from tears. 'I've known you since I was twelve. I've loved you for a lot of that. Immature love, I'll grant you that, but I believed in it.'

'You don't know me. If you knew what I was really like, you wouldn't love me at all.'

'I'd love you whatever. Please stop talking crap. I don't care that you don't want children; all I want is you. The children thing we can work out at a later date.'

'There won't be a later date. I'll *never* want them. And if I keep getting pregnant, I'll just get rid of it. I can't do this; I'll never be able to do this.'

Wild sea rushed inside my head, waves bashing against my skull. Elation coursed through my veins as I rode a surf of pure anger, not giving a fuck what words spewed up next.

'OK. I'm going to go now. I'm sorry you feel like this. You're obviously suffering after what you've been through. I was going to say I'll come down to-morrow; I've got the day off tagged onto the weekend. Thought we could spend some time together. But I'm not sure you'll want to see me.'

My heart stalled, but I ignored the warning. The anger still hadn't run its course. 'No, I think it's prob-ably better that way.'

'Fine. I love you, even if you won't let me.'

'You wouldn't if you really knew me.'

'I do know you. You're sweet and gentle and kind.'

'I'm not. I got rid of your baby.'

'You had to do it to save you. It was for the best.'

'Not this time. The other time.'

'What other time?'

'When I had my first abortion, I got rid of both your babies. Now you hate me, don't you?'

'Cordy? What? How?'

The tempest finally blew itself out.

'I have to go. Bye, David...' I put the phone down, covering my lips with my hand as the deluge fell. It was like I'd popped to the shops while a changeling stepped in, hurling hate-filled words. I really was proper mental, just as I'd always suspected.

## 47

### DESI IN THE CHANNEL

The last twenty-five years had zipped by in a blink of a gravelly voiced film trailer: *young American buck flees to London seeking high fashion, but also found clubbing, drugs and boys before falling in love at an orgy while eating lemon basil chicken drumsticks. Five years later, his heart pulverised to pâté, he retreats to the seaside where he finally meets his life partner cold-water swimming with Eastbourne Egrets. The End.* However, the end wasn't remotely in sight. He was in the middle of the Channel accompanying his much-loved but somewhat maddening cousin having talked her in to this insanity in the name of the National AIDS Trust, his film-trailer life footing this entire mission. When Cordelia had called it off with Ian (or perhaps Liam?), he'd cajoled her into joining him for a midwinter dip.

'Honestly, Cordy, you'll forget all about the guy the minute you plunge into the water. It's like a baptism – washes you clean. Ian who?'

'It was Stuart, actually. And it's not really about him; it's those fucking apps. I'm done. Everyone my age's married on the sly or actually septuagenarians jacked up on Viagra pretending to be fifty. I've made more U-turns in Costa than the bloody government. Celibacy is the new tantric sex, so I hear.'

'Well, whoever, you'll never need to go on an app again. The sea can be your soulmate.'

Since he first floated the swim, she'd raised eight and a half thousand pounds in under eighteen months, pestering people over social media, through work, on the local radio, and with an appearance on *BBC South East* news, shivering on the seafront in her swimming costume. These actions would have been inconceivable in the past – the looming half a century certainly kicked her into touch.

He and Alan had set up a *Cordelia Franks Swims the Channel* Facebook page – it had instantly drawn just under two thousand odd followers when he had asked Kerrie Ransom, a *Love Island* D lister, to share it on TikTok after he'd styled her for the *TV Choice Awards*. In between the bouts of seasickness and dips into the Channel, he and Alan updated the followers with the swim's progress.

Kindred spirits, Desi and Cordelia, hadn't ticked the boxes on whatever arbitrary list the survival of the human race hinged on. Neither were married or had kids, he owned his flat with Tim and all three of them shared Kevin. The only reason she left the safety of the cinema was because Reggie had tried to send her on a management training course.

'I don't know, Desi; it's a lot of responsibility: visits to head office. It was only meant to be a holiday job.'

'Then try something else?'

She backed herself into a loose chain of low-paid jobs that she could do in a coma, running each time she got offered promotion or a tricky role leading away from the routine and into the fire. Then July 2011, Desi styled a Christmas stationery shoot for *Red* magazine, discovering the Journal Co.

'They're about to expand and desperately need an office manager. No more public-facing duties or working Saturdays. Also, it's tiny, just you, the owner and an office junior. Joan's adorable too – I think you'd like her. What do you think?'

After she'd worked there a while, he campaigned again. 'You'd earn so much more in London, you know... You've practically set that company up for bigger things single-handed. You could name your price up here.'

Cordelia had a way of sincerely nodding whilst at the same time ignoring him. He'd learned to stop suggesting things.

When Aunty Lois sold Villiers Road, Cordelia rented a small flat just off the seafront in Latimer Road, finally cutting the apron strings. The opportunity materialised to buy the place a few years ago and this time, he crusaded against her vacant nodding.

'The flat will always be yours and no one can make you move, ever again, unless you default on the mortgage!' The rock-solid stability eventually appealed to his cousin's neurotic aversion to change. However, Baz's announcement that he was returning to Australia swiftly turned the tables. With his father slowly dying, Baz wanted to be there to take over the family catering business.

'You can come too but you'll have to be my "friend" in front of Ma and Pa.' Baz's traditional

Greek immigrant parents were blissfully ignorant about his 'disgraceful' sexuality, but Desi had assumed he would tell them one day, that day being now! 'Everything will come out in the open as soon as Dad passes over,' Baz assured him, 'but that could be anything up to two years at this rate.'

Desi took a step back, searching for signs to join him. He'd just accepted separate bedrooms were a given after this length of time. 'You snore, darling,' he'd been baldly informed. 'I need my beauty sleep.' Unsurprisingly, sex had dried up to a drizzle. Nobody put Desi in a corner.

'I can't believe you're willing to bin the last six years,' Baz had protested.

'I can't believe you're still in the closet at forty-one and expect me to leave *my* family and jump back in a closet on the other side of the world!'

They'd fought for two hours, Baz throwing down a last desperate plea. 'What if I give you the secret lamb koftas recipe you've been begging me for for years? Will you come then?'

Desi paused uncertainly before sealing his fate. 'I prefer the Ottolenghi ones... Sorry, I couldn't tell you before.'

Raging silence.

'Fine,' Baz eventually recovered. 'I hope you and the *Ottolenghi* koftas live happily ever after.'

Desi moved out the next day. Heartbroken and disillusioned, he escaped to Eastbourne and slept in Cordelia's bed while she took the sofa bed. 'Desi, I owe you a million sleeps in my bed for every disaster you've ever saved me from.' Aunty Lois had offered her spare room in her tiny cottage, but Stone Cross was purgatory. At least there were a few decent pubs in Eastbourne. The seaside hiatus wasn't supposed to be permanent, but then he'd met Tim.

Alan's whistle cut short his ruminating, dropping him back in the icy Channel, the shock as sharp as if he'd been unexpectedly launched from a cosy bed. Desi turned away from the whisper of French coast goading them on the horizon. He'd just spotted an impressive obelisk on a hilltop, some kind of war memorial perhaps. If only he could lasso it, haul them into shore, but beneath its placid surface, the water rolled to its own rhythm, tugging and pulling anything incapable of resistance. Cordelia needed to force her way across this wolf in sheep's clothing. The few times in life she'd found personal Nirvana, she'd thrown wrenches rather than accept it. Not this time. He had to save her from herself. If necessary, whip out the tough love he'd stashed in his swimming cap.

'Literally, you can say anything, anything at all. Just get me to the finish line.' She'd given full permission to administer as and when.

* * *

He and Alan cajoled as best they could and had almost cracked her, but then the jellyfish stung, worse than before. This time, they were meatier, trickier to swerve with compromised limbs and diminished mental acuity. He watched helplessly as she thrashed away from the translucent stingers, lips drawn into a silent scream, *Boudica* looming closer.

'I'll go check, see if there's more.' Alan walked as quick as he could to the bow, leaning over as far as gravity allowed, scanning one hundred and eighty degrees. 'There's a few incoming starboard, big buggers, so you should see them. They appear to be in threes. Tread water; they should pass either side of you. The current's pulling them with it. I'll throw out some painkillers.'

'Cordy, you're getting too near the boat,' Desi cautioned.

She stared past him.

'Cordy, did you hear me? You need to move, just enough to stay put. You're drifting.'

Alan reappeared with the goggle case. 'Take the painkillers. They've got caffeine in; should help with energy.' *Boudica* was near enough for Alan to lower the case into the water near her hand; it floated out of reach almost immediately.

'Cordy! Grab it!' Desi ordered, reaching for it and spinning it across the surface at her. She placed her hand over it, keeping it still.

'My legs...' *Boudica*'s hull was almost within arm's reach.

'The money, Cordy. All that cash for AIDS research. You're just cold and exhausted. Take the pills; they'll stop the stinging.' Alan handed Desi some water. He shook it at Cordelia like a maraca. 'Don't self-sabotage now.'

She chewed her lip and grabbed the bottom of the bottle, fumbling with the pills.

'Cordelia, the Facebook page is going ballistic. So many messages,' Alan encouraged. '*Love Island* Kerrie's done a live on that TikTok thing; apparently, more people are donating.' Alan's eyes flicked between Desi and Cordelia. 'She's told Jeremy's story, how his death affected Desi – it's steamrollered the total. It's over ten thousand pounds and climbing. You're amazing.'

Cordelia closed her eyes again. 'The current's too powerful.' She swallowed the painkillers and kicked her legs, just stopping herself from touching the hull. Alison dutifully logged everything in her notebook. Cathy had slipped away from the helm and parked herself next to Alan.

'Cordelia, listen... I've done hundreds of crossings, not all of them completed. This one's had some drama, I'll give you that. The current *is* strong, but that won't last all the way inshore,' she said with confidence. 'I'd be the first person to say if it was impossible. I'd love to say I know the Channel like the back of my hand, but it's forever changing, just like life. Staying still is easy, but you'll never get where you need to go. If you can eat some more chocolate, or get some cake down you, anything for energy, the painkillers'll kick in and hopefully ease those cricks and twinges. Of course it hurts, you've swum bloody miles, but it's the final push now. The mind will always give in way before the body tells it to. If you're ready to throw in the towel, do it knowing you've already achieved so much, but I'm telling you it's there for the taking. Sprint for an hour. Then the seabed will start coming into view and I guarantee that will be all the encouragement you'll need.'

Cordelia released the water bottle and goggles case. Alan drew them in as carefully as if reeling in a lobster pot. Now was the perfect moment for Desi to unleash his smash in case of emergency gilded rocket to shove up her ass. She'd yet to pull down her goggles; it was still all to play for. His cousin was indeed curious. Just when you thought you understood her, could predict how she would react, what path she would carve, she'd confound you, and rarely in a good way. Self-destruction curdled her blood, leaving powerless onlookers gasping in disbelief. Just ask David Plimpton or her school friends whom she'd ghosted. To this day, David remained the yardstick Desi (and Stephen) measured all of Cordelia's subsequent boyfriends against.

'Right, Cordy, I'm ready.'

She stared at him impassively, teeth chattering.

'You're always saying you've never achieved anything in life; this is what this entire thing's about in the first place.' He rolled the dice, a wave slapping his cheek. 'Prove to your younger self you have a future, that everything until now has been building up to this moment. The false starts and big mistakes were all part of the master plan. This is your chance to finally do something worthwhile, *be* something. Are *you* ready?' He held his breath.

Alison the observer paused her pen over her pad and watched, eyebrows raised.

'Failing that, just stop fucking around and finish this cos my balls have given up the ghost. Are we good to go?'

Cordelia rearranged her goggles and plugged up her ears.

## 48

### FRIENDS REUNITED 2003

The wedding invite oozed classic Michelle. Tasteful cream watercolour card with a perfect deckled edge, her and Rob's initials entwined in a rose-gold crest, embossed within a delicate gold heart. Still afflicted with people pleasing, Michelle had granted me a plus one despite my current single status. 'You won't know anyone and I don't want you feeling left out. The best man's single too.'

Michelle had been happy to saddle herself with the lion's share of texts, emails and phone calls sustaining our long-distance friendship. I just stepped up enough to prevent it being glaringly obvious. Her London life buzzed with glamorous parties, weddings, work events and pricey skiing holidays. I was embarrassed I had nothing special to invite her to. Claire's leaving drinks at Eastbourne Constitutional Club couldn't compete with charging around Soho burning through wads of twenties on a Saturday evening. I often wondered what Michelle got from me in return. We talked non-stop when we did meet, sarcastic gallows humour plugging any gaps, and we both regularly vowed not to leave it so long next time. I always loved seeing her but was also perfectly happy knowing Michelle in the peripheral way some friendships conduct themselves. The annual Christmas card, birthday card, occasional text and, more common now since the explosion of coffee shops – meeting for a tri-yearly latte and a dusty biscotti.

'I'd love you to come to the wedding and the hen do,' Michelle had gushed in Eastbourne Costa, giddy with the first flush of excitement about her much-anticipated special day. 'We're hoping to do it at the Grand; that's the purpose of this visit: to check it out and talk to the vicar at St Saviours.'

'Of course I'll be there,' I'd replied, chinking her coffee cup, a poor substitute for a champagne glass. 'Wouldn't miss it for the world.' *Wasn't that what people said?*

* * *

'You're going!' Desi said sternly the week before the hen do, when I had yet to concoct a viable excuse. I'd run burst appendix, temporary blindness and sepsis of the big toe past him. 'Michelle's nice. You might meet some new friends.'

'I don't need new friends. I have you.'

'I *have* to be your friend; your mom pays me.'

I hit him in the arm, while feigning a limp for the sepsis diagnosis.

'She probably does, to be fair. You always were her favourite child.'

He laughed in the knowledge it was true.

'Just pull a French exit when no one's looking. They'll all be so plastered, they won't notice.'

Be at Rockwell for 5 p.m. – we're starting early with champagne and cocktails before moving on to Criterion. Dress to impress, but make sure you can dance – surprise disco to be revealed.

Sarah and Tammy, the bridesmaids, had released a joint statement on the round-robin email. I anxiously noted all the impressive email addresses attached to intimidating City jobs: Chief Enablement Officer, Trade and Transaction Analyst, Loss Control Consultant.

'You look fabulous,' Baz said as I walked into the living room, picking my roomy Bridget Jones knickers out of my bum. 'Give us a twirl.' Desi had 'found' a scarlet slip dress from French Connection in the back of the fashion cupboard, a size too big as instructed.

I did feel surprisingly OK after staging an eighties diet revival, consuming mostly celery and boiled eggs, placing all my trust in their sulphuric hands to deliver a four pound weight loss. They didn't disappoint.

'This is Cordelia, one of our old friends from home.' Sarah introduced me to a woman with enviable glossy, thick black hair, her name instantly vaporising. I nervously said hello, clutching a welcome glass of champagne (by the stem as Mum had taught me) daunted by the elegant bar. Cosy red velvet tub chairs and terracotta leather banquettes lined the long room, spiky palms and Rococo gold lights strategically punctuated the low tables, enormous picture windows overlooking buses and cars, taxis and motorbikes skittering round the incessantly hectic Trafalgar Square, a stone's throw away. As the only hen do, we dominated the space, high-pitched voices ricocheting off the tall ceiling while a few quiet couples drank cocktails and tourists posed for photos. The elderly aunt inner critic was having a field day. *So much flesh on show, and not all of it welcome.* I was in complete veneration of Michelle's friends flagrantly parading fake-tanned, cottage cheese thighs. Mine never saw the light of day.

Michelle looked stunning wearing a discreet pearl tiara and a bodycon, electric-blue bandage dress showcasing her minute frame that by my calculations must have been whittled away on five hundred calories a day. A ludicrous stab of jealousy twisted the knife; at least Sarah still had a massive arse. *Bad thoughts, Cordelia! Stop that right now.* Well, she *had* gratuitously scoffed chocolate and crisps when we were at school as if another body hung in her wardrobe taking the calorie hit. Good for her, she looked happy. Imagine the sweet liberty of not giving a shit.

Being here contravened the confines of my comfort zone. I edged nearer the perimeter of the group towards the entrance. *Was it too early to execute the French exit?* I was prepared to abandon my Zara jacket if it meant evading detection. Michelle cackled, throwing her head back, surrounded by gleaming show-pony friends fawning over her. I shouldn't have come. My gut had swirled and juddered all week; why hadn't I taken heed? I could be at home now with a DVD – *About a Boy* and *The Pianist* both awaited at Blockbuster. I'd get a cab as soon as we left the Criterion, say I had a bad period and couldn't stand up. Bad periods accounted for so many last-minute wobbles leaving the house.

The bar door swung open. I automatically turned to look, my glass slipping from in between my fingers. I recovered in time, clasping it tightly so it tipped at an angle, spilling an inch of fizz down my dress.

Oh crap. Of all the sodding gin joints in all the world, he walks into this one. Obviously, it should read 'she', for dramatic purposes, but I was beyond pedantry that evening.

'Cordelia...' David's voice was an octave higher than I remembered. He cleared his throat, regaining composure. The black hollow pit I'd crawled out of after we broke up beckoned from the corner of the bar. I'd feebly fought the remorseless heartbreak, feeling I didn't deserve to wallow when I had made my own bed, yet the pit hadn't discriminated. Shagging Graham, a PHD student working at the multiplex, just further drove home what I had let go. Conversely, approaching David and asking forgiveness never crossed my mind. The fissure had been too deep.

'Hello, David. I'm here for Michelle's hen do.'

He was wearing smart dark trousers and an expensive-looking navy shirt. I was inevitably drawn to the woman he was shepherding into the bar, her pregnant belly stretching her black clingy dress as taut as a drum. I barely registered her face other than she was blonde and pretty.

'David?' the woman asked, smiling expectantly. 'Are you going to introduce us?'

'Steph, this is Cordelia... an old... school friend.'

'Please to meet you, Cordelia.' She offered her hand; I took it limply.

'Cordelia, this is my wife, Steph.'

My throat dried up as if blasted by a sandstorm. A Casablancan sandstorm.

'David!' Michelle screeched across the bar, allowing me a moment to swallow loudly before speaking.

'Pleased to meet you, Steph.'

'Oh my God, David! What are you doing here?' Michelle cried. 'Did Sarah invite you?' She threw herself at him hugging him tightly. 'I haven't seen you since you and C—'

'Michelle, congratulations, I hear you're getting married,' David said rather enthusiastically, patting her back. I was magnetised by Steph's perfectly rotund bump. I necked what was left of my champagne and slyly observed Michelle, the bubbles enthusiastically tickling my insides.

'I see you need congratulating yourself.' She turned to Steph, smiling broadly. 'I'm Michelle, an old school friend of David's. When are you due?'

'Next month, July the twentieth. She'll probably be late though. Most first babies are.'

'Aww, you guys, that's so sweet. Won't you come and have a drink with us?' As an afterthought, she threw me a wary glance through a champagne-fuddled haze. I shrugged indifferently.

'It's your hen do,' David protested. 'No men allowed.'

'You don't count. I've known you since you wore shorts.'

Steph's tinkling laugh grated against my teeth.

'Come on, darling, it'd be rude to turn the bride-to-be down. Let's have a drink.'

David shot me a startled look. I smiled; the edges of his mouth began to twitch in reciprocation before he thought better of it and frowned. 'After you,' he said and waved me forwards after his wife into the screeching babel of sequins.

* * *

'You awake in there?' Desi called through the door. I could only whimper; my head throbbed at the base of my skull – an odd spot, as too was the soft dent where my ear kissed my neck. The door opened and Desi stood in the frame with a can of Coke. 'I don't want to hear any crap about only drinking diet shit. Full fat is the only thing that can save you right now.'

I hauled myself upright, the sun trying its hardest to sneak through the gap in the curtains and par-boil my brain. I took the can, hands shaking. Desi sat on the foot of the bed, Baz's tuneless whistling from the kitchen strangely comforting.

'You OK?' Desi asked. 'I've never seen you in that state, not voluntarily anyway.'

'I can't really remember what happened. A few flashes here and there.'

'Do you want me to remind you? Or would ignorance be bliss?'

I opened the Coke and gingerly sipped it. *Proceed with caution.*

'Tell me.'

'I don't have all the details, just what Sarah told me.'

I winced, preparing for the Cloak of Shame.

'Sarah found you crying in the toilet in the first bar after David left. You then apparently drank "like a pirate on shore leave" at the restaurant and almost passed out on Michelle's boss. Sarah tried to get you to go home, but you refused, then never made it to the night club. At one point you thought you were in Brighton. Sarah put you in a cab just after you barfed on the pavement. Luckily, you'd given her your phone and she called me. I met you outside and carried you up here.'

'I'm so sorry. I'll make it up to you.'

Desi shrugged.

'How can I go to the wedding?' I lay back down, abandoning the Coke on the bedside table. I checked my phone where a few text messages awaited: Sarah, Michelle, Mum and an unknown. I scrolled to the mystery number, pressing open.

Are you OK? You were quite drunk by the time we left. Hope you had fun. David

No kiss.

'Fuck,' I slapped my head, instantly regretting it. 'Michelle invited him and his wife to the evening do.'

'I know, you wouldn't stop going on about it,' Desi judiciously paused. 'He texted me too last night. You never replied and I think he was genuinely concerned.'

David – I'd not seen him properly since March 1998, when he'd dropped by with my stuff.

'I couldn't find your bracelet, sorry. No idea where it got to.' He'd hovered on the doorstep of 17 Villiers Road, the new For Sale sign screaming at a host of lost opportunities. 'Why are you doing this?' he'd asked one last time, eyes smudged with tiredness. 'I don't care about what happened; I still love you. You could easily move in with me when your mum sells this place. If you hated that, you could live nearby, or I could find somewhere here, rent my flat out, move back home and we carry on as before until you're ready.'

'Until I'm ready for what?' I'd sniped, unfathomable rage simmering in the tender cave of skin at the base of my throat. Usually, all David had to do was kiss that spot, unknotting me as if he'd whispered *open sesame*.

'Moving in together. We could get a hamster called Epiglottis? I don't know. Pretend to be grown-ups. Or not. Do you prefer gerbils?' He paused, as if considering another angle. 'Or we could just wait until you're ready to leave Eastbourne.'

I squashed down the sensible voice muscling in. *He's offering you a life! Take it. You love hamsters.*

'I mean, I know we were at school five minutes ago, but we have something real. Don't let this blip ruin it. You're my best friend, Cordy. No one else could possibly make me laugh like you can with a medical dictionary. I thought I'd end up marrying you one day or at least live with you. Stupid me.'

David handed over a dented Heinz tomato soup cardboard box filled with a few DVDs and video tapes, spare knickers, two bras, some Boots lip balms and a couple of T-shirts.

'I'm sorry, David. This isn't a blip. I'm just...' I spotted the *Romeo and Juliet* DVD I'd given him on our first Christmas, jammed between two battered VHS tapes. It punched a hole through my heart. On our very first date on Brighton Pier, he admitted something I'd long since suspected.

'You know I performed that soliloquy from *Romeo and Juliet* just for you when we were at school. I thought I was in love with you.'

I'd impulsively kissed him, propelling us towards a second attempt at a relationship... Just over a year later, teetering on the lip of a break-up, I could barely bring myself to look him in the eye.

'This is real life. I can't help how I feel. Most first loves don't work out. What makes us so special? All that fizzy madness wildly misconstrued to feel like something it never was in the first place.'

*Stop this!* the voice cried. *You love him! You're being mental!*

'Sometimes you just have to take a chance, see what happens. I could throw in surround-sound TV *and* a gerbil?'

I slowly shook my head.

'No? Matching weekend pyjamas? Too much? OK, I can't believe it's ending like this... It's shit.'

My eyes never left his Adam's apple.

'Bye.' He gave up and walked down the path, shoulders miserably hunched beneath his jacket, the nape of his neck exposed to the cold like a baby bird. I fought the compulsion to run after him and pull up his collar to protect it.

*What the fuck have you done?*

That had been the last time we had spoken, apart from an unexpected text four months later on my birthday – I'd stared at it for half an hour before deleting it, a dull throbbing in my chest, guts twirling a fandango. I saw him in the street once in Eastbourne, very early spring 2000. I'd just left Marks and Spencer's during my lunch break from Waterstones – I'd recently got a job in charge of the cookery and health sections – laughable really. He'd been walking past, head down, wearing a heavy winter coat. A javelin pierced my chest. I'd almost followed him with no firm plan of what I would actually say had he turned round.

Yet he'd texted me this morning, even though he was married and about to have a baby. Everything I'd ever denied myself landed on my lap while Desi quietly observed from the foot of the bed.

'*In vino veritas*,' he said mysteriously.

'What?'

Before I could dig further, the flat phone rang. Baz answered it.

'Desi, Cordy, it's Aunty Lois!'

\* \* \*

'Why are we even here after what happened?' I hissed, even though I had agreed to it. '*Your* mum isn't here.'

'It's a long way to come for a funeral of the man that threw you out the front door with just a T-shirt on,' Mum answered for Desi and her sister. 'Anyway, I need the support.'

'You could have just not come,' I said, as we milled about in front of picturesque St Hilary's C of E Church in Warningham village, battleship-grey clouds incoming, creamy roses shedding petals like confetti from the crown of the lychgate further down the path.

'I need to see he's actually dead, the old bugger.'

Mum had received a phone call from Mr Henry, her father's lawyer. He had succeeded his father, also called Mr Henry at Henry and Sons Solicitors in Leicester. He'd gone against protocol ringing, but felt it necessary to inform Mum her father had died and that her mother was now alone, albeit living in the Big House under twenty-four hour care. No one visited her and she was practically catatonic with dementia, next in line on the grim reaper's list. Mr Henry, the pub landlord, the cleaner and the gardener made up the meagre congregation.

Stephen had refused to come. 'I'm not waving off that miserable old racist twat.'

We huddled in a row at the back of the medieval stone church, three wise monkeys. No matter what time of year, churches were always cold, all that stone leaching the warmth from old bones. I hadn't stepped inside many churches since the Tin Pot Cathedral but the few I had smelled the same: wood, polish and the heady odour of sanctity. I pulled my thin black jacket around me, feet gradually icing up in strappy sandals. I should have worn my black work shoes, but they didn't go with Mum's classic Dior navy linen dress I'd borrowed. 'It's years old, got it in a charity shop when I'd just had Stephen. Kept meaning to get it taken in. Should fit you perfectly; it's a tent on me.'

'If I'd managed to hoodwink him until now, we'd all be very rich,' Mum whispered as the pallbearers shouldered the coffin down the aisle.

'You'd have to kill Grandma first before she uses it all up on home care,' I said.

'She'll be gone soon,' Mum said ominously. 'Mr Henry said she was on her way out.'

I zoned out of the service; Grandpa's overhyped attributes didn't deserve my attention. I stared at the stained-glass windows behind the altar, possibly depicting the life of St Hilary blessing lowly pagans with blissful faces, unequipped with matching halos. I chose to remember Grandpa fondly as the iniquitous shit who had almost murdered us.

A choir had been hired to save the embarrass-
ment of mumbled words, hymns gracing the heady
heights of the rafters. Once outside in the watery
sunlight, a tall, middle-aged, Dickensian-looking
gentleman in a sombre suit and black tie picked his
way across the tufted grass as we inspected gravestone inscriptions, not quite sure what we were supposed to do next. I stood next to Arthur Milton who
had died at the age of thirty in 1905, leaving behind
five children and a wife. He was only a year older
than me. How had he accrued five kids in such a
short space of time?

'Ms Franks?' he said, as he approached. 'Mr
Henry, we spoke on the phone.'

'Ah yes.' Mum held out her hand and he took it.

'I'm to give you this, under the instructions of
Mrs Simpson.' He handed her a cream envelope.
'Sorry it's not in more formal settings, but thought I'd
kill two birds with one stone.'

'Should I open it now?'

'It's up to you. I'm just at the end of the telephone
should you need to talk anything through if you
prefer to open it in private.'

\* \* \*

'Will you read it at home?' Desi asked as we rode the ghost train back to London. Grandpa had deemed wakes utterly profligate, unless of course he attended someone else's. If he couldn't be there to ram down as many Marks and Spencer's egg and cress crustless triangles, then he'd be damned if anyone else could.

'No, I'll do it now! Sod it.' She ripped along the top, unfolding a piece of A4 cream watercolour notepaper onto her lap. I recognised Grandma's spidery writing from birthday cards. Mum turned the paper over when she'd finished as if expecting more, the Basildon Bond watermark appearing like cipher in the sunlight.

'Well, the horse sanctuary's still getting all the bloody money.' The joke didn't merit the thin smile she pulled.

'What did she say? When did she write it?' I asked.

'Here, have a look. Dated eight years ago, probably before she started losing her marbles.'

Dear Lois,

By the time you read this, your father will be dead, which gives me certain freedom to contact you. Mr Henry has been instructed to *keep this until the right time. I trust you are well and still enjoying your TV career. I watch you every day – your father has no idea. He's always busy at that time of the morning. I must say, I am so very proud of you. I know over the years your father has been difficult. I have tried to get him to back down about the whole divorce situation, but he won't. You know how stubborn he is. I also didn't want you or your sister to go to boarding school and this feels the same all over again. At the time, I begged him but he insisted you went. He wanted you both to have the opportunities that he had missed out on and to make him proud. I often wonder about Elizabeth and hope she is well. You two were thick as thieves growing up, I never knew how to talk to either of you. You were in your own little world, so self-sufficient, there was barely any room for me. I used to listen at the door when Elizabeth read the nightly bedtime story and wish I could come and sit with you on my lap, but I didn't know how to. I know this sounds silly, a parent shouldn't be scared of their own children, but I was terrified. In the end, I didn't do anything and for that I am sorry. I hope that Stephen*

*and Cordelia are well. If you speak to your sis-*
*ter, do send regards from me. I can't change*
*the will; everything is in his name. It was never*
*my money in the first place.*
    *With love,*
    *Your mother*

When Desi and I glanced up from the letter, Mum was staring out of the window, her face pinched.

'You OK, Mum? That's an odd letter. It feels like she's blaming you.'

'It's not really an apology,' Desi agreed. 'It's a justification for behaving like she did.'

Mum nodded, lips wedged into a thin line. When she turned to meet us, her eyes glistened.

'How was she scared of us?' she said quietly. 'How were two little girls scary?'

I shrugged.

'Because you weren't dolls?' Desi offered. 'Because you were real people who needed nurturing and she didn't know how? Because she was ruled by her husband who wouldn't know nurturing if it bit him on the ass?'

Mum patted his hand gratefully. 'But she could have just said something?' she said, exasperated.

'Why didn't she say anything?'

'Because sometimes, that's more frightening than saying nothing at all,' Desi replied.

I stared out of the window, a lump forming in my throat. 'She tried, Mum. She used to ring, remember.'

'It wasn't enough.' She took the letter from Desi and shoved it back in the envelope. 'Families!' she cried. 'They fuck you up!'

'Aunty Lois, you never swear.'

'It's an emergency. I wish the old boot had managed to reroute the will to make up for everything. Who knows what'll happen now?'

'It was neither of their money!' Desi insisted. 'He stole it, remember? It's better we never had any of it: bad karma!'

'Well, at least your mother might reconsider coming back home when Mum finally dies?' Mum said, ever hopeful. 'She always refused to live here as long as they were still breathing the same air.'

A week later, as predicted by Mr Henry, Grandma died. This time, no one attended the funeral.

'Who got all the money?' I asked when Mum got off the phone. 'Did Mr Henry say?'

'Yes, off the record, perhaps to save me another journey. Even after the sale of the house and chattels, with Mum's twenty-four-hour care over the last five years, there'll barely be anything left. What there is will go to Peter, the gardener and his family. At least the bloody horse sanctuary didn't get it.'

## 49

### THE CHANNEL

The mercurial Channel continued to dole out all manner of chicanery. One minute supremely calm, my arms slicing water like a hot knife through ice-cold butter, then one thousand and eight hundred elephants later, I was swimming over ploughed fields, furrows two bodies deep, water smashing my face with the force of a shovel. Disconnected limbs, sinews stretched beyond their capabilities, it was as if I were a martyr on the rack. Which in a sense, I was. I didn't have to do this; I could call it a day at any given moment. The overwhelming temptation to touch *Boudica*'s hull and invalidate the entire venture was like fighting a nervous tic.

I stared at Desi, his face unreadable after delivering his clarion call. In the past, admitting defeat had been standard. *Give in, give in, give in* and all this will cease: the cold, the pain, the puking, the jellyfish stings. Gone in the graze of a hand on steel. I could practically taste the delicious respite of being coddled in a fluffy towel beneath my Dry Robe instead of this viscous salty soup drowning me from the inside out.

Deferring had always been vastly preferable than difficult conversations, awkward situations, unwelcome change. Sometimes, it was better to stay in and watch a film, indulge in a fictional life observing others' pain rather than actually suffering it. I'd become so adept at *not* seeking discomfort that acting out of character was commensurate with flashing my boobs in Costa and squashing them against the windows like a couple of iced Belgian buns.

Occasionally, when I lay in bed toiling with another sleepless night, limbs prickling, a work conundrum bugging my brain or rehashing a Tinder date's text, *it's not you, it's me, I need more than you can give*, I'd contemplate the ultimate surrender. Mindful it was just empty speculation, I often envisaged being dead: no more trying, no more change, just rhapsodic eternal darkness and quiet, permanent relief from my own head... It did seem rather drastic. I could just move to Slough.

So far, I'd swam through every chronological stumbling block and they had drained me in ways that the sea or Desi's tough-love soliloquy could not. The past, my existential Channel, pressed so deeply into my psyche, stewing in its own juices, a forgotten cine film gathering dust in an attic. I summoned the same genie that had sustained my self-destructive preoccupation. If that resided in me, then by law of duality, I had the capability to harness it for victory. Before I rearranged my goggles, I peered at the horizon, the sea and sky smudged into one another without corrective lenses. The air pulsed and danced before my eyes, a living, breathing thing delivering a wistfulness for the babies I'd never had, for the paths I'd not taken, for the lives I'd not lived, for the people I'd discarded like soiled tissues into a bin. This precise moment, treading water in the Channel, all extremities anesthetised, Elvis started strumming his guitar and began singing 'It's Now or Never'.

I popped the earplugs back in. 'Let's go!'

No time to waste being affronted by Desi's call to arms. I hadn't got to almost fucking fifty without some modicum of self-reflection. Only now I was stuck with an annoying earworm that had morphed

into a 1980s Walls Cornetto TV advert. *It's now or never, give it to me, delicious ice cream, from Italy...*
*Head down, four strokes, breathe out. Bubbles.*

* * *

'You're swimming the what?' Mum had asked when I revealed my plan over Sunday lunch cooked by Aunty Liz, who, driven by her love of food, would hesitate at serving low-fat vegan fake meat or watery gravy. She'd made a glorious nut roast swaddled in golden puff pastry. 'You can't even commit to whether you'll come for Christmas or not. How will you swim the Channel? It's a long way.'

'Thanks for the vote of confidence, Mum.'

'Lois! Let the girl at least try!' Aunty Liz had chastised, shovelling another roast potato Mum's way in a bid to shut her up. Mum ate a full plate whenever Liz cooked. It was as if the ancient sibling hierarchy had been resurrected the minute she moved in with her five years ago. Maria, Liz's life partner, had tragically died of cancer and she had dutifully cared for her like she had for Jeremy. But her age (a spritely seventy-three) plus the fact that Edward had also passed away the year before, forced her to reassess life after. Wouldn't it be nice to see out her days how she had begun them? By living side by side with her younger sister, reading stories, having adventures, the two of them against the world as if they were nine and eleven all over again except this time turn their lives into a podcast? Why not, everyone else was doing it!

'You know what I mean, Cordy,' Mum continued, shooting her sister a death stare. 'You've hardly ventured out of Eastbourne on your own apart from holidays. It's not just about swimming; it's about being mentally tough. I'm sure it's a lot harder than you realise.'

I assumed at least Dad would be behind me. Diplomatic Netty would no doubt employ some tact. He'd scratched his chin and given Netty a pained look over the Viking table in the Pink Palace kitchen.

'If you think you can do it, good luck to you,' Netty had replied, cutting Dad off at the pass. 'We thought you were going to announce you were getting married after the cryptic text message,' she had said hopefully.

'To whom?'

'That nice chap from Pontypridd, the one you met on the walking holiday in Wales.'

'That ended ages ago; I've dated two other people since then.'

At least Stephen had initially been a bit more re-sponsive.

'Wow, that's amazing. Well done for signing up.'

'It's not like doing cross country. I don't get picked by someone – I've had to pay three and a half grand for the pleasure.'

'What? So you're *really* doing it? You weren't just saying it?'

'No! I'm properly doing it! What did you think I meant?'

It was hard to gauge Stephen's genuine reaction because we were on the phone, and not FaceTiming because he hated it. To be fair, so did I, constantly getting distracted by my pear-shaped head and prominent nose if I didn't get the camera angle just right. Which was never.

'I don't know, Cordy,' he sighed, scrabbling around for something appropriate to round off with. 'You know what you're like; you don't always finish stuff, do you?' I could almost feel him wincing. 'Sorry, that was mean... Did Desi put you up to this?'

'It was his idea, yes. But he made me see it would be worthwhile.'

'It's a lot of commitment, surely? Training, focus...'

'Yes, Stephen, it is. I have the ability to focus on

things and stick to them. Just in the past it's not been the right stuff.'

'Right, yes. Well, good luck. Are you doing it for any particular reason?'

'For myself, but also for AIDS research. It feels like the right cause.'

'Yes, it does. Well, send me a link to the Just-Giving Page and I'll share it round work; Kallie will too. Just let me know what I can do to help.'

I front crawled after Desi, just like I had been doing ever since he'd grouched his way into my life straight off the Chicago redeye. The needling in my thigh slowly began to ease, the painkillers also loosening up my shoulders. Sprint for an hour, they'd said. That was three thousand and six hundred elephants. I began to count, the elephants falling into a steady rhythm within the thrum of *Boudica*'s engine. I'd managed to successfully keep down a small square of Battenberg cake and another sweet coffee in addition to the earlier chocolate. Calories in, calories out.

Cutting through the lateral current was like arguing with the wind. I visualised myself as an unwavering arrow aiming for France, gliding over the obstreperous undercurrent. Within my rapidly diminishing mind's eye, I staggered from the water, unfeeling of cold or nausea, a victor planting her feet on wet French sand. In order for this to become reality, the green cotton thread of grass capping the sand dunes, and brutalist gun turrets guarding Wissant beach needed to pull their weight and creep nearer.

Four hundred and one elephants, four hundred and two elephants. *You can do this, Cordelia. Finish this and life will be different. You made that promise, remember? Find the joy in trying. Find the joy in discomfort. Feel the hurt, experience the inconvenience, allow your body to take you places you've never been before because it's strong, it's powerful, it's a magnificent engine that needs to be fed delicious and heart-warming food. An army can't march on an empty stomach. If you survive this, just think of the things you'll be capable of. It's never too late to change.*

I'd seen a quote on Instagram from Roman philosopher, Marcus Aurelius: *The universe is change; our life is what our thoughts make of it.* I'd tacked it on the fridge at home, in the same vein Mum had stuck the wooden pig magnet delivering the caustic, *A fridge pig stays big*. Mum had been trying to stand out, and I had been trying to disappear.

*Head down, four strokes, breathe out. Bubbles.*

## 50

---

### STEPHEN

'The M25's a bit snarled,' Kallie said, checking the sat nav. 'It hasn't suggested a different way though. Shall we just drive at it and hope for the best?'

'We have no choice, so I guess the answer is yes!' Stephen replied with a smile in his voice. He loved Kallie's optimism, among other things. It bled from her like lights through cracked floorboards. She wasn't nauseatingly optimistic; that would have been infuriating – everyone needed a real moan about life occasionally. There was nothing worse than some cheerful twat harping on about how there's always someone worse off than you. *But I've just lost both my legs in a combine harvester accident.*

*Think of the person in the* Daily Mail *who had all four limbs eaten by a chainsaw and now manages to paint Picasso replicas with their penis.* Yeah, those people could fuck off. Kallie knew when to let complaining run its course without interjecting with a 'being grateful for your lot' diatribe.

'Are we nearly there yet?' Evie piped up from the back seat where she and Finn were listening to one of the *Harry Potter* books.

'Another hour and a half according to sat nav,' Kallie said, turning round. 'You know you can't keep asking because Dad might stop the car and make you get out and walk.'

'He'd never do that. Then we'd miss Aunty Cordelia win the Channel race thing.'

'It isn't a race; she's swimming it on her own,' Kallie said.

'That's not strictly true,' Stephen corrected her. 'She has a support boat guiding her and Uncle Desi is next to her on the boat the whole time, cheering her on. Show them the Facebook page.' Kallie opened it on her phone and let Evie and Finn crowd it like flies round a compost heap. Stephen had been strict about screens from the off. If you didn't want the hassle of kids (and fuck me, they were a massive hassle. The toddler years had been like surviving a dictatorship), don't have children. They weren't for the faint-hearted. But if you could hold off screens for as long as possible, you'd reap the rewards in the long run. He had observed this with his godson, Calvin, now nineteen and the most engaging young man who knew how to hold beguiling conversation with adults and wasn't constantly jerking every time his phone tasered him from his pocket.

Stephen had genuinely expected marriage and kids to pass him by like it had his sister. He'd almost accepted his fate, so it was a candid surprise that he actually met Kallie in real life and not online or on Tinder, as was the nascent trend in 2013. She was standing in a tedious self-checkout queue in Wandsworth Sainsbury's Local when she dropped her purse. He bent down to pick it up, his cheeks reddening as he handed it to her. She was perfect in every way, like Mary Poppins, if Mary Poppins had been Beyoncé, with jet-black corkscrew curls and green eyes. He made a lame joke about her bruised cauliflower and she took the piss out of his Prawn Bhuna ready meal for one. He'd forgotten the exact details of the exchange now, the unforeseen trauma of flirting overriding everything, but Kallie had considered him sufficiently charming enough to accept a drink afterwards. Thank the gods of dating that he'd body swerved the whole Tinder scenario and its pretenders to the throne.

'I love you' wasn't a phrase Stephen heard growing up, unless it was in a soppy film Cordelia had bullied him into watching while Mum was being brainwashed at the Tin Pot Cathedral. He'd gathered that folks said it to one another only in romantic situations. It wasn't something parents whispered to their offspring or siblings blithely announced to each other. Cordelia had been his idol growing up. He sought her approval for everything, which he now understood was his way of seeking confirmation that she loved him without having to actually ask it out loud. She was the one who had cosseted him when their childhood nosedived into a soap opera.

When her mental health declined, he had been distraught and for a period ignored it. His mother seemed unaware so how could he suggest she frog-march his sister to the doctor? He could hear Cordelia turning herself inside out (his bedroom was next to the bathroom) until practise rendered her silent, the only clue being the heavy cloud of air freshener. Her bulimia was something he couldn't fix and in his impotence, he almost forgot it cohabited with them until she left for Manchester and he breathed a sigh of relief, no longer having to deny its existence. He'd not realised how draining it had become grappling with fake insouciance after each disappearance to the toilet at the end of a meal, or during a film when Cordelia had eaten her own bodyweight in crisps and Boost bars. He'd been complicit in her disorder; the guilt weighed heavy. If he'd just asked her if she was OK, stood outside the bathroom door and forced the truth out into the open, things might have been different. It had been like living with the mad woman above you in the attic, terrified any moment she would escape and you would have to confront her once and for all.

As much as the first abortion saga had been hideous, it had been a blessing in disguise for his sister. The second one less so. He'd liked David's familiarity and composed demeanour; it was so obvious how good he was for Cordelia. However, when David left the scene, she rarely introduced future boyfriends, though there had been Dylan, ten years younger but a decent chap. Teacher if he remembered rightly. Occasionally, Desi would meet one on a night out, but no sooner had they shaken hands and swapped a few jovial words about their common denominator than they were axed and Cordelia would be single once more.

All Stephen wanted for his sister was peace. On the surface, she appeared fine regardless of the perpetual yoyo dieting, and endless hobbies abandoned the instant more solid commitment was required. The book group had lasted a few months before it was her turn to host *Wolf Hall*. She also joined the Ramblers but realised after two walks that she was the only one not drawing a pension. Cordelia was the type of person who never pressed the button on a pedestrian crossing, dreading underusing her allotted time and causing a road-rage incident. She'd rather dodge cars.

Despite being a functioning adult with a job and a flat, he sensed a greedy void, like she was searching for an indeterminate something. He didn't want to be so crass as to suggest it was about meeting the right person. It was more than that. You had to love the bones of yourself before considering another, which was probably why he and Kallie worked so well. They'd met when he was older and wiser and less prone to introspective self-doubt which from witnessing his sister, could strip potential joy from life.

Kallie was younger than Stephen, an actual millennial born in 1985, the year before his parents had decided to up-end their lives as they knew it. He struggled to remember what life had been like before his mum turned psychotic and joined the Tin Pot Cathedral, fabricating that Dad lived in Australia so she could keep her eyes on the cash prize that never materialised.

'I think you're too hard on your mum,' Kallie said after she'd first met her. 'She's just a product of her time.'

'Nah, I don't buy that. She actively contributed to Cordelia's terrible eating disorder, her breakdown, her self-sabotage, and all the things Cordelia didn't achieve because of all of the above.'

'You can't blame your mum for everything; she must have some good qualities. My mum cites your mum as the reason she shed all her baby weight after me and Alex. If she hadn't watched her on *TV-am* every morning and started doing those Slimnastic workouts in our tiny flat, she says she would have lost her mind trapped at home with two kids. There weren't decent workout DVDs then; women didn't have time for themselves between squeezing in jobs and childcare. Your mum was a lifeline to so many. She made exercise normal rather than something for athletes or keep-fit freaks.'

'You weren't there. I'm telling you, she was undermining in ways she wasn't with me. It wasn't until I got older that I realised how fat phobic she is.'

They'd been driving back from Eastbourne to Wandsworth in Stephen's clapped-out baby-blue Golf that was held together with a wing and a prayer by Arnold's Garage on Garrett Lane. Stephen didn't want to concede any ground about his mum. He had his set opinion, saw her only as much as necessary and didn't understand Cordelia's obligation to someone who had so clearly savaged her self-esteem.

Kallie shook her head at him, bemused.

'What?' he'd barked, not meaning to shout so sharply.

'You've made your mind up about it all. Have you thought about how your mum ended up like that? Desi doesn't see her like that. It's probably not as black and white as you think.'

'Desi was always her favourite.'

'Oooooh.'

'Now what?'

'Someone's jealous.'

'Oh my God, I am *not* jealous of him being Mum's favourite! He deserves to be; he had so much awful shit going on.' Stephen sucked in a deep breath, his shoulders sagging. Kallie kept quiet; it was her super-power: allowing truth to ferment during a heated conversation rather than rushing to prove she was right. The perfect temperament for a tech start-up human resources manager. Brushing up against all those strapping egos was like facing down Goliath with your pebble. 'OK, yes, I admit, Mum was supportive of Desi and kept him and Aunty Liz from financial ruin for years, something we knew nothing about until years later. *But* that doesn't negate how she treated Cordelia.'

'And ultimately you. Living with someone with a mental illness is damaging and stressful. You will have masked all that for years. She basically initiated a divide-and-conquer technique lots of parents turn to with siblings to try and keep them from unifying against them. It would have all been subconscious, of course. Most likely formed from her own childhood trauma. How was it, do you know, her childhood?'

'Oh Jesus wept, we're not even going to discuss how fucked up her parents were. Let's save that for another day when there's nothing on Netflix.'

* * *

'It says on the Facebook page that Aunty Cordelia's reached the Separation Zone. What's that?' Evie asked, looking up from the phone.

'About halfway, I think,' Stephen answered before muttering to himself, 'I hope she's OK.' He was surprised to find himself swallowing back tears. Discomfited, he firmly set his jaw against them breaking the surface.

'What is it?' Kallie asked, noting the sallowness of his knuckles gripping the steering wheel for dear life. The traffic had thankfully slowed to a crawl, creeping in the middle lane bumper to bumper, the sat nav indicating a thick red line ahead for the next couple of junctions.

Stephen shook his head, unable to speak. What if something happened to her in the Channel? He'd never forgive himself. He should have done more, should have been there instead of running away to London. He'd not even told her he loved her that morning on the text; he'd sent love from Kallie and the kids, but not from himself. *What was he scared of?* He tried to articulate it, but tears just poured from his eyes, his throat throbbing from holding back the river. Kallie yanked her handbag up from the footwell and rummaged around inside, producing a scabby pack of tissues, handing him one.

'Let it out,' she whispered. 'It needs to come.' She placed her hand over his on the steering wheel, gently massaging it, drawing out the splinter from the past.

'Why's Daddy crying?' Evie asked, trying her hardest not to cry herself. Finn stared out of the window, still listening to the *Harry Potter* audio book.

'He's feeling sad,' Kallie said.

'Why?' Evie asked, her voice wavering.

Kallie side-eyed her husband, who was biting his lip so hard, she was worried he'd draw blood.

'He thinks he's the reason Aunty Cordelia's swimming the Channel. That maybe he wasn't there for her when they were children and she's proving something now.'

'Where was he then?'

'He was being a child; he did enough. He doesn't need to feel guilty. She knows he loves her.'

Kallie always talked to the children as fully formed people. 'Knowledge is power, Stephen. If we arm them with information, they'll be able to make more informed decisions later on.' Most of the time Stephen concurred, but occasionally it backfired, like explaining the concept of squatters' rights. Stephen had been discussing a work issue in the kitchen with Kallie and Evie had asked what squatters' rights were as she took a yoghurt out of the fridge for her pudding.

'So I can go and put all my stuff in Finn's room and then it's mine?' There had been issue with the size of bedrooms when they moved a year ago. It was Finn's turn for the bigger room (by one metre and twenty centimetres) and Evie had taken every opportunity to complain ever since. An hour later, Stephen had had to intervene using his top-class negotiating skills after Evie had barricaded herself in Finn's room with a clutch of Barbies and Roland the elephant, her favourite plushie, as back up. When the softly, softly approach didn't deliver, he'd submitted to employing brute force, carrying her out of the room as she hurled her Barbie Dreamtopia trio at Finn, who slipped her the finger. 'Squatters' rights!'

Kallie smiled reassuringly at Evie in the back seat, who nodded as if understanding entirely the complex tributaries of adult lives.

Stephen brought the car to a standstill in the traffic. No one was moving. He touched his forehead to the steering wheel. *Keep Cordy safe. She didn't need to do this to prove she's the best. She's always been the best.* Kallie stroked his back as it juddered.

'Tell her when you see her,' Kallie whispered.

After a minute, he collected himself enough so he could speak. 'How do you always get it so right?'

he sniffed, wiping his nose with the sodden tissue as Kallie handed him another. 'You're a bloody freak.'

'*Psychologies* magazine subscription. Reckon I could out-Freud Freud now.'

'I only cry once a year. She better finish it after all this.'

'Daddy, you don't need to worry,' Evie assured him, clearly relieved balance had been restored. 'Aunty Cordelia's brave. She's swimming the Channel, and all those people have given her money for Uncle Desi's charity. Of course she's going to finish.'

'I hope so, Evie.'

'Aunty Cordelia's the best,' Finn suddenly said. Like most boys, Stephen assumed he hadn't been listening. 'I drew her a picture.'

'Let me see,' Stephen asked, turning round in his seat.

Finn opened his little Spiderman rucksack on the seat next to him and pulled out a crumpled drawing of two rudimentary stick people holding hands, one with long black hair, the other with spiky brown hair, surrounded by carefully drawn pointed blue crenellations. A smiley sun beamed benevolently from the thin strip of sky at the top of the paper.

'Who's that?'

'You helping Aunty Cordelia out of the water when she finishes because she's too tired.'

'Why's Daddy crying again?' Evie asked, annoyed at Finn for causing more upset with his stupid picture. 'I thought he was OK.'

'He just wants to see his sister, that's all.' Kallie patted Stephen's arm. 'The traffic's moving again.'

# 51

## THE CHANNEL

It wasn't my imagination. The grey concrete bunkers rooted on Wissant beach were definitely nearer, as if I'd suddenly zoomed in with a camera. I'd been determined to concentrate on my strokes, neglecting the grinding throb in my right shoulder. It's just another swim, that's all it is, one thousand and fifty elephants.

The sun scooted across the sky regardless, not one cloud hampering its glorious trajectory. Now dipped in early-evening ochre hues as the west beckoned, it had been my unwavering companion and my guiding north star. Counting elephants helped pass these final slabs of time when concentrating on film narratives felt beyond my capabilities.

Spotting an opening, Britney Spears threatened to make a comeback bigger than her Las Vegas residency. I blocked her with a fresh round of elephants.

The stubborn undertow had finally switched direction and instead of battling the ebb and flow, I was being guided by an invisible hand, drawing me steadily inshore, just as Cathy had predicted. Desi had left the water an uncountable pile of elephants ago. Time was irrelevant anyway, wasn't it? I'd no precise idea of how long I'd been swimming. A lot of fucking elephants was a decent guess, but finishing was what mattered, not how long it took.

I had measured myself in weight for far too long (light – good, heavy – bad), but I also measured myself in time. Comparing others' milestones, I found I fell drastically short. By thirty-five, after consistently chasing a starkly absent longed-for familiarity, I still hadn't had a serious enough boyfriend to warrant the landmark label 'being in a relationship'. Lifting up the turf on the situation, I found I only marginally cared, and that bothered me more than the fact itself. Surely I should be aiming for something? A family? But until Stephen had children, I honestly had no meaningful contact with any.

With no audible biological clock ticking (possibly drowned out by body dysmorphia), I was divorced from nascent broodiness tugging on my heartstrings. When Evie arrived in Stephen's life, turning it upside down, I had my first ever panic holding my newborn niece, staring at her delightfully elfin face. *I'd missed the boat.* Experiencing my brother as a father gave me so much joy, but I spun into the dark revisiting the abortions, particularly the second one. The baby would be in their twenties now, might even be in a relationship, working towards their own future. I had never played this game, refused to wonder 'what if' about either pregnancy, but maybe it was time I did.

The further I crept from my reproductive window, the easier it became to say no, I didn't have kids, it had never happened for me, pushing the blame on the enigmatic perfect relationship perennially hovering just out of reach. Perhaps in a parallel universe where I had keenly folded into motherhood, I would have fought my way through the obstacles I'd thrown in my path because I had no choice. Because I had to provide stability for a child.

And then there was David. He got to have the family he'd wished for. I was glad; it let me off the hook. Almost.

A whistle punctured my musings. 'Cathy said you've got another few hours, so unless there's some drama, you should be home and dry before dark.'

Desi executed an elaborate jazz hands routine before a sudden lurch almost sent him overboard. Alan cackled and launched a bottle of Maxim towards me. We had left all the large ships behind. There was the odd small yacht in the distance, scuttering across my eyeline, and a few sail boats joining my journey inshore.

'Some more good news: the total's gone up to nearly fifteen grand. I've been scanning the donations – Michelle pledged two hundred pounds. I'm assuming it's the same Michelle – her surname is Wilkins? She also posted on the Facebook page. She's super proud, and has sent it round work, drumming up business. Tracey Bates donated five quid – can you fucking believe it!? She said, "Go Streaker, Go!" Sends her love, if that's possible. Jesus – fuck her, we'll take her cash though!'

Every muscle in my body, even the ones governing my thumbs, required my full attention; I couldn't squander vital energy speaking. *Fuck you, Tracey, with your five quid.* That was less than twenty-five pence a mile.

A couple of hours didn't seem long, yet I'd been here countless times before, hadn't I? Crashing at the final hurdle had always been my department, losing sight of everything, forgetting that life could blissfully fly past the post even if you came in last. *Even if you absconded from your oldest friend's wedding, you could have remained in touch. Even if you aborted the love of your life's baby, you could have explored where the next road took you instead of pre-emptively throwing away the cards life had dealt you. You might have held a royal flush, but you'd not bothered checking.*

*Head down, four strokes, breathe out. Bubbles.*

## 52

# EVERYTHING THEN AND IN BETWEEN

I sat at the very back of All Saints behind a particularly elaborate flower arrangement stuffed with lilies, their cloying, soiled-nappy smell irritating my nose.

'Lilies are for funerals,' Desi hissed, shaking his head in disgust. 'Why do people persist with them?'

'We'll stay and see her get married, then we'll leave,' I'd said the week before.

'Er, no. We've been invited to the whole thing – it's rude to leave. She probably had a back-up list of people and we're stealing two spaces from Aunty Mo, or whoever has been sat for weeks in their best clothes awaiting a drop-out. These things are expensive, believe me – I've styled enough shoots to know what they cost. Anyway, I want to go. This might be my one shot of going to a proper posh wedding!'

'She won't know if I'm there or not.'

'That's not the point!' Desi had tutted as he pulled out a selection of outfits he'd 'borrowed' from a shoot. 'You're wearing this!' And he proffered a delicate turquoise, Ghost sheath dress, a used dishrag on the hanger with alchemic transformative powers.

'I can't wear that; it's so clingy. My boobs!'

'You can. And you will. About time you stopped hiding inside sacks and showed the world your beautiful shape.'

I rebelled and wore a black suit jacket over the top, a walk-of-shame air about me.

Michelle glided down the aisle in a frothy white-bodiced, full tulle skirt studded with miniscule diamantes, every step an exploding tiny flash bulb. Sarah and Tamsyn in rose-pink tulle followed behind with two young flower girls struggling to keep up, one scowling fiercely, tear marks tracking her downy cheeks.

\* \* \*

I walked out of the toilet cubicle and straight into a blonde woman stretching her dress under the drier while wearing it, taking up more space than someone ordinarily would drying their hands.

'Oh sorry!' I jumped back, bashing the side of the cubicle with my elbow.

The woman looked up, brows furrowing before bursting apart in recognition.

'Cordelia!'

A fist grabbed my heart, squeezing until I squeaked.

'Steph!' Another fist crushing my lungs.

'Are you OK? Not been drinking again, have you?' She pulled her lips back in an insincere smile, purple smudges beneath each eye.

'Gosh no!' I shuddered when in reality, I would have jumped through a ring of fire to neck a double shot of tequila there and then. I flicked my gaze towards Steph's stomach, but the dress fanned out like a lampshade.

'Frankie puked all down me as we walked in. Typical!' She motioned to her dress, under the feeble hand drier incapable of blowing out a birthday candle.

'Frankie?' I asked before I could stop myself, realising immediately.

'Our baby.'

I nodded enthusiastically. 'Sorry... Congratulations. She must be tiny.'

'She is. We weren't going to come because the party was so close to her due date, but she arrived two weeks early, just after we saw you in fact. She's six weeks today.'

'Wow...' I floundered around for some fitting words, edging towards the basins hoping for a swift exit with wet hands if necessary.

Steph abandoned the drier, letting the dress drop to the floor. I noticed a small bump protruding below her empire line.

'David told me what happened with you guys,' she said meaningfully, head to one side, pursing her lips and scrunching her eyes to deliver whatever level of sympathy she felt I was due. 'Why you—'

I sharply inhaled. 'Let me stop you there.'

Steph jerked her shoulders back as if I had in fact shoved her.

'I'm fine. It was an accident and we've both moved on from it.'

'From what?'

'The abortion. I didn't want children; I don't even think David did at that point. I'm glad it worked out for him in the end though. I'm happy for you both.' I turned the tap rather harshly, pressing the soap dispenser with the inside of my wrist like a surgeon prepping to scrub before carving open a gowned-up square of flesh. I glanced from the sink into the mirror, catching Steph's startled reflection, ashen face, lips parted. 'Fuck, you didn't know. Shit.'

Steph shook her head. 'I felt sorry for you when David said you were probably so drunk in that bar because your brief relationship had ended badly. I'd no idea you were even an item. He'd never mentioned you before that night.'

'It was a long time ago. Both of us were way too young. We've moved on... evidently.'

I twisted the tap, wavering on a mudslide of emotions, and shook my hands in the sink, splatters hitting the mirror.

'Sorry.' I brushed past Steph and out into the foyer, where I spotted Desi chatting to David, who was carrying a baby bundled inside a frilly outfit.

'Have we met before?' a voice that could open cans asked me. I turned round, coming face to face with a glazed, middle-aged, pork pie of a man stuffed into a grey shiny suit one size too small. 'I recognise you.' I'd never seen him before in my life. 'You been to one of our Michelle's parties years ago? Uncle Malcolm.' He extended his hand but I just stared at

it. It looked like a corned beef sandwich. Inner Aunty
was on patrol.

'Sorry, can't, got to go, bye...' I walked swiftly to
the impressive porticoed entrance larger than my
entire flat and out into the early-evening sun, the first
bars of 'Can't Take My Eyes Off You' ringing out from
the ballroom somewhere in the bowels of the hotel.
The high tide over the road was clearly visible above
the railings, an optical illusion giving the impression
that any moment, the sea was going to breach the
sturdy wall and flood the town.

* * *

*Dear Cordelia,*

*I'm so sorry about the whole wedding/hen
do thing. Steph didn't even know about us.
Then we bumped into you in that bar and you
went from nought to sixty on the drunk scale, I
don't need to remind you. She picked up
something, women's intuition or whatever it
was. There was no way I would ever divulge
what had really happened. I'm sorry, we
should have left like I wanted to. And we
shouldn't have come to the wedding. But if I'm
honest, I really wanted to see you and apolo-*

*gise in person for the hen do, and everything*
*else. I still feel like I did something wrong but*
*don't know what it was. I hope you're OK.*
    *David*

The letter had preceded an epic binge of such
Titanic proportions, it had taken an hour to gather
supplies in Tesco, carefully choosing the old familiar
favourites – Boost bars, Walkers Cheese and Onion
crisps, cinnamon bagels and Philadelphia, Dairylea
Cheese Triangles, Melba toast, Jammy Dodgers,
French Fancies (no brown ones, I'm not an animal)
and an entire deep-pan, thick-crust McCain
Margherita pizza for nostalgia's sake. I'd mindlessly
pushed the trolley down aisles, planning menus, fan-
tasising I was shopping for the week, secreting the
contraband amongst commendable bags of spinach,
brown rice, a pack of Quorn sausages and a lone but-
ternut squash.

* * *

I refused to witness what I'd just done. Panting, eyes
screwed shut, tears damp on my cheeks, I flushed the
chain, the stench repugnant. The immediate relief
I'd been flooded with in the past no longer impor-

tant. I cleaned methodically, spraying every surface in sight, wiping away spatters with toilet paper, eradicating the smell and creeping shame with Dolce & Gabbana Light Blue.

Downstairs, I bagged up the half-eaten pizza, the bagels (I'd managed one), half the pack of Melba toast, all the leftover cheeses and biscuits (only two Jammy Dodgers remained), and threw it all in the back of the car then drove to the large commercial Biffa bins by the small row of shops next to the chippy two roads over. I ditched the lot, swamped by guilt that people were unable to access food to live, let alone binge and purge. When I returned home, I opened a bottle of Tesco's Finest Merlot and sunk the entire thing, staggering to bed at ten, waking at 1.15 a.m. to vomit, this time not by my own hand.

Michelle had tried to contact me several times since getting married but my wall of silence sent a clear message. I never replied to David. Just like Michelle, and ultimately Sarah, I stepped away from those formative years, shedding my skin of all, apart from Desi, who had been my Arthur to his Martha from the second we trauma-bonded over absent fathers and *Roman Holiday*.

'You're the only person I would ever let abandon me at a wedding,' he'd said afterwards when he'd met me in the Stage Door still in my wedding regalia. He'd left the reception soon after he'd received the text. 'Anyone else, it would be instant dismissal. But there's something about you, Cordelia Franks. You got under my skin years ago.'

## 53

---

## THE CHANNEL

*One thousand five hundred and ten elephants, one thousand five hundred and eleven elephants...* Boudica cruised slightly ahead. The sea swelled with stiff peaks the nearer we rode towards the shore. I dived through a few, head down, while others pushed me practically perpendicular. Feeds were administered every half an hour, keeping my furnace stoked.

'I can't believe you're almost there,' Desi said at each pause. 'I'm so proud, Cordy.'

I had no words; they took effort. Effort equalled energy. Energy now equalled cheques my body was struggling to cash. Heavy as a hippo walking on dry land, my entire being needled and twisted, cracked and creaked, an ancient wooden sailing ship battening down, its masts leaning into the wind, releasing its sails, welcoming the elements' assistance. If only I possessed sails. What I did have was a hard-won half a stone, likely chipped away by the sea. I'd surrendered the pretence of the weight being 'just for the swim'. How would life feel to be this free forever, starting in my fiftieth year? No more scolding internal monologue. No more stepping on the scales first thing, the disposition of an entire day balancing on being within a perfect narrow margin between gain or loss.

'Ever thought of giving therapy another shot?' Desi asked, almost too nonchalantly, one Sunday after a particularly blustery trawl across from the Langham to the pier and back. I'd been shimmying out of my wet costume underneath my Dry Robe, pendulous boobs hanging like two marbles in a sports sock, scraps of seaweed and delicate shells stuck to my damp, goosebumped skin. My boobs, along with my thighs, were once the hangman, now just another body part that had lost its fight with gravity.

I smiled at him. 'This is my therapy, and best of all, it's free.'

'Fancy a quick game of Crazy Golf on the way home?'

'I think you'll find it's just golf to me.'

*Head down, four strokes, breathe out. Bubbles.*

# 54

## IS THAT YOU?

Have you checked the Facebook page?

I initially didn't see the WhatsApp message. Desi and I communicated through a multitude of social media platforms, often switching between WhatsApp and iMessage with the nimbleness of today's tech-dextrous teenagers. If I failed to answer a text in iMessage or WhatsApp, Desi would scattergun direct messages all over the socials.

I'd spent the morning focusing on booking slots at trade fairs up and down the country for next year's products release. My new favourite was the Swimmer's Diary (I had suggested it, and Joan had agreed to donate 10 per cent of sales to AIDS re-search), with facts pertaining to swimming heading up each date entry, including some Channel swim-ming trivia.

CORDELIA

What am I looking for?

DESI

A direct message.

CORDELIA

There aren't any new ones.

DESI

That's cos I opened it. Go and check.

CORDELIA

Oh, fucking hell.

DESI

I know, right? What you going to do?

CORDELIA

I have no idea. Feels weird.

DESI

I think you should go. Just see.

CORDELIA

Really?

DESI

Yeah, really. Let me know what happens.

CORDELIA

Obviously. I don't fart without letting you know.

DESI

Lol

\* \* \*

I pushed my sunglasses up, resting them on my head, and scanned every face in Costa. He wasn't here. I hovered just inside the door, the air con blasting my skull. He'd said midday; it was five past. Teenagers were milling around with freebie vouchers on their phones while young families evaded the early-May heatwave. I stood in line, turning my head towards the door every few minutes. I reached the front and was about to place my order when someone tapped my shoulder.

'I'm so sorry I'm late.'

'You're just in time. What do you want?'

'Oat milk latte? Do you mind, I can pay, got one of those loyalty cards.'

'Me too. Don't worry, it's on me.' I smiled momentarily, thrown by his couched familiarity, fine lines bursting from the corner of each eye, dimples fighting away from gently creased skin, hair thinning at the temples. No matter, David had aged well. He had lost weight. Silently picking apart people's appearances remained a putative tick. I was the first to lay into myself; why should everyone else get let off the hook? It wasn't like I told them; I wasn't Mum or Grandma. 'Why don't you find us a seat. I'll bring them over.'

'Thank you.' I watched him weave through the pushchairs and skateboards, finding us a spot at the back. When I joined him, I planted myself in complete neutrality; the passage of time allowed it. I placed his coffee in front of him; he had twisted three napkins into rigid twigs. He was about to model another one when I sat down. He dropped it and picked up his coffee, taking a sip even though it was hotter than the surface of the sun. Forgotten nuances rose like cream to the top, his impressive asbestos mouth being the first. I bet he could still grab hot trays out of the oven without using gloves or a tea towel.

'So nice to see you. What are you doing down here?'

He'd drunk almost half of his latte already.

'Dad isn't well. I've been down from London a few times in recent months. That's when I saw you on the telly talking about your cross-Channel swim.'

'Feels like ages ago now. I can't keep track what with all the training. Is your dad OK?' I blew on my coffee.

'He's got prostate cancer. They caught it, but he's been in and out with various infections.' David's fingers inched towards the napkin.

'Oh, I'm so sorry to hear that.'

'He'll be OK, I hope.' He picked the napkin up but thought better of it. 'Brenda said you'd been on the radio too. Well done, you're doing such an amazing thing.'

'Thank you.' I sipped my drink. 'How's everything, apart from your dad? How's work, family?'

'All OK. I'm working for EE now, MD, doing OK. Not as exciting as swimming the Channel! Frankie's at Bournemouth University studying Media Production; she wants to work in film or TV.'

'Oh, how wonderful. I wish I could go back and do that now.'

'It's never too late.' Shadows of the past.

'Got to get this swim out of the way first. Really can't think about anything else at all.'

'Is your husband not worried about you doing this?' he asked, touching the napkin with his fore-fingers.

'God, no. I'm not married or anything like that.'

He laughed unexpectedly, eyebrows shooting into his receding hairline.

'Sorry, didn't mean to laugh. You just looked like you'd stepped in dog poo.'

I chuckled. 'It is a bit like that. No dating for me – the swim is everything at the moment.'

'You're not into all those dating apps then?'

'I was. Not any more. They're freak shows flooded with married creeps pretending to be single, or saying they're getting divorced or separated when their wives think everything's tickety-boo. Then there are the ones who've got divorced five seconds ago and think they're ready for a new relationship, but they're rebounding, using you as the diving board for the next person. I'm better off with Kevin!'

'Kevin?'

'The dog share...' I explained Kevin's life story as well as Nimrod, Mince and Pie and Finneas and Snook. Over the next hour conversation flowed, slip-ping back to an anodyne time and space preceding our relationship. I didn't reference David's written apology I still used as a bookmark, folded into three equal vertical sections, ink faded, words unreadable, yet I knew them off by heart. It currently held my place in *A Little Life*.

'So, you still wear shorts then?' I teased him.

'I'm super offended you're still harping on about that! I had to have years of therapy to get over all that childhood bullying.' David folded his arms across his chest, narrowing his eyes.

'Oh my God, I'm so sorry, that was so thoughtless I—'

His lips twitched at the corners while his eyes twinkled with scantily disguised mirth.

'You fucker, I can't believe you got me!' I screwed up a napkin and threw it at him, laughing.

'Couldn't resist, sorry.'

When we'd stopped sniggering, I enquired after Steph's health and he reported back she was well, working in publishing now having left telecommunications, the business that had thrown them together.

I reluctantly checked my phone. 'I have to leave in a minute if I want to make the lunchtime swim.'

'That's OK, I promised to go to Tesco, get some bits for Dad.'

'I actually did think of you the other day. I was in

a charity shop looking for jeans. There was a massive medical dictionary for sale. I almost bought it.'

We smiled, eyes colliding. I snatched mine away first. I pushed my chair back and stood; David did the same. Once outside, I slipped my sunglasses over my eyes, staring discreetly at him for a full minute. *Was he happy?* It was hard to tell.

'Really lovely to see you,' David said. 'Perhaps we can catch up again when you've done your swim. I'll make sure to donate.'

'Thank you, that would be nice.' After an interminable pause during which I could think of nothing other than the port wine stain on his right bum cheek, David leaned over and hugged me. He'd obviously retired Acqua Di Gio, smelling of something woodier, fittingly classic for a man in his fiftieth year.

'I'm this way.' I pointed towards the seafront. I waved then started walking, turning round once to find him staring after me, his hand shielding his eyes against the bright sun.

My phone rang. Desi.

'Why are you ringing me? You never ring me.'

'I can see you've left Costa.'

'Find My Friends is not so you can stalk me.'

'What else is it for, then?'

'So you can find me still alive if I get attacked on a Tinder date.'

'Whatever. So?'

'He can probably hear me.'

'Walk quicker. Is he watching you leave?'

'He was.'

'Is he still?'

'I don't know.'

'Look.'

'No!'

'Do it, that's an order.'

I glanced nonchalantly over my shoulder for a second time. David hadn't moved.

'He's still looking.'

'The torch's still burning.'

'Desi! He's married, anyway, I was kidding, he's not looking at all.' I side stepped an elderly lady pushing a tiny teacup dog in a buggy. *Was that my future?* 'I'm going, I'll see you later.'

*I wonder if David still pees sitting down. Does he still like having his nipples tweaked and his shoulders nibbled during sex?* I'd known the answers twenty-six years ago; maybe they still stood.

\* \* \*

I awoke from a dream, the back of my head damp, a sticky pool of sweat collecting between my breasts, both of which were squelching their way out from my clammy armpits like damp mozzarella balls. David had been kissing my neck in the toilets at the back of Costa, the long-forgotten stirring in my groin a welcome surprise. Unable to remember the last time I had spontaneously burst with sexual longing of any degree, I took it as a strong sign. I rekindled the apps, just to window shop... How about younger like last time? So much easier and less chance of being married. *How about now? Really?*

'My vagina's in danger of taking up knitting if I leave it much longer,' I muttered, scrolling through Hinge. Kevin had slept over last night and I owed him a walk along the beach. Maybe someone would like to join us?

* * *

'I love dogs!' Jamie said, beaming, leaning down to ruffle Kevin's head. Kevin took it in his stride; people always patted him. He had perfected his 'just glad to be here' face.

'Good. Do you have one?'

'Mum and Dad do.' Jamie was a bit like a

Labrador: eager to please, bouncy and enthusiastic. I'd relit my profile and within half an hour, I'd been contacted by three men asking me out for a 'coffee'. Of them, Jamie was the only one available that lunchtime. He was also the cutest as well as the youngest at twenty-eight. I brought Kevin along as insurance. We met at the same Costa I'd met David the previous Saturday.

'What do you do, Jamie?'

'I'm an IT recruitment consultant.' He smiled as if it made him a better person. 'What do you do?'

'I'm a nurse.' I had a selection of jobs I rotated on dating apps. Nurse was by far the most popular. The next best job was teacher, then swimming instructor; after that, they were all pretty much equal. I always had to match the job to the date because what if they were actually the fake job themselves and started asking technical questions? 'Nurse, intubate!'

Two hours later, we lay in my bed, Kevin banished to the kitchen. 'He's not one of *those* dogs, is he? A watcher?' I stared at the ceiling. Relationships were... time consuming. Scratching an itch was all well and good, but Jamie had to leave. I hated this part and side-eyed him, settled in for the afternoon, scrolling Deliveroo for some lunch.

'What can I get you? My treat,' he said magnanimously, as if he were the Wolf of Wall Street offering champagne and oysters, instead of Maccy D's and Pizza Hut.

'Look, I didn't say earlier, but I have a twelve-hour shift starting in an hour and I need to get on. It's been lovely.' I crossed my fingers in my mind's eye. *Sorry, Jamie, you were very sweet.* One other thing troubled me. David. I swept him away as I shooed Jamie out of the door with a peck on the cheek, my indifference instilling the poor boy with a keenness he was arguably unprepared for. He'd revealed I'd been his first older woman; from the glint in his eye as he left, I wouldn't be the last. No eggs to fertilise, no dreams of wedding dresses, no expectations, just sex and a bit of a laugh in the house of fun.

Kevin barked from the kitchen. I opened the door.

'Sorry, Kev, I forgot. I won't do it again.'

Kevin jumped up and licked my hand.

'And I won't do *that* again, either. Look at the time! I should be at the gym; it's arm day today. Desi'll kill me.' I grabbed Kevin's lead and texted I was on my way. 'It wasn't even worth it. You're so lucky having your balls cut off. They can't make any bad decisions for you... To be fair, I thought my bits had shrivelled up.'

As I shut the front door behind me with Kevin on his lead, humming the words to his theme tune under my breath, 'Kevin, from heaven, you're our baby boy,' my phone pinged in my back pocket.

> I'm assuming you're on the same number? David

'What's going on?' I asked next-door's hedge. 'Do I reply?'

Kevin barked.

'OK, that's a yes.'

> It's me, yes.

I started walking but a ping soon stalled me.

> I'm down tomorrow visiting Dad, you around? Could do coffee again. Want to hear more about the swim. We barely covered it last time.

Kevin sat down while I exhaled, worrying a stubborn hangnail with my teeth. Why now? I didn't want to be part of some weird tryst or even just friends. Beneath my hard-earned insouciance was a jumble of unexpurgated emotions that I'd not dealt with since the nineties. I had to live life in the now, not in the back then.

> Hi David. Lovely to hear from you. I'm training all day tomorrow. I'm concentrating on that at the moment. Hope to catch up after the swim.

I waited for a texting type bubble. There was none. I gave up and started walking. Just as I reached the gym, Desi sat on a bollard outside, my phone pinged again.

'You'd need a lot of lube for that thing,' I said, eyeing the bollard as he stood up.

'You're so gross. And late!'

'Yeah, got distracted, sorry, won't happen again.'

He stepped into my personal space, taking the lead from me. I averted my eyes; he always knew.

'Someone's had sex.'

'How can you tell?'

'You're limping.'

I hit him on the arm.

'You just look... different. Tell me, was it David?'

'What? No! He's married.'

'Never stopped you before.'

'I never did that on purpose.'

'Bet you wish it had been David though.'

'No! Jesus. I'll see you tomorrow.' I kissed the top of Kevin's head and Desi's cheek and headed inside the gym.

I remembered the text message as I rammed the rucksack in a locker.

Sure, no worries. Good luck with the swim. David xx

## 55

## THE CHANNEL

The war memorial jutted from the approaching coastline like a homing beacon. Alan threw towels and my Dry Robe into the yellow rib before edging in off *Boudica*'s stern, Desi gripping his arm, keeping him steady.

'This is it, Cordy! Almost there, you got this,' Desi shouted. Alison the observer grinned from ear to ear, perched on the deck. The sun celebrated alongside us, burning bright, the spectral Channel moon prematurely rising. Even though land sprouted from the horizon as tangible as my own fingers, my fire had already begun to fade. Why wasn't I stunned with joy at this personal capstone of achievement? More people had climbed Everest than had conquered the Channel; I was soon to join an exclusive cadre.

*Everything you have ever wanted is just there, waiting for you, Cordelia. The moon on a stick draped with a delicate mesh of stars twinkling inside a universe so expansive that anything is possible. All dreams come true now. Even if that dream is wishing a painlessly swift death from hypothermia for Peter Bradshaw, the Guardian film critic, in order to procure his job. Finishing this means keeping promises to yourself, means trying and not giving up, means moving forward and leaving the confines of your little life because one day, not long from now, you might regret this fear that kept you safe all this time.*

'Don't be afraid,' I whispered, a mother to myself, having birthed this line in the sand I was on the brink of crossing. 'But I am,' I answered back. 'Totally terrified.'

*Head down, four strokes, breathe out. Bubbles.*

## 56

### EVERYONE'S ROOTING FOR YOU

'My daughter's swimming the Channel today,' Phil proudly announced to the man behind the petrol-station kiosk as he handed over his card. The man made the appropriate remarks. They had a nice little chat about it, then moved on to Brighton's shoddy performance in the last home game at the end of the season before another customer started queueing and he took it as a sign he should leave.

Phil had never pictured making it to eighty-one, let alone to still be driving. He'd sworn to Netty he'd hand over his licence as soon as he got to seventy-five.

'Can't be one of those Mr Magoos squinting

through the windscreen before mowing down a bus queue.'

'Hand it over,' she'd joked as she gave him his Brighton FC football sweatshirt on the big day.

'Still got twenty-twenty vision, love. Not giving anything up yet.'

Eighty came and went, he passed the eye test, still good to drive. He had a few years left in him yet. Now that Cordelia was a year off fifty, he could no longer hoodwink himself, his knee and hip creaking like rusty gate hinges. Maybe next year, he'd stop driving.

When the nurse had handed him a bundle of rage in the hospital, he'd balked, not sure how to handle her, and it had been like that ever since. Red and blotchy, mouth searching for a nipple or some sustenance, cantankerous at being born. He loved her, no doubt about that, but it hadn't been instant. He was too afraid in case she departed again. He rarely thought about the one that didn't make it, no point now. Little girl. May. He'd not seen her; he couldn't bear to.

'She was perfect, so tiny; her little fingers even had teeny nails. You didn't even say goodbye! You never wanted her!' Lois couldn't forgive him. She'd come and gone on the same day, very hard to take. Of course

Lois had been broken. Beatrice hadn't come and looked after her; not even Liz knew what to do. How do you console someone whose breasts are leaking milk for a baby born sleeping? No such things as paternity leave in those days. They'd never been the same since, despite their flying start of around-the-clock sex. Futile thinking if things had been different.

He'd met Netty when she visited the office with her range of Avon products, would his wife be interested? He'd asked if she had anything for men, not even alluding to an innuendo, but she read between the lines anyway. She'd encouraged him to pick up the pen again four years ago, short stories, poems, a couple printed in the local rag. Netty always checked his grammar and spelling. The buzz of seeing his name in print was almost as thrilling as that time she had seduced him in the back of her car when he'd bought the new range of gift-boxed shower gels. She'd been everything for him, a ball of positivity, light and fun after years of not knowing what was going on with himself or with Lois. All he'd wanted was for Lois to be happy because if she'd been happy, then maybe he would have had a shot at it too. Ridiculous, the hoops he'd jumped through. Anyway, that was gone now.

Would she be staying in the Premier Inn too?

Though he could predict she'd be horrified at the idea. He'd not seen her since Stephen's wedding. She'd mellowed with the passage of time, though he knew better than to mention age in her presence. Still dying her hair at seventy odd, why? Her mother had been the same – suspiciously dark-brown hair for a woman of sixty-five. Netty made the best of herself, but fighting the ticking clock was a race no one was ever going to win. One thing he would say about Lois, she wasn't afraid of hard work. Her *Golden Years* podcast, started as a hobby with Liz, had gathered traction since she'd become an internet meme, especially after Gloria Hunniford had mentioned it on *Loose Women*. Amusing that her serendipitous fart had in fact led to her second stab at stardom. He and Netty had listened a few times, it was rather good; they had plugged The Swim on there too: every little helps. He had enjoyed the episode on how to avoid the snipers' alley of elderly ailments – he'd give yoga a miss, though had tried the memory game website they had endorsed. It was vital in keeping the old grey matter from shuffling into an open grave.

'She's three quarters of the way,' Netty said excitedly, waving her phone at him, open on some social media app. 'Can you believe it? I think she's actually going to finish it.'

He eased himself into his seat, his hip clicked and he let go of the roof, landing in his seat with an 'oof'. He kept forgetting to take the cod liver oil pills Netty bought for him. Like they'd make any difference.

'I *can* believe it, you know,' he replied. 'She's been looking for something to finish her whole life. Why finish something small when you can finish something huge?'

'I know what you mean. I've never seen her so focused. Talk about leaving it for the third act.'

'What do you mean? The third act is always the best act! That's when I met you.'

Netty picked up his hand and kissed it. 'Let's hope her third act is going to be as good.'

\* \* \*

Lois checked Facebook again; Desi hadn't updated it for an hour. The swim couldn't be much longer, surely. Cordelia had been in the water over thirteen hours. She and Liz had checked into the Premier Inn by the ferry terminal the night before to be with Cordelia, Desi and Tim, bit of moral support. She'd not stayed in a Premier Inn before, concerned about bed bugs, blocked toilets, or worse.

'What on earth are you buying?' Liz gasped,

peeking over her shoulder in their cosy cottage kitchen the week before. 'An LED stain finder? Jesus Christ, Lois, it's a Premier Inn, not a brothel!' It lurked in her Amazon basket all week, should her anxiety escalate without scientific knowledge her sheets were surgically clean. Attempting to pin the anxiety on the state of the bedding was typical of her. Even in her seventies, she found embracing real life emotions equally tedious and embarrassing. She shouldn't be this concerned about a grown-up daughter; her mother had thrown her and Liz to the lions, expecting them to fend off the jaws of death without so much as a whip between them. She should have let go by now but found herself agonising the closer she rumbled towards the grave, unable to isolate what she was worried about. She'd not fretted this way about Stephen. He was always going to land on his feet, no matter how far the fall. He'd never needed her, especially now he'd hit the jackpot marrying Saint Kallie. Lois adored Kallie, who never failed to message her with the latest news about the children with accompanying adorable photos and love sent from Stephen.

She'd not felt this apprehensive since Cordelia had driven herself to university in 1992. Not even losing all her money in the property scandal came close. A tight knot had settled in her stomach the week before she left for Manchester and had refused to shift, wrenching every time she pictured Cordelia alone in her room. She fretted Annette had been right and she was in fact making herself sick. If it had been up to her, she would have let her deal with it in her own time. Surely bulimia was something you grew out of, say like wetting the bed or crying when you cut your finger? She'd never understood people's obsession with food – just don't eat very much if you want to stay thin? It was quite simple. Easy for her, she supposed; Lilliputian meals at the Big House had set her blueprint for life.

'Lois, we have to say something. Don't accept her pretending it's not happening. It very much still is! She needs help, even if she can't see it!'

The mere consideration of Annette solving the whole issue without her had sent her into a guilt-ridden tailspin. So she tackled her at breakfast a week before she was due to leave.

'Let's just get Dr Singh to have a little chat with you. You've had so many fillings too. Your teeth—'

'If you say one more thing, I'll never talk to you again!' Cordelia had growled and slammed her way out of the house. *Well, she had tried...* And then the dreadful phone call from Liz. Cordelia had almost died from septicaemia. Lois tarred and feathered herself; she needed no help from Annette with that.

'Lois, Tim just texted; he's in the bar,' Liz interrupted. 'Do you want to go down and have a drink? Steady your nerves?'

'I'm not nervous.'

'OK. Shall we meet him?' Liz asked.

'Yes, just let me put some lipstick on.'

'Netty and Phil are on their way, as well as Stephen and the gang. A right little family reunion!'

Lois inhaled up from the soles of her feet while it occurred to her, Cordelia would probably never get married; this was her wedding of sorts. A day all about her. She glanced in the mirror and applied her Dior Red 99 lipstick, the shade that Rebecca, the make-up artist on *TV-am*, had pressed upon her for her screen debut. 'We need to see your lips when you're jumping around. Red will work better than a nude colour.' She'd worn it ever since, even though senior ladies weren't supposed to wear red lipstick. She prodded her eye bags; they'd been held at bay for years by Dr Sebagh, but she'd had to forfeit Botox once Miss Slimnastics was sent packing and she'd ended up with a face for radio. 'You know if you ate a little more, you'd not have to worry about all this,' Alvin had said, waving his hands theatrically over his face like Marcel Marceau.

'I'd rather be a thin wrinkly carrot than a fat dimpled peach.'

'I'd rather die happy as a peach,' he'd scoffed at her thinly veiled insult. Poor Alvin, he'd died ten years ago of a heart attack while having dinner at the Dorchester. At least he got the dramatic gastronomic ending he'd always wanted.

Refusing to take the lift as usual, Lois remained silent until they reached the bottom of the stairwell. Liz grabbed her arm before they walked through the fire doors and into the designated lobby space. Lobbies were an extension of the glorious dream you were buying into when you stayed in a hotel. Lois typically found them to be an elaborate hoax because the rooms never ever lived up to the glamour and capaciousness of the lobby unless you were rich enough for the penthouse (which she had never been, even in her heyday). Lois had scoffed when they'd checked in to the Dover Premier Inn, believing she was buying into a low-budget, service-station nightmare based on the purple-festooned lobby and vending machine peddling crisps and chocolate. No wonder the country was in the grip of an obesity crisis. However, when she opened the door to their room, she was pleasantly surprised. It boasted a super king bed with a giant TV and a nice clean bathroom. The Premier Inn was elevated to the canon as she ate her words.

'Spit it out,' Liz said in front of the fire doors.

'What do you mean?'

'I know something's up. She'll be OK, you know. Desi won't let anything happen to her.'

Lois bit back her answer twice before relinquishing it. 'She won't need me again if she does this.'

'Ah. OK.' Liz let her arm go and stood back, appraising her. 'She doesn't need you anyway, Lois. She's not a child.'

'But what if she moves away? Decides to travel the world? All that will be easy compared to this.'

'So what if she does? That would be a good thing.'

'I know.' She paused, words crowding her mouth. 'They grew up so fast, her and Stephen, and it was all such a mess when they were little. You were miles away, Phil and I were broken beyond repair and then I was on TV, and I just forgot they were there; I had to in order to do my job properly. I missed so much. And I couldn't cope with what I *could* see. I feel like a reckoning's on its way.' Lois panted, as if she'd just run up all four flights of stairs. This swim was taking it out of her.

'Lois, you have to let her go. Because she needs to fly now. It's been a long time coming. You also have to stop making everything about you. As much as I love you, you can be too self-absorbed.' Liz smirked. 'I think I indulged you way too much when we were kids.'

Lois blinked hard. Tears brimming. 'It feels so difficult though.'

'Letting go is never easy. But we have each other, Lois. Not a lot of families can say that. You've been a rock to me; let me be the same for you.'

Lois nodded, wiping her eyes. Liz drew her in for a hug and they stood quietly for a moment, cloaked within their sisterly bond that had refused to fray.

Liz pulled away and squinted out of the window into the car park beyond. 'I can see Phil's car. They must be here.'

'OK, I'm ready.' Lois pinched her cheeks.

'Be nice to Netty.'

'I'm always nice.'

'Sure you are.'

## 57

## ONCE MORE ONTO THE BEACH

'Dad, they've just updated the page; it says she's going to land in the next half hour.' Frankie surveyed the littoral carpet from the top of the steps, a tremendous sweep of sand that ran to a ledge of dunes bordering the coast. 'That could literally mean anywhere. How are we supposed to know?'

David scanned Wissant beach. People walked beside the water's edge; their lanky shadows drawn thin as the sun prepared to set. A few families had thrown kites into the plucky wind, bobbing like albatrosses on thermals, children running with them. David had parked in the town a short walk away and he and Frankie shared a delicious late lunch of seafood risotto in Hotel L'Escale.

'We could jump in the car, get on the Eurotunnel and be in Wissant by lunchtime,' Frankie had said the night before. 'I looked; there are spaces for the ten-twenty morning crossing. Or we go later in the day, but it depends on whether she's set off or not and whether you want to chance it. For the record, I think you should.'

Frankie had been nurtured on a diet of *carpe diem* and romantic comedies while pretending to love Art House cinema, a future requirement in order to be taken seriously. Fuck *Battleship Potemkin*; how was it a classic? Give her joyously quixotic *Amelie* any day. Cinema was supposed to entertain as well as inform, otherwise just watch the news, teeming with war and destruction. What would happen if the powers-that-be only reported about heart-warming events instead? Doctors beating cancer, cats adopting orphaned squirrels and people swimming the Channel for a worthy cause. Surely the world would be a happier place if no one gave airtime to unscrupulous deeds? Psychotic world leaders mightn't invade countries if no one was watching.

'Francesca, it's the equivalent of stalking.'

'Dad! You haven't been standing outside her house for ten days straight or posting dead rodents through her letterbox. You're showing support!'

'In a creepy, weird, fucked-up stalker from school way. I may as well be airdropped into the Channel in budgie smugglers and swim next to her in that case.'

'You're scared of sharks; that would never work!' Frankie changed tact. 'Come on, embrace the unknown, be spontaneous – all she can do is say thank you and get back in the water. You never have to see her again.'

David dallied the same way he did at Nando's, perennially undecided about what level of spice he fancied. Extra hot in this instance.

'Sod it, OK, let's do it!' What on earth had happened to him?

Frankie had happened.

They'd visited his dad after the operation, the local TV news flickering soundlessly in the background. He just happened to look up at the exact moment the screen cut from the studio to an outside broadcast. There she was, instantly recognisable, shivering in her swimming costume on Eastbourne seafront, the redundant caption handily informing him: *Cordelia Franks, Channel Swimmer.*

'Oh my God! Oh my God,' he'd yelped. 'Where's the remote? I need to hear this.'

His stepmum jumped up as much as a seventy-year-old with a gammy knee could manage. Between them and Jonah, his brother, they lifted up blankets, scrabbling around for it, all the while Frankie quietly observed like the beady-eyed sponge that she was.

'That's the same Cordelia?' his dad asked hoarsely as they all watched the screen.

David nodded, listening to her speak about swimming the Channel in July and how she was raising money for AIDS research in the name of her uncle Jeremy who had died of the disease. 'I just wish I could have met him,' she declared to camera before running into the surf. When they switched back to the studio, the newsreader said they would keep the public updated with how Cordelia got on in the Channel, and they flashed up her JustGiving page.

'The one that got away, hey,' Jonah said wishfully.

'What did you mean, Uncle Jonah?' Frankie had asked.

'She was your father's first love,' her grandpa butted in.

'Dad! Really? Now she's going to swim the Channel. That's so cool!'

'Yeah, it was a long time ago.' David dismissed the whole thing, his heart dancing the Macarena in stilettoes, sweat beading in his armpits. *Cordelia Franks*.

'Cordelia still looked hot,' Jonah said on the drive from the hospital.

David didn't reply; he'd been thinking the same thing, though it felt vastly inappropriate in front of Frankie. 'I used to have a massive crush on her when you two were sneaking around upstairs. I kept the packet of Monster Munch she bought me for years after I'd eaten it.'

The next day, Frankie conveniently cornered her dad in the car to London.

'I've not seen you like that about anyone before,' she said, stealth nonchalance her specialism, second only to critiquing romantic comedies.

'What do you mean?' he asked, conscious of a bear trap.

'Excited, like you might actually like her.' She inspected her nails, chewing a non-existent strip of dry skin, side-eyeing him the entire time.

'I used to, but it was a million years ago. I haven't seen her since 2003, just after you were born.'

'Did I meet her? You told me about her once, when I was little.'

'No. You met her cousin, Desi. He thought you were cute.'

'Why don't you contact her?'

'What?!' he cried as if the exact idea hadn't been badgering him since yesterday.

'Dad, contact her! It's a sign. This could be it!'

'You and your bloody signs. Honestly, life isn't one giant meet-cute, you know.' He'd only just learned what a 'meet-cute' was, when Frankie had been immersed in *Romeo and Juliet*. He'd expressed horror at her claim that act one, scene five was the perfect setting for the most celebrated meet-cute ever. 'Shakespeare would be turning in his grave with you sullying his craft with one of your soundbites. It's a tragic love story, not a Gen Z TikTok post.'

'Shakespeare would be all over TikTok and Netflix if he was alive today!' *Many a true word hath been spoken in jest.*

Yet when it came to it, he'd been transported back to the nineties as he'd sat opposite Cordelia in Costa, palms clammy, coaching himself to breathe, fretting he was staring. She was older, they all were; expecting her to retain the dew of youth was sexist and also quite frankly unrealistic. She was still Cordelia who had shown him kindness in the dinner queue, Mum's saintly death having ripped out his plumb line, rendering him a temporary orphan while his dad shut himself away. Mum had delivered her parting gift a week before the end.

Voice cracked and dry, she'd delivered the words that had incited the infamous recital of Romeo's musings in the vain hope of catching Cordelia's attention.

'Son, always tell a girl if you like her. Promise me that. Don't hang about; life's short.'

He'd been as powerless against her dying as with Cordelia leaving. Mum eventually slipped off during *Countdown* while a contestant celebrated finding 'endocrine' in the jumble of nine letters on the board. She had loved word games.

Cordelia must have an anthology of battle wounds and war stories rooted inside her since they'd last met. But he'd sensed she was shut up behind those walls again. So they talked briefly about the swim before she disappeared to the Sovereign, leaving him painfully reflective. With Frankie hungry for every single detail of the Costa meet up, she'd insisted on a FaceTime the minute he returned to his dad's house.

'And she definitely said she wasn't looking for anything, even though she's single?'

'She couldn't have been clearer if she'd had a flashing neon sign on her head.'

'But she might have been playing it cool.'

'Believe me, she wasn't. She's sick of being hassled by married arseholes on Tinder and ones using her as a rebound after getting divorced.'

'But you're not just divorced, Dad. You've been single for years.'

'Centuries.'

'Remember in *Say Anything*, John Cusack stood outside Ione Skye's window and blasted "In Your Eyes" from a boom box? He won her round.'

'He'd get done for harassment these days,' David replied darkly. She'd run like a scalded cat twenty-six years ago; why would anything be different now?

'I think you should text her again.'

He deliberated a few weeks and finally scrounged up the nerve to send one. Naturally, she politely declined like he'd expected. He was flung back to her doorstep early 1998, his guts swilling with battery acid, handing over her box of things, praying to a god he didn't believe in that she'd change her mind.

He'd never forgotten her branding first love as fizzy and crazy (which of course, it is), tricking young lovers into believing it was something more dependable. 'Most first loves don't work out. What makes us so special?' A flimsy sapling with shallow roots, deracinated by one puff of wind. And, yes in a way, she had been right – the abortions felled them with one swing of the axe. Yet he had been willing to shoulder that. She'd been worth it.

Getting over Cordelia had been a withdrawal of sorts. He'd long for the flickering in his chest, the delicious twist in his stomach when she turned the key in his door, the faint floral smell of her hair, her full-throated laugh, how she peeked in his eyes for a whip of a second when he entered her before closing them in her own private ecstasy. No need to sift through pug-ugly photos of unflattering perms and terrible eighties monochrome jumpers with a view of tracing her provenance – they had lived it side by side since they were twelve. Over half his life. In spite of that, he'd been conscious she stowed away a part of herself, sometimes folding into a busy silence without warning, the grave set of her face uninviting. He'd sincerely assumed living together would open that to him.

It was months before he weaned himself off re-living their best bits, recklessly missing entire marketing meetings, Cordelia teasing him from the edges of a daydream. That didn't stop him shagging several other women; he was still under thirty and hadn't earned his bus pass just yet. Kate at work, who was a sexy, cat-eyed, suggestive ball of want, had been like fucking an ironing board. She had fabricated a persona to meet the needs of the fantasy she believed men were looking for: the exact opposite of Cordelia. David took no pleasure from someone performing; there had to be a purpose, a motivation for mutual gratification. Even a one-night stand could be meaningful if both parties were honest and let themselves be seen.

That was how he'd met Steph: a one-night fling after a sales conference that then bled into a week. She was the first woman that he didn't tacitly compare to Cordelia. Steph didn't instil any of that first-love lunacy in him. His time with her was measured and fun, they talked about work and politics, their bodies jig-sawing in a way he hadn't experienced since Cordelia.

He latched onto their ease, suspecting this could be his first grown-up relationship. He'd been pretending to be an adult for much longer than he cared to think about, way before his first step onto the career ladder while everyone else chugged pints of lager at university. When Steph fell pregnant after six months, time punched open a portal to the past, dragging them into a familiar void where he was gifted the chance to do the right thing.

Nonetheless, he soon discovered that in sickness and in health didn't apply in this time portal.

Bumping into Cordelia just before Frankie arrived unstitched a wound he had considered thoroughly healed. He'd not lost his ability to read her and felt helplessly responsible when she speedily dissolved before his eyes. Frankie was on her way and he loved Steph. But not how Steph expected to be loved, so it turned out.

'You're so distant, unconnected. I don't know who you are any more.' Frankie had exploded like a hand grenade in their life. He never blamed her, would gladly have walked under a bus for her. But he'd no previous idea parenthood was so all consuming. So punishing. It lay traps for future discord, burrowing into niggles and gripes, forcing them into the open where they stole oxygen from the relationship until the whole marriage became a dry carapace with two people rattling around in two halves of a house, politely enquiring how the other was while not really listening for an answer. They lasted until Frankie was seven, and then he razed it to the ground.

'Classic twatty bloke!' Steph screamed at him from across the kitchen after finding the text, a tin of tomatoes in her hand. He'd take the tin, and anything else she wished to throw; he warranted it. He'd not hidden the affair; he'd just not disclosed it. It had been stupidly easy, a get-out clause; time was hurtling towards Steph peeking behind the curtain. He blanked out his own mother's notional disappointment. This wasn't his modus operandi, and he couldn't explain it, even to himself. The divorce was done and dusted in a year, half of everything and a fresh start. He'd breathed a sigh of relief and eschewed dating, instead concentrating on being the best dad he could to Frankie, his own father's shining example hard to eclipse. Steph met her second husband, Harry, rather quickly and they had two more children of their own. Frankie wasn't made to feel like the Elf on the Shelf, but she couldn't help identifying.

'I think you should get a girlfriend,' Frankie announced one afternoon before she was due back at Steph's. She'd been ten.

'Why, out of interest?' he'd asked amused.

'Because you'll get boring. And Ryan Reynolds wouldn't be single forever.'

'The last time I looked, I wasn't Ryan Reynolds.'

'I watched a film with Mum last weekend, and Ryan Reynolds told his daughter all about his ex-girlfriends and then he found a new one and they lived happily ever after. Mum asked if you'd met anyone, and I said I didn't know. You never tell me.'

'Well, let me be honest, if there *was* any one, you

don't need to know. You're the number one girl in my life. Though before you and Mum, there had been Cordelia.'

David's immersion in dating since the apps took over was a baptism of fire and he hated it, though needs must if he was ever going to have sex again. 'It's so fake!' he railed when years later, Frankie made him write a profile. She even took the picture, from above, no dominant chins, and made sure the lighting was flattering.

'Dad, it's the only way you'll ever meet anyone. You're always at work.'

He put up with a year online before deleting everything and returning to the real world, which was snail-paced and just as full of pitfalls. He met Trudy, a single mum to two boys, and they limped along for three years, having fun, but dating with kids was a minefield. He didn't need to parent anyone else's children; one was enough for him! He wasn't looking to get remarried and when Frankie reached fifteen, her mum moved to Hertfordshire for Harry's job, and Frankie opted to live with him rather than disrupt her life. No more Elf on the Shelf. He relished becoming a full-time dad and, if he was per-mitted some vainglory, he was rather good at it. But it did relegate his rather sporadic sex life to the laundry bin.

\* \* \*

In the spirit of *Say Anything* and John Cusack's iconic declaration, David stared out to sea while Frankie scrolled the Facebook page in search of a picture of the support boat, *Boudica*. A couple of vessels rode the water further out, but they needed binoculars to identify for sure which boat was the correct one.

'Dad, I know you're worried this is over the top. It kind of is—'

'Now you admit it!' he cried, dumbfounded.

'Let me finish. She's just about to complete a mammoth achievement, and something as momentous as that deserves another huge gesture in return. Sending her a well done text isn't going to raise you above all the other twats who will be vying for her attention after this. You've got to go in big or go home.'

'I get that, but I'm also worried about coming on strong when she's not looking for anything at all. I'm not even sure what *I* want – I *think* I just want to get to know her again. We may have nothing in common and this is all a huge mistake.'

'Dad! You're not some idiot on Tinder who's swiped right hoping you'll take her for a coffee and a shag behind the Wissant beach gun turrets!'

'Jesus, Francesca!'

'Sorry.'

'I think you're blinded from watching too many romantic comedies and I've been swept along with the madness. What was I thinking?'

'Maybe, but—oh, oh, look, over there, in the middle!' She jabbed her finger towards the centre of the rolling surf. 'That boat looks a bit like *Boudica*. It's navy and white. There's a yellow dinghy following someone in the water.'

'How can you even see that?'

'Cos I'm not old like you. Come on, this is it!'

With no time to hastily construct a rousingly innocent explanation, or back down from this insanity, David couldn't help but trail after his wonderfully optimistic, enduringly romantic daughter as she took the steps two at a time, landing on the sand, kicking off her flip-flops. She ran into the head wind, sand stinging, towards the waves breaking on the beach. Gulls screeched overhead, soaring like untethered kites. What if Cordelia thought he was a twat?

He sprinted as fast as he could to keep up, the

damp sand yielding under his weight, trainers sinking into the striated ridges.

Frankie drew to a halt at the edge of the water, scraping her hair out of her face. The yellow dinghy bobbed in the distance. Thirty metres ahead, a person wearing a red swimming cap fiercely vied with waves crashing over them as they swam towards the shore.

His breath stalled; what if he'd got this so utterly wrong?

Frankie turned round, a beaming smile revealing her dimples.

'Don't look so scared, Dad. Just blame the whole thing on me!'

# 58

## THE CHANNEL

*Boudica* was behind me now, astern to be seafaringly precise, waiting for me to plant my feet on French sand clear of the water's lacey verge. My body blazed, rushes of tingles pulsed through my limbs, pins pressing into flesh, reminding me I was alive. I swam with bunches of waterlogged carrots for hands and phantom feet unsure if they were still there. I had dispensed with the elephants once Alan climbed into the rib. He was port side lagging just behind, allowing me the lead. The swollen sea seemed intent on spitting out ferocious trains of waves, determined to decapitate me, disrupting my stroke. I glanced down through bottle-green water, the once undetectable seabed gradually rising up to meet me. I paused after a particularly brutal swell carried me skywards, briefly dipping below the surface, unable to feel the sand. Still way too deep. I resumed swimming, limbs leaden, the urge to continue carrying me forward. I was going to do this, to actually finish. I *wanted* to finish, more than landing my dream job as the *Guardian* film critic, or even starting a degree. My chest heaved, tears swilling inside my goggles.

This. Was. It.

*Head down, four strokes, breathe. Bubbles.*

'Baby One More Time' made a second attempt to bulldoze its way into my head. *Not today, Britney.* What song did I want to be singing as I staggered onto the beach, triumphant? What? No! Not that! Too late...

Monty Python's 'Always Look on the Bright Side of Life' trampled over all the other musical numbers vying for my attention. Hysteria bubbled in my throat as I took in a mouthful of water trying to whistle along with Eric Idle. Another wave drum rolled me up and over into freefall, feet crashing into the seabed, ankles almost snapping like saplings in a storm. I fleetingly grazed the floor before being scooped back up, levelling out. Yet it was still too deep to wade. At first, the beach had appeared deserted but dots soon emerged along the shore like ants, then shimmered and grew into people the nearer I crept. I spotted a couple running towards the sea; were they going to join me in the waves? I practised French in a sing-song voice matching the tune's iconic chorus: *Bonjour, je viens de parcourir la Manche de de de de de de de daaaah*. Along with that, I had dredged up *Je voudrais un vin rouge s'il vous plaît* and *pour allez à la gare s'il vous plaît*. GCSE French had slipped through the net a lifetime ago.

I reached down with my hands just as some rather violent foam smashed into my shoulders, the beach within easy reach. My fingertips scraped along the seabed, nails scooping gritty sand. I tested the depth: waist height, shallow enough to wade. Upright for the first time, my knees crumpled, feet awash with pins and needles, forcing me to paddle ashore. Before me, the operatic curve of golden coast burnished with dying light sang with a feast of conflicting colours in stark comparison to variations on a theme of monotonous surging water. How did sailors cope weeks on end without a tree's leaves sighing in the wind or a field of verdant grass to soothe their weary eyes? Even a tower block offers some sweet relief of stillness.

'Cordelia!' A lanky young girl in a white vest top and denim shorts splattered with water hopped over the gentle rollers, looking for a moment as if she might dive in. I popped out the earplugs whilst attempting to stand knee deep, but buckled once more. 'You did it!' She waved her flip-flops at me excitedly. Concentrating on the girl's face proved tricky through splattered goggles. I couldn't place her. A man had reached the water line just behind. I yanked up my goggles, smudging my vision, reducing the girl's delicate features to a daubed impression.

'Let me help!' the girl cried, wading out to where I knelt in the water, waves breaking gently as they fizzed round my waist.

'No! You can't; I have to walk by myself.' The man hung back; I barely gave him a glance. 'My legs just need to come round.'

I pushed my hands into the sand, leaning all my weight on them and slowly unfurled until my legs straightened out. Temples pulsing, nose streaming, I was a veritable fish out of water. I unglued one hand from its shallow grave, and then the other, gradually lifting my head, mindful of blacking out.

I flanked my ribs with my elbows to mitigate the shivering and grasped my hands tightly in front of my chest. Placing one foot in front of another, I tentatively swished through the water.

'How do you feel?' the girl asked, walking backwards. 'You must be so relieved.'

'I don't honestly know.' Weary tears filled the back of my throat. I wished I could see without my goggles on. Two more steps and I'd cleared the water before turning round, stretching the goggles back over my eyes and waving both hands in the air as if guiding an aeroplane into its hangar. Alan piloted the rib nearer to the beach and Desi and Alison yelled, jumping wildly on *Boudica*'s deck while Cathy sounded the horn. A small crowd had gathered, chattering in what could only be French. They backed away as I left the surf behind.

'*Bonjour, je viens de parcourir la Manche,*' I announced, hefty gusts sandblasting my skin. They burst into a spontaneous round of applause, a few people taking photos. The mysterious young girl had melted into the crowd and I searched for her. How had she known my name? After I'd accepted everyone's congratulations in the form of handshakes and one wet hug (two older women had kissed me on both cheeks – *Bien joué!*), I spotted the girl chatting to a man with his back to me, the nape of his neck unsettling.

'Hey, I just wanted to say thank you for the welcome. Have we met before?'

The man turned round and removed his sunglasses.

'Well done, Cordelia. That was pretty impressive to say the least.' He smiled, revealing those dimples.

'David?'

'Before you freak out, it was all my idea,' the girl said. 'I'm Frankie, but call me Francesca if you want; that's what I'm called when I've done something really wrong.'

'My middle name is Francesca.'

# 59

## THE AFTERMATH

Alan must have hauled me inside the rib like a dead seal; how they got me on board *Boudica,* I'll never know. The journey back to Dover passed as a series of shuttered moments. I'd lain down on deck eating Cadbury's buttons, swaddled in my Dry Robe staring up at the encroaching dusk, tangerine clouds shrouding a wispy back drop of faint stars.

'Will we talk about David?' Desi had asked at one point before we docked.

'I don't think I can. I don't understand.'

'You do if you really think about it.'

Quayside in the marina, Stephen had told me he loved me for the first time in my life, Mum had actually mentioned the words 'proud' and 'brave', swiftly followed by 'a chip off the old block', Aunty Liz administering a sharp dig in her ribs. Dad and Netty had given me a big squeeze, Dad saying he'd believed in me all along and Netty telling me this was the beginning of the rest of my life. Maybe it was.

BBC South East patiently waited behind my family, ready to pounce with questions, lights, cameras and microphones. I'd stared, eyes dry, mouth answering automatically, brain playing catch up.

'Any plans for future challenges?' the journalist asked as if I was now spokesperson for ultra-marathons of all persuasions.

'I want to go to university.' I took a sharp intake of breath. I'd *never* meant to say that.

'Wow, good for you. And what will you be reading?'

'Film studies.' Again, who was this speaking?

Kelley, the journalist, had signed off with the latest total of money raised: nineteen thousand, five hundred and two pounds. I wearily leaned on Desi, eyes filling faster than I could wipe them. 'I couldn't have done it without you,' I whispered hoarsely. He kissed my salt-crusted cheek.

\* \* \*

Two days later, at home in my little flat amidst a flock of cards proclaiming *Congratulations, Well Done, You're a Star*, plus two flower arrangements, one from Joan (pink roses), and one from Michelle (thistles and ornamental cabbages), and a few bottles of fancy champagne, the enormity of what I had achieved finally filtered into my consciousness. Everything, even my toenails, ached, throbbing with proof that I had swum the Channel using just my body. A body that I had starved, purged and shunned under tented jumpers. Furthermore, even with such notions in the past, the voice still managed to take me to task about an extra slice of pizza or two mince pies instead of one, or preferably none. Enough! I shuffled into the bathroom and picked up the scales. I grabbed a bag for life from the back of the front door and placed them carefully inside. I needed some fresh air anyway; the British Heart Foundation charity shop was only round the corner.

On my return, I stood in front of the full-length mirror outside the kitchen, naked apart from my least disgustingly dull Tesco's big knickers. Even this pair was plagued with holes and loose elastic. The light wasn't the most flattering but I forcibly cross-examined myself, not shying away from puckered skin and bobbly bits. My strong thighs dared to kiss beneath my gusset while my breasts had actually firmed up from the weight training, inching away from my ribs. Not quite the hefty cantaloupes I'd pegged them for aged fifteen, more like pink grapefruits flecked with silver stretch marks, crepey skin creeping from my armpits, a badge of honour others weren't so lucky to achieve. My campaign of tyranny against these parts of me so utterly improvident.

'Thank you,' I said to my reflection and all the other reflections I'd ever railed against. 'And sorry. You are enough; you were always enough. I promise you can eat the cake, drink the wine, live.'

Later that morning, a journalist and photographer from the local paper arrived to interview me, embedding the experience further. It hadn't been a dream, even if huge stretches of the swim had sunk without a trace. I – Cordelia – who had never actually finished anything in my life, had completed that. If truth be told, I hadn't started *that* many things, littering my past with an assortment of abandoned projects. Abandoned people: that was another matter.

Aunty Liz phoned the day before I returned to work.

'How are you feeling?'

'Less creaky. I think I might go for a swim in the sea.'

'Good idea…' I waited for Liz to continue and right before the awkwardness forced me into small talk, Liz cleared her throat. 'Your mother doesn't know I'm ringing.' I loved Aunty Liz's voice; she always sounded like she'd just toked on a massive spliff, years of chain smoking kippering her vocal chords. 'You need to harness this moment.'

'The swim?'

'Yes. It has its own energy right now. It had different energy before you started: anticipatory. But right now, it's fizzing with all possibilities and opportunities, it's opening doors you can't even see, waiting for you to step through them.'

I held my breath, picked up a pen and began doodling circles, eyes and hearts on an envelope next to the kettle.

'Are you listening to me?'

'Yes, Aunty Liz.'

'If you don't run towards those doors, they won't stay open, you know what I'm saying?'

'Kind of.'

'Life will settle back down into the old ruts; nothing will have changed. But if you just take one step forward, the road will rise up to meet you, like the seabed did. You gotta do it now though, or you'll lose momentum – time is of the essence.'

'OK, Aunty Liz, thank you, I will.'

'Go for that swim. See you Sunday.'

Before I could say goodbye, the phone went dead.

\* \* \*

Sauntering back from the beach, a post-swim glow pinching my skin, I passed a shop I generally dismissed: Mermaid Lingerie; soft satin and lavish lace undies were not for the likes of me. The ornate panelled fascia and pilasters were painted a lush Verdigris and posing in the window, two curvaceous mannequins dressed in the most beautiful lingerie enthralled me this sunny afternoon, stopping me in my tracks. One wore substantial silvery-grey silk knickers edged with a rose-pink lace frill, delicate neon-pink bows sewn on either hip with a matching bra. The other wore deep-navy satin knickers trimmed with scarlet Ric Rac ribbon, a sexy diamond panel of suggestive red lace slap bang in the centre and an accompanying satin and lace cupped bra. A man waved from inside, shimmying from behind the counter to open the door, a bell tinkling above.

'Hello! I recognise you,' the young man said, welcoming me in, his throwback pencil moustache set on hypnotising me. 'You're the wonderful lady who swam the Channel, aren't you, raising all that money? I saw you on the news... I'm Eric, a friend of Reggie's, who used to manage the cinema? I think we may have met once at his birthday a few years ago?'

An hour later, I walked from the shop swinging a glossy grey carrier bag, electric-pink tissue paper cradling the two lingerie sets from the window and four extra pairs of knickers, all bought with a 20 per cent discount and promise of cocktails after work with Eric and his crew. 'No saving for best, make best your every day!'

When I got home, I unwrapped everything, finding a free local newspaper secreted at the bottom. There had been a stack by the till. I flicked through, mostly adverts when something caught my eye: University of Sussex clearing dates had just been announced with lists of courses candidates could apply for. I carried on skimming until I reached the houses for sale at the back. I needed a shower.

Once dry, I slipped on the soft grey lingerie set, admiring myself in the mirror. As well as being pretty sexy, the new garments were super comfy: essential if wearing daily. Eric was right. I grabbed fistfuls of baggy bottomed, loose-elastic atrocities from my drawer and rammed them in the kitchen bin. Gone! I swept up the newspaper, ready to chuck it in the recycling, but stopped.

*　*　*

'Dad, you can't just *not* do anything,' Frankie said. 'Send her a text.'

'Francesca, I think you've done enough damage. Cordelia has enough on her plate without me adding to the mix.'

'Dad! She hugged you even though she was soaking; she was pleased to see you.'

'She was puzzled. She liked *you* though.'

'Everyone always likes me.' Frankie laughed confidently as her boyfriend, Louis, rolled his eyes. 'You have nothing to lose, go on.'

'No! Sleeping dogs should lie down or whatever it is.'

'OK, go back on Tinder then.'

'Absolutely not. I don't know what this fixation is with finding me a girlfriend. Stop her, Louis.'

Frankie bit her lip and Louis glanced up from the TV. 'What *is* your obsession with happy ever afters?' he asked, shaking his head.

'I just want Dad to be as happy as we are,' she said, tongue firmly in her cheek.

'Oh Jesus, I'm going to chunder,' David groaned.

Yet a spark had ignited in her chest witnessing her kind dad, whom she adored, crackle at the sight of Cordelia on the TV. In that case, maybe Cordelia really was 'the one that got away' and that had been her parents' eventual undoing. She understood enough to know Dad had been no angel, her mum huffing once or twice about playing second fiddle without disclosing to what or whom.

'Why did you choose the name Francesca?' she'd asked Dad countless times.

'Because I've always loved it.'

If she'd been a lawyer, she'd have presented his answer as undisputable evidence of an eternal flame, M'lud.

One of Frankie's favourite romcoms, *Sleepless in Seattle*, hugged a golden nugget of a plan firmly in its core. All she had to do was bide her time.

As soon as Dad retired to bed, Frankie pilfered his phone from the kitchen drawer, opening it with the password she knew off by heart. He should be more discerning; their birth dates were not exactly foolproof.

* * *

My phone beeped just as I was climbing into bed after the first day at work post-swim. Joan had taken me out for lunch at eleven.

'Look, I know you have other plans now, but what I want to say is—'

'I don't have any plans,' I countered, worrying not for the first time that I had the beginnings of dementia; I found my phone in the fridge the other day. 'What plans?'

'You said you wanted to go back to university.'

'Oh yes, that rings a bell now.'

'Don't you remember the BBC interview?'

'I can barely recall anything after the swim other than I could have slept on a bed of nails on the M25 central reservation.'

'Didn't you watch the interview?'

'Jesus Christ, no way! I can't listen to myself on a WhatsApp voice note let alone see myself on TV having just swum the Channel covered in Vaseline.'

'Fair point. OK, well, if you *do* decide that you want to do that, I'm here to say we would support you in that decision, should you need to stay in gainful employment. I'm sure we could work something out, pare you back to part time. You're a valued part of the Journal Co, Cordelia.'

I could have sworn I heard a creak suspiciously like an old door easing open behind me.

\* \* \*

I reread the WhatsApp message.

> Hello! Hope you've recovered from the almighty swim. Well done on your amazing achievement. Sorry I was so tongue tied – Frankie is a force of nature and didn't really give me time to think it all through. It seemed like a good idea at the time. We had a nice lunch out anyway, so that was good! Wondered if you fancied having a catch up when I'm down your way? I'm there most weekends visiting Dad. Take your pick! BTW, I'm divorced from Steph, have been for some years. Sorry I didn't mention that before, it felt too presumptuous. All the best x

Instead of being floored by David's sudden availability, I now half appreciated what lay behind his grand gesture on Wissant beach. But he didn't feel like a door; he felt like an excuse not to stride through one. *Time is of the essence...*

My phone pinged again, this time Desi.

> Heard from David yet? You want to chat?

How did he *always* know? I needed to reply to David or I wouldn't sleep. I rolled Joan's generous offer round in my head while pondering Liz's wise words. I picked up the free dog-eared paper from a few days ago already folded open on the University of Sussex whole-page advert, coffee rings obliterating some text.

> Hi, David, nice to hear from you. I'm busy at the moment, but it was a lovely surprise to see you at the end of my swim. I really appreciated your huge effort, sorry I was so speechless, I might have been a bit tired. Frankie was a delight. You must be so proud of her. I'm sorry I can't meet up. Cordelia x

My thumb hovered over the send arrow for a full two minutes while deliberating if this truly was the right response. Before my head could fret further over shutting a door, I recklessly added, *Maybe we'll bump into each other one day soon*, and pressed send. Argh! *David is typing* appeared at the top of the thread almost immediately. I gritted my teeth, closing my eyes at the same time anticipating the ping.

> You can't blame a guy for trying. If you change your mind, let me know, my door is always open.
> David x

'Doors, doors, doors!'

I'd better reply to Desi or he'd hound me. I reached down and slid my laptop from under the bed, flipping it open on the University of Sussex clearing page. I clenched my fists as if I was just about to dive into an ice-cold breaker on the beach. My application form was almost filled in.

# 60

## FOUR MONTHS LATER

I squinted, walking out of the dark cinema and into the foyer of the Duke of York theatre. I much preferred old cinemas, the Baroque cornicing, intricate ceiling roses and ostentatious Grecian pillars adding a sheen of glamour to a wet Wednesday afternoon screening of *One Flew Over the Cuckoo's Nest*. I wished owners would restore these theatres instead of handing them over to Wetherspoons to be sucked dry and turned into pubs. Though now I was a student, the affordable wine was very much appreciated.

*Poor Things* had thrown up all sorts of valid questions about my own rather peculiar upbringing, my parents limitations cultivating my own, my ingrained shame, unmet desires, while at the same time pushing me towards realising I had fostered my own rebirth. Weren't all parents like Dr Frankenstein, creating mini monsters who would go on to live lives branded with the scars of experimental parenting? I identified with Bella Baxter – I too had been given a second chance but at my own hands.

*This* was why I embraced film; it possessed the ability to hold an unflinching mirror up to the human race in a more accessible way than the written word. Not that I had anything against books, I adored them, but the way the attention-deficient human race was heading, film was the most tenable media with which to drum up a revolution.

'That was soooooo good,' Martha said from behind me. 'I love Emma Stone; she's got such an expressive face: those eyes, the strong brows! She pushes boundaries most people would be too scared to even lean against.'

'She's great, isn't she? I loved her in *The Favourite*. She's an Oscar contender, surely?' I checked the time on my phone. 'Are you staying for the drinks afterwards?' I nodded my head towards the bar upstairs.

'I don't know, I have work tomorrow.' Martha, another mature student, waitressed in a vegan café in the Lanes. At twenty-three, I was old enough to be her Mum, but Martha didn't engender those feelings. In fact, the handful of students I'd gravitated towards all welcomed me with open arms, reminding me strangely of Frankie, whom I had met only briefly under such dramatically cinematic circumstances. Frankie sporadically popped into my head whenever a fellow student ardently fought a corner for a particularly doomed theme during an essay debrief. I'd admired her tenacity, fruitlessly wishing I'd possessed that kind of diligence at her age. I was where I was.

Lex, Frida, Sunil and Oscar followed us into the dimly lit foyer, chatting animatedly.

'I loved how it flipped the Frankenstein visuals. Willem Dafoe looked like the monster from the 1931 film.'

'Do you think it was a play on *The Bride of Frankenstein*?'

'Did any of you read the book? It was nothing like it. It was supposed to be set in Scotland.'

'Cordelia?'

I turned round.

'I thought it was you.'

The unexpected dimples sideswiped me. Why God, why did I choose today to wing minimalist make-up?

'David! What are you doing here?' With no Frankie to shepherd us through stilted conversation, my stomach instinctively clenched.

In our shared past, suits had redressed David as my all-time peerlessly elegant leading man, Gregory Peck, causing me to drop concentration and cast a predatory eye over him. Several times we'd not left the hallway in his Brixton flat once he'd slipped off his backpack, suit jacket crushed beneath our joint weight on the wooden floor. My cheeks blazed. *Bugger*.

'Not stalking you. I promise Frankie didn't put me up to this!'

'Is she here?' I asked hopefully.

'No!' he laughed. 'EE are one of the film festival sponsors.' David flicked his eyes towards the Greek chorus of students gathered behind me.

'Oh wow, how cool. Did you enjoy the film?'

Before he could answer, a young man, also in a dark suit, and a stunning brunette woman wrapped in an elegant burgundy dress, approached. The woman's striking green eyes discreetly roamed over me before she turned to David, resting a proprietorial hand upon his arm.

'We're going to go back to the hotel, freshen up before dinner. See you there for welcome drinks?'

'Yes, of course, I won't be long.' He smiled at her retreating back, eyes lingering. 'Are you having a drink here? The first one's free I believe, just show your ticket at the bar.'

'We'll see you upstairs if you get time?' Martha interrupted, touching my shoulder, eyes broadening, twitching her lips in a blink and you'd miss it pouty kiss.

I waved them off and turned back to David. 'Are you staying?' I crossed my fingers inside my coat pockets.

'No, I need to go. We're hosting a dinner for the festival organisers.'

My chest forcibly sunk.

'How have you been since the swim? I can't imagine how exhausted you must have felt. What an achievement. All that money for such a good cause. You must be so proud of yourself.'

'Good, yeah. Thank you for donating, very generous of you.' I swallowed so loudly, my ears squelched. 'I've been doing a film studies degree at Sussex University. Started in September. It's going well so far.' *Just ask him for a drink.* 'Did you like the film?'

'Sorry, I did, yes, a brilliant story. Original. Surprisingly accessible for a left-brained twat like me.'

He trained his eyes on my right shoulder. 'You finally made it to uni, then?'

'You're not a left-brained twat. I bet you can still remember every word from that Shakespeare monologue.'

'Nahhh, haven't thought about that for years. I don't have an artistic bone in my body.'

*Tell him how nice it is to see him.*

David lowered his chin, scrunching his features. 'I'm truly sorry about the whole Wissant-beach fiasco.' He cleared his throat. 'Can we pretend it never happened? Draw a line? Friends?'

I hunched up my shoulders, our story rushing at me like a camera rolling on a dolly. I was seconds from confessing that when I'd dived back into the Channel, it had taken an inordinate amount of gumption to do so instead of blabbering a long overdue apology for everything, for running from probably one of the best things in my life.

But I didn't.

'Of course we're friends. I told you we'd bump into each other again,' I said flippantly, covering my footprints in the sand.

His face unfolded. 'You never said that!'

'You messaged me after the swim and I told you then.'

'I never messaged you.'

'You did!'

'Uh-uh, no way. I haven't got dementia just yet.'

'Look, I'll show you.' I scrabbled around for my phone returned to my pocket. 'Here!'

'I need my glasses.' He patted his pockets, re-trieving them from inside his jacket, perching them on the end of his nose. His eyes widened.

'What?! That wasn't me!'

'Well, it says it's you! That's your number!'

He pulled out his phone and retrieved our What-sApp messages, scrolling to find the last one. It had disappeared.

'Frankie!' he hissed. 'I'm going to kill her.'

I started laughing.

'Please don't, I rather liked her. I'm afraid she's done a *Sleepless in Seattle* on us. But, to be perfectly frank, I always preferred *An Affair to Remember*, Nora Ephron's original muse. Always loved Cary Grant in a suit.'

David set his head on one side, then shook it hopelessly. 'Is it weird to say she reminds me of you? I don't know where all her creativity comes from.'

'Well, we do share a name.'

A rattled Cary Grant observed us from within a *North by Northwest* framed poster on the wall behind, his Hollywood cleft chin a cousin to David's twin dimples.

'I need to go. It was good to see you.' David brushed my cheek with his lips, a parting shot. 'Well done for everything. For chasing your dream. I told you it's never too late!'

I watched him stroll towards the exit. He didn't look back.

## 61

### IT IS THE EAST, AND JULIET IS THE SUN

He didn't remotely resemble his picture. His forehead didn't have its own postcode on Bumble. *Cordelia! That's mean... He's nice.* I wouldn't have swiped right otherwise. Yes, yes, I'm six months off fifty, and should have learned my lesson. It was all Dr Khan's fault. Honestly, no, it was Netty's fault. If she hadn't sent me to Dr Kahn as an early Christmas present then I wouldn't be trapped in the Buskers Bar sitting opposite Ben, the Easter Island statue, while people sang karaoke.

'Your testosterone's on the floor,' Dr Khan had said, studying the blood test results. 'You should be taking that as well as oestrogen and progesterone. How's your sex drive?'

'Well, it used to be pretty rampant, but it's recently dropped off a cliff.' Dr Khan's obvious pragmatism invited a cosy fireside chat. 'Adam Driver could appear in front of me naked, begging for a quickie but I'd prefer cleaning out the fish tank.'

'Ooh, Adam Driver? You like them quirky looking.'

'The quirkier the better.' But no foreheads bigger than the National Debt. *Sorry, Ben.* I wasn't exactly Audrey Hepburn, now was I?

'Let's see if we can relight that fire.'

Dr Khan needed her own YouTube channel.

Two weeks of daily testosterone cream and I woke in the night searching for Claud in the bedside table after a particularly raunchy dream about David of all people.

'I think you should start dating again if Claud's come out of hiding,' Desi suggested in the kitchen, dropping off Kevin. 'It's a sign. But someone your own age this time. Where's David when you need him?'

'Will you shut up about David? I told you he's moved on. I'm pretty sure he's shagging someone at work.'

'He wouldn't have given up that whole "I'm just a boy standing in front of a girl who's swum the Channel, asking her to love him". It was only five minutes ago.'

'Almost five months, actually.'

'Minutes, months – whatever.' Desi had stared at me; Mince looked like he was laughing from his ladder resting against the glass. 'Tell her, Tim. Oh, you never met David. We all loved him.'

'Sorry, Cordy, just give me the nod and I'll drag him home.'

Christmas was always a dangerous time to rekindle the apps – they were teeming with desperados (myself included) trying to bag that special someone for the zombie betwixtmas period as well as New Year's Eve. I shouldn't have come. *Take responsibility for your own mistakes, Cordelia.* I'd learned about steaming wood for building guitars – Ben's livelihood. At least he wasn't boring.

'Do you want to go somewhere else?' Ben asked after a middle-aged woman had finished murdering 'You Got the Love'. 'I'd no idea karaoke was on tonight; it's normally decent singer-songwriters on a Thursday.'

*Abort, abort. Initiate phone call.*

I'd already texted Desi when I nipped to the loo. He and Tim were at dinner round the corner. My phone rang.

'Sorry, I need to get this.'

Ben nodded.

'Your mum's ill; she's asking for you,' Desi hammed up his lines.

'Oh no, is she going to be OK?' My angst-appropriate response was worthy of an understudy proposal from The Old Vic.

'We've called an ambulance. Meet us at the hospital.' He even tacked on a mournful wail before whispering: 'We've just got the bill but could come and join you for a glass of wine in ten minutes?'

'OK, thanks for letting me know.'

'Everything all right?'

After a swift recap, I had to firmly assure Ben I didn't need him to accompany me.

'Desi, my cousin's, coming to get me. I'll wait here.'

'I'll stay with you until he gets here.'

'Honestly, it's fine. Go, you don't need to stay.'

'But your mum's on her way to A&E; you're probably in shock.'

'Trust me, I'm OK. She does this all the time.'

'She does? What's wrong with her?'

'Have you got all day?'

It would have been so much easier to have told the truth, or to have disappeared to the loo. I'd climbed out of a sizeable collection of toilet windows over the last decade. Trust me to swipe right on someone who was not only nosy (a first), but actually interested in my life (a dodo). I managed to shoehorn him out the bar with a promise to DM him news of Mum's recovery.

'Don't forget. I hope she's OK!'

An old man stepped up to the mic; the opening bars of 'Non, Je ne regrette rien' filled the pub.

'Oh my God, Cordelia?' I had just exited the ladies' toilets when I was accosted. Desi was two minutes away according to Find My Friend. I glanced up from my phone.

'Frankie!' I automatically went in for a hug. She reeked of fried food and garlic.

'Ooh, sorry, I stink.' Frankie leapt out of my arms almost immediately. 'I don't want to transfer it on to you.'

'What are you doing here?'

'Working, though I've just finished my shift. You'll see Dad; he's coming to pick me up.' She smiled broadly. 'I just need a wee; where are you sitting?'

'I was just about to leave, actually.'

'Wait five minutes? I'll come and find you.'

I nodded dumbly. Stunned, questions firing on

all cylinders, I sat back down at the table before jumping up less than a minute later.

'There she is!' Desi called across the bar, weaving through tables, shaking his umbrella. There had been no takers for the next song. 'The old-lady ambulance is here.' Tim kissed my cheek first.

'What you drinking?' Desi asked. 'I'm thinking mullered wine, cos you know, it's Christmas!'

'We need to leave,' I hissed. 'Now.'

'What? Why? Is Mr Bumble still here? Are we having a quad date?'

'No! Shit, too late.'

Frankie approached the table.

'Hello!' Desi said, eyes wide, shooting between me and Frankie.

'This is Frankie, David's daughter. Frankie, this is Desi, my cousin, and Tim, his partner.'

'Oooooh, pleased to meet you both,' Frankie cried. 'Are you the cousin that was on the support boat?'

'I am indeed. You don't look like your dad,' Desi said. 'Something I'm sure you're relieved to hear. I always think it sounds like you're comparing someone to a drag queen before they've done their make-up.'

A minute of small talk blocked my escape.

'Listen, I really need to go,' I said, butterflies, ele-phants, antelope all careering through my belly.

'But Dad'll be here any sec. I know he'd love to see you.'

Before I could even contemplate a getaway through the bathroom window, David appeared.

'I saw Desi before I even saw you, Frankie.' He shook Desi's hand enthusiastically. 'How long has it been, mate?'

'Twenty years? This one was a tiny pickle!' Frankie grinned. 'You down visiting your dad? How is he? And Brenda?'

'I thought you knew? We've moved down here,' Frankie said.

'What?' Desi and I cried. Tim looked on, bemused.

'Yeah, Dad's been struggling,' David explained, sheepishly. 'Brenda can only do so much, she's get-ting on as well, and Jonah's about to have baby number three living in bloody Cardiff, so I made the change. Let the flat out, renting a house near Dad. See what seaside life's like.'

'How long have you been here?' I asked, praying he wasn't on the apps.

'Since I bumped into you last time.'

Oh.

'You never said.'

'You never asked.'

An ungainly silence descended.

'Let me get some drinks,' Desi said, clapping his hands together. 'If I remember rightly, red wine all round?'

'I'm just going to the loo,' I said.

'Didn't you just go?' Frankie asked, puzzled. 'Can I have a Coke, please?'

'Oh no you don't, you're coming with me.' Desi linked his arm through mine and hauled me towards the bar. 'I know your game.'

I looked over my shoulder. David stared after me, his brow furrowed, lips pinched.

'Why didn't he tell me he was living in Eastbourne?' I hissed.

'He was probably scared you'd swim back to France.'

'Fair. But he could have told me.'

'He doesn't have to tell you anything, does he? A bottle of the Merlot, please and four glasses and a Coke.' Desi flashed his winning smile. 'Thank you so much.'

'What if he is shagging that woman? It'll be so weird.'

'More weird than you meeting with Mr Bumble when you could have been with David?'

'That's different.'

'No it's not. Come on.'

But I couldn't find any words. Desi and Tim took up the mantle and kept conversation flowing through the shallows of Christmas plans, New Year parties, Frankie's degree.

Someone tapped the microphone behind us. 'Excuse me,' the young man with a Father-Christmas-in-waiting-style beard interrupted. 'We've got a few spaces for some singers if anyone's interested. No one's signed up for the last two slots. Any takers?'

'Yes, this one here!' Desi called, pushing me forward.

'No, no, no.'

'Come on, I'll come with you. We can do 'Freedom'; you love George Michael.'

'Desi, no!'

'You like karaoke!'

'Since when?' I death stared him and he deflected it right back. 'Fuck's sake, I'm going home.' I grabbed my scarf from the back of the chair.

'Stay,' Frankie pleaded.

'Sorry, I—'

'Look, it's my fault. I should have mentioned I

lived round the corner.' David put down his wine glass. 'Stay for a drink?'

I shook my head. The Christmas tree mocked me with its sparkly tinsel and baubles, everyone's distorted faces dangling in a sinister house of mirrors. Why had I thought I could date again? This was a circus. Unaccountable rage took hold. Desi grasped my hand but I shook it free.

'I'm going. I'll see you soon.' I stalked to the door but got trapped on the threshold; biblical rain machine-gunned the pavement outside. I prodded inside my bag. Fuck, I'd left my umbrella by the chair. Not even Gene Kelly would have braved it. I lingered, undecided, irritation bubbling, a geyser ready to shoot skywards. I kicked the umbrella stand in frustration, accidentally upending it, the parked soggy umbrellas tipping sideways all over the floor. 'You absolute twat,' I mumbled to myself. Huffing dramatically, I bent down to ram them back in but they flailed like a colony of bats in flight, spokes jabbing me.

'Er, hello, I'm not going to sing. I wouldn't inflict that on you. I'm going to recite a poem.' Booing echoed from the back of the bar area, others shushing the dissenters. 'It's for a friend of mine who recently swum the Channel and raised thousands for charity. She's amazing. This is for you, Cordelia Franks.'

Face aflame, I levered myself to standing, a wet black umbrella in hand, and turned towards the back of the pub. David stood behind the microphone stand in front of the fireplace, dying embers in the hearth. The two old blokes on a small round table put down their pints with interest and nodded heads encouragingly. 'Go on, lad.'

David cleared his throat. 'Let's see if I can remember this...' He fiddled with his watch.

> *'But, soft! what light through yonder*
> *    window breaks?*
> *It is the east, and Juliet is the sun.*
> *Arise, fair sun, and kill the envious moon,*
> *Who is already sick and pale with grief,*
> *That thou her maid art far more fair*
> *    than she.*
> *It is my lady, O, it is my love! O, that she*
> *    knew she were!*
> *She speaks, yet she says nothing: what of*
> *    that?*
> *Her eye discourses; I will answer it.*
> *I am too bold, 'tis not to me she speaks:*
> *Two of the fairest stars in all the heaven...'*

David paused; you could have heard mice breathing under the floorboards. The bar staff leaned on the counter, heads cocked on one side, cheeks resting on hands, absorbing David's touching delivery. 'Hang on, hang on, I think I've forgotten...' Shuffling feet, glasses clinking, conversations resuming.

I hastily googled the words.

> *'Having some business, do entreat*
> *her eyes*
> *To twinkle in their spheres till they*
> *return.'*

I shouted the words above the low chatter.

David grinned and mouthed, 'Thank you,' beckoning me to the mic. I weaved my way from the doorway through tables towards the fireplace, reciting *Romeo and Juliet*.

> *'What if her eyes were there, they in her*
> *head?*
> *The brightness of her cheek would shame*
> *those stars,*
> *As daylight doth a lamp; her eyes in*
> *heaven...'*

I reached David, showing him the words on my phone, the screen prompting his memory.

> *'Would through the airy region stream so*
> *   bright*
> *That birds would sing and think it were*
> *   not night.*
> *See how she leans her cheek upon her*
> *   hand!*
> *O, that I were a glove upon that hand,*
> *That I might touch that cheek!'*

He finished, smiling reticently at me.

Silence.

'Oh my God,' Desi cried, tears streaming down his face. 'You two!' Gentle applause rippled out from the bar area until it gathered force, the room eventually bursting with the kind of ovation reserved for football heroes, George Michael (RIP), or two old school friends reciting Shakespeare in the pub on a wet Thursday evening in December. We bowed awkwardly then I curtseyed, styling it out with some jazz hands.

'I didn't think you could remember it,' I whispered in his ear, mindful of the mic. 'Hadn't thought about it for years?'

David flicked off the mic and grabbed my hand, placing it on his heart. 'It was always in here. I just needed a bit of a nudge, that's all.'

Spontaneously, before pre-swim Cordelia could hold me back, I reached up on my tiptoes and kissed him on the lips, the dying groundswell of applause reigniting until I saw myself struggling out of the water on Wissant beach, waves smacking the backs of my knees, David waiting on the shore.

# EPILOGUE

'Cordy, where's your bouquet?' Aunty Liz asked. Standing on the threshold of the council chamber, its impressively ornate wooden doors as tall as a ship's sail. I held up my posy of antique pink roses, not a lily among them. 'Good. Desi, breathe.'

'I'm OK, I think. I need something to hold.' His hands shook; I took one in mine and lifted it up to my lips. His purple velvet suit was almost papal in its vigour; the canary-yellow shirt popped like a splash of sunshine.

'You look so handsome. I love you. Thank you for asking me to do this huge honour.'

Tim and his parents had already walked down

the aisle and shuffled into place at the front of the oak-panelled council chamber underneath the overly large oil painting of a past Mayor of Eastbourne resplendent in a scarlet tunic and black tricorn hat.

I peeked down the aisle and caught David's eye as he stood on the end of the front row next to Mum and Frankie, Stephen, Kallie and the children on the row behind. Evie beamed, clutching a basket of rose petals for the photos later on. I recalled the card David had given me yesterday on our one-year anniversary, *Third time's a charm* written inside. The year had sped by so quickly. Time flies when you're having fun exploring the world in between studying, working and keeping a miniature zoo alive. He winked at me. Despite my nerves and the stately surroundings, my loins snapped to attention. David in a suit naturally led to trouble. I'd spotted a dark antechamber on the way in that looked in need of christening.

While Alan and the rest of the Egrets took up three whole rows, Reggie and his gang were halfway down on the other side. Michelle, Rob and the two girls perched at the back, almost level with me. She took a picture while we waited for the signal. I was so glad she was here.

'You all look gorgeous,' Michelle mouthed to us, then made a heart with her hands.

'I'm so proud of you, Desi,' Aunty Liz said, kissing his cheek. 'You are the most wonderful son and human being. Your father would be beside himself today, watching you marry the love of your life. I wish he could see you now. I wish he had been able to do the same for himself.'

'Mom, stop, my nerves are shot as it is. I can't remember my vows.'

'Hey, look at me. Your vows are in here.' She tapped his chest. 'Look what you've achieved – a whole room full of love. I know people who'd have a queue of haters wanting to stab them, but that's another story. Everyone in that room is rooting for you.'

The celebrant raised her hand, giving the signal. The photographer jumped into action, ready to capture our entrance while the opening bars of 'Somewhere Over the Rainbow' tinkled through the speakers.

'Are we ready?' Aunty Liz asked.

'Ready,' I said.

'Ready,' Desi agreed.

'Let's go.'

\* \* \*

## MORE FROM JANET HOGGARTH

Another completely unforgettable book club novel from Janet Hoggarth, *Us Two*, is available to order now here:

www.mybook.to/UsTwoBackAd

# BOOKCLUB QUESTIONS

1. What do you think are Cordelia's reasons for swimming the Channel and can you identify with them? Does The Swim and its aftermath live up to her expectations?

2. The Swim explores several different relationships in Cordelia's life. Which relationships do you think have shaped her the most as a person?

3. Did you find the film references worked as story prompts? Did any stand out as particularly powerful?

4. Which characters do you find the most compelling and who was the most perplexing?

5. How does the theme of 'loss' manifest throughout the book?

6. How far (if at all) do you think the world has moved on from body shaming?

7. Has the author managed to capture the essence of swimming the Channel and does it matter that she did not actually swim it herself?

8. What piece of advice would you like to offer Cordelia as a child? And do you think she would listen?

9. Did the novel end where you wanted it to and what do you see happening for the characters in the future?

10. What does the Channel symbolise in the novel?

# ACKNOWLEDGEMENTS

Thanks to Neil as always, for giving me the space to write this. And to my agent, Charlie Viney, for his wise words and guiding hand. Thanks to Sarah Ritherdon at Boldwood and everyone else there who works tirelessly to get our books out into the world. Thank you for loving this as much as I do.

This book wouldn't have been possible without Sarah Hoggarth pointing me in the direction of Holly Manktelow, who swum the Channel in August 2022. Holly is a remarkable person who raised money for The Youth Counselling Project in Seaford, East Sussex. Holly's experience underpinned the sea-swimming narrative for this story because I have not swum the Channel! I love sea swimming and have braved it quite a few times in mid-winter to gain in-sight into the process and training for something as intense as a Channel swim. I also listened to count-less podcasts, watched many films, TV programmes and read cross-Channel swimmer, Mark Ransom's, account of swimming the Channel – *Keep Calm and Swim to France.* All very inspiring!

Special thanks to Bob Reynolds for all his inside track on growing up in Chicago, and for letting me bend his ear for hours about American TV shows (Vanna on the *Wheel of Fortune!*) and general eighties popular-culture references. I am also grateful to tutor, Gio Iozzi, and fellow students on the Creative Writing and Education MA at Goldsmiths University, for such insightful suggestions.

Lastly, thanks to Dad for his knowledge of Liverpudlian Baptist church, the Tin Pot Cathedral (not its real name).

*We need a bigger boat.* (*Jaws,* 1975)

# ABOUT THE AUTHOR

**Janet Hoggarth** is the number one bestselling author of *The Single Mums' Mansion* and the highly successful *Single Mums'* subsequent series. She has worked on a chicken farm, as a bookseller, a children's book editor, a children's author, and as a DJ (under the name of Whitney and Britney!). She lives with her family in East Dulwich, London.

Sign up to Janet Hoggarth's mailing list for news, competitions and updates on future books.

Follow Janet on social media here:

**f** facebook.com/JanetHoggarthAuthor

**X** x.com/Janethauthor

**O** instagram.com/janet_hoggarth_author

# ALSO BY JANET HOGGARTH

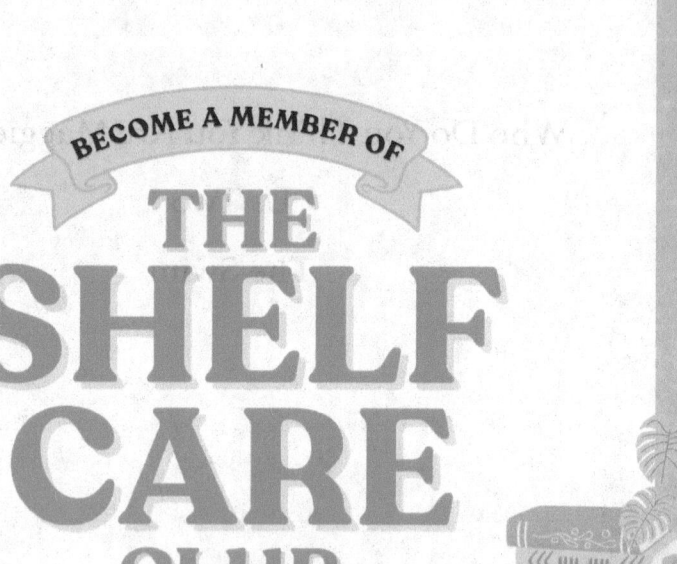

# Boldwood

Boldwood Books is an award-winning fiction publishing company seeking out the best stories from around the world.

**Find out more at www.boldwoodbooks.com**

Join our reader community for brilliant books, competitions and offers!

Follow us
@BoldwoodBooks
@TheBoldBookClub

Sign up to our weekly deals newsletter

https://bit.ly/BoldwoodBNewsletter

www.ingramcontent.com/pod-product-compliance
Lightning Source LLC
Chambersburg PA
CBHW010655100726
47900CB00010B/2672